Shadows of Old Town

Shadows of Old Town

T. Olsen

Dedication

To my husband, who never questioned it when I called my writing a second job, and always accepted that I needed to put those hours in.

And to my kids, in the hope they chase their dreams as hard as I have.

Table of Contents

Acknowledgements

When I started writing novels I thought it was a private and personal thing to do. It was something one person struggled to produce, then sent out into the world. Then I realized it took a village. A slightly neurotic, caffeine-fueled, self-doubting village.

Many people contributed to the creation of this book. More than any others, my family supported me. My husband and kids put up with the hours of writing in the evenings, and the weekends where I let the dishes get all crusty and gross because I was in the zone. They put up with my complaining when my back hurt and I had tension headaches because I hadn't moved from my chair in six hours. And they listened to me prattle at 3x normal conversation speed about some plotline or character that was giving me problems.

The rest of my close friends and family supported me completely. My mom bragged about me a LOT. She was always proud of me, and not afraid to tell literally everyone about it.

And of course there is the Nebraska Writers Guild. I'm not in Nebraska, but they took me in anyway. I met a ton of people there, had great times at the conventions, and learned a lot about writing. Why don't all conventions have writing sprints?

I also have to thank the bottomless depths of Book Twitter. Back in its prime, during the heyday of pitch contests and manuscript games, I found my people. It was a wealth of unsolicited advice and blind encouragement, both of which needed to be taken with a pinch of salt, but a few people stand out.

My first beta reader, Maria. You were a harsh critic and I loved every bit of it, even when you made me cry in frustration. This book was a mess when you first saw it, and you gave me the push I needed to turn it into what it has become.

The people who met Gray along the way: Steve, Sophia, Bubba, Kyle, Ren, Sarah, and Dale. There's a little bit of each of you in this book, and your help was invaluable.

Ian, who gave me an edit letter anyway, and made me believe this wasn't a waste of time.

And last, but never least, my wenches in the Plague Year Query Squad. The world was falling apart, and we found each other. For the last few years we've laughed and cried together. We've shared tea and pet pictures. You all "get it" when nobody else does, and for that I thank you. You've all touched this book in some way, either critiquing the first pages, query, or the entire manuscript, and I'm so thankful for you all.

Chapter 1

I glanced back at my pursuers and heaved a sigh at how far behind they'd fallen. If it weren't for the greasy streetlamps pushing back the dark, I'd have already lost them. Once again I slowed a little, forcing myself to remember this wasn't the Copperguard after me, but a couple of overweight, whiskey-riddled, stiff-legged dock workers. Honestly, it was amazing they were still running. I'd been worried they were going to get tired and find a bar somewhere before we even got within sight of the river.

But here we were. I leaped to the slick, uneven boards and made a show of clattering along the dock to draw their attention. It was much darker here. Only the ends of the docks were lit, like glowing tips of wooden fingers stretching into the current of the river, reaching for the opposite bank that was lost in darkness. I purposely chose a path that would dead end, forcing me to turn onto one of the fingers. The water rushed beneath me, dark except where it reflected the light of the lamps. It was their home turf.

Should make them cocky.

Near the end, I skidded to a stop and windmilled my arms when it was more slimy than I expected. I'd have to be careful how much I played this up. Didn't want to end up in the river with them.

They thudded onto the dock after me, shaking the entire thing as they came up to where they thought I was pinned down. They were grinning. Sneering really.

The one in the lead was puffing hard, wheezing through his crooked nose, but still cracked his knuckles with as much menace as he could muster. "End of the line, pretty boy."

I held my hands out, glancing one last time to fix the distance to the edge of the dock in my head. "Are you idiots ready to apologize for your gross misconduct?"

Crooked Nose laughed and grinned at his ponytailed comrade, giving him a not-so-subtle sign to move in. "You don't like us hittin' women? We'll just hit you instead. Mush up that cocky face of yours."

The smile tugged at the corner of my mouth, but I forced my expression into something more nervous, trying not to ruin it by laughing. "I'd hate to have to resort to violence."

The man bared his teeth. "Don't worry, it won't take long." He reared back, winding up a punch with an arm that was as big around as my thigh.

I waited for it, then swatted his drunken punch aside and responded with an uppercut to his chin that staggered him away from me. Damn, that felt good. I shook my knuckles to get rid of the sting. "I'm gonna tell you one last time—"

Ponytail slipped past his friend and swung as well, but I leaned away from it, then sucked in my middle as he tried again. The third wild swing I just ducked under.

This was too easy. "You need to treat the ladies with respect."

Ponytail snarled, pushing forward. "They're whores. They don't deserve no respect."

I narrowed my eyes and the pit of anger in my stomach hardened. "They don't deserve to have to cater to the likes of you."

The man spit on the dock between us. "It's what they're paid for."

Time to finish this.

One.

I darted forward and swung as hard as I could at Ponytail, my fist connecting with his sternum and sending him stumbling back to land huffing on the boards of the dock, making the entire thing shudder.

Two.

Crooked Nose growled and lumbered forward and I sidestepped, letting him stumble past and hitting him in the back with my elbow to add enough to his momentum to send him right off the end of the dock and into the cold, black river.

Then Ponytail staggered to his feet. His face twisted in drunken fury as he rushed me.

2

And thr—

I twisted and shifted my weight in preparation to send him after his friend, but a slick spot made my foot shoot out from under me and landed me on the wet dock on my ass. When I looked up a buoy was flying directly toward me. It hit my raised forearm with a numbing thwack, then grazed my forehead before it clattered across the dock and off the edge.

I cursed and squinted against the sharp sting above my eye, glaring at the thug that was advancing to finish me. As he reached down, I rocked back and set my boot in his belly, grabbed his forearm, and catapulted him over to land in the river with a second massive splash.

As I climbed to my feet and brushed myself off, the sound of shouting and splashing began to fade. The river was carrying them away. Not quickly, but quick enough I didn't need to worry about them coming back to bother me.

My pants were covered in wet grime. I scowled after the thugs.

Lighter footfalls came from the docks behind me and I turned to see Saree, breathing hard as she got closer. She put her hand on a wood post halfway down the dock and leaned against it, frowning as she caught her breath. "Where did they go?"

I hooked a thumb over my shoulder. "They took my comments about hygiene to heart and decided to take a bath." I walked to meet her, my boots making hardly any sound on the planks now.

In the soft light of the lamp I could see the bright red mark on her cheek and the darker cut that had split her lip. The blood had been wiped away. I had the urge to follow along the bank and hit the morons a few more times as they dragged themselves out of the river, but I smiled instead and offered her my arm. "Would you like me to walk you back to the brothel?"

She peered in the direction of the faint screaming and splashing downriver. "Are they going to be okay?"

"Of course, I didn't hurt them." I followed her gaze and snorted. "Honestly, it was more like they hurt themselves."

She sighed and slipped past my offered arm, strolling to the end of the dock.

3

I gazed after her. I didn't think it was those thugs that had her all gloomy. Anyone that worked in Old Town was used to violence, and she'd been working here for almost as long as I had.

If I had to hazard a guess, she was thinking about home again. Somewhere across the river was the farm her family worked on. She'd mentioned it a few times, and how she missed it. I quietly joined her at the edge of the dock, letting the silence grow and waiting to see if she wanted to talk, or just think.

Her voice wasn't much more than a whisper, but my thief ears picked it up over the ripples of the water below us. "You're bleeding."

I wiped at the cut above my eye, checking the smear of blood on my fingers. "Barely."

"You don't need to get into trouble over me."

I scoffed and leaned against the post at the corner of the dock. "What trouble?"

"If you don't get yelled at by Senyr for interfering in brothel business, I'm sure Deidre will have a few words for you when you get home."

"We're on the docks, not in the brothel."

She raised an eyebrow.

I let her have that one. Hopefully Senyr wouldn't find out anyway. "And Deidre isn't my mother or my wife. We're just friends. She can complain all she wants."

"She cares about you. For *some* reason." She crossed her arms over her chest and turned away from the light, her voice dropping to barely above a whisper. "You shouldn't have gotten involved."

"I couldn't *not* get involved. This is my district." I nudged her, leaving the snark out of my voice. "And you're my friend, too. Those assholes had it coming."

She snorted. "Thanks."

"No problem."

I waited, wishing I knew what else to say. She seemed more troubled than this discussion warranted, but I shouldn't pry. Life at Odele's could be hard. The Six knew life in Sangarie itself wasn't easy, and any number of things could make her scowl like that. It just wasn't like her to let it churn around in her head for so long.

She shook herself and plastered on a smile. "I suppose you're right about getting back to the brothel, at any rate."

I frowned. She didn't fake shit with me, so the business-as-usual smile was like a slap in the face. Especially after I'd just dunked a couple of good-for-nothings on her behalf. "You sure?"

"Yeah. You have rounds to get back to anyway, enforcer."

I took her offered arm and led her toward Odele's brothel. Without really thinking about it, my steps followed my usual route. She was quiet, leaning on me as we strolled with a comfortable familiarity, her thoughts far away.

After a few blocks, my curiosity and worry won out. "Something else wrong?"

She sighed, deep and long. "I don't know yet."

"Ominous."

"Just brothel politics." She leaned her head on my shoulder as we trudged up the cobblestoned street toward the flickering lamp outside Odele's. "Nothing for you to worry about."

"I could still put a word in for you. You could transfer. You know May would love to have you at her place."

Saree chuckled. "I'm not fancy enough to be in May's brothel. I'll stick to the roughs around the docks."

My lip curled up as we neared the brothel. "But Odele's such a—"

"Gray."

I rolled my eyes. "Fine. I'll drop it."

She slipped her arm out of mine as we reached the glowing lamp. The sound of drunk laugher trickled out of the building and the lamp flickered in a sudden breeze, casting a dark shadow over her face before its orange light steadied.

A shiver rolled up my neck.

I was a very good thief. Good enough to trust my instincts. As she reached for the door I pulled her back. "Are you sure everything is okay?"

Her eyes darted to the door, then back to me. "It's nothing you need to worry about. See you around." She stood on her toes to kiss me on the cheek, then slipped a lace-edged cloth into the palm of my hand. "And get that cut treated. You're bleeding down the side of your face."

I glanced down at the handkerchief as she disappeared inside.

She could take care of herself. I knew that. Something just felt off.

Maybe she was right, and it was none of my business. Maybe I was just feeling out of sorts after that bonk on the head… or the dampness all down the back of my pants from landing on the dock. I grimaced and wiggled a bit to get the fabric unstuck from the back of my thigh. I wasn't doing any more rounds like this at any rate.

Deidre wouldn't be home tonight, so I could get back to our apartment underground and clean myself up. Despite my nonchalant attitude earlier, I didn't want a lecture about staying out of fights. Which was sure to happen if I walked home with blood running down my face. For someone who insisted upon keeping our relationship strictly business, Deidre flew apart way too easily about things like this.

I wiped the handkerchief across my temple as I searched out the nearest entry to the underground, then pressed it over the cut to stop it bleeding more. With any luck, nobody else would find out about the scuffle, so I wouldn't need to worry about Senyr either.

I could just go home, go to sleep, and dream about the dumbfounded looks on the faces of those men as I dropped them into the river. At least that had been entertaining.

***

I came to bleary consciousness the next morning when Deidre unlocked and opened the door. Even in the pitch dark of the underground apartment I recognized her by her footsteps. She turned a lamp on very low and moved quietly, trying not to wake me.

I cracked my eyes open and watched her. She was still in one of her fancier dresses, dyed the deep red of wine, and was just reaching up to release her long black hair from the tie that bound it above her head. It tumbled down to the middle of her back in waves, and I imagined if I was closer I'd have smelled the sweet and spicy scent of moonflower.

She loosened the various ribbons and hooks and laces that kept her dress in place, then stepped out of it and draped it over a chair to clean later, moving in just her sheer underclothes to pick up a long robe and wrap it around herself.

I shifted on the bed, trying to keep her in view.

She spoke without looking at the niche with the large double bed. "So you're awake."

"Not officially," I mumbled.

6

She chuckled, using her professional seductive rumble, and the sound sent a shiver through me. Her hips swayed as she came closer, and the neck of the robe slipped just enough to show the beginning of—

I scowled and pushed my thoughts back into line. "Busy night?"

"Very. I'd tease you more, but it's not fair if I don't follow through."

That got a snort out of me. "Hasn't stopped you before." I rolled onto my back and gave her space to sit on the edge of the bed.

She gathered up the front of the robe as she perched there, her head tilting and eyes tightening as she looked at me. "Have you been fighting?"

Shit. I flung an arm across my forehead to hide the cut from her view. "I'm not sure you could call it that."

She pulled my arm down and peered closer. "What happened?"

"Just a scuffle by the docks. Nothing major."

Her fingers gripped my chin and turned it to give her a better angle in the low light. "Your people?"

"No. A couple of dock workers."

She narrowed her eyes even further. "Why would you *scuffle* with a couple of dock workers?"

"Why not? They're like stray dogs. They'd punch their mothers if they got gruel instead of beer for breakfast."

Her voice lowered. "Gray."

I blew out in a huff and shifted my gaze to the ceiling. "One of them hit Saree. I got them out of the brothel, though, so if a dock worker decides to jump me on my route I'm perfectly in my rights to hit back."

There was a heavy silence.

I looked at her in time to see her bite her lip and turn her head to hide the flush on her cheeks. She sighed and rose from the bed, going to gather up soaps and a towel. "Just try not to get knifed in an alley or something. You're not invincible."

"You don't know that."

She shot me a dirty look and wagged a bottle of scented soap in my direction. "Don't be an ass or I'll never sleep with you again."

I rolled to put my back to her. "I don't believe you. All those noblemen are asses and you still keep them as clients."

She let out an angry jumble of cursing and I was just starting to chuckle to myself when a soft leather shoe thwacked into the back of my head.

"Ow!" I rubbed at it reflexively and twisted to look over my shoulder, but she slammed the door as she left. At least she hadn't thrown the glass soap bottle. I tossed the shoe to the floor and pulled the blankets over my head to block out the light of the lamp she'd left on.

Chapter 2

I spent the next few days just walking around Old Town, keeping up with my rounds and the various managerial duties of an enforcer. I didn't stop at the bars or the brothels, and stayed away from the docks entirely. Better not to encounter either of the men. Give tempers time to cool.

At least half a dozen times I turned toward Odele's, but kept changing my mind. I would have heard rumors if something had happened, and all was quiet. Saree knew how to find me, and if she wanted to talk she would. I'd give her a few days. By then whatever upheaval was happening in the brothel would have come to a head and she'd be ready to gossip about it a bit.

I woke the second evening and had a few hours until my criminal duties called me away, so I decided to head to the bar. The promise of a stiff drink and a stacked deck of cards was better than sitting alone in my apartment. Should be safe enough now. Thugs like those two had short memories.

The main tunnels were dirty and wide with uneven walls, a combination of natural erosion and chiseled rock. A damp, earthy smell clung to everything this close to the river, and had a comforting familiarity. There were quicker routes through the underground, but unless there was someplace pressing to be it wasn't worth being brained in the dark by a low-hanging chunk of ceiling, or tripping over an uneven floor. At least on the main route there was an attempt to light the way, even if half the oil lamps were always empty.

"I've been hearing stories about you, Gray."

My heart jumped into my throat and I came to an abrupt stop in the middle of the tunnel. Shifting my gaze to the shadows on my right, I was just able to make out the cloaked form of Senyr.

He sighed and his voice lowered with displeasure. "Again."

My surprise twisted into the jaunty and mischievous expression I'd practiced over the years, giving me time to swallow my heart back down where it was supposed to be. No sense inflating the old man's ego by letting him know he'd caught me off guard.

"All flattering stories, I hope?" I replied.

Senyr peeled himself away from an irregular section of wall. His age was starting to show in how carefully he moved, but he was still as silent as ever. He was the Hand of the Master, after all. He glanced at the small cut on my forehead, not quite hidden by shaggy black hair, and frowned. "Lord Rigel wants to talk to you."

A knot of anxiety formed in my gut. "I was just heading out, maybe I can stop by later."

"I think you should stop by now." He turned around and started down the tunnel behind me.

I sighed and followed him through the twisting tunnels, my steps as silent as his. "This is about those thugs, isn't it?"

Senyr's usually steady baritone vibrated with checked anger. "You threw them in the river."

"They're dock-workers. I figured they knew how to swim."

He only grunted in reply. In the last ten years, Senyr was rarely without words unless he was biting them off for some reason. It was probably best to hold my tongue before I talked him into an even worse mood.

After Lord Rigel had assumed leadership of the criminal guild, the cluster of caves and natural passages beneath the city of Sangarie had been converted into a sprawling underground that housed most of its registered members. He'd swept through, renovating and expanding, until it was pretty much a city unto itself, hollowed out beneath the very streets we worked. When we arrived at the guildmaster's chambers, deep in the heart of that maze, Senyr breezed past the two Red Hands guarding the short corridor and rapped on the door.

The assassin on the left was grizzled and steely-eyed, probably retired from street duty, but the one on the right was too young to have acquired the jaded glare most of the Red Hands sported. He was also very pretty. Quite possibly recruited to infiltrate more gentle society. I gave him an appreciative look, then winked. A blush rose to his smooth cheeks.

I was sorely tempted to ask the Red if he was busy later, but Senyr cleared his throat and I grudgingly followed him into the guildmaster's apartment.

The best stuff the guild couldn't resell came here. It was a riot of color and style. Vases, ancient weapons, paintings, statues...

A wooden mask caught my attention as we walked. It was carved into a grotesque expression and had a lattice of leather straps used to attach it to the head. The wood looked like it blended seamlessly into glass over the eye holes. I reached out to touch one of the glass eyes, and the unmistakable tingle of magic crawled over my skin.

I jerked my hand away and clenched it at my side, taking a quick step to rejoin Senyr as he came to a stop in front of the guildmaster. The tingling was slow to fade, and I scraped my fingers on the side seam of my pants trying to get rid of it.

Lord Rigel stared at me from an overstuffed chair near a matching pair of couches. His eyebrow rose, and he smoothed his neatly clipped grey beard. "It might be easier for you to hide your elfblood talent if you refrained from touching strange things."

The label made me bristle. "I'm not an elfblood. I told you, I wasn't born this way."

"Ah yes. I forgot." Rigel motioned at the couch across from him.

I hesitated, not eager for the lecture I could sense was coming, but Senyr caught my gaze and motioned subtly with his eyes for me to get moving. I sighed and sprawled into the cushions. "You wanted to see me?"

Senyr cleared his throat.

I reluctantly added, "Sir."

Rigel steepled his fingers. "I heard you got into a bit of a scuffle."

"Don't worry. I'm fine."

"Gray—you can't get into fist fights with the citizens."

I frowned as I bit my tongue. In my opinion, those thugs deserved a lot more than a few bruises and a bath in the river. They were lucky I hadn't knocked them cold before shoving them off the dock to let the river have her way with them.

Rigel scowled. "You're a Black Hand. A thief. Roughing people up is a job for the low level Red Hands."

"There weren't any around."

His tone sharpened even further. "Then you send for one. It's their job to take care of such things. At your rank you need to set an example for the people in your district."

My eyes narrowed and my jaw tightened. "I was."

Rigel glanced at Senyr, and the older thief nodded. The guildmaster leaned back in his chair. "Very well. Explain yourself."

I leaned forward. Shorter was probably better in this instance. No need to hang myself with details. "Those two assholes roughed up a Blue from a brothel in Old Town, and that shit doesn't sit well with me."

Rigel's face darkened. "Continue."

"I threatened them. They followed me. I led them to the docks and knocked them into the river."

"I see." The stern expression didn't soften. "Still, you should have come to me—or to Senyr. We'd have sent a Red Hand to deal with them. The baroness allows us to maintain our fragile peace so long as there is order being kept within our ranks. We can't have everyone doling out their own form of justice. At the very least, it would have been the brothel owner's problem. You stepped on both the Blue Hands and the Reds."

I snorted and shifted my gaze away. The situation hadn't required one of the fledgling assassins. I was more than capable of laying down a few threats.

Rigel tapped his fingernails on the arm of the chair. "We have divisions in the guild for a reason. People are trained properly, things run smoother, and accidents are kept to a minimum. Each of the divisions supports the other. In this way, we control the streets of Sangarie. We maintain an acceptable level of crime, and the baroness doesn't burn us all out like rats."

He was about to go into one of his lectures about maintaining the criminal balance. But the rules were useless if our people got hurt because of them, and I didn't see why I had to stand by and watch that shit happen in my district. It wasn't like I was carrying out an assassination. It was just a little roughing up.

"When I promoted you, it was because I saw the potential in you to be a leader."

I was careful to duck my head before I rolled my eyes so the guildmaster wouldn't catch it. I would have thought such a conversation more appropriate for Senyr, or one of the other Hands of the Master. An enforcer level thief like me was less of a leader and more of a shepherd for the criminally inclined. "I thought you promoted me because I could sense magic."

"That didn't hurt." He stroked a hand over his beard as he watched me. "You're still able to hide it?"

"It's not like I glow when it happens. And I don't encounter much magic in Old Town. It's still just you and Senyr that know."

"You won't be able to keep it a secret forever. You know this."

The old anxiety tried to rise in my chest, but I stuffed it down. "I'll keep it secret as long as I can. I'm not going to be some nobleman's stooge in their pursuit of whatever the fuck has taken their fancy for the week. I never wanted this, and I'd just as soon nobody ever knew about it."

"Hmm." He watched me a moment more, face thoughtful, then straightened up and turned all business. "Speaking of leadership, when was the last time you trained new thieves in Old Town?"

My heart sank. I'd managed to avoid *that* particular duty for quite some time. I'd been an enforcer for two years, and I had quickly realized a few of the old-timers didn't mind babysitting young thieves instead of risking their necks on hits. Rigel had said leadership was about delegation, hadn't he?

Rigel's mouth twitched at the corner, not into anything that could be called a smile, but enough I could tell he was pleased with himself. "Perhaps you have too much time on your hands."

"I really don't think—"

"Then it's settled. I've sent a couple of unmarked recruits to the Old Market already, so you can supervise them. Test them. See if they should take the Black or not."

"Lovely."

"In addition, there's a newly tattooed Black Hand I'm assigning to Old Town. Take her along when you hit the glassblower."

I scowled at him. "On an actual hit? Are you serious?"

The guildmaster raised his eyebrow. "Aren't you the best thief in Sangarie? Surely you can handle a little challenge in your work. In the meantime, I'll have a Red Hand talk with those two men."

13

I choked back any further comments. I'd pushed my luck far enough, and if I was honest, I'd gotten off light for breaking one of the guildmaster's more precious rules. Don't interfere with another division's business.

I stood and tugged my vest straight. "Is that all, sir?"

Rigel waved me away. I left quickly, before he could think of something else to saddle me with, or before Senyr could decide to follow me and continue the lecture. Now I really needed that drink.

Chapter 3

The best part about the Old Market Square was the Devil's Throat tavern, situated right at the edge, where I could justify having a round even if I was supposed to be babysitting. I slid through the crowded marketplace, hands hooked casually on my belt, never losing the lazy stroll designed to let me blend into the shoppers and put potential marks at ease.

It was a little busier than usual, and people were chattering at the stalls a bit louder than normal for this time of day. Some sort of gossip was making the rounds. I caught whispers of Craftsmans Row and Firmin, and rolled my eyes. That pampered jackass was always finding new ways to spend his mother's coin. The Six knew the baroness had enough of it to spare.

As I made my way to the tavern, a trio of kids darted past and bumped into my hip. I reached out and snagged the back of the littlest one's shirt as she tried to run off, lifting her completely off the ground and holding her at eye level. She was so scrawny it was like holding a dog by the scruff of the neck. I recognized her from the summer group of recruits, but I hadn't bothered to remember any of their names.

I sighed, holding out my free hand until she produced the coin pouch I typically wore at my belt. It was usually a decoy, but today it had my gambling money in it. Can't trick a Black Hand with an empty pouch, and my unranked thieves were supposed to be learning how to spot the difference between coins and rocks.

She slapped it into my hand. "Sorry."

"That was sloppy."

Her big eyes widened and her lip quivered. "Are you gonna cut off my hands?"

Shit, what rumors did these kids spread about the guild enforcers? I scowled and made a show of thinking about her question. To be fair, I wouldn't put it past some of the others to do it. Took themselves entirely too seriously. "I'll let it slide this time. Don't let me catch you again."

Her waifish face widened into a smile as I set her down, and she wasted no time disappearing into the crowd. I paid a little more attention as I crossed the market, and noticed a handful of dirty, eager faces sneaking peeks at me from between shoppers, but none of them were brave enough to try their luck.

I stepped beneath the shaded doorway of the Devil's Throat, taking a moment to look the place over as my eyes adjusted to the dim interior. While many such businesses were havens for filth and disease, the Throat was scrubbed and swept daily. The building creaked, and the tables and bar were worn smooth from decades of use, but it didn't have the piss and vomit smell many dives acquired. You couldn't hide the smell of ale, or the stink of the men and women who sat at the tables, but what was a tavern without that?

Even before I'd been old enough for Sans to let me drink, I'd come here to watch the gamblers. I'd learned to play a dozen different games, and how to cheat at them. This is where I'd picked my first pocket, and been caught. It was where I'd earned my first honest coin by scrubbing the hearth—and my last honest coin once I realized gambling and stealing paid better. It was the closest thing to a home I could remember having.

I caught sight of the old bartender, leaning on the far end of the bar as he talked with a pair of men. "Hey, Sans!"

The rosy-faced barkeep looked up and his grin widened. "Gray! We missed you yesterday. Need a drink?"

I nodded, but stayed in the doorway, glancing across the market for my would-be pickpockets as Sans filled a tin mug with ale. When he called out, I cast a final backwards glance over my shoulder and stepped up to the bar. He limped over and set the drink on the polished wood. After a long swallow, I wiped the foam from my lip with a thumb and sighed.

"I needed that."

Sans chuckled. "Where have you been?"

"Had a minor encounter with some locals."

16

"Nothing serious I hope." The barkeep glanced at the cut above my eyebrow.

I grunted and leaned my forearms on the bar. "Nothing I *took* seriously. Just a couple of thugs that needed to be educated. Rigel wasn't thrilled about it, so he insists I spend my time more productively by training new recruits." I took another drink and looked out the open door at the marketplace full of people, flicking my gaze from person to person. "Damn waste of my time."

The barkeep grinned widely, his sparse white hair sticking out at the sides of his head. "Don't forget, you were a new recruit once. And if I remember correctly, you were a damn waste of Senyr's time too."

I raised my mug in mock salute. "I still am, old friend."

Sans shook his head, buffing the inside of a tin mug. "Normally I would disagree, but I can't help but notice I'm doing your job lately."

"Oh? Do tell."

"Overheard some interesting gossip being passed along yesterday. Seems a couple of thieves are asking around for anyone interested in picking up an extra score. Off the books, so to speak."

"Is that so?" I took a swallow of ale and glanced around for anyone that might overhear. It wasn't busy, but there were a few handfuls of people enjoying the afternoon. A couple of them were mine, but they paid me no mind. A pair of Blue Hands waved from a table where they were playing a card game and I smiled back. "Did they mention who it was?"

"The conversation never got that far. But the group talking about it seemed to want no part of it."

"The experienced thieves know better than to try something like this. Did they have a hit in mind?"

He sighed. "I don't know that either. I think they're still hoping to convince someone to help carry all the gold."

"If you hear any more about it, let me know. I'll do some digging."

The barkeep nodded. "Do you have time to sit a while? Detano will show up after he's done sweating last night's alcohol out on the docks, and he asks about you every damn day. He wants to win back the hundred you took from him last week."

I chuckled at the thought. Poor Detano. All these years and he still hadn't managed to catch me cheating, though not for lack of trying.

Maybe fleecing a full hundred had been rubbing it in too much. "Technically I'm working." I swilled the last of the ale and pushed the mug across the bar. "Have to make sure these brats don't get themselves hanged."

Sans picked up the mug. "Shouldn't be too hard today, if you keep em around here. Copperguards will be busy holding back crowds for a guest of the baroness's son. He's supposed to be arriving soon."

That must have been what the gossip was about in the market. "A guest of Firmin? Someone would want to visit that brainless ass?"

"Apparently a noble from the other side of the kingdom. Warden ordered the Coppers out to clear the streets not long ago."

Sans was one of my better sources of information, whether he intended to be or not. The man loved his gossip as much as he loved his bar. "Is he coming in the River Gate?"

"Seems that way, but they'll be getting him out of Old Town fast as you please. It sounds like they're cutting up to Craftsmans Row where the streets don't have so many broken cobbles. Wouldn't want him to get his boots dirty."

"If he's anything like Firmin, he'll have a sachet of posies pressed to his nose to avoid the stink, and a flock of landless nobility waiting to lick his boots clean."

"Sounds like a tempting target for you."

"As much as my fingers itch to relieve the nobility of their financial burdens, I'll have to let this one pass me by. I'm supervising the youth."

Sans chuckled. "Like the one glowering at everyone from across the market?"

I glanced out the door and sighed. "The very same." I trudged out the door and into the crowd, sliding past people that were browsing the storefronts and carts.

Sans was right, it would be ideal for pick-pockets. People were distracted. Security was low. Unfortunately, none of that was enough to compensate for a lack of skill. I made my way to the boy lounging against the wall of a shop and took up a place beside him.

"You're too obvious."

The boy glared up at me. "I'm doing everything they told me."

I sighed and rubbed my temple with the tips of my fingers. "People will think you're trying to pick their pockets."

18

"I am."

"Yes, but you're not supposed to look like you are."

The boy rolled his eyes, a belligerent tone in his voice. "So what am I doing wrong?"

"For one thing, you're staring at people."

"I'm looking for something worth stealing."

It was assignments like this that made me wish I was still a common burglar. I'd been good at stealing shit. Now most of my time was spent watching other people fuck it up. Pushing my fingers up through my hair, I spoke more slowly, hoping the boy would understand better. "You need to learn how to spot your objective at a glance. Ideally, the person won't even realize you've noticed them, or their purse. For instance…"

I flicked my gaze over the crowd, catching sight of a middle-aged man wearing a well-tailored doublet and carrying an armful of wrapped packages. He was standing near one of the carts looking bored and watching another man rummage through the merchant's wares.

I smiled and turned toward the boy. "There's a man standing by a scarf merchant's cart about thirteen paces behind me. He isn't paying close attention to his surroundings, most likely because his partner has dragged him up and down the market for hours. He's probably more concerned with what he'd rather be doing than with how heavy his pocket is. He keeps his purse beneath his doublet on the left side, attached to his belt, and by the looks of the bags he's carrying, and the size of the bulge at his hip, it's half full of silver and copper."

Crossing my arms over my chest, I continued. "The poor sap is asking to be picked."

The boy blinked, nodding at everything I said, then started to look over at the man. I held up a finger. "Don't look right at him. Glaze over him as if he's nothing more than scenery, then look at something else."

The boy nodded and tried to do as he was told.

It was all I could do not to sigh out loud at the expression of concentration on the kid's face. I gripped the back of his neck and dragged him along the edge of the market.

"Hey! What are you doing?"

19

I kept him moving, smiling and nodding at people we passed. "Saving my sanity." *And getting you out of the market where you won't ruin anyone else's chances at working.*

"I'm supposed to be practicing."

"We can practice later, when people forget about the scowling little brat drooling at the sight of their purses. In the meantime, we're going to watch a parade."

"What for?"

"Research," I lied.

"For what?"

"By the Six, do you ever stop talking?"

In reality, I was itching with curiosity about who would call our nasty lordling a friend, and how heavy his purse was. As one of the top thieves in the city it *was* my business to know where the gold was. I made a beeline for the northern part of Old Town, where Craftsmans Row cut through this district and continued into the next. Lionel's district of Crafthold.

As we got closer we had to push our way through curious spectators jostling us from all sides. Copperguards were peppered throughout the onlookers, their hands on their weapons and their eyes hard. The chest insignia over their dark red tunics was more orange than copper, but mentioning it to one of them was the quickest way I knew to a cracked skull. I recognized a few of them, and avoided catching their gaze. I was high enough in the guild ranks now that they weren't supposed to harass me, but it was better not to tempt them. After a long day of dealing with crowds, just about anyone would push back.

Here and there I caught sight of a Silverguard, gazing calmly over the crowd for trouble. They stuck to the wider streets, unwilling to mingle with the unwashed masses. I could imagine them bitching under their breath, eager to be back in the civilized parts of the city and leave Old Town to the Coppers. There was no easy way to get through this crowd, and by the half-hearted cheers ahead, the procession was already nearing the edge of Old Town anyway. I'd have to get ahead of it somehow.

I glanced at the kid beside me just as he slipped his hand under a man's tunic. *Opportunistic little shit.* I gripped his wrist. The man glanced at us, and I mumbled an apology and pulled the boy to the side, then leaned down to hiss in his ear. "Keep your fingers to yourself or I'll chop them off."

"But he wasn't looking."

"And if he *did* catch you, you'd have nowhere to run. It's too crowded, and the Coppers are too close. If you want to become an *old* thief, you'll realize easy doesn't always mean smart."

I dragged him into the next alley. There was a low roof nearby and a few iron spikes driven into the wall beneath it, spaced just close enough together to let a person climb quickly onto the roof. I motioned at the spikes and waited for the kid to scramble up, then swung lightly after him and brushed my hands off. Now that we were above the crowd, the going would be quicker and I wouldn't feel so penned in.

I led the way. The rooftops of Sangarie were referred to as the Thieves Way and I was intimately familiar with the peaks and walkways. I was in no hurry today, so I picked out a casual route, finding the flat roofs and gentler peaks as I crossed out of Old Town and toward the center of the city. There were discreetly placed rope holds and makeshift ladders to make the going easier. I made note of a footbridge that had been ripped down from the five foot gap between two buildings, probably by one of the owners to deter thieves.

Before I could detour past it out of sheer laziness, the boy darted forward and launched himself to the other side. He landed with an echoing crack of wooden shingles and a grunt, his hands stopping him from sprawling into the slope in front of him. He looked back at me with a slanted grin.

Cocky little shit. I jerked my thumb to the left. "Nice jump, but we'll go this way." I turned and followed the edge of the building, leaving him to make the awkward jump back across with impressively colorful language. Petty? Yes. But it made me feel better about having to drag him along.

As I strolled along a narrow parapet wall I glanced down into the alley below. I immediately knew which alley this was by the color of the bricks, the angle of the crooked buildings, and the timbers crossing between them like scrawny arms held out to keep two drunkards from staggering together as they walked.

A shiver ran up my back. I also knew what *this* particular alley had looked like as a snot-nosed kid when the blue glow of a cursed gateway

21

reflected off the bricks and timbers. It had lit up the shadows like mystic's fire. I remembered the pressure across my skin when I had broken the clouded surface and stepped inside.

My foot slipped off the parapet and I stumbled, thankfully onto the roof side and not the alley side of the wall. It jarred me out of the memory and I registered that I was breathing too fast and my heart was racing. I glanced in the boy's direction, but he was too busy staring at his feet and grumbling to notice. I got his attention and crossed to the other side of the building, finding a route that didn't require looking down over that particular alley.

The Thieves Way took us all the way to Craftsmans Row, giving me time to forget about uncomfortable and unwanted memories. I sat on the edge of a brick chimney that afforded me a clear view of the road and the clump of people headed this way from the river. The boy scrambled up next to me and we waited in the orange light of the late afternoon sun.

The visiting noble traveled with a little army. One of the baroness's open carriages must have been sent to meet them at the River Gate, and inside it rode a well-dressed man, looking just like any other pompous nobleman. His arms were crossed and he ignored the noise around him, his nose wrinkled at the smell of the docks that I could pick up even here. An elder sat beside him, wrapped in so many layers I couldn't tell if it was a man or woman. They were dirty layers, however. Common, rough-spun cloth. An odd pair, for sure.

The rest of the entourage seemed to be normal guards, except for a knight that rode his horse in front of the carriage in half plate armor that was dented and scratched and not at all shining. The place on the front of his breastplate where a coat of arms should have been was damaged and bare, as if all identifying decoration had been pried off.

I scanned the guards. Some of them wore the dark red tunics of Sangarie's baroness, Lady Karyn, with silver or black insignias on their chest. Impressive. They'd even called out the Ironguard. Ignoring the Silvers and Irons, I counted twenty-three outsider armed guards and the stiff in a tin suit. Who would visit a friend with a guard contingent like that? Foreign royalty?

The boy smacked my arm and pointed further back down the street. "What's that?"

It was the Warden's prison wagon, escorted by another dozen or so of the visiting guards and just as many of the baroness's. Normally it was just a cage on top of a wagon, but they'd fitted boards in between the bars on the sides, probably to keep people from seeing who or what was inside. I raised an eyebrow. "Now why would they bring a prisoner? And why hide them?"

The kid scrambled up to stand on the chimney edge for a higher vantage point, using my shoulder for balance. "Maybe it's someone who insulted the baroness. Sullied her honor. And they chased him down in the wild and now they're bringing him back to be hanged come morning."

I raised an eyebrow. Kid had a good imagination, I'd give him that much. I watched the prison wagon rattle closer. They hadn't bothered to fill in the iron bars over the top of the cage, and from my vantage point on the roof I could see a hunched figure curled into a corner inside. They wore a heavy cloak of good quality, and I caught a glimpse of braided white hair, but the figure itself didn't seem to be old.

The folds slipped away from the figure's face as they looked up, and their eyes locked onto mine like they'd known I was there. Greenish tinted skin, bright emerald eyes, a bloody lip.

An elf.

A shiver went up my back. The gaze felt entirely too familiar, like someone you passed on the street everyday but never interacted with. I held my position, years of thieving urging me to remain frozen and silent, glad they were in a cage and I was high above the street.

Of course I *knew* elves existed. Any human with a magical "talent" had an elf somewhere in their bloodline. There were stories of elfish settlements surviving deep in the forests or mountains, never found by the soldiers that had sought them out centuries ago during the wars. Travelers in the bars told tales of meeting solitary elves on the road, then losing chunks of memory or having terrible dreams for months after.

But to see an elf here, in the city, caged and sullen… and picking me out above the crowd like I was the only person here…

The wagon rolled by without incident, and I watched the crowd disperse in its wake, hurried along by the Coppers. The boy jumped down from the chimney and walked to the edge of the rooftop to keep it in sight.

23

I was being paranoid, maybe because we'd passed by that alley earlier and crazy magic was on my mind. There was no way I would recognize some elf being dragged into the city. I'd never seen a living elf before, and I could count the number of elfbloods I'd seen in my life on one hand.

It was a coincidence. A visiting noble had caught himself an elf and was bringing them here to show off to his rich friends. They'd happened to glance up and catch my gaze at just the right moment. Nothing more.

The sun was warm on my back and I shook off the unease and stretched, watching the kid's eager expression as he leaned over the edge of the building. It reminded me of myself when I was young, dreaming about all sorts of daring escapades. I had been obsessed with following rich folk.

I smirked. At least I wouldn't have to babysit him if he was chasing down carriages. "Hey kid."

The boy scowled back at me. "What now? You gonna buy me candy to go with the parade?"

"No. I'm going to give you an assignment. Like a real thief."

His eyes went wide, as if I *had* given him candy. Perfect.

"Follow that carriage. See where it goes, count the guards, see if there's anything they unload worth stealing. But—" I held a finger up. "Don't get seen, and don't actually steal anything. We don't steal in another enforcer's district."

The boy nodded eagerly and took off across the rooftops.

I watched him go. I was getting better at this whole leadership thing.

My eyes darted in the direction of the jailer's wagon, just able to pick it out as it rounded a corner and disappeared from sight. The elf's emerald eyes were stuck in my head. I would have expected them to be pleading, pained, or furious. All valid in that situation. But instead they'd been... intensely patient.

Chapter 4

I wandered my way back to the Old Market, thinking I could spend the rest of the afternoon in the Devil's Throat and maybe get some gambling done before I had to go out for night rounds. As I strolled along I heard my name, and turned to run my gaze over the shoppers.

Deidre was working her way through a crowd of people clustered around a food vender, apologizing as she squeezed between them. The long black waves of her hair were pulled back and tied, but a few strands had escaped to ring her face. She was in a simple, unadorned dress, which told me she wasn't working. Most of her clients were the kind of rich assholes that couldn't recognize beauty unless it was draped in satin.

The sight of her warmed my chest and chased away the last of the unease I'd been carrying with me. I waited for her to join me at the edge of the square and gave her a wicked smile. "Hello, lover."

Her smile was more wry than wicked. "I hope you aren't causing too much trouble."

"Not yet. I plan on divesting a few people of their hard-earned silver at the Throat this evening. Care to join me? You can sit on my lap and distract them for me. I'll even give you half my winnings." I winked at her.

"Actually, I need your help with something." She took my hand and drew me along the edge of the square, her dark eyes lowered invitingly.

I chuckled and let her pull me along. There was *one* reason I'd happily dive back into the underground on such a nice evening, and the thought of it made me grin.

She took me to one of the entrances to the underground, leading me down the cellar stairs and into the dim tunnel. I kept hold of her hand as I followed her, and my thoughts turned to what I hoped she'd do with me once we reached our apartment. I thanked the Six for the shortage of rooms in the underground, and her willingness to pair up. Letting her practice her skills on me was a sacrifice I was more than willing to make.

"Is this the kind of favor I'm going to enjoy?"

She looked over her shoulder, flashing me a smile in the light of a lamp we were passing, but didn't answer. When she opened the door to the apartment the lamps were already on. I walked in and paused at the sight of a young woman shooting up from a chair at the table, the wood scraping on stone.

I recognized Beth immediately and my mood crashed. Her long blonde hair was pulled back and tied behind her head. Her face was youthful, her skin still showing some of the benefits of the pampered life she'd led before coming to Sangarie and falling into the guild about a year ago. She was avoiding my direct gaze and wringing her hands, shifting her weight as if she wanted nothing more than to run past me and out the door. It was a stark change from her usual cheerful and overly-friendly attitude toward me.

I raised an eyebrow. "Somehow I don't think we have the same kind of favor in mind."

Deidre let go of my hand and went to the young woman, giving her a hug. They spoke in low voices. Low enough even I couldn't hear them with my trained thief's ears.

That suited me fine. I didn't care what they were hatching. They spent way too much time together in my opinion, and none of it needed to involve me. Beth was pushy and had retained too much of her noble snobbery for my tastes.

Plus, she reeked of magic. Unlike elves, humans couldn't do magic naturally. They had to use a source of power created from a special ore found deep within the earth called motherstone, which is what I could sense with my so-called gift. Motherstone was used to make trinkets or jewelry to help humans use magic.

Some magic-users powdered it and inked that power source directly onto their bodies as elaborate tattoos, preventing it from being stolen or lost. Beth had been particularly clever. Her ink was scattered across her body as freckles. I hadn't realized it until she hugged me one day and it had felt like I was about to be struck by lightning. Even then, it had taken a while to figure out where it was coming from, as I couldn't let anyone else know I could sense it, so I couldn't very well ask her.

Against the wall on the other side of the table stretched a line of carved cupboards that served as our kitchen. I opened one of the upper cupboards and took down a bottle of good whiskey and a glass. With a casual twist, I pulled the cork out of the bottle and poured my glass half full.

Deidre gave Beth one more brief hug, then turned to me. "Beth has something to tell you."

Of course she does. "Hold that thought." I reached for two more glasses. I had a feeling this news would go over much better with a drink. At least for me. I poured and held one of them out toward Beth, automatically giving her the charming fake smile I used so often in my line of work.

Personal feelings aside, she was part of Old Town, and the Black Hands and the Blue Hands had always worked closely with each other. Safer that way. I kept my eyes away from the tiny dots scattered across her exposed cleavage, even though I knew I wouldn't be able to feel the magic unless I got *much* closer to it.

She stared at the glass, a blush spreading across her cheeks. "I really shouldn't. I'm not supposed to be out."

I set her glass on the table and handed the second one to Deidre with a gentlemanly nod. She accepted it and seated herself out of the way, avoiding my gaze to indicate this was my problem to work on.

Damn her. I picked up my glass and sloshed the whiskey around inside. "So you snuck out, risking Odele's temper, to talk to me?"

She nodded and ducked her head, crossing her arms tightly over her chest. "I heard something. People let their guard down around a Blue Hand—say things they probably shouldn't."

I raised an eyebrow. "Go on."

"I heard two men plotting to steal enough gold to be able to leave the city."

The conversation with Sans popped into my head and I sat against the table edge, crossing my ankles and sipping at the whiskey. She kept talking, stumbling over her words, as if she didn't think I'd believe her. I pieced together the fragments and quickly realized the two men weren't just talking, they had a plan already in place. This was much different

27

than daydreaming about a big score. This required I exercise the "enforcer" part of my rank. If I let it get so far as the Coppers, it'd be bad for the entire guild.

Damn it.

Her voice was artfully hysterical now. "I didn't know what to do. I didn't want to get anyone in trouble, because maybe it was just bragging and they wouldn't really do it, but—" She stepped forward and gripped the sleeve over my forearm, dramatically raising her large brown eyes.

A vague feeling of discomfort arose at the closeness of her. There was at least a foot between her chest and mine, but it didn't seem like nearly enough. If I shrugged her off too quickly it would seem odd, so I stared back at her and let my skin crawl.

Her eyes bore steadily into mine, searching. "I'm afraid. They knew I was there, and if they find out I told you—"

"You did the right thing." I pulled out of her grip, then picked up the glass of untouched whiskey on the table and pressed it into her hand. Anything to keep her from hanging on me. I needed to focus, or I'd give myself away. "What are their names?"

She immediately took a step back, clinging to the glass so hard I wondered how it didn't shatter between her palms. "I don't want them to know it was me."

"I'm not going to tell them."

She nodded, but it was still a few moments before she spoke. "Evin and Adriel."

It didn't surprise me. Unranked Black Hands, both of them. Evin was lazy and careless, always claiming to be better than he was and never following through. Adriel was impatient, and frustrated that he'd been tattooed for over a decade without gaining his first bar. Neither of them were likely to rise in the ranks as long as I was their enforcer.

And neither of them was going to work in Old Town ever again. I just had to catch them at it, and send them off to the Red Hands. I still didn't know what their hit was, or if they'd managed to drag anyone else in on it.

Most likely they'd be branded as outcasts from the guild and encouraged to leave town. Rigel wouldn't authorize killing for the first offense, and I doubted either of them would have the balls to commit a second.

Beth sipped her drink, her pale cheeks flushing red. "It's terrible feeling so helpless… being caught in the middle of something scary. If Odele finds out I'm snitching on clients…" She looked like a cornered bird.

I gazed down at the finger of amber liquor still in my glass. I might not like her—or her magic freckles—but I wasn't heartless. She was clearly worried, even if she was playing it up a little. "Why don't you rest here for tonight. I'll pay your fee so crackpot Odele doesn't have anything to bitch about."

Beth's face lit up. "Really? Thank you so much! With Saree gone the madam has been twitchy about us spending time away from the house."

My stomach tightened. "Where's Saree?"

Her face crinkled, as if the question had confused her. "I'm not sure? She left two nights ago and hasn't come back. Maybe she has a secret suitor."

I frowned. A suitor? Fucking nobles. Even if you took the money and power away and inked a hand on them they sounded pompous. But—Beth's noble inclinations aside—I doubted Saree would skip out on her brothel to meet with a personal lover. Saree had aspirations, but she was dependable.

Also, two nights ago was when I stepped between her and those thugs. I'd watched her go inside the brothel door, so I knew she'd gotten back safely. Could she have turned around and left after I walked away? Why would she have done that?

Deidre rose and pulled me aside. When we were out of earshot an amused smile crept onto her face. "Long-suffering hero, eh?"

"Yeah, sure." Maybe Saree had finally left the city and gone home, like she kept talking about. She'd seemed upset about the brothel, and acted like she was trying to make a decision. I wished her well, but I would have thought she'd come to say goodbye.

"You already knew about those men, didn't you?"

I turned my attention to Deidre, setting aside musings about Saree's whereabouts. "Some. I didn't realize it had gone this far."

"I thought as much once she started talking." She ran a finger teasingly along the open front of my vest. "At least this time you'll be sticking your nose into your own business. Rigel won't be able to scold you for interfering."

29

The conversation I'd had earlier with the guildmaster surfaced again and I groaned. She must have been talking to Senyr. "He likes to make my life miserable."

"You do that to yourself." She glanced pointedly at the cut over my eye.

I scowled back.

"Do you work tonight?"

"A small job." I didn't mention how much of a nightmare it was going to be. Taking an amateur along on a robbery ranked right up there with gouging my eyes out on the list of things I wanted to do tonight.

"Did you have plans for later?" she asked.

Marisso would be waiting at May's brothel for me. Deidre obviously wasn't going to follow through on her teasing while Beth was around, but maybe the night wouldn't be a total loss. The Six knew I needed to clear my head somehow, and Marisso was good at that. "I do. You didn't need anything, did you?"

"Beth and I can manage by ourselves. Just don't expect to come home and climb into bed with the two of us."

I knocked back the rest of my drink. "Yes ma'am."

Deidre frowned. "You know I hate it when you call me that."

I smiled and bent close, ignoring her disapproving glare as I whispered. "That's why I do it." The smell of rain and moonflowers lingered in my nose. She always smelled like the nighttime should—not the night of the streets and rooftops, with sweat and piss and tar—but the crisp night of the dark sky and quiet gardens.

Her eyes gleamed from underneath long lashes. "Say hello to Marisso for me."

And just like that, the effect was broken. I snorted. "Hmm. Because that will go over *so* well."

When I turned around, Beth was watching me intently. As soon as our eyes met she dropped her gaze. Her cheeks flushed and she fiddled with the glass, which was now almost empty.

I smiled politely and went to put the whiskey bottle back where it belonged. "When I come back in the morning, I'll take you home and pay Odele."

She nodded.

I grabbed my dark cloak from a hook beside the door and slung it over my shoulders, adjusting it so I had easy access to the pair of knives sheathed at the small of my back under my vest.

Deidre called out from the table. "Be good."

"I think I left good behind a long time ago." I waved over my shoulder as I left, making sure the door was shut behind me.

Chapter 5

I walked through the halls of the underground, nodding at people as they greeted me and doing my best to avoid full-fledged conversations. A few young thieves waved and giggled, and I smiled politely, rolling my eyes when I'd passed them. The list of things I hated about my rank in the guild grew daily. I must have been drunk the day I accepted the promotion to enforcer. It was hard to be invisible when so many people recognized you.

I went topside through an abandoned warehouse, checking to make sure no one was watching as I left the building. Other than the beggar sprawled across the alley guarding the entrance from casual citizens, the way was clear.

I traveled the dark streets like a shadow, my footfalls making no noise on the cobbled stone. I ran Old Town, the district where the original village had once been. Sangarie had developed out from there, growing into the largest city in the kingdom. There were now nineteen districts, plus the walled Estates, but the largest district by far was Old Town. It was a patchwork, grungy, unruly village nestled in the armpit of the city. And fate—in the guise of Lord Rigel—had handed it to me.

Its thieves, at any rate. The other divisions of the guild had their own leadership.

The Blue Hands ran four brothels in Old Town. I had designed the path of my rounds to pass each of them, just so I could make sure everything remained quiet. The wealthier districts used bouncers in their brothels—usually strong men, but sometimes dangerous women—who did double duty in the bed as well as at the door. Old Town still resorted to daggers under the mattresses. The clientele around here weren't in any position to complain.

I had a good working relationship with each of the houses, providing the occasional backup in return for safe landing for my own people in a pinch. I even thought about stopping at Odele's as I did the rounds, but the woman always put me in a foul mood, and I didn't want to be off my game later with a freshly inked thief at my heels. So I passed her brothel by, wondering if Saree would be coming back, and why she'd gone off without telling her madam. More of the brothel politics she'd mentioned?

As I walked, I ignored the Yellow Hands for the most part. Their network of panhandlers and beggars was scattered loosely across the district, mainly appearing down by the docks and around the brothels and taverns, where outsiders might spare a few coins or let slip a little information. I recognized many of them, but even the few that were ranked didn't bother talking to me unless they wanted something, and the less information you gave the beggar-spies, the better.

I wandered along my route, taking note of everyone on the street. I knew all my thieves by sight, if not by name. Here and there I'd stop and talk to one of them, catch up on the gossip, and give a few pointers. The more experienced thieves, those with the single bar under the black hand tattoo that marked their rank, I greeted a little less rigidly. If a thief wore the single bar in Old Town, it was because they could handle themselves, despite their many short-comings.

As I neared Tanji's brothel I noticed a handful of people gathered out front. The roof extended over the door, supported by four upright timbers. A wooden platform ran along the entire front of the building to create a narrow porch. It was a popular place to stop and chat out of the mud and the weather, and Tanji usually stationed a couple of Blue Hands outside to lure in customers.

My natural stride was silent enough I was within hearing range without any of them knowing, and I was easily able to recognize the throatiness and slight northern accent of one of my ranked thieves. Culley was telling a story, and if I was hearing it right, it was a story he shouldn't be telling in mixed company. People knew about the existence of the guild—simply because it was impossible to keep an organization like that secret—but we preferred they go through life without many details. There was a big difference between knowing there was a criminal underbelly and being given an intimate look into the workings of said underbelly.

I sidestepped into the shadow of the buildings, continuing my forward progress with a mind not to be heard or seen. Culley was explaining in great detail how—four nights ago—he had picked the lock of a warehouse near the docks and lifted two cases of the finest Dreaming Weed he'd ever seen.

I crept into the shadows nearby and crossed my arms over my chest, listening. One of the Blue Hands glanced my way and stiffened, prodding her partner, but I put a finger to my lips and they merely stepped closer to the brothel door.

Culley belched. "They have it all in the underground now. Never let you keep none of the good shit." He laughed and took a swallow from a flask in one hand.

One of the listeners, a man wearing the short pants of a fisherman, spit on the wooden planks and swayed. "Fuckin thief. You was the greasy-fingered bastard that cleaned out Jarpenny, weren't you?"

My stomach dropped. I had planned on letting Culley dig himself into a hole with that story, then giving him a proper lecture, but the idiot had managed to find a more attentive audience than I think he intended.

Culley's face bunched up in irritation. "What'd you just say to me?"

Another man swayed forward into the light, focused so intensely on Culley he probably didn't notice me standing in the shadow of the post. He waggled a meaty finger in the thief's face, his bare muscular arms sporting tattoos of crisscrossed lines like fishing nets from wrist to shoulder. "Your whore mother should have swallowed you. Yer a fuckin plague on honest folk. Along with all the other criminals in their holes beneath the city. The Six take every last one of ya."

Culley spluttered a litany of colorful words, slurred by drink so I could barely pick out the insults. Definitely not going to end well.

The Blue Hands had retreated through the open doorway of the brothel now, and I could see a few curious faces peering out. On the porch, three men were positioning themselves around Culley and two more that looked a little panicked were scurrying out of the way of the impending scuffle. I needed to get this under control—now.

Just as I stepped into the light, all three men started moving. Culley was too drunk to react except to put his fists up in a bad imitation of a fighter's stance. My plan was to shove the nearest man out of the way, let Fishnet, who seemed to be the ringleader, get a good punch or two in on Culley, then separate everyone. Culley needed the lesson, and I doubted these men would leave without blistering their knuckles at least a little bit.

My mistake was in thinking everyone was as drunk as they seemed to be. I stepped into the path of Short Pants, and instead of shoving him to stumble into the street, I only managed to stagger him. He tried to catch hold of me, but I twisted away.

Fishnet didn't seem at all surprised to find me in his line of sight, and shot his meaty hand out with more speed than I expected. I blocked his blow, but it pushed me backward into the man I'd just evaded. Short Pants caught me and staggered, then slipped his arms under mine and lifted until only my toes touched the wooden porch and my arms were bent awkwardly at the shoulder.

Two quick punches from Fishnet landed square in my gut, and the air left my chest with a wheezing huff. The man holding me was pushed back a step. I gritted my teeth and swung my feet up despite the pain in my stomach, planted my heels on Fishnet's chest, then shoved with everything I had.

He staggered back and the man holding me stumbled off the edge of the platform. It was enough to throw him off balance, and I freed one of my arms. Within seconds a knife was in my hand and I slashed a long, shallow cut across his arm to get him to back off.

I pointed the knife at Short Pants and reached for a second one with my off hand as I tried to suck air back into my lungs. Fishnet had recovered and was focusing in on me. Beyond him Culley was on the floor with the third man standing over him.

I threw a knife past Fishnet, so it thunked into the post next to the head of the man bearing down on Culley. He jerked back in shock and looked at me.

I extended my remaining knife and pointed at each of them in turn. It took a few more moments to catch enough breath to speak. "You don't want to do this." I bent with a wince and slipped a third knife from my boot so I held two again. "And I don't want to explain why I had to kill you."

35

The men growled curses under their breath. Fishnet looked like he would have risked it, if his two friends hadn't decided to turn tail and run. He followed with more decorum, spitting insults until he rounded a corner and disappeared from sight.

I bowed my head and resisted the urge to clamp my arm across my aching gut. Instead I slipped my knives back into their sheathes and went to pry the first one out of the post. The extra spectators had disappeared at some point during the scuffle, but a few Blue Hands were now leaning against the outside of the brothel with smirks on their faces.

When I was sure the men weren't going to come back for more, I sheathed the final knife at the small of my back and went to where Culley was climbing to his feet. I even offered a hand for him to steady himself.

He nodded at me, his nose bloody and one eye already darkening. "Thanks boss."

I let him get his feet, then drew back and threw my shoulder into a right hook, splitting his lip. He fell back on his ass again, spitting blood beside him.

I shook out my hand as I glared down at him. "You need to watch what you say, Culley. I don't want to hear you talking about your hits again."

He glared at me, muttering under his breath as he tried to get back to his feet.

I watched, this time not moving to help at all. My gut was all twisted up and my knuckles were throbbing, but I kept an impassive expression on my face. Even the Blue Hands behind me had gone quiet.

When he was finally standing again, I shook my head. "Get the fuck out of here, and stay away from those men." I gave him one last glare and deliberately walked past him, continuing on my rounds. I felt like throwing up. What had started as such a quiet night was quickly turning into a fucking mess.

Chapter 6

I turned away from the docks onto a street of dark warehouses, crossing to the opposite side to avoid the building where Blind Bob kept a lamp glowing night and day like a white star over his door. The Temple of Six in Old Town had burned down decades ago, and as the ranking White Hand in the district, Bob had quietly moved his mystics into a warehouse and claimed the title of priest for himself. None of the other temples in Sangarie cared enough about Old Town to challenge him.

To be fair, hardly anybody in Old Town went to temples anyway. Blind Bob's place acted as a safe house for the White Hands to land. It was full of seers, fortunetellers, and magic-users with a more criminal outlook on life. But to the general public it was an orphanage for the poor street kids, and Blind Bob was a harmless old priest who dedicated his service to the downtrodden.

While I appreciated what he did for the brats on the street, I still avoided him whenever possible. If it weren't for a good number of my young unmarked pickpockets bedding down there, I might have left his block out of my rounds. He was a creepy bastard.

The Green Hands ran two black market shipping companies and half a dozen fencing businesses near the docks. Although wealthier merchants preferred the newer dock at Clifton district, most of the underground commerce happened in Old Town. To save myself time, I'd worked out a deal with the Green Hands. They each had a small wooden tile placed inconspicuously on the front of their buildings. One side was green, and the other was black. If they had business to take up with me or my thieves, they'd turn their tile to black, otherwise it stayed green.

37

I was glad to see them all showing green tonight by the light of their security lamps. That meant none of my people had picked the wrong pocket, and none of the Green Hands wanted our services. Thank the Six for small blessings.

About twenty minutes later I'd finished my rounds. The pain in my stomach had settled into an ache, and my knuckles were a little swollen, but at least I was breathing normally again. I recognized one Red Hand as I was crossing back through the district, but he made no move toward me.

The Reds always seemed to pop up when someone went looking for them, as if they already knew you were looking, and noticing one when you weren't was considered bad luck. I didn't go so far as to hold my breath or kick a stone or anything else meant to ward off untimely death, but I passed him with my head down, watching for any signal he had business with me.

He didn't stop me, and I turned at the next corner to get out from under his gaze. I shared enough responsibility with the Reds not to be overly superstitious, but I was a thief, and I didn't like people staring at me.

Eventually I crossed into an area of shops with apartments above them, headed for the glassblower. I'd recently found out the old coot was stashing gold away and lying about his profits to the tax collectors. It was the perfect hit. He couldn't report the theft because he'd be taken in for tax evasion. Many of the large hits assigned to the Black Hands were carefully chosen by their enforcers to avoid fuss and keep a check on the criminal activities of the citizenry. Or so the guildmaster said when he lectured me. I just tried to keep from pissing off the honest folk, and took advantage of the greedy ones.

And tonight I had to bring along a freshly tattooed thief.

I was still a couple of blocks away when I heard a *psst* from the shadows of a building, followed by my name in a loud whisper.

I stopped in the middle of the street and waited. There was faint movement in the shadows and the thief edged along the building and looked up and down the street in an obviously furtive way, then scurried out to meet me. I rubbed a hand over my face. The Six were punishing me.

She was dressed in roughspun clothes with a ragged cloak that went down to her knees, the hem frayed at the bottom. Her mousey brown hair was shoulder length and partly concealed her eyes, and a worn pair of goggles with yellow lenses hung around her neck. She was tiny, and I couldn't tell how old she was behind the dirt smudging her face, but I was guessing she hadn't even hit her teens. What had Rigel been thinking, sending a little kid out here? She should be pissing me off in the market square, not assisting with a robbery. How had she even earned her ink at that age?

She whispered loud enough I could have heard her a block away. "I walked past the shop an hour ago, Mr. Gray. The craftsman is asleep."

"Good to know."

"I'm Ruena."

"Uh-huh." I frowned as I tried to catch her gaze, leaning to the side a bit and angling to get a better look at her, but she tucked her chin so her hair fell even further forward. I raised an eyebrow. "You're acting like a skittish mystic. Look at me."

She wrung her hands and raised her head.

Her face was normal enough, with dirt smudged on her cheeks and forehead, but her eyes were unlike anything I'd ever seen. While other people had blue or brown or green eyes—hers were the color of pearl, neatly blending into the whites, with wide black pupils that stared back at me.

My brow crinkled. Occasionally mystics would use magic to change small things about their appearance, but magic was expensive and I didn't think a street kid would have access to that kind of thing. There was also the possibility that one of her great-great-great ancestors had poked an elf and this was how the elfblood presented itself in her. "Are you—"

She ducked her head again, breaking my gaze. "Yes sir." She gripped the goggles in both hands, shoving them up into place to cover her eyes.

As I stared at the top of her head, the only thing I felt was my own nerves. There was no cringey, flesh-crawling sense of magic at work.

I clung to the practical. "Can you see well enough?"

"Yes."

I pointed at the ridiculous googles. "Even with those?"

"Yes sir."

I nodded and took a step back. "Good." I cleared my throat and nodded again, doing my best to pretend the sight of her eyes hadn't shaken me. "That's good."

I started down the street again, with her keeping pace behind me.

I could see why she kept them hidden. Growing up on the streets like that, she'd have been bullied mercilessly. Street kids were superstitious brats, and they would have blamed her for everything bad that happened. And a lot of bad shit happened.

Even worse, if she demonstrated an elfblood talent, someone could simply pluck her off the street and put her up for "adoption" to whoever offered the most coin. The rich and powerful were always on the lookout to forcibly employ the rare elfblood with innate talent, and it was rumored the baroness herself kept a handful of them for special use. If they ended up having no magic, they were never seen again. It was why I kept my cursed gift a secret.

I understood Rigel's habit of trying to fix things. He'd changed many people's lives for the better—mine included—but, once in a while he went too far. I don't know what good he expected to come of sending this kid to me. Old Town was a shithole, and I barely managed to keep it in line on a good day. If he wanted to help her, he should have sent her to the mystics or the beggars so she could stay out of trouble.

I reached the shop and walked past it, covertly taking note of everything from the amount of light in the windows to whether there were any stray cats hanging around. At the next corner I turned, and the girl had to scurry to catch up.

"Wait for me!"

I glared back at her. A small part of me knew I was being unfair, but it was also unfair that I was being saddled with this kid for a hit. Some of my single bar thieves wouldn't have been able to pull off this job. How did Rigel expect me to take a thief whose ink was barely dry?

She hit a piece of cobblestone with her toe and sent it skittering through the alley. "Sorry."

"First lesson. No talking during a robbery."

She nodded, biting her lip.

As we came to an alley I motioned her inside, then followed. I cast off the casual citizen pretense and crept through the twists of the alley as

40

it made its way around the buildings. Ruena was moderately quiet, as long as she wasn't whispering or kicking rocks.

I'd looked the place over earlier in the day and knew exactly where to go. At the back of the building was a large vent in the wall near the ceiling of the ground floor. It was to allow hot air from the craftsman's workspace to escape. At night the fires were banked, and using the crates nearby I would easily be able to crawl into the building. The old man's apprentice, underpaid and addicted to the pleasures of the brothels, had told one of the ladies where his master hid his gold. I wouldn't even have to look for it. It was a straightforward job for an enforcer, but I was nervous bringing in an amateur.

I turned to Ruena and leaned close, pitching my voice low. "I go first. You follow after a couple of minutes. Once inside, take my lead. Remember, you're just here to watch how it's done."

I took off my cloak, hiding it in the alley and retrieving the small pry bar I'd stashed earlier. I climbed the pile of crates, easing my weight up to avoid making any unnecessary noise. A grate over the vent kept stray animals out, and I pried it up and pushed it aside enough for me to fit through. If I'd been any larger, I would've had a hard time of it.

I backed inside, holding myself up with my arms as my feet sought purchase on the top of the giant oven. There was a tense moment where my stomach spasmed from the abuse earlier, forcing me to pause and breathe through the pain, but it passed. The oven, though dark for the night, was still very warm and I quickly got to the floor. Once there I squatted next to it for several minutes, listening for any sign that I'd been heard. I could hear nothing but the snoring of the glassblower upstairs.

Then I heard the scuff of shoes against the wall outside. The girl's head popped into the opening of the grate and she scurried through like a monkey. She'd left her cloak outside too, and now her goggles were hanging around her neck again. When she lowered herself on top of the oven she gasped and started shifting from foot to foot.

I grimaced and waved at her to get down.

She squatted, then jumped down. Her feet slapped on the stone floor and I flung my hands out in a *What the fuck was that?* gesture.

She cringed and crouched down as we waited to make sure the craftsman was still sleeping. If I could hear the man snoring, he'd be

41

able to hear almost any noise we made. These old buildings weren't insulated like some of the newer districts, and it made thieving in Old Town that much more dangerous.

After a few minutes I crept into the back room, Ruena on my heels, to the sacks that held coal for the ovens. Slowly, and as quietly as I could, I began to move them, taking care to remember exactly how they'd been stacked. She tried to help, but they were heavy enough they dragged on the floorboards when she moved them, and I mimed at her to leave it and stand out of the way.

Every sack I moved forced me to clench my gut muscles, and I silently cursed Culley for being an incompetent buffoon. There were a lot more than I'd seen earlier in the day, so they must have gotten a shipment after business hours. By the time I'd reached the floorboards I was sweating and my arms ached almost as much as my gut. Ruena stepped close and stared at the floor with me.

"Now what?" she whispered.

I glared at her and put a finger against my lips.

I pushed carefully on each board until I found the one that was loose, then used the pry bar to lift it up. I slipped the bar back under my belt so it wouldn't be in the way. In a hole dug into the dirt under the floor were seven small boxes.

I reached for one, but Ruena grabbed my forearm in both hands. "Wait!"

My brow creased. I kept my voice as low as I could and jerked my arm out of her grip. "What are you doing?"

She stabbed a finger toward the boxes. "There's something there. I can see the magic."

I narrowed my eyes. "What are you talking about?"

"There's an extra lock on one of the boxes. A magic one. I can see it on top of the metal... waiting." She reached inside and set a grubby finger directly on top of a box. "This one."

So there *was* more to her eyes than just the strange color. No human blood carried a gift like that. Someone in this girl's family tree had definitely spent some naughty time in the forest.

Was that why Rigel had tattooed her so young? Being able to see magic would save her a lot of trouble if she became a burglar. Strange he hadn't sent her to the White Hands, though. I would have thought the mystics would have been itching to get an elfblood apprentice.

I waved her off and reached in to touch the box she'd pointed out, running just the tips of my fingers across the lid toward the clasp. Sure enough, my fingers tingled and the hair on my neck stood up.

If I hadn't been looking for it, I might not have noticed in time, especially as irritated as I was at having the kid along. My sense of magic needed close proximity, and I certainly couldn't *see* anything different about the box under my fingers. It could have been a very stupid mistake.

I also didn't have any ability to counteract whatever it was.

It didn't matter. All I was after was a little of the glassblower's surplus earnings. He could keep his secrets. There were six other boxes and none of them had locks on them, so I opened each in turn to check their contents, choosing one that was all gold coins, and carefully picking gems out of the others to add to it. Lifting it out of the hole, I handed it to Ruena.

She wrapped both hands around it and started to pull it to her chest, which made the coins and gems cascade to one end with a metallic slithering noise. I grabbed it and pulled it back level, then shook my head.

She nodded, hunching her shoulders.

I replaced the board and began to stack the coal back the way I'd found it, breathing through my teeth because of the nausea. I was almost done when the snoring upstairs turned into a grunting snuffle, and I froze and gazed at the ceiling as I listened.

Ruena crept closer to me, her breathing fast and her grip on the box making it shift and rattle. "He's gonna wake up and catch us!"

I narrowed my eyes and clapped my hand over her mouth. I gave her the most frightening glare I could and put a finger to my lips, then moved it across my neck in a cutting motion.

She nodded.

I removed my hand and motioned her to move back to the wall, out of my way.

I waited a full five minutes before moving the rest of the sacks of coal. Just as I was settling the last one into place there was a loud snort from upstairs and Ruena squeaked and bumped against the shelves on the wall.

A single bottle toppled from the shelf and I lunged to catch it, but was too far away. It hit the floor and shattered.

I held my breath. There was a moment of total silence upstairs, then the creak of a bedframe and the muffled thud of bare feet crossing the floor.

Fuck.

I grabbed the box from Ruena's arms and pulled her into the front workroom, pushing her back into the corner behind the oven and squeezing in after her. It was away from the back room, away from the shop door, and entirely in shadow. I crouched in front of her and curled in as close as I could to take advantage of the shelter the oven provided. It was uncomfortably hot at my back and my gut ached in protest.

Her heart pounded against my side, and I knew mine wasn't any calmer. One of my arms was behind her head, and my knee was drawn up in front of her. We were packed tight into the corner, and if he saw us, there was no way we could escape. She was shaking and I put my mouth right up by her ear and whispered, "Be still."

The glassblower stomped down the stairs, carrying a small lamp. I watched the play of shadows as he raised it and peered around the room, praying to the Six he wouldn't shine it high enough to see the open grate, but the light didn't reach past the stove where we hid. He stepped into the back room and swore, probably at the broken bottle on the floor. For a few minutes I watched the light moving on the floor as he poked around that room, then it brightened as he walked back to the main workshop.

He stood for a moment more, then sighed and headed back to the stairs, muttering under his breath about mice. The light slowly faded until he closed the door at the top and left the workshop mostly in darkness again.

I heard the muffled footsteps across the floor and the creak of the bed, then nothing.

Ruena started to shift, but I tensed around her and shook my head.

I waited, occasionally hearing the bed creak above us like the man was tossing and turning. Eventually the snoring started back up. I let out a measured breath and unwound from the girl, careful not to burn myself on the side of the oven. My back was covered in sweat.

My muscles had stiffened, and I stretched my thighs and shoulders as the girl made a comical effort not to make noise crawling out from behind the stove. When she was clear, I motioned at the grate and held a hand out to give her a boost. She scrambled up and out.

Tucking the box under my arm, I braced a hand on the wall and took a hopping step up to the top of the oven. Shuffling my feet from the heat, I set the box on the sill and pulled myself up. After I'd slipped through the window and replaced the grate, I climbed down, retrieved my cloak, and slung it around my shoulders. The box was concealed the best I could with the folds of the fabric.

Ruena had her cloak on and opened her mouth to talk, but I held a finger up and shook my head, then pointed down the alley. She started walking and I stepped into line beside her.

I guided her out of the alley and down a few more blocks before I was finally able to relax. "Okay. You can talk now."

"I'm so sorry."

I took a long breath and gritted my teeth. "No talking during a hit."

She sighed and nodded, staring at the street as she walked beside me.

"Always wait and listen. Always be aware of your surroundings. Don't shake the fucking box. Don't overestimate your ability."

"Yes, Mr. Gray."

The formality irritated me. This is why I didn't like being the boss. I mean, yes, it had its perks, but did I really want people fawning over me like they did with Rigel? If I had the scum of Sangarie bowing and scraping at my feet, I think I'd turn myself over to the Copperguard.

We walked silently for a few minutes.

It could have gone worse. We could have been caught.

She sniffled and I put a hand on her shoulder, leaving the irritation out of my voice. "You weren't that bad. Go home. I'll take it underground."

She nodded and fell back, spinning on her heel and darting into the shadows in the opposite direction.

Chapter 7

The walk back to the underground was uneventful. The entrance I chose was concealed near the back of a warehouse, and I waved at the beggar guarding it before I slipped inside, not missing the glint of steel from the darkness before the man had recognized me. A trapdoor opened onto a ladder that let me below the city.

Striding through the underground, I went straight to the treasury where everything the thieves brought in was sorted. The front room was well lit and held only a large table that served as a desk, with a chair behind it for the Green Hand that recorded takes. Behind the desk was the treasury itself. It was protected by a massive iron door that was kept locked at all times. I placed the box on the table and opened the lid, revealing the gems and gold coins. The weaselly little woman behind the table licked her lips.

"Ah, Gray, you've done well tonight." She reached for the box.

I pulled it out of her reach, digging in it with one hand and bringing out a small handful of coins and a few sparkling gemstones. I shook them out in my palm so the woman could see them. "Eighteen gold, and I'd say about two hundred worth of gems."

The woman glared and pulled the box away, tucking it protectively beneath her arm. "That's more like three hundred worth, and that's more than your cut allows."

Picking the coins out and dropping them into a secure pocket inside my vest, I shrugged. "You cheat me out of my cut whenever you can. I ignore it for the most part." I shook the gemstones out on my palm, peering more closely at them.

"You're right, it is more like three." I slipped them into another pocket of my vest with a smile.

The woman hissed at me, but didn't push the issue.

46

I spun away and walked out. I'd have to find Ruena later and give her a bit of coin. Probably not gold, because it'd just make her a target for pickpockets, but if I leaked her some silver over the next few weeks it would be enough for decent food and maybe some better clothes. She might not have done much when it came to the actual burgling, but I didn't want to know what would have happened if I'd opened that box with the magic lock on it.

The more I thought about her talent of seeing magic, the more certain I was that Rigel had put her with me because of it. He knew I wouldn't give her away, because I was keeping the same secret. Best guess? He was hoping I could teach her to survive with it.

I still thought it was a bad idea. She was too young, and I didn't want a pint-sized shadow. As I made my way through the halls, I debated going home despite my plans for the evening. I was exhausted. My gut ached. My hand still hurt. After the fight, moving all that coal, and the stress of nearly getting caught, a big part of me was tempted just to pass out for the rest of the night. I went so far as to start down the hall that led to my apartment, then paused.

Beth would be there, and the woman irritated the fuck out of me. Deidre was probably asleep. The thing I needed most right now was to relax and unwind. Marisso was waiting eagerly to help me do just that. Besides, I had promised him a visit.

What the hell. I took a different route and came up in an alley in Lionel's district. The beggar lying in a heap near the door chuckled as I walked by, wishing me a good hunt.

I smiled, but didn't respond.

I made my way to a building without windows, but I could see light coming from under the door. Walking inside, I glanced around as my eyes adjusted to the light. The room was decorated in rich tones of red and gold. It was warmed by a large fireplace, and couches were scattered around, some of them occupied by customers looking for someone special to spend a few hours with. Many brothels tended to be gaudy and over-decorated, but the madam in charge of this one was a simple woman, and she made the front room look classy.

In a nook to one side, lounging in an overstuffed chair and watching the fire in a second, smaller hearth, was the madam. May was an older woman, her hair graying despite the dye she used, and her skin was covered in soft wrinkles. Beside her rested five cases of wine, the crates stamped on the side with the image of a monstrous horned head tipped back to accept a stream of liquid from a goblet. She looked up when I drew close and smiled, pushing herself out of her chair to greet me.

"Gray! Welcome." She took my arm and led me to a chair facing hers, seating me before resuming her place. Smoothing out her skirts, she smiled at me. "What have you been doing?"

I leaned back in the chair, enjoying the small comfort after the night I'd had. "I've been busy with guild business. I'm more interested in why you're stockpiling what appears to be some of the Throat's best wine."

She laughed, a sound that once had been captivating, but was now a little scratchy. "If I don't buy it early, there's none left. The Night of Shadows is less than a month away and it's one of our biggest nights."

My gut clenched at the mention of the festival and I took a few moments to make sure my voice wouldn't waver when I spoke. "I try to forget about that."

She cocked her head and her voice softened. "That was a long time ago, Gray."

My heart was fluttering against my ribs and I gripped the arm of the chair as I fought to keep my face neutral. From sunset until sunrise on that night, the entire population of Sangarie stayed inside, keeping their fires lit to ward off the shadows. A few stupid kids always tested their courage, running between houses with their hearts in their throats as they watched out for the blue glow of the gateways. A few unlucky kids had no houses to hide in.

I had been both stupid and unlucky. At that age you didn't turn down a dare, not if you wanted to keep your place in the pecking order. A few older kids had strongly suggested I walk into one of those gateways.

The nightmares still plagued me. The massive slithering beast... the ash and dust in the air choking me... the twisted humanoid figure with dripping black skin and glowing green eyes... the screaming man who pushed me back toward the gateway as the giant monster came crashing forward...

One of the logs in the fireplace collapsed and sent shadows dancing on the wall behind May's chair, and for just an instant I saw the black tentacles rising above her. The crackling fire sounded like the jaws of the beast clacking together. I could smell the ash...

48

She leaned forward to touch my knee and I flinched, bringing my mind back to the classy red and gold curtains, the little fire that warmed the side of my leg.

Her face was sympathetic, and I took a ragged breath and drew on all my training to smile back. I didn't want to sink into those thoughts tonight. My way of dealing with the entire festival was to lock myself in my apartment and drink until I passed out. Just thinking about it was making my skin crawl.

"Does it still bother you?"

"Like you said—it was a long time ago."

She nodded. "If you say so." She was too clever to be fooled by my reassurances, but not cruel enough to press me further. "You're always welcome to join us."

I felt a rush of warmth at her offer, and the smile came easier. "Thanks. I'll keep it in mind."

A younger woman sauntered up to May's chair, giving me an appreciative once over. Her thin dress left hardly anything to the imagination, and the scent of cloves and cinnamon followed her. I shoved the last of the memories out of my head, breathing in her perfume and grounding myself in the cushioned chair.

May patted the woman's hand. "Fetch Marisso would you my dear? He has a visitor."

She gave me one last glance before walking toward the stairs. I turned my attention back to the older woman. "He isn't occupied is he?"

She chuckled. "No, no. He got your message, dear. He's been waiting for you." She gave me a long look. "Seeing you makes me wish I were twenty years younger."

I shook the last of the shadows away and laughed. "You don't want me, May. I'm a bad influence."

She smiled. "Did Deidre tell you that?"

"Among others."

May leaned forward conspiratorially. "I heard a rumor about your Marisso."

"Oh yeah? What's that?"

"I heard," the madam went on in a lower voice, "that Lord Rigel was going to call him down to be an escort soon, like Deidre."

I smiled and picked casually at the arm of the chair. "Where do you hear your gossip, May? That process is highly exclusive. Even I'm not party to those musings."

She snorted. "Like I believe that. You have more of Lord Rigel's ear than Lord Rigel himself. Did you suggest it? You know, that would make thirteen escorts to come from my house. Deidre was one of mine as well."

"I admit Lord Rigel sometimes asks my opinion on placements, but I had nothing to do with Marisso's selection."

May slapped her wrinkled hand down on the arm of the plush chair. "Ah-ha! I knew it! He's one of my best boys and I'd hate to lose him, but he really does deserve better than this. He's only twenty-two, and he has so much life in him." Her smiled widened like a cat's. "Are you going to remain with Deidre or move in with Marisso?"

I gave her a pained look. "May… Deidre and I have an arrangement. We understand each other."

She waved my protests away.

The talk of moving nudged up another worry, and I leaned forward, lowering my voice. "I also heard an odd rumor."

The old woman raised a perfect, graying eyebrow. "Oh?"

"You remember Saree?"

"I do. She turned down my offer to get her out of Old Town. No offense, dear boy, but that place is a shithole."

I cracked a smile. "None taken. But I heard she walked out and hasn't been home for a couple of days. She didn't change her mind and come here, did she?"

"You know I wouldn't outright poach a girl, even to get her out of Old Town. If she was moving here, it'd be through the proper channels with the approval of the Attendants, and her madam would have been in on the discussion."

I eased back in the chair and sighed.

May touched my knee again. "Are you worried about her?"

Was I? Saree was good at taking care of herself. She was scrappier than I was. She'd always wanted to leave Sangarie and return to her family, but I thought she would've said goodbye first if that was the case. "Yeah. A little."

Quick footsteps on the stairs caught my attention, and I stood as Marisso ran down the steps and across the floor toward me. He was shirtless, but wore sheer linen pants that tied at the waist and rested low on his hips, clinging to his legs as he moved. When he reached me, he flung himself at my chest and wrapped his arms around my neck, his unruly blonde curls bouncing and tickling my nose.

I grunted, easing him back so I wasn't supporting his weight. "Gods, Marisso, I ache all over."

He leaned against me and ran his hands up my chest, putting on a pouting face. "Did you have a bad night at work?"

"Yes, as a matter of fact, I did." I didn't push him away though; he smelled too good. Like sun and citrus. "Plus, this afternoon Deid—"

"Oh, to crap with Deidre!"

I frowned at him. "*Deidre* brought a Blue Hand home that warned me of some trouble, so I'll have to sort that out later."

Marisso's face turned more serious, his expression a little guilty. "Oh." He sidled closer and pulled on my sleeve with his thumb and two fingers. "You're here though, so come up and spend some time with me."

I looked back at May and nodded a goodnight before allowing Marisso to lead me past envious glances and up the stairs. We went to his personal room. He locked the door once we were inside and turned his back to it, running his eyes over me. Then he slipped over to the table and poured a glass of dark red wine. "So, why do you ache so much?"

I unclasped my cloak, shaking it out and flinging it over a chair. "I got into a scuffle during rounds. Then I had to bring a new thief along on a job tonight. My damn hit covered his hidey hole with a ton of crap I had to move. He almost caught us, so I was scrunched in a corner for what felt like an hour." I backed up and sat on the edge of the bed, raising an eyebrow. "I don't know if I'll even be able to hold myself up."

Marisso sauntered forward with the glass in his hand, his eyes narrowed and his cheeks highlighted by a rosy blush. He lowered his voice to a sultry rumble. "Then I'll just have to do all the work." He stepped close and set the wine on the side table, sliding my vest off my shoulders and down my arms. I shrugged out of it and raised my arms.

With a sly look, he dropped his hands to grasp my shirt and pull it up and over my head, tossing it behind him, along with the vest.

He frowned at the sight of my stomach. "Did someone hit you?"

I glanced down to see the blush of red that hadn't yet faded from the punches I'd received. His fingers brushed over the mark and I pulled his hand away. "I'll be fine."

Running his hands over my bare shoulders, he slipped behind me on the bed and started massaging tense muscles.

I groaned and closed my eyes, letting my head fall forward. I was *soooo* glad I hadn't gone home tonight. In addition to the more obvious skills a Blue Hand practiced, Marisso was a damn good masseur.

He worked his hands along my shoulders and down my upper arms, every so often kissing between my shoulder blades. His chest rubbed against my back and I smiled at the contact. He sighed, trailing his hand across my skin and tracing the tattoo on the back of my right shoulder. It was a black handprint with two dark lines underneath it, symbolizing my rank as an enforcer. He had one of his own—a blue one with one bar—where his thigh met his hip.

He edged around to my side, stretching one leg across my lap and stroking a hand along my cheek. His nails scratched at the stubble and his gaze rose in a languid way that set my blood pounding.

I ran a hand along the sheer fabric over his thigh and leaned in to meet his kiss. He tasted like wine. His arm slipped around my neck and he shifted until he was sitting on my lap, facing me. He pulled back enough to look at me, his forearms on my shoulders and his fingers curling through my hair.

"You know it really isn't fair," he said.

I tried to ignore the uncomfortable pinching in my pants. "What's not fair?"

"That a scoundrel like you is so pretty."

I laughed, the heat rising in my face. "Pretty?"

He stroked a hand down my cheek. "Your eyes are bluer than mine, and no matter how disheveled you are when you show up here, I can't keep my hands off you."

I pulled him closer, gripping the soft angle of his hips beneath my fingers. "That sounds pretty fair to me."

He kissed me once and eased away, crawling behind me.

I turned to watch him. "I thought you were going to do the work tonight?"

He smiled in return and knelt in the center of the bed, his back arching slowly. "I changed my mind."

Chapter 8

Shortly after sun-up, neither of us having slept, Marisso watched as I rummaged for my clothes. I was tying my pants when he sat up, letting the blanket slither to his lap and exposing his smooth chest and the taper of his hips. "Leaving already?"

I looked at him and smiled, shaking my head. "Cover it up. I need sleep and I still have errands to run before I can go home."

Marisso pouted, but didn't pull the blanket up. "When are you coming back?"

I snapped my belt buckle into place and adjusted it on my hips, then walked over and leaned down to kiss him. Just as he was melting against my bare chest, I pulled back, grinning. "Don't know." I looked around the room before I caught sight of my shirt on the floor and picked it up, shaking it out. "Why do you always ask me that?"

"Just in case you give me a different answer someday."

I shot him an accusing look as I pulled the shirt over my head, then reached for the vest at my feet. I hated it when he started in like that. I'd made it clear to him—many times—that I wasn't interested in anything formal.

He chuckled. "Don't worry, I don't need the lecture." His voice deepened in a mocking parody of mine. "*I'm too young to settle down with one person. When I'm old and nobody wants my cock anymore, I'll find a hag to babysit me.*"

I forced a laugh. "A hag, eh? Are you applying for the job?"

He threw a pillow at me—which I sidestepped easily—then he sank back under the covers. "Go home, Gray."

I turned my back to him, shrugging into the vest before I grabbed my cloak. With a final wink in his direction, I left and closed the door softly behind me. It was too early in the morning for most of the workers to be up, and I trudged down the stairs with a grimace. I wanted to go to sleep. I was used to being up most of the night, but this was late even for me. At least the ache in my gut had gone.

May was sitting in her chair, finishing a breakfast of toast and fruit. I strolled up to her and gave her a peck on the cheek, dropping a couple gold coins next to her plate and picking up a piece of toast.

She scowled at me. "What's this for?"

"Please—I'm taking up valuable time, so I'll pay like everyone else."

"Marisso isn't working when he's with you."

"We aren't a couple, May."

She caught my sleeve before I could move away. "Does he know that?"

"Of course he does. I've told him as much."

She sighed and shook her head.

I gently removed her fingers from my sleeve. "There's no place in my life for that." I pulled up a grin, hoping it appeared suitably roguish despite the fatigue and irritation I felt. "I have too many hearts left to steal."

Her scowl followed me all the way out of the building, but I knew she understood. May was a businesswoman, and she'd give the coins to Marisso, just like she did every other time. Nothing in this world came free. I bit into the toast, determined to enjoy the taste of honeyed apple jam.

The damn sun seemed brighter than usual and I squinted as I made my way through Crafthold. It was a longer walk than I liked to Odele's brothel. I had to cross a district and a half before I caught sight of it in the glaring morning sun. It was built much like May's place, but more run-down, less inviting. I rubbed a hand down my face and blinked my eyes to wake myself up, then went inside.

A few women and one pouty looking man were lounging around, and they sat up curiously when I entered. Like everything in Old Town, they were a little worn. I didn't make a habit of frequenting Odele's brothel, mainly because of the madam, but I knew most of the men and women from the streets or the taverns.

There was no sign of the madam herself. And no sign of Saree.

"Morning," I said. "Can one of you wake your boss for me?"

One of the women was shoved off the couch by the others and she blushed as she stumbled and glared back. She headed off to the rear of the building.

I waited in an uncomfortable silence. Odele's place was never overly friendly to me, but this felt almost hostile. Saree had always come outside to meet me, so I didn't have to endure the madam's displeasure. She even came out to join me on my rounds occasionally, standing with me at the docks and staring across the river as we talked about life. I couldn't imagine her just walking away from the brothel, though. Not without telling someone.

I didn't have to wait long before the madam lumbered out. Over the years her hips had gone bad and she'd gained weight. She walked with a pained shuffle and stopped beside a couch so she could grip the back of it.

Odele's voice was high and scratchy, and she looked me up and down like a slab of meat. "Well... to what do we owe this dubious honor?" She settled a lady's pipe between her lips, the long stem discolored from use.

I bowed extravagantly and cocked a lopsided grin in her direction. "Mistress Odele. You're as pleasant as ever."

"Cut the shit, Gray."

Nothing would have pleased me more than to throw insults back and forth with the woman, but I was too tired to prolong it. I reached into my pouch and pulled out a few gold coins, holding them up in front of her. "I have one of your women at home. This should cover last night and probably a few more as well, so don't expect her back for awhile."

She snatched the coins out of my hand. "Which girl?"

My smile twitched, but I held onto it. "How many are missing?"

She glared at me, rubbing the surface of a coin with her thumb and taking another draw from the pipe. "Not your business, thief."

She was right. As much as Saree was a friend, it was decidedly *not* my business to ask after a missing Blue Hand. Once I walked in the door, I had no jurisdiction.

"It's Beth," I said. "I picked her up last night."

The woman's brow creased, and I heard Beth's name being whispered by the Blue Hands on the other side of the room. My thief's ears were sharp, but brothels were designed to muffle sound and I

56

couldn't pick up anything else over the noise of the madam wheezing and shifting her weight. Odele's beady eyes were calculating. "And when can I expect her back?"

I smiled as politely as I could manage and shrugged. "When I get tired of her."

The woman pursed her lips until I was sure she would suck her face into her mouth. "One more night."

My face flushed and I glared back. "Are you fucking kidding me? Those are gold coins, you blind old—"

"Consider it a hassle fee. This isn't an escort service. Next time, you do it here. My workers have more important duties to perform than playing house for the likes of you."

I wanted to tell her off. I wanted to rip that damn fingerpipe from her hand and snap it in two. Every eye in the room was focused on me and I could feel the accusation in those gazes. Were they on edge because Saree was missing? Maybe I was overtired, and Odele was just trying to keep her people safe.

I bowed and turned to leave.

"Oh, and Gray?"

I paused, looking over my shoulder.

"Why don't you teach her a few tricks while you're playing with her? I've heard you're pretty good at that."

I ground my teeth and walked out the door without a reply. The sun hit my eyes again and I cursed, stalking down the street towards the closest passage underground. How that woman ever managed to move up in the ranks of the guild was beyond me. I couldn't imagine spending time alone in the same room with her, much less touching her. She had the personality of a gutter rat, and probably the bite of one too. As I walked, I rubbed my fingers over the bridge of my nose, trying to ease the ache in my head.

By the time I descended into the underground, I'd shrugged off most of my bad mood. Now I was merely tired. I made my way to the audience hall where Lord Rigel held court during the morning hours, intent on laying out my thoughts about taking fresh thieves on hits. Once there, I caught the guildmaster's eye and settled down on a bench to wait until I was called forward.

The audience hall was an extravagant name for the cavern that was originally called "the den." When Lord Rigel had assumed the guild seat, he'd made them scrub it clean of the blood and filth, then decorate it to look like the court of a nobleman. Six massive banners hung from the walls, three to a side. Each one depicted the color of one of the divisions of the guild: black for the thieves, red for the assassins, yellow for the beggar spies, blue for the prostitutes, green for the marketeers, and white for the mystics. People came and went at all hours of the day, bustling around at Lord Rigel's pleasure.

Rigel was the center of that bustle. It was rumored among the members that he'd been real nobility once, long before he came to Sangarie. He certainly conducted business like a real nobleman. The guild didn't mind it. They lived for the show, after all, and they loved to play court. Despite my usual disgust for nobility, I had to admit Rigel inspired loyalty and service.

His three Attendants, the highest ranked Blue Hands of the guild, encouraged the spectacle. They arranged social gatherings, managed Rigel's calendar, and kept order in the hall. At least a dozen Red Hands stood guard throughout the room, and two more were stationed at the bottom of the dais that dominated the far side of the hall. Rigel sat in a large chair on the raised area, a smaller chair for the Attendant of the day placed to his right and unoccupied.

By the time they called for me, I had dozed off, and another supplicant had to shake me awake when the guildmaster repeated my name. I rubbed a hand over my face and made my way toward the dais.

The guildmaster laughed as I approached. "Gray, you look awful."

"Thanks." Ignoring the protests of the lord's guards, I walked up the two steps onto the raised platform and seated myself in the smaller chair, slouching back tiredly and covering my mouth as I yawned.

Rigel waved the indignant guards away, turning in his seat to face me. "What's on your mind?"

"Currently?" I muttered low enough only he could hear it. "Wondering why I don't retire to a little village and spend my days cheating at cards in the local tavern."

Rigel smiled, but the steadiness in his eyes told me he was merely tolerating my quips. "I haven't been asked to buy your freedom from the Warden, so I assume your hit went smoothly enough."

"I'm not sure you *could* buy me from the Warden if she ever got her hands on me. She'd give her right arm to see me hang." I shifted to get more comfortable in the hardback chair. "I've made fools out of the Coppers too often. I'd accidentally fall into a noose before you knew I was arrested."

"The price of infamy."

"I'm more irritating than infamous. But thank you for the compliment."

"So what brings you to my hall? As you can see, I have a full morning."

My eyes narrowed. "I know what you're doing with that fresh ink."

"I'd be disappointed if you hadn't figured it out."

"Why give her to me? I can see how her talent might be useful, but Old Town is a stinking rat's nest of a place. She's too green to be inked, and my streets are even less friendly than the rest of the city."

"*You* grew up there."

"And look at what an ass I turned out to be."

"I've decided you're the best person to teach her what I want her to know." He brought a hand up to stroke his short beard. "I want you to train her personally. Give her the skills she needs to survive. Keep her out of trouble."

I grumbled and slouched back in the chair.

"Besides, teaching someone else to respect guild law should remind you how to do so as well. You're concerning yourself too much with things beyond your duties. It's a delicate balance, keeping the guild from spiraling out of control and bringing Lady Karyn's wrath down upon us."

He continued lecturing, but I wasn't listening to most of it. I didn't care about the politics of the guild except where my job was concerned. Inevitably, whenever I tried to have a professional discussion with the guildmaster, he would start going on about the day to day of running the largest and most complex criminal guild in the kingdom. I didn't care about the ramifications of illegal trade on the economy, or the sweet spot when it came to bribing the baroness's guards, or the social impact of providing food in the slums, or whatever else he was trying to teach me.

I tuned him out, staring at the tapestries hung on the wall that depicted the colors of the guild divisions. I'm not sure why he always saw fit to explain politics to me. If anything, he should be teaching this shit to Senyr. He was the natural choice to take over the guild once Rigel was gone.

"Where is she now?" he asked.

I brought my attention back to the guildmaster. "Who?"

He frowned and sighed. "The young thief."

"I sent her home," I muttered.

He nodded. "Your concern is commendable, Gray, but I'm sorry. She's yours to train, and I expect it to be done well."

I leaned back in the chair and glared out at the milling guildmembers, the so-called scum of Sangarie.

Lord Rigel's voice changed to a carefully casual tone. "Are you ready for the Under Ball?"

My mood darkened even more. "I'm not going."

"Gray—"

"It's ridiculous."

"The members are really looking forward to it. I'm told this year will be the best one yet." He lowered his voice until I could barely catch the words, mindful of the thieves and assassins in the room. "Don't tell anyone, but the theme this year is the Night of Shadows. My Attendants got the idea from one of the brothel workers. One from Old Town, if I remember correctly. They're so busy with the preparations, they don't even come home in the evenings."

A shiver crawled its way up my back. I definitely wasn't going now. The last thing I wanted to do was prance around like an idiot in a hall decorated like the worst night of my life. I wiped my sweating hands on my pants, my mouth gone suddenly dry.

Rigel was babbling under his breath. "I can't believe we didn't think of it sooner. The Attendants have recruited some of the Yellow Hands to dress as monsters, and the White Hands are working on decorations so it feels authentic."

Fuck no. "Absolutely not going."

"You're an enforcer, Gray. You should be there."

"Not a chance." I rose and bowed. "Thank you, my lord. I'm going to bed now."

Lord Rigel sighed and waved me away. "Goodnight then."

I turned and left, heading for my room, my feet scuffing on the floor the entire way. Rigel knew about my odd little knack for sensing magic, but he didn't know about my issues with the Night of Shadows—at least, not that I knew of. Not many people *did* know, and I tried to keep it that way. It was hard enough keeping my ragged bunch of criminals in line without giving them fodder to mock me.

The walk to my apartment seemed to take years. After I finally shuffled inside I stopped and stared, letting the door inch shut on its own behind me. The apartment was spotless, everything picked up and put away, the dishes all clean and in the cupboard, the furniture wiped free of dust and the air smelling like citrus. I looked to where the ladies sat at the table, both watching me expectantly.

My voice held a hint of sarcasm, probably just a side effect of my lack of sleep and shitty mood. "Well, my gold was well spent after all."

Deidre frowned, tossing a card onto a growing pile in front of them. "Don't be so rude."

I sighed and threw my cloak over a chair. "If you don't mind, I haven't slept yet and would like a few hours of unconsciousness."

Beth hopped up from her chair and blushed. "Of course. I should go."

I shrugged my vest off my shoulders and folded it sloppily before dropping it on top of the dresser, then perched on the corner to take off my boots. "Just so you know, I paid for tonight as well."

Deidre's mildly disapproving look twisted into something more sweet. "Wonderful. Then she can stay here again tonight." She ignored my scowl and rose to guide Beth toward the door. "Once he's gone out for the evening, we can eat together and spend the night relaxing. You won't have to worry about running into those thieves at all."

It felt like she was planning on booting me out of my own apartment, but since I didn't want to spend a lot of time around Beth anyway—and I had to catch my wayward thieves—there was no point in making an issue of it.

Beth beamed back at her. "Thank you so much. I knew you'd understand."

"I told you before, I'm here for you." Deidre gave her a quick embrace. "You've done so much for me, the least I could do is make sure you feel safe."

Beth tightened her arms around Deidre's shoulders. "It's so wonderful to have a friend like you. It makes me not miss home as much."

They muttered a few more things that I didn't bother listening to, then Beth bounced cheerfully out the door. Deidre came to stand beside me near the dresser. "Everything go well last night?"

"I have a new shadow. I'm to *personally* teach her how to be a thief."

"As if one of you wasn't enough."

I ignored the jibe. It was basically the same thing I'd said to Rigel. I pulled off my belt with the knives and set it on top of my vest, then dragged my shirt over my head. "I don't suppose I could charm you into bringing something for me to eat later tonight?"

She held out her hand, palm up, and raised her eyebrow.

I sighed and fell onto the bed, rolling into place and not bothering with the blankets. "Can't you put it on my tab?"

"I'm not a fucking barkeep, Gray."

"Please? I'll get the next one."

"Fine." She started getting ready for the day, doing her hair and face, choosing her clothes. For a few minutes I listened to her moving around the room, the sounds familiar and soothing, and then I was out.

Chapter 9

I woke in the early evening, as sore as I'd feared, and sat up to flex my shoulders. Thank the Six I didn't have another job tonight. I did, however, have to look into those thieves Sans and Beth had mentioned. When you were in charge of a gaggle of criminals wrangled primarily by bluffing and boasting, you were constantly having to remind them who was boss.

I got up and was digging through the dresser when the door opened and Deidre came inside. I could smell the roast and fresh bread immediately and grinned. "Your timing is perfect."

She set a small canvas bag on the table and started pulling out food. "Are you getting ready to head out?"

"Yeah. Have you seen my heavier leather vest?"

"One drawer up and to the left. What are you planning?"

I found the vest and shook it out, then slid the drawer shut with a knee. "Planning? Why am I planning something?" The corner of my mouth quirked as I shrugged the vest up my shoulders. It was much stiffer than the cloth, but it'd give me some slight protection against nasty surprises. "I'm headed for the Devil's Throat to play dice with the guys."

She raised her eyebrow as she ripped the loaf of bread in half and started filling it with roast and soft cheese. "Be serious. Are you expecting a fight from those men?"

"You never know. They may have forgotten how to respect the authority of their enforcer."

Deidre frowned. She stepped up to me, gripping my arm so I'd look at her. "Don't get into trouble, okay?"

"What trouble could I get into at the Throat?"

"Gray…"

I took hold of her arms, peering into her face. "Don't *worry*. I know how to handle myself. It's just a couple of misbehaving thieves."

Her eyes were wide and looked oddly vulnerable. My chest tightened and I started to pull her close, then hesitated. I didn't want to read more into it than there was. *Was* there more to it? I had this crazy urge to fold her up in my arms until she was smiling again. My voice cracked as I broke the silence. "Are *you* ok?"

She nodded, shoving me away and holding out the stuffed half loaf. "Can't I worry about my idiot friend?"

I caught my balance easily and took the loaf from her hand, swallowing past the hitch of disappointment in my chest. She was refusing to look at me, fidgeting with her half of the bread so that crumbs fell to the table.

What the fuck was wrong with me? I shook myself and went to the door to grab my cloak. One hand was engaged in keeping grease from dripping on the floor, so I just slung it across my arm for now.

She spoke with a strained casual tone. "Be careful."

"I'm always careful."

"And it's your turn to buy lunch tomorrow. You can't keep expecting me to feed you all the time."

I waved at her over my shoulder and slipped out the door into the underground. I needed to get back on my game, especially if I was going to be confronting rogue thieves tonight. I didn't know what had come over me back there. I knew better than to get too close.

I ate as I walked, mumbling around mouthfuls whenever I met someone. I had finished the last of the meal and licked the grease from my fingers by the time I walked into the open air of Sangarie and slung my cloak on. It was still early enough in the night that hints of music and laugher drifted to me as I walked through the streets. As I neared the Old Market where the Throat was, I could also hear light footsteps coming up behind me. I took the next right, into a narrow alley, and moved into the shadows to hide and wait.

Sure enough, the figure soon peered around the edge of the building. It paused for only a moment, then darted forward, unknowingly stepping past the shadow where I waited. It was my little thief, Ruena.

I called just loud enough for her to hear. "What do you think you're doing?"

She jumped like a rabbit and skittered to the opposite side of the alley, shaking like it was the middle of winter. To her credit, she didn't run away. Instead she peered into the shadows and bit her lip.

I stepped away from the building.

She took a deep breath and closed the distance to stand in front of me, staring down at my feet so her hair hid her face. The goggles were hanging uselessly around her neck again. "Lord Rigel said you were going to teach me how to be a good thief."

"Listen, kid, I have a lot of nefarious things to get up to tonight. I don't have time to babysit you."

"I understand, Mr. Gray."

I frowned and blew out in exasperation. "Don't call me that."

"Mr. Gray? But isn't that your name?"

"My name is Gray. Just Gray."

"Lord Rigel said to follow you. Even if you don't want me to."

"That asshole." I ran a hand up through my hair and glanced around the darkened street, hoping a solution would reveal itself. I didn't want a pint-sized shadow when I went to the Throat tonight. I needed information, and she would only distract from that. Besides, I couldn't be intimidating with a sheepish little girl at my side.

And the Six forbid she saw me slip a card off the bottom of the deck and asked how it was done. "Okay fine." She wanted a lesson, I'd give her one. "What you're going to do—" I tried to meet her eyes, but her hair was in the way. "Look, kid… I know you're trying to hide your eyes—"

"People think I'm a freak."

I bit my tongue before I told her she *was* a freak. It wouldn't help matters, and I remembered all too well what *that* felt like as a kid. "Tell you what… you keep your head down around everyone else, but I want you to look at me when it's just us. Got it?"

Her face flushed and she wrung her hands as she nodded.

"Okay. First lesson—"

"No talking during a hit. I know."

I narrowed my eyes. "Fine. Second lesson, don't interrupt the teacher."

She nodded quickly.

"Third lesson, people will pay attention to someone who looks like they're sneaking around. We don't creep or dart or stalk if we can help it. We walk like honest folk."

"Senyr can disappear into the shadows."

I glared at her. How did she know Senyr? "The Hands of the Master are skilled enough to pull it off. You're not."

"Are you?"

"Are you going to keep mouthing off, or are you going to let me teach you something?"

She put a hand over her mouth and gazed back at me.

I breathed deep, my nose wrinkling at the undercurrent of piss and fish that was uniquely Old Town. I caught the scent of death beneath it—a combination of blood and decaying flesh. I glanced around, peering into the shadows where a pile of crates clogged the narrow alley, thinking it was probably a rat or something.

Near one of the crates I saw a foot sticking out, with a lady's shoe stained dark where it rested on the ground. The cracks between the broken cobbles were darker than they should have been as well. My chest tightened, even as I told myself it could be a beggar sleeping back there.

Ruena came up beside me, following the direction of my gaze. "What is it?" She saw the foot and gasped, moving toward the crates. "Someone's hurt."

I grabbed her shoulder and pulled her back. "You stay here."

"What if they need help?"

"I told you to stay here." I strode past her, bracing myself for whatever I'd find on the other side of the crates, and stepped over the dark area on the cobbles.

I drew in a sharp breath at the sight of the body, and got a stomach-turning whiff. My hand came up to my nose automatically, and I clenched my jaw and turned away.

"Gray? What is it?"

I pushed her back, swallowing a couple times until I was sure I wouldn't vomit at the smell. "Go get a Red Hand."

"What's wrong?"

"Just do it!"

She turned to run off, but I grabbed her arm and swung her back around. "These don't help if you have them around your neck." I grabbed the front of the goggles and snapped them over her eyes.

She reached up to adjust them.

"Go."

Her footsteps echoed off the walls of the alley. I glanced at the body again and my eyes narrowed. There was a horrible weight in my chest, but I had to be sure. I pulled a handkerchief from my pocket and held it over my mouth and nose as I squatted down to get a better look.

A simple dagger was buried hilt deep in her abdomen, angled up under her ribs. Her chest and stomach were dark with blood, but I could make out part of the blue handprint tattoo on her bare midriff, between the bottom of her corset and the waist of her skirt. A single bar beneath it meant she worked in the brothels. I braced a hand on the nearby crates for balance and reached across to turn her head so I could see her face, praying I was wrong.

It was Saree.

I bit my lip at the sight of her slack-jawed face and staring eyes. Other details stood out, and I focused on them instead, trying not to picture the woman as I'd known her—soft smile, deep eyes, warm heart—but seeing the yellow bruise along her jaw and the scraped skin at the ridge of her cheek… that was worse.

Her clothes were dirty, like she hadn't changed in days, and the back and hem of her skirt had dried mud caking it. As dirty as this alley was, she hadn't gotten covered in mud here. The murder had happened here, though, judging by the stain on the cobbles. The dagger—at least what I could see of it without pulling it out—was simple and unadorned, like something you'd see on the hip of anyone walking the streets of the city.

Who could have done this? Those thugs had been stupid, but I doubted they'd have killed her. She'd been so uneasy… acting strange and dwelling on something. If only I'd pressed her about it. Brothel politics my ass.

I should have checked in on her. Gone out to look for her when I heard she was missing.

Fuck.

I ran a hand over my face, surprised at how much I was shaking. When I shifted my gaze away, I caught a glint beneath the corner of a crate in the faint light of the moon. Picking my way around the blood stain, I fished out a gold coin that had slid beneath the wooden crate.

I almost dropped it again. The tingle of magic creeping up my fingers was like tiny insect legs. I cringed at the feeling, but flipped it in my hand, staring at the strange symbols on either side. It was like no coin I'd ever seen in Sangarie.

The sound of light footsteps came running down the street nearby. I had enough time to step away from the body and slip the coin into a pocket before Ruena came sliding around the corner. She was out of breath, and beckoning at someone still in the street.

The man that strode into the mouth of the alley was cloaked, a hood hiding his features. He barely paused before walking toward me. Ruena was at his heels and I gestured at her to stay back.

The Red Hand took a quick look behind the crates, then back at me. "You found it?" His voice was full of gravel, and not at all shaken by the sight of the body.

"Yeah."

"Did you touch anything?"

I hesitated, thinking about the coin, then shook my head. "Just looked. Her name is Saree. She works at Odele's brothel."

"I'll take it from here."

I nodded and spun away, reaching out to snag the kid as I passed. She stumbled until she got facing the right way, and I dragged her out of the alley. I didn't let go until we were walking down the street and I couldn't smell death anymore.

She walked beside me, trying to match my silent steps. "That lady was dead?"

I hummed an affirmative.

"What are we gonna do?"

I had my own work to do tonight. The Red Hands could worry about the dead. It wasn't like I hadn't seen bodies before. The streets weren't an easy place to grow up, and you didn't get as far as I had in a criminal guild without seeing your share of death. Without experiencing your share of loss. Saree knew that too. We all did.

I shook my head and clenched my jaw, forcing myself to believe that. I'd done my part by turning it over to the Red Hands, and now I needed to forget about it and do my own job. After all, I had some ambitious thieves that needed my attention. Dwelling on this would make me slow. Make me miss things.

Fuck.

I breathed deep through my nose, blinking away the sting in my eyes. Life was hard. These things happened. I just had to keep doing my job… stay on my game. There was nothing I could do for her now.

Ruena hopped a little beside me, like a kid out in the market with her parents. "Are you gonna show me the third lesson?"

I frowned. "Third lesson?"

"People pay attention to someone sneaking around, so we walk like honest folk. Are you gonna teach me to walk quiet?"

"Maybe another time. I have business tonight, so you should go home."

"But you didn't teach me anything."

I sighed and stopped in the middle of the street, folding my arms across my chest and shoving thoughts of Saree out of my mind. I couldn't afford distractions when I was working, and I had work to do tonight. I could do this. "Fine. Show me how you walk."

She hopped back a few steps, grinning and quivering like a puppy. Her hand came up to adjust the goggles and I realized they were probably a little too big for her. Then she straightened herself up and strolled across the broken cobbles. They cracked under her shoes, even with her slight weight, and I could hear the occasional slap as she set a foot down.

"Ease your weight forward. Your legs aren't sticks, so you don't need to jab them at the ground. Set your heel down, then roll your foot into place. Don't shift your weight until your foot is planted."

She spun and came back the other way, slowing down and staring at the ground as she tried to do as I said.

I watched her feet. "The weight should be mostly on the outside of your foot, not spread all the way across. And loosen your knees."

She looked like a drunk walking down the street. I watched her do a few turns and tried to keep the amusement out of my voice. "Watch where you step. If you put your weight down on a broken stone or gravel, it'll crack. You need to choose where to walk so you don't step on things."

69

Her steps got even more erratic as she swerved to find the best places to put her feet down. She *was* quieter though. Maybe she'd get the hang of it with practice. She had her tongue stuck out between her teeth and was staring intently at the street beneath her with one hand on the goggles. "Is this what you do?"

"Yes." *Mostly.* I'd always been light on my feet. This *was* how Senyr had taught me to sneak, except he'd been a lot more patient.

She did a few more passes and I took a long breath. "Okay. I want you to practice walking quiet tonight. Walk the district. Don't skulk."

"Where should I go?"

"I don't care where you go as long as you stay in Old Town. We don't work or practice in another district. Got that?"

She nodded.

"Then get going."

She turned and darted off.

"*Walk*! You sound like a horse galloping away."

She slowed without looking back at me and I grumbled and turned to continue the way I'd been headed. This was an absolutely valid form of teaching. If Rigel bitched about it, I'd say I was giving her missions. They just happened to be missions away from what I was trying to do.

Chapter 10

The Devil's Throat was already full when I walked in. Sans waved at me from behind the bar and I wound my way through the tables in that general direction, greeting people as I went. When I finally reached the bar, Sans had a mug ready for me.

"Nice to see you out, boy."

I raised the mug in a salute. "Nice to be out. Thought I'd entertain Detano for a bit and see what everyone's up to."

Sans nodded somberly. "You've come to the right place." He leaned forward and lowered his voice. "See the pair to the right of the hearth?"

I didn't look. I'd noticed Evin and Adriel as I came in, but I wanted to hear it from Sans. I spoke low enough the noise of the crowd would drown out my words if they carried. "Yeah. A couple low-level idiots."

"*Ambitious* low-level idiots."

I smiled, glad to have the confirmation of Beth's story. "Noted."

He wiped his rag across the bar, more in a habitual gesture than any real need to clean it. "How are the streets faring tonight?"

I took another drink, checking once again that my words wouldn't carry past the bartender's ears. "They're decidedly unfriendly. I found a body dumped in the alley behind Mina's shop."

Sans's hand stopped moving and he stared at me in shock. "Murder? Or the work of the Reds? Do you know who it was?"

I saw the scene in my mind again and took a long pull from my ale. "Saree. From Odele's." I kept my face neutral and distanced my thoughts from the memory of the woman. "It wasn't pretty. And the Reds wouldn't have left the body of a guildmember in an alley."

Sans' face was tragically sympathetic. "Oh no. Did you tell the Red Hands?"

"Of course I did. Some faceless man in a cloak showed up and told me to get lost."

Sans nodded, his hand starting to move again, though he wasn't watching the rag or the bartop anymore. "Bad business. I hope they catch whoever did it soon."

"Me too." But I had done my bit. The rest was up to the Red Hands. I raised my glass, pitching my voice a little louder and cheerier for the benefit of the patrons around me. "Wonderful ale! As always, my friend."

Sans nodded at me with a final worried glance and moved on to another customer.

I turned my back to the bar as I looked around the room, relaxing with an elbow on the counter behind me, pretending to be enjoying a well-earned evening of fun. It was no use dwelling on thoughts of murder when I had my own problems to solve. Killings were the business of Red Hands, and burglaries were my business. I couldn't help Saree now.

Some of my people were in the crowd, which was typical considering the Throat was a guild-sponsored business, but many of them avoided my gaze tonight. Truth be told, I was a little irritated it had been Sans and Beth to tell me about the rogue thieves, and not my own people. Not surprised, really, but still irritated. Back in my younger days, I wouldn't have said anything to my enforcer either. Thieves didn't rat each other out.

Dock workers, however, had no qualms about it. As long as it benefited them in some way, or they got some entertainment out of it. My gaze rested on the table where Detano and a few others were throwing dice. If I could push him just right, I'd find out everything I needed to know. He collected rumors like most drunks in Old Town collected fleas. He would have made an excellent beggar spy.

I wound my way through the crowd, placing myself on the side of the table that would allow me to keep an eye on my rebellious rogues. I spoke up to get Detano's attention. "Good evening, friend. Have a spare chair?"

Detano stared up at me and made an effort to look indifferent, though his hands clutched at the edge of the table in one of his many nervous habits. "I guess." He waved at the men across from him to make room.

I seated myself with a smile. *Good old Detano*. The current game was still underway, so I leaned back in my chair and waited for them to finish. Knowing Detano, he wouldn't have more than insults to say to me right now unless he thought he was going to make back his money. I didn't dare ask about the rumors around a gambling table, but I could possibly soften him up and draw him away with the promise of a better payout.

As the pot was cleared, Detano looked across at me, his face stern. "Let's raise the stakes some, eh? Four silver ante."

He was already eager. That was good. I sat forward and pulled the pouch from my belt, digging into it dramatically until I found four silver pieces among the small stones meant to make the pouch look heavier for my pickpockets. I tossed them into the center of the table and eased back into my chair again, glancing across the room at the pair of men by the hearth. They didn't show any indication of moving.

Detano shook the dice cup and spilled them out onto the table, watching nervously as the three cubes bounced to a stop. He pulled a five out and rolled the remaining two. He took a four from that one and rolled a five for his last dice. His face lit up. "Fourteen! Beat that!"

As the two men to the left of Detano took their rolls, I kept my attention mostly on him. I didn't really care whether I won or lost at the dice game. I was more interested in playing the dock worker. It was both more fun and more useful. I needed to make sure he was desperate enough to leave the table.

Both the men between us had rolled themselves out of the game now. I picked up the cup and slid the three dice in one at a time, deftly tipping the last one into a six and pinning it against the rim of the cup when I placed my fingers over it. Shaking them gently, I stared at Detano while I held the single die secure, hidden under my fingers. "How's your luck been tonight?"

He'd been smiling, but now it faded. "Fair."

I nodded casually. "That's good." In one quick motion I flipped the cup over and let the two free dice fall out while making sure the pinned one dropped onto the six. When I pulled the cup away I grinned. "Lucky roll."

I moved the six aside and scooped up the dice, pinning another one to the rim. "So, heard any interesting news lately?"

Detano was frowning again, watching my movements very closely. "Nothing *interesting* happens in this shithole."

A woman nearby grunted and nudged him from behind. "That's exactly what your wife says."

The rest of the men snickered and Detano made a rude gesture at her before she kept on walking. He frowned at me and dropped his eyes to the dice cup in my hands again, staring at it as if I was a street performer about to pull one over on him.

Which, to be fair, I was already doing.

Detano growled and slapped his hand on the table. "Roll already!"

I flipped the cup and slipped my fingers out, but kept the dice hidden. "You know, this really is a bad habit you have, Detano. What does your poor wife think about it?"

"Shut up and show yer roll!"

I shrugged, lifting the cup and revealing my six and a four. "That makes sixteen for me. I'll hold there." I slid the dice to my right and set the cup down beside them.

Detano's face had turned red and he glared at me as the last man rolled a total of ten. I smiled in return. The poor man must be really upset about losing all that money to me last week. This would be easier than I'd hoped.

I reached out, picking up the silver in the middle of the table one piece at a time. When I'd finished, I stood and edged around the men seated to my left, tipping an imaginary hat to the table. "I don't think I feel like dice this evening after all."

Detano stood and trailed me to the bar. "You ain't gettin' out of it that easy, Gray! I finally got ya at a table and we're playin' til I get my silver back!"

"Settle yourself, Detano. We could always play a private game. Just the two of us." I reached the bar and held two fingers up. Sans nodded and started filling mugs.

Detano leaned on the bar. "If ya think I'm using *your* dice, yer stupider than ya look."

I smiled darkly. I just had to apply the right pressure. "We're going to play a new game. Let's call it—tell me what I want to know or I'll tell Marla about the cute little wench who plays with *your* dice."

Detano blanched. "You wouldn't!"

74

"I would. I'm a scoundrel, remember?" I took one of the mugs Sans held out, gesturing for the trembling Detano to take the other.

He did, swallowing half of it immediately. The foam was still on his short beard as he looked up at me. "Marla'll kill me if she finds out about that! You of all people should understand—"

I cut him off with a gesture. "I really don't give a damn about your personal life, Detano. What I do care about right now is what my people are trying to do behind my back." I took a drink, flashing the other man a wide grin. "So, are you playing?"

Detano shot a glance in the direction of the hearth and I snapped my fingers. "Keep your eyes over here, please."

He narrowed his eyes and glared. "I'm not one of yer *people*, Gray. You can't order me around."

I chuckled and settled an arm over the man's shoulders, turning him toward the bar and away from the thieves. All it'd take was one suspicious look and they'd probably bolt. "My friend, I'm not attempting to. I only want to play a simple game. I know those two have been recruiting in here, and I know you've been in here every day. So tell me, who are they hitting and when?"

"I still don't see why I should tell *you* anything."

Stubborn old goat. I raised my mug and called out across the bar, "Sans! Another for my friend." I ignored the barkeep's raised eyebrow and looked sideways at Detano. "I can make it worth your words."

Detano's eyes lit up and he fairly quivered with greed. "How much?"

Sans walk up with the mug. He set it in front of Detano, giving me a stern look. I winked and slapped most of my winnings onto the bar. Sans scooped the coins up and shook his head, walking away as he slipped them into his pocket.

Detano stared at the barkeep's pocket as he walked away. "How much money?"

"Hmmm? Oh… how much did you lose to me last week?"

"A clean hundred silver."

I smiled and took a sip of ale. "Really? That's too bad. It really is. You should consider giving up dice." I pretended to put the rest of the coins in my pouch as I palmed them. All that was in there now were stones, copper, and a few stray silver pieces.

Detano's face was getting red and he turned to leave, but I stopped him. "Tell you what, I'll give you everything that's in my pouch if you tell me what those two are planning."

He glanced down at my belt, took a gulp from his own mug, and nodded. "Fine. They're gonna rob the goldsmith in Crafthold district tonight, near about midnight. They haven't found any help, so it'll be just the two of em."

I grinned widely. "Thank you very much, my friend." I took the pouch from my belt and held it up between us. "Now, you'll take this and leave for the night. I don't care where you go, but stay away from here."

Detano snatched it up and smiled. "No problem, *friend*." He downed his ale and tried to bow, but swayed forward.

I pushed him back upright, holding him until he steadied. "Go home, Detano."

"That really is some fine ale, barkeep!" He straightened, smiling widely. He started to walk away, but turned back to look at me. "Not a word about any of this to my wife."

I raised both hands. "Not a word."

"Hmph." He walked out of the bar, whistling tunelessly.

I turned back around to lean on the bar. So, they were looking for an easy hit, were they? Did they really think going out of the district would let them get away with it? Taking one last swallow of ale, I set the mug down and put the handful of silver I'd kept hidden in my palm on the bar. "Sans."

The barkeep wandered over, looked down at the silver, and scowled. "I don't suppose Detano thought this money was in the pouch you gave him?"

I shrugged, an innocent look on my face. "How the hell should I know what that man's thinking? Put this toward my tab, would you?"

Sans was cursing under his breath as I walked away. I lifted a wide-brimmed hat off the back of a man's chair as I walked past, stuffing it under my belt for later.

Chapter 11

I set off toward the north, using the light of a nearly full moon to guide my steps. Once I was sure I wasn't being followed, I took a sharp right and headed for the edge of my district. To try to pull a solo job *here* would have been bad enough, but to go to another part of town would make me look like an ass for not being able to keep a handle on my own people.

I crossed out of Old Town and into Lionel's district of Crafthold. Most of the district consisted of craftsmen's shops and homes, but here and there you could find a brothel or a tavern. Lionel kept his people in line and expected them to know the rules. I merely walked down the middle of the street and trusted my presence would be noticed soon enough.

I didn't have long to wait. Two thieves paced me from the shadows, watching to see what business I was about. If I had continued to a brothel or a tavern, they likely would have wandered away, but I stopped in the middle of the street and waited.

A figure stepped out of the shadows of a building in front of me, meandering up to block my way. A throaty female voice cut through the night just loud enough it wouldn't carry to the shops nearby. "What do you want, Gray?"

I moved forward until I was standing quite close to the woman, then stopped and hooked my thumbs in my belt. "I was looking for your enforcer, actually. Maybe you could point me in the right direction?"

The woman didn't back off, but her voice was a little more respectful now that I seemed to be on guild business. "He's got a job tonight."

"Still a little early to be working, isn't it?" I tilted my head as I heard the scuff of a boot behind me, but didn't make an issue of it. "Why don't you take me to him. What I have to say won't take long."

The woman hesitated, shifting her eyes to whoever was behind me. "All right, follow me."

I walked after the woman, keeping one ear on the person who slinked along behind. We made our way into an alley, then crossed the street into another alley and entered a courtyard sandwiched between buildings. The moon provided enough light to see the tall, older man in the center of the space talking to two others.

I stepped past my guide, despite the woman's whispered objections, and sauntered up to Lionel. "Well met, old man."

Lionel glanced at me, no change of expression evident on his face. He motioned for the two men he'd been talking with to back off and they joined the others at the entrance to the courtyard. Lionel crossed his arms over his chest and stared me down. "What brings *you* here?"

I smiled and looked at the buildings surrounding us. "Nice little cove. Old Town is so compact, more like a maze."

Lionel sighed. "I've got work to do tonight, Gray. Tell me what you want or go away."

I shrugged. "Is your goldsmith in bed yet?"

Frowning, the other enforcer glanced at his people, then back to me. "Probably. Why?"

"A few of my thieves have taken it into their heads to go against the system. Would you mind if I handled it, considering you have a prior engagement?"

Lionel's mouth had hardened back into an impassive line and he didn't answer right away. I waited patiently, knowing better than to push him. When he did speak, it was in a soft tone that made even *me* uneasy. "Are you going to kill them?"

I stared at him for a moment, wondering if he was trying to make a joke. Then I realized he was waiting for an answer. "No?"

"Why not?"

"Because I don't kill people?" I lowered my voice even further, mindful of the thieves waiting at the entrance to the courtyard. "Shit, Lionel, what the fuck is wrong with you?"

"That's not what I heard."

My brow crinkled and I tried to imagine who would have told stodgy old Lionel I killed people. "What are you talking about?"

"Didn't one of your lovers go missing, only so you could find her in an alley earlier tonight? Convenient."

I knew the shock was clear on my face, but all I could do for a few seconds was stare at him with my mouth open. "What are you—" I cut myself off and glanced back at the other thieves, dropping my voice to a whisper. "I don't know what you heard, but I didn't kill that woman."

Lionel raised an eyebrow, his hard expression turning more calculating. "Interesting."

"What the fuck is that supposed to mean?"

"What are you going to do about your errant thieves?"

"Don't change the subject, Lionel."

"I don't care about your bedroom drama. People die all the time in this city. What are you going to do about the two thieves planning to rob my goldsmith?"

There was no manipulating Lionel. He always steered every conversation, no matter who he was talking to. It was why he was an enforcer. He was done talking about it, and I wouldn't get another word from him on the matter. Not unless he came looking for one. I snapped an answer back. "If you let me borrow two of your men, I'll catch them at it and bring them into the Red Hands. They like witnesses. It makes everything a little more black and white."

"You aren't going to punish them yourself? This makes you look bad, Gray. Letting your people cross into another district for an unsanctioned hit—you look incompetent."

I glared at him. "I didn't ask for your spin on it, just your permission to work it out. If I stop them before they do something wrong it won't solve anything."

Lionel waved his hand absently. "Very well, take the two that brought you here."

I forced a polite smile. "Always a pleasure working with you." As I turned and walked back to the alley, I gathered up the man and woman Lionel had loaned me. "Let's foil a robbery."

The woman grumbled, but her partner whispered back at her and they fell into line.

I took them to the goldsmith and we hid across the way to wait for the would-be thieves. Lionel's people shot grumbles and glares in my direction, but I ignored it. My own people would be just as pissed if they had to follow Lionel's orders. The personality that made for a good thief made for a poor soldier. I really didn't care what the two thought of me, as long as they did what I told them.

I was more concerned with where Lionel might have heard about Saree's murder mere hours after I found her body. Red Hands didn't make a habit of talking about their work, and Ruena would have been scared shitless to even look at Lionel. Sans wouldn't have said anything. As far as I knew, those were the only three that were aware of it.

Unless one of the Yellow Hands had been watching. If that were the case, there was no telling how far it had spread. Information traveled as fast or as slow as the beggar-spies wanted it to. But the thing about the Yellow Hands was they only dealt in facts and left the guesswork to the buyer. And it wasn't like Lionel to jump to conclusions. So someone had fabricated that story and fed it to him.

Shortly after midnight I set my musing aside as my two rogue thieves slunk into sight, creeping along in the shadow of the buildings. I shook my head. They looked like idiots. Why did Lord Rigel feel it necessary to put all the slow-witted amateurs in *my* district? I waited until they were inside the building and motioned Lionel's people forward.

I positioned them on either side of the door and waited a few more minutes, making sure the two would be caught *while* they were stealing. When I judged enough time had passed, I gestured my helpers forward. The woman pushed the door open wide and they both walked in, knives in their hands. The two inside jumped at the noise, one of them dropping the bucket he was holding and spilling gold coins onto the floor.

I stepped inside to watch, and to make sure I would clearly be seen by my thieves. I shook my head again at the racket they were causing. Within moments Lionel's people had the two trussed up and had replaced the coins in the bucket and set it on the workbench. The two ambitious thieves glared at me from the floor.

I shook my head. "I was hoping you'd come to your senses. Probably would have let you off easy, too, right up until you went inside. But you had to follow through for the first time in your miserable lives."

They just glared back at me.

Muffled sounds could be heard from the second floor of the building and Lionel's people looked to me for orders. I smiled. "Hold up a moment, boys."

The woman spit at me under her breath. "I'm not a boy."

Footsteps crossed the floor over our heads and I straightened my vest and pulled the crumpled hat from my belt. It was a little too big, but I stuffed as much of my hair under the wide brim as I could and pulled it down low on my forehead. "You may not want the smith to see your faces."

The two positioned themselves accordingly and lifted their captives up, getting ready to leave. I could hear one of them whispering something to the other and I shushed them.

The smith rushed in through the door in the back, a lamp casting shadows wildly around the room. He looked at me, standing calmly in the center of the shop, then at the two people tied up and being supported by two more. "What's going on here? Who are you?"

I deepened my voice, giving it a more gritty accent like the merchants from the west, then waved at Lionel's pair. "Take them away, boys. They won't be causing any more trouble in this city." I crossed over to the goldsmith as the two were pushed out the door, distracting him from taking too close a look. "It's a good thing we were passing by, sir. These men were trying to rob you."

The smith's eyes widened. He stepped forward and took my arm, leading me to the heavy workbench near the anvil as he eyed the room to make sure everything was still there. "I can't think you enough, sir. I don't know how much I'd have lost if those thieves hadn't been stopped."

I smiled and pulled the hat further down, letting it make shadows across my features. "I couldn't just look the other way. Someday it may be me they're after." I looked around the room as well, my thieves' eyes taking in everything. "You really should take better measures against this sort of thing, what with all the gold lying about."

The smith sighed. "You're probably right. I thought the new locks would be enough."

I nodded, picking up a coin from the bucket the thieves had been trying to take. It made my fingers tingle with magic and I turned it around, staring at the symbols on either side. It was the same as the coin I'd picked up in the alley where Saree had been killed. It felt warm in my hand, and I got a knot in my gut looking at it. I swallowed and remembered at the last moment to use the gritty tone of voice. "You can never be too careful."

The goldsmith nodded. "I suppose you're right. Thank you for stopping those men."

I held the coin up between my thumb and finger. "What's this?"

The man's face paled and his eyes twitched ever so slightly toward the door. "Just vanity coins. I'm melting them down into bars."

"Seems to be a waste of a finely minted coin."

The smithy smiled too widely and wiped the palms of his hands down the front of his shirt. "Oh. Well. Lord Firmin brought them in for trade. Said he received them as payment for something and they obviously aren't worth more than the gold they're made from. Ha. Probably just playthings of the rich, right? I really didn't pry. Gold is gold, no matter where it comes from!"

"Right. Gold is gold." I set the coin back in the bucket—palming a different one as I removed my hand—and forced a smile. "I should be headed home. I just thought I'd stick around so you knew what was going on down here in the middle of the night."

"I appreciate it, you're a good man…"

"Jonas. You can call me Jonas."

The goldsmith held his hand out and I shook it. "Jonas. Well, thank you again. I hope you have a safe walk home."

I bowed my head, holding the front brim of the hat. "Don't worry, sir. I know how to handle myself."

"I'm sure you do. Good evening then." He ushered me to the door and it slammed behind me quick enough to ruffle the hair at my neck. I could hear him moving around inside, and the scrape of something heavy enough to be a bucket full of gold coins being dragged across a table.

Any goldsmith worthy of being called a craftsman would be able to extract the motherstone from a coin. My guess was our dear Lord Firmin was having him pull the magical source from these coins so it could be reused. I wasn't aware the lordling was into magic.

I'd show them to Rigel, and ask him to take them to a mystic or something. They'd be able to figure out if they did anything, and one of the high ranking Greens might know where they'd come from. They *were* coins after all, and the Greens loved coins. Besides, it couldn't be a coincidence one had shown up in that alley. Something more than brothel politics was going on here.

I tugged the hat off and pushed a hand through my hair. Lionel's people and the would-be thieves were already gone. As I was passing by the mouth of the closest alley I heard a hoarse chuckle. A beggar wrapped in soiled rags was partially concealed behind some crates. I raised an eyebrow as I slipped into the concealing shadows of the alley to join him.

He spoke once I was out of sight of the street. "I was wondering if you decided to rob the man yourself."

I recognized the voice immediately. "Neffery. Why am I not surprised to see *you* here?" He was higher ranked than I was, the top rank of the Yellow Hands, one of the three Eyes of the Master. If you scraped away the top layer of anything strange in this city, you'd find Neffery peering back at you.

He looked like a used up rag as he shifted on the hard ground, cursing under his breath. "I'm not used to lying in the streets anymore. I don't know why I bother helping you."

"*Helping* me? Are you saying you knew about this hit?"

The false beggar lifted the rags covering his eyes so he could glare up at me. "Of course I knew about it. It's my job to know everything."

I tossed the hat into a pile of garbage in the alley and folded my arms in front of my chest. Everything, huh? I wondered if he knew anything about Saree's murder. If the rumors Lionel mentioned originated from the Yellows—had it been from gossiping spies, or had he orchestrated the leak? Neffery liked to talk like his finger was on the pulse of the city, but I knew how hard it was to rein in Old Town.

The best way to handle the old spy was to play dumb. "So why did I have to find out about it on my own?"

Neffery shrugged, letting the cloth slip back down. "It's *your* job to keep an eye on your own people. Besides, if you hadn't got to them, I would have tipped you off sooner or later."

I huffed.

Neffery grinned, showing his black and rotted teeth. "I'm just wondering how much you actually noticed in there."

"What are you talking about?"

The beggar flicked a coin into the air and I caught it out of reflex, glancing at the same strange symbols as the ones in my pocket. The hair on my arms stood up, and I did my best not to react to the faint current of magic coursing through my fingers. Was he testing me? Did he know I'd taken it from the murder scene?

I feigned nonchalance. "So some rich bastard deals in weird shit. Who cares?"

"Have you seen it before?"

"No." I flicked the coin back at him, surprised to see him snatch it out of the air just as easily as I had.

His hand disappeared beneath the rags. "I have."

I waited, but he only stared at me. There was no accusation, and no clue as to what the man was referring to. A spy wouldn't tell me anything he didn't feel like telling me, but why had he dangled the information out like that?

Maybe the old beggar just enjoyed being a pain in the ass. He was fucking with me, and I wasn't in the mood for it tonight.

I turned around.

His next words kept me from moving. "I've seen them in the guild treasury."

That was not what I'd expected. The curiosity that was every thief's downfall flared within me. Only the three highest level Green Hands were even allowed into the treasury, and when thieves gathered to drink and trade stories, a favorite topic was how much wealth must be in that cave. No one knew who was the richer bastard, the guildmaster or the baroness herself.

If he was baiting me, it was working.

I scowled and looked over my shoulder. "Are you telling me Firmin stole a bucket of coins from the guild treasury?"

"Not at all. Four dragonoak trunks full of these coins lie untouched in the guildmaster's vault."

I ignored the implication that the master spy had recently been in the vault, and the pang of envy it raised. He could have simply asked Rigel about it. Besides, if I had to guess, he was only telling me to gauge my reaction.

I snorted and looked away again, scanning the dark street outside the alley. "Offering information for free? That's not like you, Neff."

He chuckled behind me, a grating sound that could easily have been mistaken for a cough. "Nothing is free, Gray. And not all payments are collected immediately."

"What are you after?"

"What am I always after?"

I waited silently, still facing away from him and staring out into the street. He was after better information. But what information he wanted... I still wasn't sure.

He sighed, shifting on the hard ground, and I could hear his joints pop. "I don't judge, enforcer. I only report. But that doesn't mean I can't dig a little."

"I don't have anything for you."

"Not even an explanation? Very odd, how you found that woman."

My back stiffened and I finally turned back to him. "I had nothing to do with that. If your spies had their heads even *halfway* out of their asses, you'd know that."

Neffrey squinted at me for a few moments, then smiled. "If you say so."

I wanted to go off at him about gossip and rumors, to explain what happened and demand to know exactly what had been said about me, to defend myself... but this was Neffery's attempt at digging. I didn't want him picking too closely into my doings. I had secrets of my own to keep that had nothing to do with Saree, and Neffery wasn't an Eye of the Master for nothing. If I let anger or frustration fuel this conversation, he'd dig up more than I was willing to give.

I growled under my breath, knowing full well his sharp ears would pick it up. "Fuck off."

He chuckled himself into wheezing as I walked away.

Chapter 12

I decided to go straight to Lord Rigel. I wasn't fond of magic, and the weight of the coins in my pocket set my teeth on edge. At this time of night he'd be in his chambers. I entered the area of the underground that housed the highest ranking members, including Neffery when he wasn't sleeping on garbage in the alleys above. Lord Rigel's chambers were at the far end.

Two guards sat on the dirt floor outside the door, playing dice and drinking. I stood over them and coughed to get their attention.

"He's asleep."

"It's important," I said.

One of the Red Hands blew out in exasperation and heaved himself to his feet, slipping into the chamber behind him. He came out a few minutes later and waved me through.

I stepped over their dice game and pushed the door open. As I walked inside, the guildmaster came out of his bedroom, tying a gold-trimmed robe around his waist.

"Gray, always a pleasure to see you."

"I won't take up much of your time. Just wanted to show you something."

The lord sat on an overstuffed chair and gestured at a couch.

I ignored it and slipped a hand into my pocket, palming the two gold coins there. "I found a Blue Hand dead in an alley tonight."

I had expected the guildmaster to show some shock, but there was only a tightening around his eyes and a barely audible sigh.

I squeezed the coins hidden in my hand. "You already know."

"A Red Hand was here an hour ago."

"Did they find the killer?"

The old man's expression tightened even further, and his fingers gripped the arm of the chair. "I told them to go back and look again."

My brow creased. Not the guildmaster too. "Look again? Do they suspect someone?"

Rigel was quiet a long moment, gazing at me with an intensity I hadn't seen in him since he made me an enforcer. The hair on the back of my neck stood up and I fought the urge to step back. "Sir?"

"They suspect you."

My face flushed with indignation. I wanted to protest, but only half-formed words and curses came to mind, and I couldn't very well curse at the guildmaster. He calmly watched as I brought my expression back into line. My hands were shaking again, and I realized I had pulled my hand out of my pocket, and the coins clutched in my palm buzzed against my skin.

I pushed words past clenched teeth. "I didn't."

"I don't think you did." He leaned back in the chair, finally relaxing his stern posture. "I'm glad to hear you say it though."

"How could they think I—"

"The woman has been missing for days. Her friends at the brothel said she went out looking for you, and never came back. Tonight you led a Red Hand to the body."

I shook my head. "I talked to her that night, after I dealt with the two thugs by the river, but I walked her home and left."

"I believe you." He rested his elbow on the arm of the chair and his chin on his fist. "But right now there is no other evidence, and Red Hands are quite disregarding of *feelings*. Even my feelings."

I looked down at my hand. "I found something near Saree's body."

"And you didn't tell the Red Hand?"

"I didn't. Maybe old habit, maybe a *feeling*."

He sighed. "What was it?"

I held up the coins so he could see them both. "I found one of these near her body. The other came from a bucket full of them at a goldsmithy in Crafthold. The smith says Firmin traded them to be melted down."

Rigel took the offered coins, turning them over in his hands. His eyes flashed and his jaw tightened. I was actually surprised his hands didn't shake with how much anger I sensed coming off him. What was it about the sight of those coins that would cause an even stronger reaction than hearing about a murder?

I rubbed my hand on the leg of my pants, trying to get the tingle to leave my fingers. "There's magic in those coins, or I'm a fishmonger's salty mistress."

Rigel's expression smoothed out and a shaggy grey eyebrow went up. "Colorful." He set each coin on a table next to his chair with a little *click*. "I'll have a Green Hand take a look."

I should leave it at that. Let the Red Hands investigate the murder and trust Rigel to keep them off me. Whatever connection these coins had to the baroness's son, or to Saree, wasn't my business. I could feel myself standing at the edge of something I didn't want to be involved in.

I mean—shit—those coins alone were trouble. I didn't want to be part of something Neffery was interested in personally, or something that would get the Purse of the Master looking in my direction at *all*. Those top ranked Green Hands ruined people.

Four dragonoak trunks full of magic coins. And not a single rumor as to their existence until now. I clenched my hand at my side, pressing my knuckles into my thigh. If he told me anything, he'd probably swear me to secrecy. I stared at the coins on the side table. "Sir—where did they come from?"

Rigel's mouth quirked in a knowing smile. "Can't leave it alone, can you?"

I didn't know whether to apologize or press the issue. I waited, hoping I wouldn't have to do either.

"I brought them with me thirty-seven years ago, when I came to Sangarie." He turned one of the coins minutely, so the symbol caught the light of the lamp nearby. "It was how I bought my way into the guild. A gift—of sorts—from the elves, to ease my transition into obscurity."

I sensed an entire month's worth of drinking stories in that statement, but I swallowed and refrained from asking questions. Nobody knew for sure what Rigel had been before he arrived in Sangarie and took over the guild. Nobody could say why the guild accepted his leadership so completely. If the elves had something to do with it, I didn't understand why. The only interest elves had in humans since the wars was keeping them away.

I wasn't sure I wanted to know either. If it involved the elves, it involved magic. I vaguely remembered stories at Blind Bob's as a kid, where he said elfish blood was filled with something like motherstone, the ore that humans molded into magical items.

It was why the wars had happened. There was very little motherstone to be found, and centuries ago some humans thought of using elfish blood instead, not realizing it lost its power once it left the elf's body.

Of course, the elves objected. Within a few decades there were hardly any elves left, but they had wiped out over half of humanity in return. Even finding out the blood was useless didn't stop the killing. Eventually the elves bought peace by turning over all the motherstone they had, and humanity squabbled over it while the elves disappeared into the forests and mountains.

Were these coins that old? Was this the literal blood money of the Elf Wars?

Rigel sighed deeply and knitted his fingers together, his elbows resting on the arms of the chair. "Was there anything else?"

I shook my head and turned away, but he called me back.

He stared at me a moment, his gaze narrowing, and I recognized his calculating politician's brain at work. He leaned back in the chair and set his arms on the cushioned sides. "It will take more than my word to dispel the rumors that are sure to rise up about you."

I frowned, sensing more to his musing than just dispelling rumors. "I'm sure it will settle on its own. Sangarie breathes rumor and gossip. Something else will come along eventually."

Rigel continued, his eyes shining hard and bright. "I think the best way to prove you aren't hiding anything is if you go to the Under Ball with everyone else."

My cheeks flushed and my stomach tightened. I'd been able to avoid that spectacle for years. The last thing I wanted was to parade around like a damn fool and pretend to be *civilized*. I didn't understand why the entire guild wanted to mock themselves so badly.

Besides, Rigel had admitted the theme for this year's ball was the Night of Shadows, and I didn't want anything to do with a drunken, cobbled together version of my nightmares. I shook my head, my jaw tight.

Rigel shrugged. "It is, of course, your choice. But it would go a long way toward fostering your innocence within the guild."

"Why is it so important?"

"Because you're an enforcer, Gray. It's important to show the guild there's a hierarchy to be maintained. It's important for them to be reminded of the power behind the rules we make them follow." He sat back in the chair and relaxed, like he was playing a game and just waiting for the opposing player to realize he'd lost. "To show them *you* follow the rules."

I bristled. "There are other ways of showing that."

"If you aren't there, people will talk. What is Gray doing while we're all here? Does he think he's better than us? What is he hiding? But if you're there, at my side in front of everyone, the rumors fall apart. You can show everyone you have nothing to hide."

I knew he was right. I tried to think of some fault in his logic, but as a thief I knew the best way to appear innocent was to appear in public. To hide was to invite rumor and speculation. Damn him.

Maybe it wouldn't be so bad. I could loiter around the edges, have a few drinks, stand there and look responsible while Rigel talked. It was certainly better than living with an itch between my shoulder blades because some Red Hand was always watching me. And it was one night.

"Fine."

Rigel leaned forward. "You'll go?"

I grimaced. "I'll go."

The guildmaster grinned. "Excellent. You'll be part of the grand speech with the other high-ranked members, and after that I'll make sure the guild sees how much I trust you. It should settle some of the rumors."

I gritted my teeth and nodded. Sometimes I wondered if we wouldn't be better off fighting for scraps and knifing each other in alleyways like any other city guild. Organization seemed to come with a lot of extra trouble.

"My Attendants assure me this year will be amazing. I can't wait to see you there." He stood and adjusted the way his robe fell. "Now, I'm heading back to bed. I'll speak with the Blades of the Master in the morning and make sure they keep their investigators in line."

I sighed and spun on my heel, not trusting myself to keep a decent tongue.

***

I walked into the quiet of the night and took a left. There wasn't much I needed to do except make myself seen and make sure things weren't going sideways. The thought of managing my district rankled after my discussion with Rigel. For the first time in its history, the criminal guild of Sangarie had a stable hierarchy. I had quickly risen in that hierarchy to control the largest and most unmanageable district in the city. Supposedly, Lord Rigel had "the utmost faith in me."

Now he was going to parade me around at some fancy ball where the scum of the city would pretend to be nobility. I groaned just thinking about it. We weren't nobility. That ball was a joke.

All I knew was I seemed to be plagued with imbeciles and incompetents. Every entry-level thief seemed to be given to me first. Old Town was known for its pickpockets if only because I had to sift through the ones who always managed to get caught. And now some Red Hand thought I would murder a friend in my own district. They *should* be figuring out who really killed Saree.

I grumbled as I walked until Rigel's story surfaced in my thoughts again. He'd arrived in Sangarie ten years before I was born, so I had never known the guild before Rigel remade it, except in stories from the older criminals. May remembered it. Senyr did. Even Sans, despite not being tattooed, admitted the city was better off with Rigel in charge of the underground.

Rigel had mentioned starting a life of obscurity. Had the elves forced him into some kind of exile? Had he sought out their help to escape his previous life? I wasn't sure what made me more uncomfortable, knowing that Rigel had been involved with elves and been given a fortune in magic-laced gold, or thinking the elves had some hidden motive in the workings of Sangarie.

Nobody was sure how many elves were even left. They'd hidden themselves away, fled the butcher knives of the human armies and turned the ancient forests against them. How had a nobleman managed to make any arrangements with them?

Maybe I was seeing the worst in things. Maybe he was being cryptic, and the elves weren't involved in anything. Rigel had come to Sangarie to become the King of Thieves, after all. Maybe their contribution had been metaphoric. As in, he'd stolen the coins from someone. The thought was comforting. Comforting enough I decided not to continue thinking about the problem, so as not to ruin my imagined solution.

I wandered the streets for the next three hours, escorted two women and a young man back to their brothels, helped four drunks out of the gutter, and broke up a fight between two of my own people. I went underground less than an hour before the sun was due to rise.

When I slipped inside my room, it was still dark. I didn't bother to light the lamp, since I could find my way through my own room without sight. I hung my cloak up beside the door and walked to the table as I unhooked my belt.

"Welcome home," Deidre said.

My heart jumped into my throat, but I managed not to voice my surprise. She would never let me live it down if she startled me at home. "You're supposed to be sleeping," I commented.

I heard her shifting. "I've been waiting for you."

I set the belt and my knives on the table, feeling in the dark to make sure they didn't rest too close to the edge. "Where's Beth?"

"She said she had some things to do and left not long ago."

Unfastening the wooden toggles on my heavy leather vest, I walked in the direction of the bed. "I wanted to talk to her." Maybe she knew something about Saree, and where she'd been the last few days. She was from the same brothel after all.

I shrugged the heavy leather off my shoulders and still had my arms behind me in the sleeves of the vest as Deidre's body suddenly pressed up against me. I braced my feet and slipped one hand free to come around and catch hold of her. As she pulled my head down to a kiss, I tossed the vest in the direction of the chest of drawers. It slipped to the floor with a slithering whack.

This was much better than continuing to roll worrying thoughts around in my head. I kissed her back, tasting wine and breathing in the scent of her soap. I slid my fingers through the hair at the back of her head, already loosened for sleeping, and stroked the gentle curve of her jaw just below her ear. The lack of sight in the dark room let me focus on touch... her lips on mine, her skin beneath my hands, her body against me.

After a moment she pulled back, just enough to speak. "I'm so glad you're here. I had to entertain Sir Variet tonight, and he's absolutely boorish."

I ran a hand down her back, the silk of her short nightgown impossibly smooth. "Is that so?"

"And then I had an appointment with the young Lord Garret."

I chuckled and nuzzled her neck, pulling her against me. "The younger one? He's barely old enough to shave."

"It was a coming of age present from his father. The fool was so excited I barely had time to catch a rhythm before he finished. Then he spent the rest of the time crying in my lap in embarrassment."

"What a shame."

She tugged playfully at my pants. "Would you mind if I took out some frustration on you? I thought about taking care of it myself, but there's a few things the girls and I have been talking about that I wanted to try."

"Try whatever you like, lover."

She kissed me as she tugged me closer to the bed in the dark, running her hands up my chest and across my shoulders, then behind my neck.

I pulled my head back abruptly, but couldn't see her face in the dark. "As long as it doesn't involve tying me up. We aren't doing that again."

She laughed. "No bondage. I promise."

She pulled me into motion again. I shuffled forward, and when the back of her knees met the edge of the bed she fell back, pulling me down with her.

I caught myself, the bed bouncing beneath us, and she drew me further onto the mattress. She was insistent, determined. I couldn't see her in the blackness of the unlit room, but I could hear her breath coming fast already. The little sounds she made between kisses made me want to see what other noises I could tease out of her.

She ran her hands down the front of my shirt and pulled it up until she found skin. Her touch sent shivers through me and I pushed myself to my knees between her legs, reaching up to pull my shirt off over my head as she scooted further up on the bed.

I crawled forward and hooked a finger in the low neck of the silky nightgown she wore, pulling it down until I could kiss between her breasts. I kissed lightly up to her neck, making sure to hit the spot right below her ear that made her moan and lift her hips against me. She tasted like midnight. Like rain. And the warm taste of spiced wine.

Everything I'd been worrying about fell away. I slid a hand down her side and under the hem of the short nightgown, my fingers dimpling her ass as I lifted her hips to mine again.

My pants were in the way. I growled in frustration and sat up to fumble with the ties. As they loosened, her fingers pushed mine aside and she tugged the front open. The feeling of her smooth hands on sensitive skin made me gasp. I hunched at the shudder that ran through me.

I didn't care what was going on with the guild anymore. Didn't care about Beth or Rigel or anyone else. Her breath was hot on my skin and I rolled so she was on top. There was a whisper of silk as she pulled off her nightgown and tossed it aside.

***

A satisfied shudder went through me and I swallowed against the dryness in my throat. My heart was racing, I was panting to catch my breath, and it took conscious effort to get my fingers to unclench from the blankets. Deidre settled herself onto my chest and nuzzled beneath my chin, her hair falling across my neck. The room was still black as pitch.

I raised a hand to stroke her bare shoulder and closed my eyes against the dark. After a few moments I noticed the trembling in her chest as she rested against me, and a dampness on my collarbone. I reached a hand up and found tears on her cheek. As I started to sit up, she pressed me back down.

"What's wrong?" I asked.

"It's nothing. I'm just glad you're here."

"So you're crying?"

"I've had a lot on my mind. It's nice to get a chance to—to let out some frustration." She snuggled in closer, tracing her fingers across my ribs. "Were you looking for Beth earlier?"

I didn't want her to change the subject, but I didn't know what else to say. She'd always kept her problems to herself, never wanting me to get involved in her work or her private life, but it bothered me to see her upset. I answered reluctantly. "Yeah. I—"

I didn't want to tell her about Saree right now. I swallowed and lightened my tone. "I wanted to tell her I caught those thieves. They've been given over to the Red Hands."

Her voice brightened. "That will make her feel much better."

"Hmm."

"I know you aren't fond of her, but she's really trying. It's not easy for her living like this after being raised noble."

I kept my mouth shut, running my fingers lightly over her bare shoulder.

"She talked about it one day. We'd had a little too much wine—some good stuff I'd been given after a job—and she cried and told me about how her family had shunned her and locked her away, and how they'd planned on sending her to a mystic sanctuary to live so they didn't have to deal with her."

"Is that so." I really didn't want to know anything about Beth's past. I didn't *want* to feel bad for her. As a kid I would have done *anything* to be locked in a tower just so I had someplace to sleep out of the rain. Beth's sob story of being ignored by her rich family didn't tug on my heartstrings.

Deidre went on, tracing circles on my chest. "All she wants is to make something of herself. To be her own woman and have her own power. To not be at the mercy of anyone else ever again. Is that so different from any of us?"

I grimaced. "No. It's not different at all." Many who found themselves on the wrong side of the guards were only trying to take control of their lives. That's what turned them to the guild in the first place. Freedom to choose. Freedom to say no.

By choosing the guild—choosing Rigel—I was ensuring my own freedom. My talent for sensing magic made me… valuable. Rigel helped keep my secret, and his influence would turn suspicion aside if need be. I didn't want to be used by anyone.

She sighed and snuggled closer in the dark. "Did you talk to Rigel tonight?"

It was like she could read my mind. "I did."

"I'm sure he was happy you caught them."

"Hmm."

"Gray? Is something wrong?"

95

Deidre knew a great many things about me, but I'd managed to keep my freak talent hidden even from her. However, there was *one* thing she was uniquely qualified to sympathize with. "I have to go to the Under Ball."

Deidre laughed, and I frowned. She patted my bare stomach before getting off the bed. "It won't be all that bad. You might even enjoy yourself."

"I very much doubt it. He told me the theme."

Her voice came from a few paces away, her figure not visible in the dark. "He *did*? People have been trying to figure that out for weeks."

The mattress shifted as she climbed back on. She set a hand on either side of my chest and leaned over so her hair tickled my shoulders. "Tell me what it is."

I grimaced. It wasn't even because Rigel had sworn me to secrecy. I was a liar and a thief. He had to have known there were circumstances where I'd tell someone. I was hesitant because of what the theme was. Deidre was one of three people who knew how much I hated that night.

Memories came unbidden to my mind. Reasons why those three people were party to the truth. May knew, because as a little kid I had ended up outside her brothel that night, and she had been the one to hold me in her arms as I sobbed and dripped snot, reassuring me that no monsters were chasing me.

Sans knew, because he had taken pity on a wretched brat and given me a place at the hearth in the years following, when he would have normally sent street kids to Blind Bob's. But after that night I couldn't stand to be around magic, and the mystics made my skin crawl.

Deidre knew, because once we started sharing a room, she got to witness me drinking myself into a blubbering mess on the Night of Shadows. I was sure she knew a lot more about it than I was aware of. I had a habit of babbling when I was completely shitfaced.

She wiggled above me. "Do I have to give you some incentive or something? *Tell me*."

"It's the Night of Shadows."

"Oh." She shifted to sit beside me.

I took a deep breath and cut off any consoling gesture she may have made. "I told him I'd be there. That's the end of it."

96

After a few moments of silence, she bent over to kiss my cheek. "Try to get some sleep. I'll bring supper back for you later."

"I thought it was my turn."

"I'm using your silver."

That actually got a laugh out of me. I rolled over so she could turn the lamp on low and get ready to go out.

Chapter 13

When I woke up, Deidre was setting food out on the table. My stomach growled and I pushed myself up in bed, looking around for the clothes I'd thrown off earlier. Once I'd put on my pants, I crossed the room to the table and sat down.

"Do you work tonight?" she asked.

"No, but I need to go out and do the rounds."

She smiled at me, then looked down at her food.

We ate in silence. It worried me a little, because she only got quiet when she was fretting over something. She couldn't be this upset about the ball. Could she have run into someone who knew about Saree? Maybe not telling her about it myself had gotten me into trouble. I kept my head down as I watched her—trying and failing to decide if she was upset or just quiet.

Once I finished my food, I stood and pulled on a shirt. "I think I'll hit the baths before I go out."

"I'll join you, if that's okay."

"Always." The answer had come automatically, but maybe it wasn't such a good idea. Something seemed off with her, and I wasn't sure if I was worried about her, or about what was being left unsaid. I had enough to think about with elves and balls and dead girls and magic coins and baby thieves that wouldn't leave me alone. I didn't need to second guess my relationship with Deidre as well.

The word *relationship* made me cringe. Friends worried about each other like this, right? That was a relationship, too.

She merely gathered up some clothes and towels and waited for me to join her at the door. I couldn't very well tell her no. I would never brush her off like that, and it'd probably make her try to figure out what I was hiding. So I smiled and followed her out.

The baths were located in a lower level of the underground. Under Lord Rigel's guidance, the natural hot springs in the caves had been turned into a relaxing spa where guild members could go to clean up or just to rest. He'd had them build partitions to divide the space into individual rooms, but left them open at the top to allow the steam to escape. It was the one luxury the guild controlled that couldn't be found in the city above.

This early in the evening the baths wouldn't be busy. Most people preferred to use them in the mornings when they got done with business, or in the afternoon when people gathered there in rowdy groups. Deidre and I found a room where we could be alone and shrugged out of our clothes.

I slid into the waist-deep water and she sat on a towel on the warm stone. The water was almost too hot, and I closed my eyes and crouched near the edge, leaning my head back between her knees.

Her hands came down and started to massage my shoulders and neck. It felt so normal. Maybe I was overreacting and reading more into her mood than there was. She had problems of her own. Some of them I knew about—like certain feuds with other escorts, or problematic clients, or smuggling abused servants of the nobility out of the city—but I'm sure there were other things that weighed on her.

Her voice broke into my thoughts. "When is your next job?"

"Hmm?" I mumbled.

"Your next job. There should be one coming up, shouldn't there?"

"The night after the ball."

She rubbed her thumbs down the sides of my neck and across my shoulders, repeating the motion several times. "Is it something difficult?"

"No, not really. The owner won't even be there. It should have gone to Tekken, but she's getting close to having her baby and I told her I'd handle it myself." I let my head fall to the side as she kneaded my shoulders, my cheek resting against her thigh. I was being stupid. I was projecting my worries onto her. "That feels good."

She traced my collarbone with a finger.

Letting my thoughts wander, I remembered the first time I'd seen her. I'd rushed into her room at the brothel close to morning, dived under her blankets, and whispered in her ear that she should pretend we were busy.

99

I'd barely evaded capture by the city guards that morning, and when I'd left in the afternoon it had been with a black eye and a distracted grin, both of them from her. That was eight years ago. We'd been friends ever since, supporting each other's rise through the ranks of the guild.

Good friends.

I sighed and pushed away from the edge, moving out a ways and slipping under the water. It smothered everything, prickling my scalp and face with heat, reducing the entire world to the sound of my own heartbeat.

Why did those thoughts make my chest feel like it would burst? I couldn't imagine sharing a living space with anyone but her, and if she were to leave… The thought was actually frightening. We were so comfortable with each other. Of course I was worried about her happiness. Who wouldn't be?

I came back up, standing and wiping water off my face. The ripples on the surface lapped at my stomach and I looked at Deidre.

She had entered the pool while I wasn't watching and turned away to crouch at the edge, resting her forearms on the towel and her chin on her arms. The lamplight reflected off the water and danced across her back.

I waded closer and raised a hand to reach out to her, but changed my mind at the last moment and eased up beside her instead, bending enough to rest my elbows on the edge. "Is everything okay?"

She nodded and wiped her cheeks, smiling. I couldn't tell if the wetness was from the steam or from tears, but I suspected it was both. "Of course."

"You can talk to me. If you want."

She chuckled and turned to lean her back against the side, sinking down until the water lapped at her throat. "I'm fine."

"You don't seem fine."

She sighed and stared up at the steam-filled ceiling. "You're my best friend, Gray. I don't want anything to ever change that."

It was like a punch to the gut. I'd been saying the very same thing to myself for days, but hearing the words come from her was making my hands shake and my stomach turn. I swallowed a few times to get rid of the dryness in my throat. "Nothing ever *will* change that."

My voice had only cracked a little, and hopefully she hadn't noticed.

She took a deep breath and let it out in relief. "Good." Her hand reached beneath the water and traced the outside of my thigh, then she pulled it back. "Be careful out there. You still owe me for supper."

I plastered a smile on as she pushed herself away from the edge of the pool and waded through the waist-deep water, out of my reach. Reflected light played across her skin, twinkling like stars where droplets of water clung to her back.

Good friends.

I shook my head and pushed myself out of the pool, then walked to the bench by the door to dry off and put my clothes on without looking at her. "I should be home early." My hands fumbled with the buckle on my belt and I cursed under my breath. I already knew this was how things were between us. It changed nothing. I made sure my knives were secure under the vest at my back.

With a last look in her direction as she lowered herself into the water, I slipped out of the room and headed for the surface level.

I walked around for a few hours, checking all the usual haunts, visiting with people and getting any news I'd missed during the day. Everyone I talked to seemed to want to turn the conversation back around to the ball the following evening. I even caught a couple of low level thieves staggering drunkenly through the street with arms full of puffy skirts. They snickered and belched, giving me a wavering salute as they wandered past. I probably should have stopped them and asked what the fuck they were doing, but I didn't want to know.

Eventually I started making my way toward the Devil's Throat. I was walking past Odele's brothel when I heard shouting from inside and paused to listen. As much as I disliked Odele, this was Old Town. This was *my* district, and I wouldn't stand by and let someone get hurt… again.

A man's commanding baritone broke into the night, his voice cracking in panicked indignation. "Get your hands off me, you filthy whore!"

The sound of something solid hitting the floor and glass shattering drifted out, along with the muttered protests of multiple people. One sarcastic female voice rose above the rest. "You're in a whorehouse, what did you expect? Courtiers?"

101

Another voice rose in laughter and added. "Not until their spouses go to sleep!"

I waited outside, in the middle of the street. I wasn't supposed to get involved in the business of the other divisions. Especially here. Odele would love nothing more than to complain to Rigel that I was roughing up her customers—again—and I needed to keep my distance from anything connecting me to Saree right now.

The man's voice bellowed through the building, loud enough the beggars two streets over could probably hear him. "I'm not here to be tempted into depravity. I am a *knight*. Mine is a higher calling, and scum like you will whisper my name in awe when—"

"What's your name then, tough guy?"

I could actually hear the man's intake of breath before he stuttered and caught himself. I had unconsciously moved up to the door and put my hand on the knob. I let go and stepped back, frowning. They could handle it.

"I wouldn't dirty my good name by giving it to the likes of you. Now let me through."

A softer male voice came back at him. "Just let him leave, Tilly. His asshole's too puckered even for my tastes."

Scattered laughter greeted the comment, which turned into shouts as I heard a yelp and the sound of heavy furniture sliding across the floor. I grimaced and flung open the door, one hand reaching to the small of my back to rest on the handle of a knife.

Everyone turned to look as I burst in, including the big blond man in a simple tunic and pants. He had one fist twisted in the shirt worn by one of the male Blue Hands, holding him down on a couch that had been shoved dangerously close to the hearth. His other hand was clutching a shapeless package about the size of a loaf of bread, wrapped in cloth and bound with string. The knight's expression changed from anger, to startled guilt, to embarrassment, so quickly I might have missed it if my gaze hadn't sought him out first when I entered the room.

I drew my knife, but kept it behind my back, knowing if I escalated things I'd be in even more trouble. Instead I smiled, but kept my eyes hard. "Good evening. I couldn't help but hear the shouting as I was passing by. Must be having a good time in here."

102

The man dropped the Blue Hand, wiping his hands on his pants afterward. "Not worth it."

He walked toward the door, which meant he walked toward me, and I stood my ground. He was a lot bigger than I was, and the way he moved and the calluses on his hands told me better than his bragging that he knew how to fight. I kept my gaze locked on his and tightened my hand on the knife hidden behind my back.

He stopped in front of me and looked down, a full head taller than I was. "Move."

I thought about making an issue of it, trying to teach him a little humility, maybe snapping off a witty comment about his honor. He wasn't armed. I'd give myself decent odds of coming away from it with only a bloody nose and a sore gut, while he'd be leaking from several internal organs, but I didn't want to sit through another lecture from Rigel. I shifted my weight to step aside.

He was impatient, and swung out an arm and *shoved* me.

I was already moving in that direction, so the force of it overbalanced me to the point that I had to flail wildly. The knife skittered across the floor. Even then I would have remained upright if there hadn't been a padded footstool behind me, probably pushed aside in the earlier commotion. I toppled over it, landed on my back, and immediately scrambled to my feet, but he was gone.

A few of the Blue Hands muttered under their breath, and they were all staring. For the first time in my life I felt absolutely unwelcome inside a brothel. I was sure it had to do with Saree's death. By now every one of them must've assumed she'd left the brothel to meet up with me as I walked my route... and ended up dead.

Tilly stepped ahead of the others, my knife in her hand. Her expression was cold and her voice sharp. "You dropped this." She tossed it to bounce and clatter on the floor at my feet.

Curses and mild threats rose from the group as I stared down at the blade. A few people spit on the floor. I bent to retrieve the knife and slipped it into the sheath at the small of my back, then lifted my gaze to Tilly. There had to be something I could say.

She tilted her head at the door. "Get out."

Chapter 14

There was nothing to be done about the gossip. Rigel had warned me about it, but I hadn't expected it to impact me so quickly. Or so strongly.

I knew those people. I drank beside them, gambled with them, and even slept with a few of them. I was shocked how angry they all were, and how easily they'd turned on me. Arguing against rumors never got you anywhere, but finding out who had killed Saree would fix everything. I only hoped the Red Hands could find something that led them in the right direction. It didn't bode well for me if the people in my district didn't want me around.

As I walked, I watched for the knight to be lying in wait somewhere, but I didn't get to redeem myself with a second meeting. It gnawed at my pride that I'd stumbled around like a clumsy fool.

I didn't know what a knight would be doing at a brothel in Old Town anyway, especially someone with an aversion to Blue Hands. Maybe he didn't realize what a slum Old Town was, and had wandered here by mistake. There had been a wrapped package in his hand, which he'd taken with him when he left. I don't know why someone at Odele's would have given him a package, so he must have brought it with him. Maybe he'd been trying to deliver it to someone…

Come to think of it, a disheveled knight had been traveling with that visiting nobleman. It could have been the same man. I'd have thought a guest of Firmin would have been provided with escorts, but—

I stopped in the middle of the street.

A guest of Firmin, who had come riding into town with an elf in a cage. Then Firmin suddenly was in the possession of a bucket of elvish coins to melt down. One of which I'd found in the alley with Saree's body.

Now this knight was inexplicably in the brothel where Saree had worked. He obviously disliked the Blue Hands. He hadn't been there to hire one. Was it possible he'd killed her, and was there looking for another victim? Or had returned to cover something up? Had it been guilt over his crime I'd seen when I burst in, and not just guilt at being seen in a brothel? The visiting noble could have given Firmin those coins, and paid this knight with the same—

What had been in that package? I looked back, and went so far as to take a couple of steps toward Odele's, then shook my head. They wouldn't know anything, and even if they did, they would never talk to me. My best bet was the knight himself, but I'd already walked halfway across the district without any thought to tailing him, so he could be anywhere.

I could ask the beggars if they'd seen him, but they'd ask questions and I wasn't supposed to interfere with work that was better suited to the Red Hands. I could question some of my own people, but they wouldn't have followed the man unless they decided to pick his pockets, and he'd been dressed as a commoner. Nothing worth stealing.

I grumbled and started walking. At least I was more likely to come across him if I was moving. I thought about taking the Thieves Way, but even on the rooftops it would take forever to search the entire district. Old Town was too big. And there was no guarantee he would stay in Old Town. I definitely couldn't search the entire city.

There was only one place I *knew* he'd be eventually, and that was with Firmin's noble friend, wherever the lordling was putting him up during his visit. Maybe I'd shaken him enough he'd give up for the night and go home, and I could avoid tramping around the city. The problem was figuring out where it was. It would be in the Estates, because the baroness rarely allowed visitors to stay at her own manor, but I didn't know which manorhouse it would be.

The night was clear and quiet, and I made my way toward the Old Market again and the comfort of the Throat. The rumor mill might know which house it was, saving me a lot of trouble. When I heard someone coming up behind me from a block away, I actually hoped it was the so-called knight, but a sneaky glance and a long familiarity with the dock worker's stride, told me it was only Detano.

When the man finally drew close enough, I spun around and startled him so much he almost fell over. He regained his balance and cursed.

"You cheatin' thief. That pouch was full of rocks!"

I tried to keep a straight face, but the smile crept up anyway. "Oh come on, Detano. What did you expect?"

Detano pulled a worn knife from his belt and lunged clumsily at me, but I merely stepped aside. "You're going to hurt yourself, friend."

"You aren't my friend, bastard! Marla hit me twice with a broomstick afore I could get outta the house."

I actually had to make an effort to evade his next lunge. I held my hands up and backed away. "I'm sorry about your wife, man, but you're the one who played the game."

"SHUT UP!" He ran at me, slashing with the knife.

I caught his wrist and twisted his arm so he dropped the blade. It clattered on the cobbles and I kicked it away. *That* was more like it. The knight had just caught me off guard, that's all.

Detano clenched his free hand into a fist and swung at me. I bent backwards to dodge the punch and shoved him away.

He lost his balance and fell onto his backside, then growled and spit at my feet. "You thievin' son of a bitch!"

I chuckled, holding out a hand. "Come have a drink with me."

"I should kill you!"

I kept my hand out, waiting. "Who would play dice with you then?"

Detano glared up at me, but reached for my hand anyway. "Bastard."

I helped him to his feet and waited for him to brush himself off and retrieve his knife before falling in beside him to continue to the Devil's Throat. "What was she upset about? You didn't tell her about the money, did you?"

"Of course not! Do ya think I'm stupid?" He grumbled something else under his breath, a drunken garble of words I didn't catch.

I looked over at him. "What was that?"

"She thought I robbed someone, because she saw your pouch."

I laughed as we reached the door to the bar.

"It isn't funny! She told me to give it back to whoever I took it from, afore I angered the Six by bein' a thief."

106

I slapped the man on the back as we went in. Leave it to Detano to put the world back in order. "If it's any consolation, you'd make a terrible thief."

"I'll tell her you said so. That'll make things all better, I'm sure."

I walked to the bar, still chuckling. "Sans! Two of your best for the scum of Sangarie!"

Detano glared at me. "You ain't funny."

When Sans hustled over with the mugs, he set them on the bar hard enough the ale slopped over the edge. His brow furrowed and he pulled a rag from his belt and quickly cleaned it up. "Sorry, the boy that was supposed to be helping tonight never showed up. So hard to find good help these days. Let me take care of a few tables and I'll be back." He pointed a chubby finger at my chest. "I need to have a word with you." He scurried away with his rag dripping ale.

I picked up the mug and turned to look over the crowd. It was pretty busy for this late at night, and I could see why Sans was flustered. Even with Kash, the after hours bartender, he was running himself ragged. Many of the people were criminals who had no jobs for the night, but there seemed to be a surprising number of strangers in large groups, shouting and drinking like fish. I recognized a couple of Blue Hands that looked away from me quickly when they caught my gaze.

That Sans wanted to talk to me was worrying. I had a feeling it was about Saree, and I hoped he knew me well enough to know I wouldn't kill anyone, much less a friend. But then, I would have thought all of Old Town knew me well enough not to believe those rumors.

A woman with chestnut hair straight as rain and a low-cut forester's bodice caught my gaze. She rose from her seat at one of the tables and smiled as she sauntered up beside me at the bar.

"Hello, handsome." Her voice had a rumbling undertone that promised a lot more fun than I expected to have trotting into the Estates tonight. She wasn't a local, judging by the smell of dust and horse shit.

"And hello to you, beautiful. A bit late for a lady to be out, isn't it?"

"I wouldn't know. I haven't been called a lady in years." She slipped her arms around my waist and leaned her pelvis into me.

A dull whack caught my attention and I glanced down at the bar where Detano had slapped my empty pouch. I grinned. "Thanks. Deidre gets upset when I lose things."

T. Olsen

"Curse your breath, and hers too." Detano drained his mug and motioned Kash over. "Give me another, and put it on Gray's tab."

I nodded my acknowledgment and Kash fetched another mug. The woman in front of me stroked a hand down my cheek, letting her eyes do the talking. I'd have been more tempted if she were a Blue Hand, but I avoided men and women just passing through town. It was never worth the trouble. Either they weren't clean, they had angry partners that had a habit of bursting in, or they didn't want to leave the next morning.

Detano belched. "If you're gonna pet each other, can you do it somewhere else? I'm try'na drink."

I smiled. "Maybe another time, my lady. I need to catch up with my friend here."

She pouted, running a hand down the fabric of my vest. "I could find a friend, too. We could all find a room somewhere and catch up together."

Detano waved her off like he was shooing chickens. "You heard him. Go milk some other idiot."

The woman raised her eyebrow and snorted at him. She slipped a hand behind me and squeezed my ass, whispering in my ear. "Offer's open, if you change your mind."

I winked at her and she sauntered back to her table, sitting with two other women who dealt her back into whatever card game they were playing. I made sure to check that all my valuables were still in place. While I wasn't interested in what she offered, it made me feel a little more like myself. It was surprising how rattled all this had gotten me.

Detano scowled. "They're like leeches."

I chuckled and picked up my ale. "They're just looking for a cheap bit of fun after weeks on the road."

"I'm surprised you didn't go with her. I thought you were some fancy-boy thief what all the men and women can't keep their hands off of."

"I prefer my partners to be professionals. They're cleaner, better at it, and they don't expect more than the coin they're due."

"What about Deidre? If I had a woman like that at home, I wouldn't buy it ever again."

"She isn't my woman. We just share an apartment."

Detano laughed. "You don't get any of that?"

108

"You're looking for a punch to the face, old friend."

He caught on and changed the subject, and I listened to him alternately gossip about the regulars in the tavern and curse me for a bastard. Sans was running drinks, still looking a little too busy for conversation. I did catch him glancing at me with furrowed eyebrows once in a while, and it made me even more certain he'd heard the rumors floating around. I'd love to know how those were spreading so quickly. The Red Hands usually kept such matters quiet, and the Yellows only spread rumors on purpose.

I nodded in agreement at Detano's tirade about the butcher's wife and her habit of putting her finger on the scales, taking another drink and waiting for him to stop long enough for me to bring a topic up. Before that could happen, he brought up the one thing I *didn't* want to talk about.

"Word is, you knifed a woman the other night."

I slammed my mug on the bar and glared at him. "I did not."

He held his hands up and waved his fingers. "Don't get yer dick in a knot. I told them boys you wouldn't kill a Blue. They was stupid for even passing that along."

I stared down at the bar and shook my head. Of all the people… who would have thought Detano would be the one that came to my defense?

The man continued. "Not to say you wouldn't skewer some poor bastard over a shiny new copper, but you'd never hurt none of those whores."

I snorted. "Thanks."

"Dunno who you fucked over to get this one pinned on you though."

"Me either."

"You tryna find out?"

I nodded and took another long swallow of my ale. This was as good a way to broach the topic as any. "Did you hear about that nobleman who rode in the other day?"

"I saw him go through at the River Gate. Such a fancy dandy."

"Somebody figure out why he's here?"

He nudged me conspiratorially and chortled. "Probably buffing the baroness's son in exchange for a place at court." He made a rude gesture with his hand. "You know what I mean?"

"It's hard not to, when you demonstrate so well." I raised my mug to hide the grimace.

"I hear they brought some kinda elf with em. Maybe they're making elfbloods. Heh."

I choked on my ale, coughing and tearing up. Detano waited for me to catch my breath and wipe my watering eyes. The thought of the baroness breeding elfblood babies was disturbing, to say the least. "Who told you about the elf?"

"Just heard it from people. Guards probably said something, cause they don't got no servants in that manor they put him up in. Servants would have blabbed it straight away, you know how they—"

"Did they say why she was there?"

"Nah, just that she's got greenish skin and white hair, and she's real mean."

Mean, huh? The elf in the jailer's wagon had sent shivers up my spine. I didn't trust magic—and I definitely didn't trust people *made* of magic—but it was a little too convenient this elfish prisoner showed up at the same time as a bunch of coins of elfish make. She must have some connection to the new coins that had appeared.

Neffery had said the guildmaster's coins were all accounted for, yet Firmin had acquired an entire bucket full of them. Was it too paranoid to wonder if the elves were meddling in the affairs of the city? Or was it the other way around, and Firmin and his friend were meddling in the affairs of elves?

Detano continued on with no regard for my inner monologue. "I heard a handful of Firmin's bootlickers are gonna get to have a peek at her, too."

I shifted my gaze to him. "You don't say?"

"Yeah. Showin her off like a rare critter in a zoo. I'd have my britches in a wrinkle if I had to sit in a cage and let nobles titter at me too." He took a long pull from his mug. "I'd go look though, if I got the chance. Ain't never seen a proper elf before. I mean there's that elfblood mystic in Copperton district, but he's a bit wrong in the head if you know what I mean. Maybe cus he has elfish brains and a human cock!" He guffawed and slammed his hand down on the bar.

"Even I think that's rude, Detano."

"You don't get to say so." He pointed in my face. "You're a cheatin, lyin bastard."

I shrugged and took a drink.

"Anyway, this elf is all locked up. Wonder what they're gonna do with her?"

She *was* locked up. Which hinted more that it *wasn't* the elves moving on Sangarie, so much as someone who had fucked them over. I wasn't sure if that was better or worse. It also occurred to me that Neffery hadn't mentioned anything about the elf in the cage, so either it wasn't important, or it was too important to mention to me. "Detano?"

"What?"

"Where was this visiting nobleman staying again?"

He snorted. "In the Estates. Firmin got him put up in an empty manorhouse. Lots of city nobles are crying into their wine goblets about it."

"Any idea which manor?"

His eyes went as big as eggs. "You gonna break in and steal his shit?"

"No. I'm not."

"Then why do you wanna know?" He narrowed his eyes and leaned closer, though his voice remained at the same noise level. "If you do, do I get a cut for telling you about it?"

"Absolutely not. Your wife would be appalled."

He grumbled and I heard a few curses.

I leaned closer, ignoring his stench, so it seemed I was letting him in on a secret. "I think this noble has something to do with Saree's death."

"Why would a noble give two loose shits about a Blue?"

"I found something that night. Something I've only seen in Firmin's possession." The man didn't need to know anything about the guildmaster's vault, or the goldsmith, or the faint lick of magic in the coins. But every poor sap in Old Town would grab at a chance to blame the jackass son of the baroness for something.

He took a long drink, then looked at me sideways. "It's got green pillars out front and a big stone walled garden in the back."

I finished off the mug, pushing it across the bar and calling out to Kash. "Let Detano drink on my tab for the rest of the night."

Detano flashed a dark look at me. "That doesn't make up for anything, ya know."

"I know." I tied my empty pouch back onto my belt and headed toward the door.

"I'm still gonna get you, bastard!"

I waved over my shoulder. "Goodnight, Detano."

Now I had two good reasons to pay a visit to the higher end of society. To find that asshole of a knight and see if he'd killed Saree, and to get a second look at this elf. Preferably from a long ways away. Sans would have to talk to me later.

Chapter 15

You didn't go into the Estates as a thief without a lot of planning, even if you only wanted to look around. The Estates weren't technically a working district like the other nineteen. They consisted only of the manors of the rich and powerful, and part of Rigel's agreement with the baroness was that petty criminals were kept out of the area. I *should* have found out who was guarding the inner wall. I *should* have informed a Hand of the Master of my intentions. I *should* have checked in with a double-bar Yellow Hand before going inside.

I didn't do any of that. If I was doing things by the rules, I'd have tipped off a Red Hand and left them to investigate the knight, and not gone into the Estates at all. The guildmaster wouldn't be sympathetic to me taking things into my own hands, and asking questions would only draw attention to myself.

So I was going to trust my luck. I wasn't stealing anything, so I might be able to talk my way out of any trouble after the fact.

I walked through the city, occasionally raising my gaze to the scattered lit windows of the baroness's manorhouse, faintly shining from its hill. It was in the center of the Estates, perched high to afford it a view of the city. Back when Old Town had been a riverside village, there had been an actual castle fort there, overlooking the small river settlement. Eventually people started settling around the castle fort, and a wall had been built for their protection. As the city expanded and swallowed the hill, the castle had been replaced by a modern manorhouse, the nobility had moved inside the wall, the craftholders were shoved out into the growing city, and the fort wall had become the inner wall that separated the Estates from the city proper.

There were gates at all four directions, usually open and watched by a Silverguard stationed at each. There were also hidden ways through the wall—at least three I knew of. Those were guarded by Yellow Hands, and so were even more risky than the open gates.

I'd be lying if I said I wasn't nervous. It took real effort to walk down Market Street without skulking and looking behind me. This far away from Old Town I was known more by reputation than by sight, so it was unlikely I'd be recognized. There was no disguise as effective as a confident swagger and an open smile. If you looked like you belonged, people who didn't know any better would assume you did.

I reached the nearest gate, which stood open as usual, and saw the Silverguard perched on a stool within the stone framework. He was definitely awake, and I turned briskly onto a crooked street that circled the wall. The easiest way to get in would be to find a sleeping guard. Not likely, but it'd save me a lot of trouble. I could afford to check a couple more gates if it meant not climbing the wall.

When the next gate came into sight, I recognized the Silver standing there. A smile snaked its way onto my face and I changed tactics midstride. He saw me right off, attentive and dutiful as he was, and I could tell the exact moment he *recognized* me too. It was when he took half a step back and looked to see if anyone was nearby.

I sauntered up to the gate, giving him a roguish grin and tipping an imaginary hat. "Evening, defender." I edged to the side, clearly intending to step right past him.

Just as I'd expected, he dropped his spear to block my way.

I looked at it with feigned surprise, then raised an eyebrow at him. "Is something wrong?" Before he could answer, I stepped closer, peering intently at his face. "Trivere? Is that you?"

Even in the shadows of the gate arch I could see his face redden and his gaze falter. "State your business, whore."

I chuckled. "It *is* you!" I gripped the shaft of the spear just below his hand, my finger brushing his knuckles. "Good master Trivere, how pleasant it is to see you again."

He pulled the spear out of my grip.

Trivere was at least a decade my senior, and a few years ago had been merely a Copperguard stationed in Old Town. I was still a single bar thief when I'd seduced him and distracted him from noticing a hit that had put three crooked merchants out of business. Despite it being Senyr that had spearheaded the actual robbery, Trivere had nobody to blame

114

but me. To be fair, I'd put on quite the act. I'd even had Deidre paint my tattoo blue ahead of time, earning me several weeks of snide comments from my fellow thieves until it had worn off.

From his reaction now, Trivere was still a bit sore about the entire thing. I stepped closer and raised a hand to feel the fabric on his upper arm. "You seem to be doing well."

He took a step back. "I'd appreciate if you kept your fingers to yourself. I'm not interested in what you're selling."

And he was also not aware I wasn't really a Blue Hand. Perfect.

I put a good, throaty rumble into my laugh, holding his gaze. "I'd be open to giving it to you for free. It might have to wait until the business of the night is done. When do you get—"

"Enough!" He stepped entirely out of reach, snapping the hem of his coat and doing a little wriggle to adjust himself as unobtrusively as possible. "I'm not falling for your games again. Lying whore."

I smirked. "So you don't want to meet up later, revisit old times?"

"No."

"Fair enough. I'll just be on my way. I'm working anyway, so someone else gets to enjoy this tonight." I winked at him and turned toward the Estates. It was all I could do not to hold my breath as I took the first couple of paces with as much swagger as I could pull off. I expected him to shout after me to stop, to chase me down and throw me out.

He didn't. I could hear him cursing, spitting on the cobbles, and then start pacing with the butt of his spear tapping sharply on the ground each time he turned. I was unwilling to tempt fate for long, and took the first corner available to me. I breathed in relief and chuckled at my good luck.

The streets were set up in three rings around the baroness's manorhouse, intersected by the streets leading in from each of the four gates. I'd have to walk them all to figure out which manor I was after, and they were wide open due to how far back the houses sat from the street. Nobles could afford to plant grass and flowers in front of their houses, as well as have enclosed gardens in the back. There were also posts with lanterns on alternating sides of the street. The only shadows were behind the decorative waist-high walls in front of some of the houses, and under the occasional flowering tree that filled the night air with perfume. I'd have to continue my escort charade if I ran into any more of the Silverguard, and hope they didn't ask to see proof, or question my choice of clothing.

I started around the outermost ring, taking my time and finding shadows whenever I saw a figure patrolling. When I reached the cross streets coming from each of the gates I made sure to keep out of sight. No sense inviting the Silvers to question me. I spent almost an hour working my way through the outer ring, and was a quarter of the way along the middle one, when a door at the front of the house I'd just passed opened and soft light spilled into the street.

I dove for the low wall in front of the house. Fooling a horny Silverguard was one thing, but the nobility wouldn't appreciate seeing a commoner walking the Estates in the middle of the night. I wouldn't be able to smooth-talk them before they brought every Silver within earshot down on me, and I wouldn't be able to convince anyone of my innocence at that point.

I thanked the Six the cobbles were solid under me, and not grating like gravel as I worked my way along the bottom of the wall on my hands and knees. I could hear a man's tenor and a woman's lilting giggle, though I couldn't make out their lowered voices this far away. When they were done saying their goodbyes, whoever was leaving would come out and I'd be in plain view on the side of the street. If they talked just a little bit longer, I could maybe reach the corner of the wall and turn into the neighbor's yard.

The voices stopped and I picked up the pace, setting my knee down on a pebble in my rush. I bit off a curse as I bumped against the wall, knocking some mortar loose so it rattled to the street around me. My trained reaction was to freeze, which I did, but the light footfalls moving from the manor to the street forced me into movement again. Freezing wouldn't help when that person passed through the gate in the wall and saw me.

The footsteps were nearing the gate now, and I was still too far away from the corner. I lifted myself into a lizard-like position and scuttled forward on hands and feet as fast as I could without raising myself higher than the wall.

Maybe they wouldn't look my way. Maybe they weren't paying attention.

I heard the gate creak just as I reached the next lawn, and I swung around the corner and dropped to the grass. I was panting softly and my knee was throbbing.

The footsteps started up again, headed down the street in my direction. I mouthed curses as I listened to them get closer and closer. This side of the wall was too well lit for them not to notice me if they looked, and if I tried to follow the wall toward the neighbor's house it turned again and continued to the building.

I was effectively trapped by a waist-high garden wall.

Chapter 16

I stretched myself out against the bottom of the wall, giving myself a lower profile and hoping the grass would hide me some, and that my cloak would make me look like a long pile of dark rocks or something. They just needed to walk past without looking over at me.

The footsteps stopped at the corner of the wall.

Shit. Shit. Shit.

There was a long pause and I knew they were staring right at me. I could feel the hair on my neck standing on end. It took everything I had not to jump up and run.

"Gray?"

My heart stuttered and I couldn't believe my ears. That was Deidre's voice. I raised my chest off the grass and looked over my shoulder.

She stood watching me, a shawl drawn across her shoulders and held closed with one hand. Her dress flowed in layers of cream, trimmed in red, and the red corset was tight from her hips to her breasts. Her dark hair was down, loose waves that lifted gently in the breeze.

I chuckled in relief and twisted into a sitting position against the wall to properly rub at my bruised knee.

She frowned in the light of the lamp post. "What are you doing out here? And why are you crawling around like an idiot?"

"I'm looking into something."

"Come out of Lady Shura's yard before someone sees you."

I stood and brushed myself off, then joined her on the street.

Her brow wrinkled and her lips were drawn into a tight line. It made it easy to see the smeared lipcolor at the corner of her mouth, but I ignored it. She pulled her shawl tighter around her bare shoulders. "You aren't supposed to be out here."

118

"Then it's lucky you happen to be here too. Now I'm escorting *you*." I slung my cloak off and settled it around her shoulders, over the shawl. "The city is a dangerous place these days."

She narrowed her eyes, but gathered up the front of the cloak and pulled it closed. "And where, kind sir, are you escorting me to?"

I gestured in the direction I'd been searching. "To a manor with green pillars in the front."

"Firmin's guest house?" She frowned. "Why there? What are you up to?"

How had I ever doubted my luck? "I'm so glad you know it. Lead the way, gentlelady."

"You tell me why, or I'll lead you in circles."

There was no longer a reason not to. It might even keep her safer if she knew a killer was on the loose. Maybe then she wouldn't walk all the way across the city in the middle of the night alone.

"Last night I found Saree's body in Old Town, stuffed behind some crates in an alley."

She bowed her head and glared at the street between us, growling curses under her breath.

It wasn't the reaction I'd expected. I'd thought she would tear up, maybe cover her mouth in shock or grab my arm for support. Anger wasn't even on the list. "Deid?"

"They think you did it."

I sighed. "How did you find out?"

"Beth told me."

Of course she had. She belonged to Odele's brothel, and would have known all about it. I stared at the top of Deidre's head, watched her clench her fingers in the fabric of my cloak draped over her shoulders, and caught her hard gaze when she finally looked up.

"What does Firmin's guest house have to do with this?"

"I think Firmin—or the noble he's got visiting him—have something to do with it. I found a strange coin in the alley near the body, and Firmin was having some just like it melted down in Crafthold."

She nodded thoughtfully.

I kept going. "Tonight I had an encounter with a knight in plain clothes at Odele's. He was acting strange, and I think I recognize him from that visiting nobleman's entourage. Detano told me they were staying at a manor with green pillars in the front. So here I am."

She started walking and I fell into step beside her. After a few moments she spoke with a weary undertone. "What do you expect to find?"

I didn't answer right away. The weapon had been left in the body so I wouldn't find that, and he wasn't likely to have more dead women in the manor. I mostly wanted to confirm that it was the same knight, and check on the location of the manor and the rumors I'd heard about the occupants. Maybe put a little pressure on him. Find out what was in the package he'd been carrying. The more information I had, the easier it would be to plan something later. "I'm just looking around."

She nodded. "Well, there's a garden party at the manor tonight, so I'll make an appearance and you can be my bodyguard. But we shouldn't stay long. And for the sake of the Six, try not to be yourself."

I followed quietly beside her. We passed a few Silverguard on the way, and I did my best not to appear tense as she greeted them warmly and inquired after their evenings. They gave me hard glances, but Deidre was a familiar face and a better disguise for me than anything I could have come up with.

The manor was in the inner ring, and she led me up the cross street and to the right, pointing out the estate before we reached it. I could see the light coming from the back garden, and hear the sounds of laughter and a lute. She walked right up to the front door and pulled the rope that sent a ringing bell noise throughout the inside of the house.

"I trust you, Gray."

I felt a surprising rush of relief hearing those words. What would I have done if Deidre accused me of being a murderer? If she believed I could do something like that?

She took my cloak off her shoulders and laid it over my outstretched arm, straightening her shawl and her skirts, and fluffing out her hair. "How do I look?"

I used my thumb to wipe the lipcolor from the corner of her mouth.

She blushed as the door opened.

A guard stood there, dressed in the colors of the entourage that had paraded down Craftsmans Row. "Can I help you?"

Deidre smiled brightly. "I was in the neighborhood and thought I'd drop by and greet Lord Firmin's guest."

The guard turned his gaze to me, taking my measure in an all too familiar way. I was dressed like a commoner, I had grass stains and dirt on my clothes, and my smile was in no way noble or subservient.

Deidre set her hand on my arm. "This is my protection. The streets are a frightening place at night." Her smile was warm, and her eyes shone, even in the faint light from inside the manor.

The guard moved aside reluctantly and allowed us entry. He then escorted us through the house, to a corridor that led out to the garden in the back.

I had never felt so visible. I swear half the people there turned and stared directly at me. It was disconcerting being the focus of so much attention when I spent my whole life trying to blend in.

The garden was lit by multicolored lamps, casting artful light onto the flowerbeds and benches. The combination of flowers and perfume invaded my senses and made my eyes water. The lutist was seated beneath a blossoming tree, and the melody was a haunting refrain weaving through the buzz of conversation. Children outfitted in simple white tunics and crowned in daisies walked among the nobles, carrying trays of food and drink.

Deidre set a hand on the small of my back and leaned close to whisper. "Just stand out of the way and act invisible."

"Perfect," I mumbled out of the side of my mouth.

She slipped away and started greeting people, her smile shining brighter with each encounter. Some she left rather quickly, and others she lingered with, draping her hand on an arm or touching her mouth with a finger. It was a lesson in the art of seduction, watching her mingle.

I tore my gaze away and scanned the crowd for signs of the knight. Off to the left, and given a wide berth by the party-goers, was an ugly iron cage. It was partly concealed by shrubs, and I caught sight of a figure seated on the bottom inside, leaning against the bars as far back as they could.

My skin crawled and I forgot about the knight. After a quick glance to check on Deidre's progress, I moved through the edges of the crowd to get a closer look.

121

It was definitely the elf. The heavy cloak was gone, taken from her most likely, to provide the nobles a better view. She wore heavy canvas pants and high leather boots, like a forester. There were leather plates tied to the front of both thighs, scratched and faded with use. She wore a heavy shirt as well, but the sleeves were cut off at the shoulder to reveal greenish tinted skin with black tattoos crawling down her arms like vines, the leaves of which were strange clusters of runic designs. Over the shirt was a fitted leather breastplate, also scuffed and worn.

Her hair was the white of the moon, and tightly braided down to her waist in the back. She was thinner and smaller than the average woman, almost gaunt, and her face was the same greenish tint as her arms. Her ears swept back into delicate points, and her eyes shone like emeralds. As she caught my gaze, she grimaced back at me and I noticed the pointed eye-teeth. They weren't so large as to be called fangs, but absolutely *not* human.

I came to a stop about three paces away from the cage, gazing into her eyes and trying to ignore the chill it sent through me. An instinctual spike of fear was working its way through my gut, and I knew I'd seen her before. I *remembered* her from somewhere, and every ounce of my being was telling me to run.

But *why*?

She glared back, not bothering to stand up. The colored light of the garden lamps caught her eyes and made them glow green.

Two little boys darted up beside me, dressed like miniature versions of the chattering nobles. One of them wound his arm back with an intense look on his face as he sighted in on the elf, and I saw the rock clenched in his hand. Without thinking, I wrapped my fingers around his fist and held tight before he could throw it.

His shock was comical, and he looked at me like he hadn't even seen me standing there. It morphed from disbelief into anger. I kept my grip on him as he tried to jerk his hand away, and then he started howling.

I realized what I'd done then, and who I was surrounded by. This was no dirty street kid in Old Town. I let go and the brat tumbled to the ground and scrambled to his feet, then ran off into the garden with his friend. The nearby nobles were staring at me with narrowed eyes and heavy frowns, drinks or plates clutched in their hands. I clasped my hands together in front of me and took a step back, trying to imitate a stuffy Copperguard and hoping they didn't care a whole lot about what their kids got up to.

The elf, when I glanced her way, had her eyebrow raised in surprise.

Deidre came up beside me, smiling widely, and spoke through her teeth. "What are you *doing*? I thought you wanted to see the knight?"

"I haven't seen him."

"He came in after us. He's near the reflecting pool." She tipped her head toward the other side of the garden and I followed her gaze.

Sure enough, the man from Odele's stood with the visiting nobleman and Lord Firmin, looking more the part of an attentive bodyguard than I ever could. Except that he was watching me, instead of staring off into space. He was dressed in the manor of the other nobles, if a little less expensively.

And he definitely recognized me.

I smiled wide. "I'll be right back."

She grabbed my sleeve, bringing me up short. "Don't you dare cause trouble here. Many of these people are my clients."

I plucked her hand off. "Don't worry. I'll be discreet."

She sighed behind my back, but let me go. I locked eyes with the knight as I moved through the party-goers, and he stepped away from the noble he'd been shadowing. By the time I reached him, I was comfortably certain we wouldn't be overheard unless we got loud.

The knight glared down at me, resting his hand on his belt like there was usually a large weapon hanging there and his hand liked to be on it. "What are you doing here? This party isn't for common scum."

"Oh, I came with a friend."

"I suggest you leave with them. Now."

"I was just about to do that, but then I saw you and wanted to make sure you didn't have any unfinished business in Old Town."

The knight's crooked nose, probably broken years ago and never set properly, crinkled in disgust. "I would be happy never to set foot in that slum again."

"We are of the same mind. Imagine that. You don't have anything still to be delivered? Anyone you still need to talk to? I could pass any messages along and spare you the trouble."

"Mind your own business."

"I am." I decidedly *wasn't*, but he didn't know that. I stepped just a bit closer, pitching my voice to make sure nobody would overhear. "I lost a dear friend from that brothel just the other day. Sweet girl. I don't want to lose another."

I watched his face closely, but all I saw was disdain. If he knew anything about the murder, he was hiding it better than a master cheat. He looked down his crooked nose at me, but there was nothing hidden in his eyes at all. No guilt, no elation, and no calculating return stare. For all I could tell, he just thought I was beneath him, and had no more reaction to my words than if I'd told him I had spit in all the little snacks on the server's tray.

Perhaps I'd been wrong.

The knight lifted a hand, the front of his tailored doublet pulling tight against his muscular chest as he gestured at the manorhouse. "I think you should leave, before I throw you out."

My memory flashed back to the brothel and how I'd embarrassed myself sprawling over the footstool. The heat was rising on my cheeks and it pissed me off. This arrogant goat-fucker wanted to throw *me* out? Maybe I could take out the seams of his doublet a little and make him wish that—

"Gray, dear." Deidre set a hand on my chest and nodded politely at the knight, pressing me back. "I'd wondered where you'd gone."

The knight's lip curled at the edge, but he held my gaze. I choked down my pride, knowing full well a confrontation here would likely get me arrested. If we'd been on the streets I may have risked it, but not in a nobleman's back garden.

I slipped my hand into Deidre's and broke eye contact first. "Let's get out of here."

We'd almost reached the door leading back into the manor when a lazy voice came from behind us.

"Leaving so soon, Lady Midnight?"

Deidre pulled me up short, squeezing my hand briefly before slipping free. Her smile was once again dazzling, and she dropped into a graceful bow to Lord Firmin.

I turned as well, keeping my gaze on the ground near his pointy-toed boots. I'd seen enough of his gloating, self-important, thin-lipped, snide face from afar over the years.

124

He wasn't interested in me anyway.

He took Deidre's hand, raising it to his pale lips and placing a loud, wet kiss on the smooth skin. He kept hold of it as he continued speaking. "You are as beautiful as always. A night flower blooming amongst drooping blossoms of the day. All men ache to taste your sweet nectar."

My lip curled and I glared at the man, wishing I could light him on fire with my thoughts.

Deidre giggled, slipping her hand away with some effort. "My lord, you are too kind."

"Must you leave now? If it's cooler air you desire, I could offer you a place to relax and divulge yourself of any cumbersome attire."

The blood rushed to my face and I wanted to divulge the pompous asshole of a few of his teeth. I clenched my jaw and counted my breath in and out through my nose.

"I'm sorry, my lord. I must decline for this evening. I am already going to be late for a prior engagement."

The fucking inbred toad took hold of her hand again and pulled her closer, inhaling like she was a freshly cooked meal he was savoring. His eyes followed the curve of her neck down to the swell of cleavage above the corseted top. "A pity. Perhaps another time."

With that he reached forward with his free hand and stroked the curve of her ass, then spun and walked off as he called for more wine.

Deidre caught hold of my elbow and I shifted my gaze to her, realizing I had taken two steps after the nobleman. She was shaking her head sternly, tugging me toward the manor. I shot one more glare in the man's direction, then fell into step behind her.

We didn't speak as we left the manor by the front door and walked through the Estates. By the time we were passing under the Market Street gate, I had lost the tension in my shoulders and was no longer worried I was going to crack my teeth with how hard I'd been clenching them. I sighed into the night and breathed in the normal smells of Sangarie—stale water, urine, and lamp oil.

Her voice remained low enough it wouldn't carry through the dark street. "What was all that about?"

"What?"

"You were acting like a jealous lover back there."

I avoided her narrowed gaze. "He was being a prick."

"I see. That's all it was?"

"Of course. He offends me deeply on principle."

Neither of us said anything more as we walked. She was right. I'd been way out of line, and I wasn't sure where it had come from. Her flirting in the garden hadn't bothered me like that, and her work had never been an issue between us. Maybe my disgust with the impotent lordling was the difference. Seeing him treat her like he owned her...

I led her to the closest entrance to the underground I could find. We were far from Old Town, and even I couldn't keep track of every hole in the city's bottom. She paused with her hand on the rickety cellar door and looked back at me.

"Aren't you coming?"

"I have to do one more round. I'll be there soon."

She nodded and walked into the tunnels.

I watched her until the shadows swallowed her, then closed the door. Too much was racing through my mind right now, and I needed to walk it off.

Chapter 17

I returned to Old Town and made my round, letting my head clear and my irritation run itself out, then headed underground. As I was winding through the tunnels on my way back to my room, I heard Ruena's voice echo behind me.

"Gray! Wait!"

I sighed and stopped, turning around to let her catch up. "What do *you* want?"

She was out of breath and rested her hands on her knees as she panted, her goggles once again swinging at her neck. "Down at the docks... you should... come and look."

I cursed. "Can't you see I'm on my way home? The docks were doing just fine half an hour ago."

"I found something... you need to see."

Grumbling, I started back the way I'd come, going topside again and heading for the docks. Ruena followed along behind me. When we reached the river, I walked out on the wooden planks and looked around. "Where?"

She pointed to the left where a cluster of people stood with torches, and I raised an eyebrow at her and pointed to my eyes until she raised her goggles up. Then I followed her to where a section of the river had expanded under the raised boards and onto the city side of the dock. The group of people were gathered around something at the edge of the water and I stepped down onto the muddy bank, sighing as my boots squelched a few inches into the mud. It sucked at my feet as I trudged to the crowd and shoved people out of my way.

Looking down I saw the body of a man, highlighted by the dancing orange light of the torches. His pants and v-necked shirt had soaked up the stagnant water, mud, and something darker. The tattoo of a Blue

Hand with one bar was recognizable just above his breast on the left side, like a badge. *Danial*. His short brown hair, normally teased into an artful parody of messiness, was slick with mud against his head. His perpetual smirk was now gone and his jaw slack. His eyes covered by a milky film as they stared into the sky.

I swore and pulled my cloak off, draping it over his body. "What the hell did you call *me* here for? This is something the low rank Red Hands are supposed to handle. Or even one of the mystic priests."

Ruena fidgeted. "They're saying it's one of Tanji's men."

"Go get a Red Hand, for fucks sake!"

She nodded and ran off again.

I took a torch from one of the gawkers and waved the others away. "Don't you people have anything better to do?"

They all backed off and drifted away, whispering among themselves. Some of them stared at me, rather than the body, and I could imagine what they might be saying. I wished Ruena would have left me out of this and went straight to the Red Hands. I shouldn't be here.

But it was Danial. I couldn't leave him lying in the mud with half of Old Town poking at his body. He deserved better than that. He deserved better than what had happened.

I planted the torch in the mud and moved away, waiting for the girl to return. Danial's body was half sunk in muck, and any evidence of how he'd gotten there had been destroyed by the crowd that had surrounded him. I'd never been with Danial. He liked women, and they liked him. He was Tanji's darling. But we'd been friends for years. I tried not to imagine him winking and posing with his hip cocked, surrounded by a gaggle of eager ladies.

Was this the work of the same killer? He couldn't have been here long, or a dock worker would have found him earlier in the day. There was no way the knight could have done it.

I waited half an hour before I spotted three figures in the dark, one of them pint-sized and struggling to keep up. "It's about time." I walked up to the dock to meet them, waving Ruena away and leading the other two down the bank. I uncovered the body and the two cloaked figures bent to look at him more closely. I looked away.

One of them spoke, his voice muffled. "Imagine seeing you here, *enforcer*."

128

I stiffened and checked that the onlookers weren't within hearing range. Only Ruena was nearby, and she was staring at the Red Hand, her goggles eerily reflecting the moonlight. I stepped in front of her.

The Red stepped closer. "Second Blue we've removed now, and you're involved with both of them. Why is that?"

The gall of these men. I stood tall, refusing to let him intimidate me. "Maybe because I'm an enforcer, and this is my district. These are my streets."

"Or maybe because you got bored with slitting purses and decided to start slitting throats."

I growled and grabbed the front of his cloak, pulling him forward, but whatever I might have done or said was cut off by a hard and rather pointed sensation at my midsection. I glanced down to see a blade held against my gut.

"That's right, *enforcer*. Go ahead and prove to all these people what kind of man you are."

I let go and stepped back through the mud, glaring at him.

He laughed and the blade disappeared beneath the cloak again, then he turned around and rejoined his partner by Danial's body. They shook out a canvas sheet and rolled him onto it. It wasn't until they had lifted the canvas and were carrying him up the bank that I remembered Ruena standing a few paces behind me. Her face was pale in the moonlight, and she looked frightened.

Damn it.

"Come on, kid." I walked along the dock so I didn't have to follow the Red Hands, pausing to wash my cloak in the ice-cold river where it ran black and smooth below the dock. I wrung it out the best I could and carried it along. My boots would have to wait. Ruena was silent the entire time, but she stuck close to me.

When I reached the underground I turned to her. "Are you good to go home?"

She nodded hurriedly, her lips pressed tightly together, but didn't move. The goggles on her face made her look like a quaking bug.

I sighed and tugged them down.

Her pearly eyes were wide. I didn't know what she'd been through in her short life, but I knew the last few nights hadn't been easy. I'd be heading back to my apartment, a refuge from the realities of the streets, but where was she going?

"How old are you, Rue?"

"Nine."

I wiped my hand over my face. That was even younger than I'd thought. "Where are you sleeping?"

"I have a nice spot behind a warehouse. The Green Hand said if I keep the rats away he won't burn my stuff."

It wasn't surprising for a kid her age. Blind Bob didn't have room for all of them so he concentrated on the youngest ones, and she couldn't apply for her own room in the underground until she was thirteen. There were places she could go, but most of them were crowded and full of bigger kids that had no qualms about roughing up the younger and smaller ones. It was probably better for her not to be around them anyway, if she didn't want her elfblood being found out.

"Okay." I closed the door to the tunnel and went back into the dark street. I wasn't going to let her sleep in an alley, not with a killer loose in Old Town. "Follow me."

I led her to the Throat. The streets were full of predawn shadows, and I knew Sans would be passed out after the busy night, but he'd have Kash as a stand-in, tending bar for the overnight and morning shifts.

I walked into the nearly empty tavern and eased up to the bar, motioning Ruena to sit at a nearby table. Kash looked about the same age as Sans, but where the barkeep was carrying around a little extra padding, she was all lean muscle. She dressed like a man and had her hair chopped short, and she was constantly chewing on the end of a twig. She strode up to me on her side of the bar and leaned on her forearms, shifting the twig to the side of her mouth to speak.

"You're tracking mud all over my floor, Gray."

I glanced down and grimaced. "Yeah. Sorry about that."

"What'll you be having?"

"Nothing, actually. I wanted to ask a favor."

She turned her eyes to the little girl and frowned. "Is this gonna get me a lecture when Sans wakes up?"

"Tell him it's my fault."

"Oh I will."

I rubbed a hand over my face. This night just needed to end. "Let her sleep in the back. She's a good kid, and she's already inked."

"Why isn't she underground then?"

"Because she's only nine." I leaned closer, pitching my voice so Ruena wouldn't hear. "I don't want to start over with training another one if the gangs in Bottoms get hold of her."

Kash grunted and rolled the twig between her teeth, thinking as she stared at the kid. "She's an elfblood. That have anything to do with this?"

Shit. I closed my eyes at my own sloppiness. The goggles were still down around her neck. "Is there a problem with that?"

"Not from me. Somebody might notice, though. This is a bar after all."

"She's supposed to be learning to hide it. Remind her to pull up her goggles."

After a few moments she sighed. "Fine. But she works for her space."

I slapped my hand on the top of the bar and grinned. "Deal. You're a sexy bitch, Kash."

"Don't I know it." She turned away and headed for the opening in the center of the length of bar.

I walked over to Ruena and pointed at the barkeep. "You're staying here now. She'll show you where. Get your stuff and bring it here, then get some sleep."

She stared at me with wide eyes, pearly-white and watering as her lip trembled.

"You have to help out in return, so if they tell you to do something, you do it. Understand?"

She nodded and her mouth trembled into a smile. She popped off her chair and threw her arms around my waist in a hug. "Thank you."

"Get off me. And find someplace to take a bath." I pulled a couple of silver from my pocket and dropped it into her grubby hand. "And wear your goggles all the time, got it?"

I left her bouncing on her toes, staring up at the tall form of Kash looming over her. At least I knew she'd be off the streets.

I trudged home, trying to ignore the uncomfortable looks from some of the beggars as I passed. My thieves politely greeted me, and quickly moved on, the air a little more tense than usual. By the time I entered the tunnels, I was cursing the speed of rumors.

I reached the apartment, opened the door, and slipped inside, moving through the darkness to hang my damp cloak on its hook beside the door. As I sat at the table and struggled with my boots, I heard a rustle from the bed.

"Gray?"

"You were expecting someone else?"

Deidre turned the lamp on and I blinked and pulled off the second muddy boot. I stood with a sigh and moved to the cupboard to get out a glass and a bottle of whiskey. Pouring the glass full, I returned to the table and dropped into a chair, taking a long swallow. That was two bodies in just a couple of days. Why did I feel like the Red Hands weren't doing a damned thing about it? Except trying to blame me, of course.

Deidre rose and padded across the room, standing behind me. She put her hands on my shoulders and rubbed gently. "What happened?"

I took another swallow from the glass and sighed. "Ruena found a body washed up on the bank of the river."

"No... do you know who it was?"

"Danial. From Tanji's."

Deidre's hands stopped and she walked around to look at me. "Did you tell Tanji?"

"You really think they want to hear this from me?"

Deidre shook her head, her face pale in the lamplight. Her voice was soft and sad. "I've heard the rumors about you."

I looked up at her and spun my glass slowly on the table. "So you said."

"I tried to argue with them. I don't know how they think you could do such a thing." She pressed her lips firmly together and her chin trembled as she fought for control of her voice. "You're not a killer. Anyone who knows you would say the same."

I nodded and stared across the room at the shadows where the light didn't reach. I felt like the Red Hands weren't even trying. Normally they were frighteningly efficient in tracking people down.

Deidre slid a hand down my shoulder and lifted my arm, tugging me out of the chair. "Come to bed. You look like you need some sleep."

I didn't argue. I left the bottle and the last few swallows in the bottom of my glass, letting her tug me across the room. She crawled across the blankets, and when she was settled I blew out the lamp on the bedside table and climbed in beside her. I raised my arm up and she snuggled into my side, draping her arm across my chest.

We lay that way for some time. As tired as I was, I couldn't seem to get my mind to quiet. The events of the last week flitted through my thoughts—the images of the two dead Blue Hands, the story of the elfish coins, the haughty expressions of the nameless knight and the baroness's son.

Even worse, I remembered the fierce glare of the elf inside her cage. The more I thought about her, the more certain I was that I knew her from somewhere. The emerald of her eyes reflecting the lights of the garden had stirred old memories, and was now making the darkness of my own apartment feel unsafe.

Whenever I would shift or sigh, Deidre would slide her fingers lightly across my skin, letting me know she was awake. I don't know how long we rested that way, but eventually she lifted herself off my chest, pushing her hair behind her ear.

"I have to get up and do some things today. I'll be back before it's time to go to the ball."

I had forgotten all about the ball. I sighed and nodded.

She got up and turned the lamp on low, just enough so she could see to get ready. She hummed as she dressed and brushed her hair—a soft melody that rose and fell in a soothing rhythm. I watched for a few minutes, laying on my side, but my eyes got heavy. My thoughts quieted as I focused on the sound of her humming… and in that quiet, sleep finally came.

Chapter 18

In the early evening, Deidre and Beth both showed up in their party clothes to make sure I got ready in time. Beth mostly stood out of the way, looking excited with her light blue skirts floating around her, and her corset threatening to squeeze her breasts out the top. A pendant was nestled at the top of her cleavage, twinkling in the lamplight. Her blonde hair was curled and piled on top of her head, decorated with flowers that almost matched her dress.

I didn't notice much else about her, because as soon as I saw Deidre I wished we had another hour to spare before we had to leave. She wore dark blue. The outer skirt was some kind of filmy material that shimmered in the lamplight and showed the darker color beneath. Her corset fit like skin, and the rise and fall of her chest as she laid out the clothes she'd bought for me was enough to make me self-conscious about having Beth in the room. Her hair was pulled up too, and fell in rings down to her neck, making me itch to brush it away from her skin and kiss her.

"What are you staring at?"

I swallowed and shook my head.

"We don't have a lot of time. Get dressed."

"Right." For fucks sake, it was just a fancy dress. She was still the same Deid she'd always been. Granted, she was sexy even in homespun. Even more sexy out of it. I grinned as I joined her at the bed.

The smile faded when I saw the clothes she had laid out. "Oh you've *got* to be kidding me."

"Put them on."

She'd bought tights, dark blue to match the inner part of her dress, and tall black boots that flared at the knee. There was a dark blue shirt that matched the tights, and an actual doublet like the nobility wore. It was trimmed in silver, although part of the trimming had come loose and been mended, the stitching just a little out of place. The shirt sleeves were puffy at the top and tightened with laces between the elbow and wrist, and the doublet, while sleeveless, had little protruding pieces at the shoulders. Wearing something like this in Old Town would have had pickpockets crawling all over me like lice before I could cross the market square.

I sighed and stripped out of my usual clothes, carefully chosen to help me blend in with the crowds. The tights weren't bad, but the boots I struggled with. They squeaked when I moved and brushed together at the knee, which was going to drive me mad. The puffy sleeves of the shirt felt overdone, and the doublet was a little too snug.

She stepped forward to tie the laces on my sleeves and I fidgeted and pulled at the collar of the doublet, which buttoned shut at my throat. She slapped at my hand. "Leave it alone."

"I feel ridiculous."

She fussed with my hair for a moment, then turned to pick up the handbag sitting on the table.

I grabbed my belt and wrestled the doublet up enough to swing it around my waist. When she saw me, she scowled.

"What are you doing?"

I adjusted the belt at my hips and smoothed the doublet over the two knives sheathed at the back. It fell nearly to the middle of my thighs. It'd be a pain in the ass to get to them like this, but I felt better knowing they were there. "Not optional."

She rolled her eyes and went to link arms with Beth, leading the way out of the apartment.

I followed, hoping there'd be some kind of alcohol there. At least it was for guild members only, so Sans and Detano would never see me dressed like this. I followed the two women through the underground to the massive audience hall that had been cleared to make room. I could feel the uneasy tingle of the work of the mystics even before we reached the room, and resigned myself to being on edge the entire night.

The moment the doors opened, the blood drained from my face. Rigel had been right about his Attendants creating a theme that would cause a stir. Their rendition of the Night of Shadows made my flesh crawl.

135

The lamps were somehow putting off blue tinged light, and judging by the way my hair stood on end, I was guessing it was magic rather than a mystic trick with herbs or powders. Canvas gateways had been built and painted black, edged with bright blue flowers, and hung at crazy angles from the ceiling as if they were about to drop down and swallow the guests into their depths. Some of the guild members were dressed in flowing black costumes with hideously twisted masks, and they drifted around the room, laughing and pretending to attack people. Their sleeves were long and draping, so when they whipped out their arms the fabric streamed through the air.

I wiped my sweating hands on the hem of the doublet and swallowed past the dryness in my throat. A hand closed over my arm and my gaze flicked down to Deidre's sympathetic face.

"Gray?"

She was waiting for me to say something. I opened my mouth and looked into the room again, no words making it past the lump in my throat.

Beth stepped closer, peering intently at my face with a penetrating look I'd never seen on her before. "Is something wrong?"

Deidre waved her off and tightened her grip on my arm. "Gray, is it that bad? We can go home."

Beth's expression fell, and she looked into the transformed ballroom. Her hand went to her breast and pressed hard over the pendant, and she scowled. Did my appearance at this thing mean that much to her?

I reminded myself that I had made a deal with Rigel. This was the best way to show the guild I wasn't guilty. And it was even more important with two bodies to answer for. I took a deep breath. It was only canvas and flowers, for fucks sake. And idiots running around with black streamers. I clenched my hand hard enough my nails cut into my palm and cleared my throat. "I'm fine."

"Are you—"

"Let's go." I propelled myself forward, dragging Deidre along.

I had been so concerned with the decorations and fake monsters, I hadn't really looked at the people. The higher ranked members were decked out in their second-hand finest, like we were, but the low ranked people had gotten a little more creative.

136

Hand made costumes were the norm, and hardly anything matched. A lot of the colors were dulled from years of use, and stained from past balls. I couldn't count the number of tiaras and fancy jewelry made from wire and broken glass. A number of people only had partial costumes they wore over their normal rags, and a few looked like they hadn't been able to decide on one thing and wore everything they could find. There was even a clustered group of bearded men wearing dresses and singing while they drank. One woman walked past and I saw a large brown stain from dried blood on the back of her dress, and the attempt to stitch shut a knife hole in the fabric.

The smells were enough to make me dizzy. Spicy scents of cinnamon, cloves, and cardamom. Sweet smells of fruit, sugar, and candy. Every flower scent I could imagine. And all of it was layered over the top of sweat, urine, and unwashed bodies. Too many people had decided to cover up their normal stench with perfume and my nose burned. It shamed me to think I preferred the garden party from the night before, where at least the only thing rotten had been the morals of the nobility.

There was music playing from somewhere, although I wondered if they'd bothered to practice before trying to play together, because none of them were in time with the others. People jostled me from every direction, crammed into the audience hall to enjoy their one night of extravagance.

And Lord Rigel had provided. There were tables full of food, barrels full of alcohol, and even a mountain of cakes that was being eroded by half-grown criminals. Rigel himself sat on his huge chair, his three Attendants surrounding him in sparkling dresses, staring out with contented smiles at the chaos.

As I watched him, his eyes moved and he met mine. He looked surprised, then pleased, and raised his goblet in my direction before looking away.

Deidre put her hand on my arm and leaned close to whisper. "Are you ok?"

I nodded, sick to my stomach.

On my other side, Beth pointed at the food tables. "Look! They have candied fruit. I see dates, and cherries, and—oranges! Oh I used to *love* candied oranges back home." She slipped her arm through mine and pressed her chest against me.

The magic from her tattooed freckles jolted through the poofy fabric of my shirt and sent a shiver racing up my back. I unwound my arm and stepped away.

Beth pouted, then took Deidre's arm and tugged her toward the food tables. "Let's see what they made."

Deidre's brow creased and she resisted, but I plastered a smile on my face and motioned for her to go. Her hand trailed down my arm as she walked off with Beth.

I drew in a slow breath and looked at the clusters of people. My doublet was choking me and I tugged at the neckline, wondering if Deidre would skin me alive if I opened a few buttons. A familiar voice stopped me cold and brought a whole new slew of worries to my mind.

Marisso.

I turned and saw him, standing with his hip cocked and a full drink in his hand. He was wearing a flowy yellow outfit, more like something a wandering bard would wear than a nobleman. The front of the shirt was open to his navel, showing off the perfect skin on his chest. The pants were tight over his ass, but flowed out below that to the floor, where pointed shoes peeked out. His sleeves flowed wide at his wrists and he held the drink out to me.

"Don't we look like day and night?"

I took the drink and downed half of it before answering. "It would seem that way."

"I thought she would never leave. Did she dress to match you?" He laughed and slipped his arm beneath mine.

Shit. I was so concerned with having to even *be* here, that I hadn't thought about who else would be. My eyes darted toward the food tables, but Marisso took my chin and kissed me. It was all I could do not to spill my drink. He tasted like sweet wine, and his hand slipped around until he could grip my ass.

Any other place, any other time, it would have been sexy. But here, surrounded by the pretend Night of Shadows, knowing Deidre was probably watching from somewhere, it only made me want to disappear.

I backed away, realized my hand was shaking, and drained the other half of the drink before I could spill it. "Is there more of this?"

Marisso's brow twitched as he looked at the empty glass, but he nodded. "Let's get you some more."

I had hoped he would go alone, but he linked his arm with mine and dragged me to the makeshift bar. It was decorated so the surface looked like a horizontal gateway. I closed my eyes briefly and told myself it was canvas and streamers.

Canvas and streamers.

I didn't lean on it.

Marisso ordered two drinks, and handed me a glass of whiskey while he took red wine. A couple of men and a woman were standing to the side—behind a natural stone column encircled in flowers and streamers—talking about the real Night of Shadows.

One of the men, wearing a shirt with lace sewn up the front in rows, shook his head. "No, no, no. That's not how they tell it. The labyrinth was here before men ever came to settle this land. Maybe even before the elves. But it was destroyed a long time ago."

I grimaced and tried not to eavesdrop, but it was a habit ingrained in me as a thief, and their conversation was drunkenly loud. I tugged at Marisso to get him to leave, but he only laced his fingers in mine and determinedly continued talking to the Green Hand serving drinks.

A man with a shaggy red beard gestured with his drink. "Wasn't destroyed! It was buried. The tunnels we live in now *are* the labyrinth."

The lace-shirted man sneered at him. "That's stupid. These are caves, not a labyrinth."

The woman nodded. "That's right. These are natural caves."

Lace-shirt pointed at her. "Exactly. Anyways, in the middle of the labyrinth, in a huge palace, is a priceless treasure that's guarded by the monsters. It's a ball—"

"A stone," Redbeard interjected.

"—a stone that caused the ruin of the people that lived in the labyrinth."

The woman shook her head. "I heard it was an egg. An egg from one of the monsters."

"It wasn't. It was a stone. They called it some weird name. Can't remember what it was." He gestured at the man with the beard.

Redbeard's face screwed up in thought. "Uhm... Enelly vogasurry?"

The man shrugged. "Something like that."

I took a long swallow and tried my best to ignore them as Marisso talked to the bartender. This was all hearth stories, built upon by bards and embellished over the years so people would continue to ply them with drink in the bars or the brothels all night long during the festival. The real labyrinth was dark and deadly and terrifying.

Especially for a little kid with no sense.

Lace-shirt continued. "Anyway, it destroyed the people that lived there, so they hid it deep inside the palace, to keep anyone from using it ever again. But it was so magical it opened up these gateways. So every year we have to be careful that the monsters don't break through the gateways and destroy Sangarie!"

Redbeard frowned. "I thought you said it was before people came here?"

"It was."

"Then how could it have destroyed people and been locked up if no people were here?"

The woman smacked Redbeard in the chest. "It wasn't *normal* people. It was labyrinth people."

He nodded slowly. "Oh. That makes sense."

The entire conversation was both anxiety inducing and insane. I leaned over to Marisso and whispered. "Can we go someplace else?"

He waved at me to wait and I huffed.

Lace-shirt took a long swallow of his drink, and wiped the wetness from his mouth. "The point is, this stone is so powerful it could destroy whole cities, and it's just sitting there waiting for somebody to find it."

Redbeard made a sign against misfortune, and the woman shook her head.

Lace-shirt laughed. "You babies scared?"

The woman snorted. "You go look for it. Maybe the monsters will throw back your corpse for us to bury if they don't eat it."

They all three laughed at that, and Lace-shirt happened to glance around the decorated pillar that separated us to meet my gaze. He squinted a moment, then recognition dawned and his eyes narrowed. "Look what crawled in. It's the killer Black Hand."

The other two turned my way and the woman spat on the floor and made a rude gesture with one hand. Redbeard only grunted and took a

140

drink. He said, "Can't trust no Black Hand anyway. Care more for your gold than your life they do."

I could have guessed this would happen. I pulled free of Marisso's hand, turned away from the bar, and walked toward the music, hoping it would drown out any further conversation. Marisso apologized to the barkeep and hurried after me, then slipped his arm through mine and walked along with me.

Now that I was looking for it, I noticed a good portion of the party-goers reacted the same way when they recognized me. Then they'd whisper to their neighbors, and *they* would glare in my direction. I seemed to be almost as entertaining as the musicians.

This was a terrible plan.

A hand touched my elbow and I looked down at Ruena. My snort came automatically, but her hurt expression made me attempt to cover it up by coughing.

She seemed self-conscious in the dress she wore, and I couldn't blame her. It looked as if someone had tried to make her look like a doll. The skirt went down to just below her knees and poofed out in layer upon layer of pink fabric. The top had short sleeves and a huge pink bow in the front over her chest, to match the one on her lower back. She wore her usual dirty and patched boots that reached halfway up her calf. Her face had been scrubbed until it was nearly as pink as her dress, and the goggles were adorned with pink ribbons.

At least they were over her eyes, even if it made her look absolutely ridiculous.

"Hey kid."

She grinned at me. "Kash helped me find a dress."

Marisso stared down at the girl, his eyebrow raised. "Who is this?"

"She's the newest thief in Old Town."

He held a hand out, and Ruena took it and kissed it like a noble kissing the hand of his lady. Marisso flushed and chuckled. "Well, such manners. What's your name?"

"Ruena, sir."

"Ruena." He tugged my arm closer and leaned in with an exaggerated conspiratorial whisper. "I like this one, Gray."

"She's a pain in the ass."

Her face fell, but Marisso leaned down and whispered something I didn't catch over the music. At his comment she grinned and kissed him on the cheek, then waved before darting back into the crowd.

I scowled. "What did you say to her?"

"I just told her you're a grumpy old man, and she shouldn't pay any attention to it."

"Thanks a lot."

Marisso set his half empty glass on a nearby table and turned to stand in front of me, slipping his arms around my waist. "I've heard what they're saying about you. May would have none of it, and said anyone spreading it around from her house would be kicked out onto the streets."

I smiled, despite my discomfort. I could always count on May.

Marisso tried to shift my weight into motion. "Want to dance?"

I did not. I wanted to leave, but that wasn't going to happen. I tried to step out of his arms gently, turning to break his hold. "I don't think that's a good idea."

He pulled me closer to the dancers, and I held my drink out of the way so I wouldn't spill on his outfit.

"Come on. Just one dance. Let's show everyone your softer side."

Someone brushed against me from behind and I jerked away from it out of reflex, which put me even closer to Marisso. I put a hand on his shoulder and stepped back. "It's a little crowded here for me."

His face fell, then he looked over my shoulder. "Madam, you look gorgeous."

I turned around to see May, dressed conservatively in red and silver. She walked with the help of a cane and her expression was kind and a little wistful.

I bent enough for her to kiss me on the cheek.

"Glad to see you changed your mind about coming," she said.

"I'm not."

She squeezed my upper arm and leaned close to whisper. "This setting must be hard for you, even after all these years."

"I'm trying not to think about it."

"Have the Red Hands found the real killer yet?" Her face was a bit pale, and her eyes had hardened. Her knuckles were white over the handle of her cane.

I shook my head. "You've heard about them both?"

"I heard a client talking about Danial. He must have just come from there, and he was describing it none too politely to one of my girls. I had to ask him to leave."

I could imagine. Some people got off on that kind of thing, and those encounters could turn dangerous quick for whoever was entertaining them. "Did they mention me?"

She sighed. "They described you. They didn't know who you were, but my people figured it out."

"Thanks. For defending what honor I have left."

She patted my upper arm, crushing the poofy sleeve a little. "I can keep them from talking about it, but I can't make them believe otherwise. I'm very disappointed in the failure of the Red Hands to find this killer."

"I'm disappointed in their failure to *try*."

"It does seem like they're doing their best to implicate you. I even overheard a report to Rigel about your whereabouts during the time of the murders. That means they've tapped the beggars."

"Where did they say I was?"

"They said you visited Odele's and had an argument with the old bat, then showed up at court, and then you were unaccounted for until you found Saree."

I grunted. "Convenient how sleeping in my apartment is considered unaccounted for."

"As far as Danial, they said you walked off into the city and disappeared, then you showed back up hours later doing rounds like you'd never left."

I frowned. Before I found Danial, I had been in the Estates. I couldn't very well explain *that* to everyone. It broke a number of guild rules, and Rigel would be pissed if I was investigating the murders on my own.

Her voice lowered again, and I could smell the wine on her breath. "You need to be careful. I'm sure they will have the beggars watching you now. Rigel is demanding more evidence, but others might not let him wait to find it. No matter how courtly Rigel tries to run things, the guild is populated with criminals and good-for-nothings. Get them riled up, and they will demand action, or take it themselves."

I nodded. The prickling sensation of too many eyes upon me was all too apparent. I knew what action that would be. Even before Rigel had civilized us, the guild didn't tolerate anyone preying on their own.

May reached for Marisso. "Can you help me to a seat, my dear?"

Marisso glanced once at me, but did as she asked him, wandering away to where the music wasn't as grating. I stood a moment, taking the opportunity to drink the entire glass of whiskey. It was going to be a long night.

Chapter 19

Deidre stepped up beside me and handed me a bread roll the size of my hand. "Eat this. You can't drink like that with nothing in your stomach."

I held the bread in one hand and the empty glass in the other, gazing out at the crowd and staring down anyone that tried to meet my gaze. "I hate this."

"It'll be fine. Nobody would dare ruin Rigel's party." She reached up and rubbed her thumb across my lower lip, her mouth tightening into a line and her eyes flashing.

I was sure Marisso had been wearing some kind of lipcolor, and my face flushed.

Her smile returned, but she didn't look me in the eye. "He looks very handsome tonight."

I didn't answer. She stood beside me for a while, chatting about the people flowing around us, complaining about the loudness of the music, and forcing me to eat the bread. It seemed to keep everyone else at a distance, so I let her talk. After a while I asked about Beth, and she said she hadn't seen her since she left the food table.

I grunted. "At least that's one blessing."

Deidre frowned. "She feels terrible tonight you know."

I scanned the crowd, shivering at the masked monsters that cavorted around pretending to attack people. "And why is that?"

"Because she's the one that suggested this theme to the Attendants of the Master."

I turned wide eyes on her, my face heating up. "She what?"

"She didn't know. When she saw you react like you did, she asked me why, and I told her you don't like the festival."

I glared at her.

She sighed back at me. "Don't give me that look. I didn't tell her why, just that it bothers you. She feels terrible about it, and said if she'd known, she would never have suggested it."

I tried to take a drink out of the empty glass in my hand and huffed in irritation. "Whatever. It's done."

Deidre frowned and scanned the room. "I should find her. Make sure she's okay. She really didn't mean anything by it." She gripped my arm once again in a comforting gesture, then stepped into the crowd.

I took the opportunity to find the bar again and ordered two. The first one I drank there all at once, then took the second one in the opposite direction of the musicians.

Marisso found me leaning against the wall and sidled up beside me until he was able to wrap an arm around my waist. "You look a little pale."

I smiled tightly and sipped at my drink, then realized it was nearly gone and finished off the last swallow. Marisso started talking about the people going past us and I listened to him ramble. He loved to talk—and usually I didn't mind—but I wasn't in the mood tonight. The blue light of the lamps set me on edge and the fake gateways kept catching my gaze and making my heart thump against my ribs. I didn't know which was worse, the accusing glares all around me, or my nightmares brought to life in theatrical fashion.

It was all taking me back to that night. The fear that twisted in my gut was the same fear I'd felt as a little kid. My time in the labyrinth had been short, but it had never left me. The smell of ash and dust. The slithering and clacking of the monster. The glowing green eyes of—

Culley stepped in front of me and held up a glass of amber liquid. He was wearing a tattered dress, and I raised an eyebrow at him before exchanging my empty glass for the one he offered. He laughed and swayed on his feet.

"I jus wanted to say—I'm so sorry. I shouldna got you in that fight. Please—assep—" He covered his mouth with a fist and belched, then continued. "*Accept*. Accept my apology."

"Whatever you say, Culley."

"One night a year, right boss?" He winked at me, but it looked more like an eye spasm.

I raised the glass in agreement and he spun away, toppling into a woman and immediately arguing with her about which of them had the prettier dress. I took two gulps from my new drink and settled in to listen to Marisso chatter.

By the time I finished it three and a half stories later, my hands were tingling even more and I had a vague sense of floating. Marisso was still talking, but I wasn't really paying attention. The swirling colors and scents were making me nauseous and I was mostly wondering what time it was. I didn't think I was drinking fast enough to be this drunk.

Marisso stepped in front of me and stood with his face inches from mine until I focused on him.

"Are you listening?" he asked.

"Sorry?"

He sighed and put his arms around my shoulders, playing with the hair at the back of my neck. "When this is done, do you want to come over to my place?"

I laughed, surprising even myself. "I think when this is over I'll be lucky not to be dead in a tunnel somewhere."

He pouted up at me, brushing off the statement. "You look amazing tonight, even if she was the one who dressed you up."

"Thanks. I feel like an idiot."

"Well you look great." He moved forward and pressed his lips to mine.

For a few seconds I kissed him back, but it started to feel like the room was slipping out from beneath me. I pulled back and blinked to try to clear my head. Everything was fuzzy. "I need to get a little air. I'll be back."

I slipped out of his arms and deposited my empty glass on the nearest table, trying not to stumble as I crossed the room. I just needed to slip out for a few minutes and catch my breath. I fumbled at my throat and undid three of the buttons so I didn't feel like I was choking. There were tunnels leading into the hall on all sides, and I made a line for the nearest one.

As I got close, one of the black-masked monsters brushed past me from behind and I nearly jumped out of my skin and stumbled into a man and woman standing nearby, knocking the man over. I reached for his hand while I glared at the fake monster. "Sorry. I'm really sorry."

147

He brushed himself off and raised an eyebrow at me. "Gray?"

"Senyr?" I hardly recognized him in his finery. His mop of hair was carefully combed back and he was freshly shaven, his dour clothes had been exchanged for an aristocratic outfit in green and gold, and his usual slouching posture was gone. He looked... noble.

He grinned and slapped me on the back. "You showed up! Come and have a drink with me."

I protested, but the woman with him linked her arm in mine and dragged me along to the bar. I took the offered drink and Senyr made a toast to the continued success of the guild. I drank with him, and leaned against the bar for stability as he talked about the dances I had missed, and how this one was so much better.

When the woman with him turned away to chat with someone nearby, he leaned closer and lowered his voice. "This was supposed to be a chance for you to act normal and quell the gossip. You're jumpy. At this rate, everyone here will be sure you're hiding something."

I grimaced. "Aren't we? We *are* thieves after all."

"None of your bullshit. If your brain was half as sharp as your mouth, you'd be staying out of trouble instead of finding more damn bodies and breaking into the Estates."

My stomach turned. "You know about that?"

"You'd be surprised what I hear. That's what happens when you aren't distracted by the size of your own cock."

I grumbled, but held my tongue. I looked down at my glass, and my hand resting on the black painted canvas. My vision doubled, then snapped back in place. I usually held my alcohol better than this. What was going on?

Senyr had continued, and I refocused on his words, missing a good chunk of what he'd already said.

"—haven't the luxury of stroking our egos."

I nodded, swallowing back the nausea it caused, and tuned out the rest of his lecture. My head was heavy, and my vision seemed to trail behind the movement of my eyes. I heard his words, but only about half of them registered as sensible noises. I needed to get away from the bar. "This was a bad idea."

Senyr plastered a false smile on his face as his companion returned. "Just relax, and try to enjoy yourself."

I patted him on the arm and excused myself, then walked toward an exit. The room was spinning—or the people were—as I staggered through the crowd.

Beth appeared in front of me, pushing on my chest with enough force to make her grunt. "Why are you falling down?"

"I need some air." I pushed past her and barreled out the door, into the echoing silence of the tunnel. My heart was pounding and I put both hands on the wall, bending forward and counting my breath to keep from throwing up. The floor swam beneath me. I heard the door open and shut behind me and glanced over to see Beth.

Her face was creased with worry. "Are you okay?"

"I'm fine. Just a few too many drinks I guess."

She moved closer and I straightened, turning to lean back against the wall.

She stepped right in front of me, her tight corset brushing the fabric of my doublet as she breathed. My eyes were drawn to the pendant rising and falling with her chest. This close, I could feel the magic from it as well, making the skin on my chest crawl. She put her hands on the front of my shoulders and trailed her fingers down my upper arms. "I wanted to tell you I was sorry. It's my fault they made the ball like this."

My face felt hot, and I realized it must look like I was staring at her cleavage, so I looked over her shoulder instead. "Don't worry about it."

She turned my face to hers and kissed me full on the mouth.

I froze, the blood pounding in my ears. She pulled away enough to move her mouth to my ear, leaning into me until I was squeezed between her and the wall. At least it was helping to hold me up, though my entire body was tingling from her magic.

"I'm *really* sorry, Gray," she whispered.

My brain was so fuzzy. I opened my mouth to reply—to protest—but she covered it with hers. What was she doing? I gripped her arms, thinking I should push her away, but lost my train of thought before I could do it. She pressed against me, snaking her hand behind my head. With my brain not working, my body just responded from habit.

The door beside us opened, and the buzz of the crowd grew louder. Deidre stepped into the tunnel and stared at me.

Beth pulled away and wiped her mouth with a trembling hand. She mumbled something I didn't hear and ran past Deidre and back into the hall. Deidre's eyes narrowed, and I wanted nothing more than to pass out on the floor right there. I rubbed a hand against my chest where the tingling was slow to fade.

She spoke in sharp, crisp words. "Lord Rigel wants us for the ceremony."

Shit. I nodded, regretting it as I waited for the dizziness to pass, then used the wall for support to make my way back into the audience hall. The musicians had stopped, and people watched us walk past. I did my best not to stagger or sway, but I could tell by the whispers behind hands and the smirks, that I'd be a topic of conversation for a while after tonight. I had a feeling I'd fucked up Rigel's plan.

I followed Deidre to the space in front of Lord Rigel's chair that had been opened up. I bowed, leaning on her to keep my feet as she curtsied beside me, and we separated.

There were six divisions in the guild. Each of them had three members of the highest rank, and those people stood to either side of Rigel, nine to a side. Senyr was there, as well as Neffery.

The rank Deidre and I belonged to was a little less structured. The Black Hands had nineteen enforcers, and I moved to stand with those that bothered to show up, next to Lionel. The Blue Hands had at least three dozen madams in attendance, and again that many escorts, and Deidre faded into their midst. The other divisions were clustered together as well.

When everyone had taken their place, Rigel began to speak. My eyes closed and I tried not to sway into Lionel's crossed arms beside me. Rigel was talking about the theme of the ball, and I didn't want to hear any more about the fucking Night of Shadows.

Lionel nudged me. I raised my gaze and saw the crowd backing away for the black costumed people to come forward. One of the gateways was being lowered from the ceiling by ropes.

Rigel's voice boomed theatrically through the hall. "This year's Under Ball is the Night of Shadows. Once a year the streets of Sangarie become host to the realm of shadows and ruin."

The costumed beasts began sliding around the gateway. They must have been starting some kind of skit. I felt my skin crawling as I watched, but couldn't look away. They were dancing and waving their streamer arms. The sounds around me blurred together.

A thick, black tentacle waved from the edge of the gateway, suction cups dripping. I sucked in a breath and staggered back, but the Green Hand behind me shoved me back in line. When I looked up again the tentacle was just the arm of one of the dancers. I shook my head to try to clear it. My imagination was running away with me. Must be the drink.

"Rumor has it that before men settled here, there was a great labyrinth, inhabited by fearsome creatures twisted by darkness."

The crowds parted at the side of the cleared space so people could shove ruined walls made of sticks and canvas forward, pushing them together as a backdrop. One of them was deposited just an arms length in front of me. The blue light of the lamps flared and suddenly it looked like real stone instead of glued together canvas.

The edges of the gateway hanging from the ceiling glowed and fluttered like blue fire. The blackness in the gateway cleared and I could see the walls beyond and the ash drifting through the blackened streets. A huge mass of darkness blotted it out and a tentacle whipped out of the gateway and waved over the crowd, which was laughing and cheering.

My heart hammered in my chest and I clenched my eyes shut. It wasn't real. Hallucinations? Had one of these fucking criminals added something to the booze? I swayed and a hand gripped my arm and shook me.

I opened my eyes and blinked to bring Lionel into focus.

"Are you drunk?" he whispered. "Get ahold of yourself."

I shrugged him off and glanced at the performance. Sticks and canvas. That's all it was.

"On that night each year they rip through the veil between the past and the present and walk the streets of the city, dragging anyone they find into their world."

A tentacle whipped over me and I shouted and covered my head, my entire body shaking. I staggered sideways and people were muttering and backing out of my way. Their dresses and finery were blurring together, turning them into walls of color that moved around me, penning me in.

It's not real. It's not real.

A figure stepped in front of me, thin face dripping black ooze, green light sparking from its eyes. I staggered back and the colorful wall grabbed at me, tugged at my clothes, and tried to push me toward the

151

figure. The features twisted and I saw pointed ears, a gaunt chin, and an almost human-like grimace. My heart stuttered in my chest.

It leaped for me, arms outstretched, and I swung at it. Pain flared in my knuckles as I struck its face. It fell to the ground, shrieking.

My heart jumped into my throat. It was real? The shadow creatures converged on me, blending together into one massive creature with waving tentacles and clacking jaws. I tried to pull one of my knives from the sheath at the small of my back, but the doublet went too far down my thighs and was too tight to lift out of the way with my fumbling hands.

Where was the man? Where was the man that always came after the dark figure? I couldn't remember his face, but he always woke me from the nightmare. Where was he?

The wall still grabbed at me, and I kept trying to free one of my arms enough to reach my knives. There was a roaring noise in my ears, like hundreds of people talking at once. I shouted at it to let me go.

The shadowy figure climbed back to its feet, face dripping black, eyes glowing green. It stalked toward me and I struggled as the wall behind me tightened around my arms.

It raised its arm and struck, and everything went dark.

Chapter 20

I woke feeling like my mouth was full of cotton. A jagged line of pain was splitting my skull in half and my jaw ached. At least it was dark. I rolled onto my side and immediately clenched my teeth and breathed through my nose as I tried not to throw up.

A chair scraped loudly across the floor and someone walked toward me. "Good afternoon."

I cracked my eyes open to see Deidre in her usual simple dress, holding a lamp turned down low in one hand and a bucket in the other. She set the lamp on the side table. I was in my own bed at least. I had no shirt on, but still wore the tights from the night before.

I swung my legs to the edge of the bed and pushed myself into a sitting position, and my stomach immediately tried to turn itself inside out. I grabbed the bucket she thrust into my hands and vomited. Between convulsions I slid off the bed and to my knees, hunching over the bucket and leaning against the side of the bed.

When nothing else would come up, I pushed the bucket aside and curled into a ball on the floor, holding my head in my hands. The pain was so loud.

"How much did you drink last night?"

I put a hand flat on the floor and rose to my knees, my stomach clenching but unable to send anything else up. With a grunt and a grimace, I sat on the floor and leaned back against the bed. "I'm not sure. Everything past seeing Culley in a dress is all fuzzy."

"Everything?"

She did *not* sound happy. I raised a hand to my head, making sure there wasn't an actual jagged split in my skull, and that it was just the worst headache I'd ever experienced. "What happened?"

Her face was definitely angry, but she wasn't yelling at me. I guess I should be happy for small miracles. If she'd been screaming at me, I think my head would have finished splitting in two. "Do we have any water?"

She moved to the kitchen area and I leaned my head back against the side of the mattress. I hurt all over. I couldn't remember ever feeling this bad after getting drunk. She walked back to me and held the glass out.

I drank about half, pausing once in a while to make sure it wasn't coming back up.

She continued to stand over me, her arms crossed in front of her.

Definitely angry. What had I done? I reached up and touched my jaw, wincing at the ache. "Are you going to fill me in?"

She snorted and snatched the glass out of my hand before walking to the kitchen area.

I crawled up the side of the bed and pushed myself to my feet. I got two steps toward her before the entire room started tilting and I stumbled back to sit on the edge of the bed. My heart was banging in my chest and my fingers felt like ants were crawling up and down them. "I don't feel right."

Deidre banged something on the counter, making my headache spike, and I could hear her rummaging around in the cupboards. "You're probably still drunk."

"No." I put my hand to the side of my head. The room wouldn't quit spinning. "I don't think so." If I didn't lie back, I was going to fall on the floor...

***

I woke up again and waited to move until I was sure I wouldn't vomit or fall over. Thankfully, I seemed to be suffering from just a mild hangover now. And an aching jaw. I reached across to the other side of the bed, but I was alone.

The room was dimly lit. I had no idea what time it was. I flung the blankets off and sat up, my gaze landing on a dark figure sitting at the table. My heart jumped into my throat and I reflexively tried to grab a knife from the small of my back before I realized I was both shirtless and knifeless.

Of course I was. I was in bed.

The figure turned in the chair and I recognized Senyr. I hung my head and let the tension fall out of my body. "By the Six—what the fuck are you doing in here? Where's Deid?"

"She went out."

I took a long breath and shook away the last of the surprise, then stood and stretched before making my way to the table.

Senyr turned up the lamp nearby and I could make out the deep scowl on his face, along with a dark bruise under one eye. His cloak was draped over the back of his chair and a bottle of whiskey with a half full glass rested nearby.

"Did she leave any food? I'm starving."

"We need to talk about your behavior at the Under Ball."

I passed the table and poured myself a glass of water from a pitcher on the counter. "I already told Deidre, I don't remember anything past Culley handing me a drink. She seemed upset, but I have no idea why." I glanced back at him. "Although it must have been quite a party, you even have a souvenir on your face."

His eyes flashed, and I wished I could remember what had happened. It would have been the chance of a lifetime watching Senyr in a fight after all these years. I rummaged through the cupboard, finding nothing to ease the grumbling in my stomach.

"After the shit you pulled at the ball, I think you need to lay low until this murder issue is resolved."

I frowned and spun to look at my mentor. "What are you talking about?"

"You really don't remember?"

"Not at all. I think Culley spiked my drink, to be honest."

Senyr shook his head, a blush rising to his cheeks. "You acted like a crazy man. It took half a dozen people to hold you down. If the guild didn't think you were capable of murder before, they do now."

My brow furrowed and I rubbed my aching jaw. "You expect me to just sit here in my room? For how long? Those Red Hands aren't even trying to find the actual killer."

"For as long as it takes."

I slammed the glass of water onto the counter. "Fuck no."

"You go out there now, you'll make things even worse."

I laughed. "Worse?" I crossed to the dresser and started looking for my normal clothes. "Unless those worthless assassins start actually *looking* for a killer, I could end up stuck in my room for who knows how long. I'll go crazy." I stabbed a finger in his direction. "You know that. You may as well hand me over to the Warden and let her put me in a cage."

"We can't be held responsible for—"

"Besides, I have work to do. I have a district to take care of."

"I can take over your—"

"That's bullshit, and we both know it." I pointed vaguely in the direction of the surface. "I need to be out there. You'll just have to kick the Red Hands in the ass and make them wrap this up, so I can get on with my job."

Senyr shot out of the chair and leaned on the table a moment, working his jaw like he wanted to rip into me and shout me into submission. I saw that desire fade, then he shook his head and straightened to sling on his cloak. "Keep out of trouble, boy, or even the guildmaster won't be able to help you."

"I'll do my *absolute* best."

He gave me one last grumpy look, then strode to the door and slammed it shut behind him.

I sighed and finished finding my clothes, then peeled off the fucking tights and dressed properly. I made sure my knives were secure at my back and waited a little longer just to be certain I wouldn't run into Senyr in the corridors, then I left.

The walk through the tunnels was awkward. The people I passed looked away, or ignored me, or responded briefly and hurried by. What had I done at that ball? Senyr hadn't gone into any detail.

I went topside and found it was midmorning, and the sky was full of heavy gray clouds. There was a little eatery by the docks that served early for the workers. I knew the owners and the food was always good—and it wasn't frequented by guild members—so I wandered my way there. I didn't want to eat while people whispered around me.

The old woman from the kitchen set down a plate of smoked fish, bread, a little fruit, and some tiny steamed potatoes. "You should come around more often, Gray. I have many new things to let you taste.

Clyson brings me some kind of blue fish from up north, and it has the flavor of mountain streams in its meat."

I chuckled. "Somebody works hard for my money. I can't spend it *all* on food."

The old woman cackled merrily and walked off to the kitchen.

Once I'd eaten, I started rounds. I got some strange looks, a few sidelong glances, and a lot of awkward, rushed greetings. At one point, one of my guys laughed at me, but I glared until he apologized and scurried away.

Even though I couldn't see the sun above me, I was guessing it was late afternoon when I heard my name as I walked through the Old Market. I turned, scanning the sparse crowd. If this was another thief, come to snicker about something I couldn't remember…

"Gray! Come quickly!" Breathless, Beth shoved past the people separating us and grabbed hold of my arm, pulling me in the direction from which she'd come.

Great. She was the last person I wanted to see today. I pulled back, refusing to move. "I'm not interested. Not today."

She looked up at me, tears welling in her eyes. "You have to hurry!"

"Whatever your problem is, find someone else to deal with it."

Her grip on my arm tightened and she brought the other hand up as well, tugging on me. "Deidre is in trouble."

My eyes narrowed and I pushed her into motion in front of me. "Where?"

Guiding me through the crowd, she told me about how she and another woman had found Deidre in an alleyway, bleeding and exhausted. They had started to help her up, but she had insisted they go for me instead. The other woman had stayed with her.

"Which alley is it?"

"It's behind Yardo the silversmith's shop."

I looked at her blankly.

She tried again. "Yardo's place is next to Hayl's jewelry."

I nodded and took her arm—ignoring the tingle it sent through my hand—then ducked onto a narrow side street. "I know a shorter way."

We raced through the alley and across the street into the next one. Halfway through, I pulled her up short and pushed aside a large crate, revealing the bottom of a rickety ladder. I put my foot on the first rung and looked back at her. "You go underground and have a healer sent to my room."

"But—"

"I can go faster on my own. Get the healer ready for when we get there." I turned back to the ladder and started to climb, ignoring the way the iron scraped against the brick and sent chunks of it crumbling down to the alley. I didn't bother to check whether Beth had obeyed me. The ladder creaked dangerously under my weight so I moved quickly, pulling myself onto the roof and getting my bearings.

I took off in the direction of the district that housed Hayl's shop, navigating the varied levels of the roofs with practiced ease. I was moving much faster than I would have been able to if I'd been forced to push my way through the crowds below, or follow the twisting streets. The small gaps between buildings didn't even give me pause, and I navigated around the larger gaps.

I got as close as I could on the rooftops, but eventually came to a gap I couldn't jump. No road was perfect. Sliding down a sloped roof, I braced my hands on a beam and swung out over the edge, then dropped the last five feet to the ground. I darted across the street and sprinted to the next corner. Five blocks to go.

Most of the shops in this district sold luxury items, so they weren't busy this late in the afternoon. The few shoppers that were browsing backed out of the way as I ran past. I ducked into the alley behind Hayl's and came to a stop, chest heaving.

The alley was dark under the overcast sky and I squinted to see among the crates and barrels piled behind the buildings. Without even thinking about it, I moved my hand closer to my knives. "Deid?"

A frightened female voice I didn't recognize came from my left and my head snapped around. My heart was pounding from both the run and anxiety. "Deid, are you there?"

A young woman came out from behind a pile of crates. She shifted from foot to foot, trembling and ready to bolt back into the shadows. "Are you Gray?"

I moved forward and nodded, pushing past her and slipping behind the crates. Deidre was propped against the wall of the alley with her arms tightly across her abdomen and her head down. I knelt beside her and gently lifted her chin up. "Hey, are you alive?"

158

She grimaced. "So far."

I looked her over in the failing light. Blood showed at her hairline, and her dark hair was wet with it. Her satin dress was torn and had dark stains on it as well. "How bad are you hurt?"

"I think I'll be fine. I just couldn't walk anymore."

I scowled, my hands shaking with the desire to check for myself and make sure she was okay. "Have you been stabbed? What happened?"

"Don't worry." She groaned a little as she shifted away from the side of the alley. "I'm not bleeding out. It just hurts."

I nodded and slid an arm beneath her knees and the other behind her back. "Let's get you home." I lifted her carefully, shifting her weight to carry her better. She slumped against my chest.

The other woman mumbled some excuse for leaving, then scurried off before I could reply. I hadn't recognized her, but that didn't mean much. Deidre worked all over the city, and the girl could have been from anywhere.

Trying not to jostle her too much, I began walking toward the closest entrance to the labyrinth of tunnels that made up the underground. A few times I had to stop and carefully shift her weight. By the time I walked past the beggar guarding the entrance my arms ached with the strain. I went quickly through the tunnels, and when I reached my door I stopped to fumble for the handle. Deidre drew in a hissing breath, squeezing my arm.

"Sorry," I mumbled. Shifting her weight, I reached again and my fingers finally caught it. With a little creative balancing, I managed to turn it and give it a slight push. I adjusted my hold on her again and kicked the door open with my foot.

Inside, the lamps were already lit and Beth was talking with one of the guild healers. I glared at them as I hooked the door with the back of my foot and slammed it shut. "You couldn't have left the door open for me?"

The healer motioned at the bed in the alcove to the left. The covers were already turned down. Her face didn't show the least bit of an apology. "We didn't hear you until just now. Put her here. Gently."

I walked over, mumbling under my breath about what I would *gently* do to the two of them. Deidre pinched my arm.

"Ow! What the hell!"

159

"Shut up," she said, her voice trembling.

I clamped my mouth shut and sat on the edge of the bed, easing her down. She moaned once, but managed to nod up at me when I stood and backed out of the way. The healer shoved past me and immediately began assessing her wounds.

There was a rage in my chest. I wanted to run back across the rooftops and find whoever had done this and drag them into the street and—

I stalked across the room to the table and shrugged out of my vest, which was stained with drying blood. There was a bit of blood on my linen shirt as well, but I could live with that until I had a chance to change properly.

I glanced at the bed, seeing nothing but the healer's broad back as she examined Deidre. My hands were shaking and my jaw ached from being clenched. I had an overwhelming need to move, and started pacing, staying close to the table to keep out of the way.

Beth was standing nearby, watching me with a flush on her cheeks and a furrow in her brow. "Are you okay?"

I put both hands flat on the table, leaning into it and taking deep breaths. "Did you see who did this?"

She shook her head. "We found her on the street."

"You don't know where she came from?"

Beth shook her head again.

From the other side of the room, Deidre called my name. I crossed to the bed, looking down at her. Her chest was wrapped in bandages and the healer was applying ointment to the last few cuts on her arms. I shook my head, narrowing my eyes. "Do you want to tell me what the hell happened?"

She frowned at me, pulling the coverlet further up her chest. "No, I don't."

I glared back. "Whoever did this can't just get away with it. Tell me who it was and I'll—"

"You'll what?" she snapped. "Tell Lord Rigel? Go after the guy yourself? Come on, Gray, you know you'll only get into trouble."

I leaned down, my voice harsher than I intended. "Probably, but whoever it was will never hurt you again. Or anyone else for that matter."

160

She shook her head. "I won't take any more jobs from him, and I'll have the madams blacklist him. There's no need for you to get involved."

"Stubborn woman! That guy needs to be taught a lesson."

"Not by you!" she yelled back. She winced and relaxed into the bed, her eyes smoldering beneath her long lashes. "Drop it, Gray. I'm not your wife. We're only friends, remember? I can take care of my own shit."

I grunted and leaned against the post at the foot of the bed, not meeting her eyes. Her words had stung more than I expected.

After a moment of silence, she spoke in a softer tone. "You threaten people and you steal things. You cheat at dice, and you drink too much, and—" she gestured at Beth across the room "—and you flirt as naturally as you breathe. But you're no killer. Let someone else handle this." Her voice softened and I could hear the tears she was holding back. "I don't want you to do something that will make you look even worse right now."

I didn't trust myself to speak.

"Please, Gray. Just let it go."

I shook my head and spun on my heel. I could still feel the burning in my chest and I didn't want to yell at her, so I grabbed my cloak from the hook by the door and walked out, slamming the door shut behind me.

Chapter 21

As I went through the tunnels I kept my head down. I noticed the looks and the way people stepped out of my way, but I didn't acknowledge any of it. It felt like there was a lead weight in my chest, and I wasn't sure if it was anger or fear or something else entirely. I thought about Deidre's hair matted with blood, the cuts and bruises on her arms, the bandages that had been wrapped around her chest, and the way she'd pressed her arms into her belly.

I slammed both hands into the door that opened onto the street, nearly taking it off its rusted hinges. Two people were dead. Deidre could have been the third. If she hadn't gotten away—

I pushed my way through the crowd, running over the memories of the dead Blue Hands in my mind to see if there was any clue I might have missed that would lead me to the real killer. There was the coin, but that had gotten me nowhere. The scene by the river hadn't revealed a weapon, although he'd been stabbed as well.

Why weren't the Red Hands finding who'd done this? What the fuck were they doing? How many people had to die before they did their damned jobs?

I rocked to a stop and looked up at the door to May's. Had I intended to come here, or was it old habit? I took a breath and thought about Marisso. I thought about his sunny smile and his soothing fingers. Intentional or not, I was here.

When I strode through the door, some of the Blue Hands flinched. The room went quiet and I wondered how crazy I must look for them to stare at me like that. There was no sign of May at the small hearth, and I searched the familiar faces with a sinking feeling in my gut. Most of them were unfriendly, if not outright hostile. I was still deciding what to do when I heard light footfalls upstairs and looked to see Marisso peek his head down the stairs.

He looked uneasy, and glanced at the assembled Blues before taking the steps in a rush. By the time he reached the bottom he wore a polite smile, and he crossed to the door where I stood and took my arm. "Gray. Good afternoon."

"Good afternoon? Why are you so—"

He stepped between me and the other people, putting his back to them. "Why are you here?"

I faltered. The anger over Deidre was still hot in my thoughts, and the strained smile on Marisso's face was a stark contrast from how he'd been at the ball... to how he always was. "I wanted to talk to you. Something happened and I wanted to—"

"You really shouldn't be here. People are saying all kinds of things about us, and I don't think this is the best time for you to visit me."

It felt like something in my chest broke loose and fell into my gut. I stared back at him, not knowing what to say.

He steered me toward the door. "Having you here will make me look bad. The others are talking and I don't want it to affect my work. You know how rumors spread. Lord Rigel said I'm on the list for becoming an escort, and I can't risk ruining that."

I stumbled into the doorway, still staring at him like an idiot.

He stood, framed in the red doorway, eyes brimming with tears and biting his lip to keep that fake smile on his face. "I'm sorry." He reached out and brushed my hair over my ear with trembling fingers. "Let everything die down a bit, then you can come back."

He stepped back into the building and closed the door softly in my face.

I couldn't do anything but stare at the door for a minute, trying to sort out the flood of emotions fighting for attention. I was still full of adrenaline from arguing with Deidre and seeing her hurt, but now I also felt horribly betrayed.

May's had always been a sanctuary. Even before Marisso arrived. To be pushed out the door and... I wasn't sure what I felt.

I slunk back toward Old Town, sticking to the shadows when I could and keeping my head down. Fuck him. If making escort was that important to him, then... fuck him.

The rage was coming back. I welcomed it. I was tired of the sideways looks and the whispering. I was tired of the accusations. Most of all I was tired of my life being upended and shaken, leaving me not knowing who I could trust or where I could go without being blamed for something I didn't do.

I needed to get rid of some of this energy.

The Throat wouldn't do. The way I felt now I'd just end up starting a fight, and Sans would have Kash kick my ass. A fight in general would probably be a bad idea, considering my circumstances. That left sex.

I had reached Tanji's brothel before I even considered the thought that Danial had been from there, and they might look at me the same way the Blues in Odele's had done. I stood outside the door a good long while, debating whether I went in, or tried to find someplace across the city where they wouldn't know me.

I didn't have to do either. A woman sidled up to me with a half-smile, eyes shining, and I recognized Vin. She had a sleeveless dress on, cut low in the front, and her upper arms were ringed by tattoos. Bangles clinked softly on her wrists as she stepped in front of me and put a hand on my shoulder. "Hello, Gray."

"Hey Vin." She was one of Tanji's. Must have gone out for something and just returned.

She swept her fingers through the hair behind my head. "Are you looking for something today?"

It was at the front of my mind, and I wasn't going to be comfortable until I said it. Besides, Vin pulled no punches and she'd tell me what she thought whether it cost her a client or not. "You aren't worried about me? Because of Danial?"

"Fuck no. Those rumors are bullshit." She gripped the back of my neck and gazed hard into my eyes. "You'd never have hurt Danial. Or Saree. Anyone who believes that doesn't really know you."

I swallowed and nodded. The surge of relief in my chest would have been sweet, but there was still so much anger there over Deidre. Over the thought of someone hurting her.

I grimaced at the feeling of possessiveness that boiled up. I had no right to it. Deidre had said it herself. We were friends and nothing more.

"Well? You come here to fuck, or you just want to stand around?"

"Yeah. Let's go upstairs."

She grinned and led me inside the brothel. I kept my gaze down or on Vin, avoiding any poisonous glances that might have given me second thoughts. She must have understood how I felt, because she wasted no time in dragging me through the front room and upstairs, heading straight for her room.

I closed the door behind me and unhooked my cloak, tossing it to a nearby chair. I had left my vest at home in my rush, and I tried to shove the annoyance aside and focus on the woman in front of me.

She ran her hands up my chest, then pushed me back against the wall with enough force to rattle the shelves. Her mouth found mine and she kissed me hard. I flinched at the lingering pain in my jaw, but it felt good so I followed her lead.

I pulled the dress off her shoulders, running my hands down her back and slipping one down to cup her ass and pull her closer to me, kissing her like a drowning man gulping for air. She tugged at my belt, unfastening it before I could try to help, and letting it thunk to the floor with my knives. I stopped kissing her long enough to fling my shirt off, then wrapped my arms around her shoulders again as she worked at my pants.

There was an urgency to her movements that fed the need in me. The more frantic she became, the more I lost myself—and I desperately wanted to lose myself right now. I wanted to let everything fade away in the heat, even if it was just for a little while. I pushed her dress down past her waist and gripped her ass in both hands, pulling her against me as she wrapped her arms around my neck.

***

After I had thoroughly exhausted myself, I lay back in her bed with my arms crossed behind my head. She was still sprawled over my lower body, tracing patterns on my stomach.

"I'm glad to see your reputation remains intact."

I laughed, trying to hold onto the euphoria as long as I could. Eventually I'd have to get dressed and be responsible. A soft rushing noise from outside caught my attention and I stared up at the ceiling and sighed. *Shit*. It was raining.

She crawled higher up my body and kissed my chest. I closed my eyes and listened to the rain.

165

Her voice broke me out of a light doze. "Some of us were wondering if you got in trouble after the ball."

There it went. Afterglow completely gone. "For what?"

Her kisses stopped and she raised herself up to look at me better. "For hitting Senyr? Not many people have the balls to punch a Hand of the Master."

I frowned and sat up, moving her off to the side. "Hold on. I hit *Senyr*? Are you sure?" I pictured him sitting in my apartment with a black eye and a grouchy glare, talking about how it had taken half a dozen people to hold me back. I had wondered why he was blushing.

Vin picked up my hand and traced the split knuckles. "Pretty sure. He hit you right back though, and you have the bruise to prove it under that scruff."

I put a hand to my aching jaw and struggled to pull up the fuzzy memories I had from the ball. I vaguely recalled seeing my superior, and I think I might have talked to him—but I did *not* remember hitting him. No wonder every thief and beggar was looking at me like I was crazy. *Shit*.

"You must have been really drunk."

"I must have." But I didn't think I had been. I remembered every excruciating detail up until Culley gave me that drink, then everything got fuzzy. Maybe the bastard really had drugged me.

Vin leaned close, her breasts sliding against my chest. "Do you have one more in you?"

The rain outside was getting louder, and the talk of the ball had put me completely out of the amorous mood. I took her chin in my hand. "Sorry, I should get back to work." I kissed her lightly, giving her a charming smile that was nowhere close to being genuine, then slid out from under her.

I cleaned up and dressed while she lay on her stomach with her knees bent and her ankles crossed in the air, watching me. Thankfully I had coins instead of stones in the pouch at my belt today, since I had left my vest with its more secure pockets in the apartment. I dug out more than I needed, dropping them in a small bowl on the table with a tinkling sound.

"Come back soon, Gray." She winked. "I have things I still want to do to you."

That got a real smile from me. "Thanks. For everything you *did* get to do." I went downstairs and avoided the gazes of the Blue Hands still in the front room, then raised my hood and stepped out into the rain.

I hunched into my cloak, immediately regretting leaving the brothel. I hated the rain. Most thieves lived for the added concealment, but I thought it was a wretched state. The drumming on top of my hood, the puddles that soaked my feet, the water that always managed to trickle down my neck... it made me antsy and pissed off, ready to snap at anyone.

I was supposed to have robbed a place the night before, but had apparently been too drugged to get my ass out of bed. It wasn't a big deal—this time—because the merchant would still be gone for at least one more night. Just to be sure, I walked past the house. I never slowed my steps or turned my head, but everything checked out to my satisfaction and I continued on.

Every time my brain tried to bring up Deidre, I squashed it down. Beth was there with her, and there were healers taking care of her, so she was fine. I didn't trust myself not to say something stupid, so it was better just to stay away for a while. Occasionally my thoughts turned to Marisso as well, and I squashed those just as quickly. Nothing I said to him right now would turn out well either.

I walked through the door of the Devil's Throat and looked around for a few minutes as the water dripped off my cloak onto the floorboards. As I angled toward the bar and the mug Sans was already pouring, I noticed the card game going on in the back. I smirked, thinking cards sounded good for the rest of the evening.

Sans kept hold of the mug as I neared the bar. "I've been trying to talk to you for days."

That's right. He'd wanted to talk to me the night I questioned Detano about the Estates. I had ditched him, more concerned with finding that asshole in the tin suit. "I've been a little busy."

"Well I've been kicking people out of my bar for saying shit about you. The least you can do is find the time to speak with me."

My eyebrow went up and I glanced around the room. Sure enough, the sidelong gazes I did see were carefully neutral and wavered between the barkeep and me. Nobody wanted to get on the bad side of the man with the best booze in the district. It was a huge relief, and I smiled as I reached for the mug. "Thanks."

"Red Hands. Never liked those assassins and thugs. Your guildmaster is a fool to trust them with policing anything." He reached under the bar and brought up a jar with a lid, along with a small wooden bowl. Without any prompting he poured a mix of nuts and dried fruit into the bowl and slid it over to me, then put the jar away. "They aren't trying very hard to find the truth if you ask me."

"They seem set on blaming it on me. The rumor was spreading within hours, and that's fast even for Old Town."

"Well, not all of Old Town believes it."

I poked at the mix in the bowl, looking for the dried berries. "Not all of Old Town has to. Things are plenty complicated with just most of them believing it."

"One of the beggars was in here asking questions about you. I'd have thrown him out too, but he seemed a little too intense to be fishing for gossip. Asked when you'd been here, who you'd talked to, lots of things."

"Any idea who it was?"

"Nobody I recognized, so probably not from Old Town. He had a shadow, though. Hooded fellow. Stayed by the door and just made everyone uncomfortable until they both left."

"Red Hand?"

"I'm guessing so. I don't get many of their kind in here."

"That you know of."

Sans scowled and glanced around the bar as if a Red Hand would pop up any moment with daggers for fingers and a toothy grin.

I took a drink to hide the twitch at the corner of my mouth.

"Point is," he continued, "you're being watched. Your every move is being accounted for. Funny thing though, the next day another beggar showed up. Different guy. This one bought drinks for a few people, and he was mighty interested in hearing all the gossip about you."

I grunted. "It's the newest pastime around here."

"Well, when he finally got around to talking to me, he asked a lot of the same questions the other fellow had. I made a comment about wasting my time repeating myself, and he clammed right up. His face got red and he walked out."

"Embarrassed?"

"More angry, if I'm any judge."

"That's odd." The beggars were usually efficient to a fault. If they were digging up information about an enforcer, they'd be sending the higher ranked people, and those people kept track of each other. It was unlikely they'd mistakenly send two Yellows onto the same source.

Unlikely... but possible. It could also have been Rigel interfering with the natural order of things. Or someone fishing around for their own reasons. Or someone trying to get ahead in the ranks by finding out new information.

Sans shrugged. "They can snoop all they want. I don't belong to the guild, and I can serve who I please. If I want to pour ale for a no-good scoundrel, ain't a Hand that can stop me. I've been too busy lately anyway, so if people don't like it they can fuck off."

It was the best I'd felt in days. I could always count on Sans to have my back. "I appreciate it, old friend."

"Your little thief has been a delight to have around, by the way. I have to try very hard to look grumpy and unsatisfied with her."

I chuckled. "She's a hard worker. I'll give her that much."

"She's a load more polite than you were at that age. Better at everything I ask her to do too. And she's thoughtful. And—"

"I get it. I was a pain in the ass."

He plucked a walnut out of the mix in the bowl. "I asked Kash to buy her some things. Put it on your tab."

I took a long drink, but didn't protest. I'd intended to give her some coin anyway. Hopefully Kash wouldn't go overboard with it.

Sans picked at the nut in his palm. "I heard about Deidre."

And there it was. Why did people always know just what to say to ruin whatever good mood I was courting? "Word travels fast."

"Was it the same killer do you think?"

Anger heated my face, but I kept my tone casual. "I don't know. But you can bet I'll be looking into it."

"Good." He picked up his rag and walked off, going to serve other patrons.

I *would* dig into it too, just not right now. It was raining out, and I had a hit to take care of later. Plus, I might *actually* kill whoever had done it, considering the mood I was in. Grabbing my mug and food, I strode to a table near the back, watching the players finish up their hands. They were all people I'd played with many times before, and none of them seemed upset to see me, which meant they weren't putting much stock in the rumors—or they didn't care if they were true. When they were done with the current hand, they made room for me and I sat down and threw in my ante.

About half an hour later, Ruena appeared beside my chair, poking the goggles that hid her eyes more firmly into place and shifting nervously from foot to foot. "Gray?"

I picked up the cards the dealer threw out one at a time, arranging them in my hand. "What's up, kid?"

"Are you okay?"

I snorted and listened to the other players bidding. "I'm fine."

She sighed loudly and flung her arms around my neck, leaning her head on my shoulder. "That's good."

I scowled and shrugged her away. "Get off. What are you doing?"

Her face was all smiles now and she stood with her hands tucked behind her back. The man on the other side of her was glaring and holding his cards close to his chest.

I threw a silver piece into the pot to call, then slid a couple of cards out of my hand and held them face down on the table. "If you're going to stand there like a fool, at least stand behind me so these gentlemen don't think I'm using you to cheat."

Her eyes widened behind the goggles and she darted behind me, her hands resting on the back of my chair as she looked over my shoulder. "Sorry."

"You might as well pay attention. No questions though, or I'll send you outside to memorize buildings or something."

"Okay."

I tossed the pair of cards into the pile in the center of the table and accepted two more, settling in to play. I was more interested in relaxing than making money, and I didn't want Ruena to give me away, so I didn't bother cheating.

The game was going fine. In another half an hour I had almost doubled my money—even without slipping cards from the bottom of the deck—and my mood was improving, when the noise level in the room suddenly dropped. People were migrating toward the door. I watched them funneling into the rain and frowned.

I picked up my cards as the dealer tossed them out, glancing again at the door. I could hear shouting from outside. *Damn it*. Why the fuck couldn't people cause problems on *sunny* days?

The noise outside grew louder and one of the men standing just inside the door glanced back in my direction. Cursing, I threw my cards onto the table and stood up. Ruena started to follow, but I pointed at the table. "Sit."

She deflated, but backed up to the table and plopped herself down in my empty chair.

I walked to the door and shoved my way outside into the light rain, pushing through the crowd until I had a clear view of the spectacle.

An old woman, dressed in layers of rags and a hooded shawl, stood in the center of the mass. The crowd had left her plenty of room and she paced before them, arms flailing with the passion of her words.

"You will all be damned for your arrogance! When the time comes that my mistress takes this city, her magic will wash it clean of your filth! You will all bow to my mistress or you will die!"

I grunted and started to turn back to the bar, but someone grabbed my arm.

"Can't you do something about this? You're an enforcer."

I looked at the old woman once more, shaking my head. "It's not within my jurisdiction. The mystics will handle it." I waved an arm extravagantly in the air. "They've probably already *foreseen* it anyway." I shrugged off the man's grip and turned to go back inside again, the old woman's voice grating on my ears.

"The first of the evils to be purged from this city will be the guild of thieves and assassins that lurks the streets at night!"

I paused at the door, turning my head to listen.

"They will be flushed from their underground burrow like the vermin they are. My mistress will free you from their greedy hands and bloody knives. The people will be set free! The head of the foul bandit king they follow will be raised on a pike over the city walls as a testament to the new era!"

She was directly referencing Lord Rigel now. Stirring shit up against the guild. I didn't know who this woman was, or what she wanted, but I

171

couldn't let her talk in public like this. It would undermine everything Rigel was doing. It would throw my district into chaos. It would bring the Coppers around to reassure people the guild was under control and they would try to make examples to prove it. With that one little comment, the old crone had made it my business. The Six be damned.

Sighing, I turned and walked back into the crowd, stepping into the cleared area the old woman paced though. I smiled my most charming smile, walked up to her, and bent down so I didn't have to speak too loudly. The smell coming from the old woman hit me like a wall, even over the rain, and I could feel some kind of magic tingling across my skin, but I did my best to ignore it. Most mystics had one or two minor sources on themselves at all times. Usually for stupid shit like lighting torches by snapping their fingers or rattling windows to be dramatic.

"Hello there. Can I have a word with you?"

The old woman glared at me, but paused her tirade.

I smiled politely despite the rain that was soaking my hair and clothes. My cloak was still on the back of my chair in the bar. I didn't even have my vest, and tried not to shiver as the breeze cut through my shirt. "Let me get right to the point. Are you registered with the guild, ma'am?"

The woman hissed, her eyes boring into me. "I despise your rotten guild!"

I nodded, scratching the stubble on my cheek absently. "Yes, well, therein lies the problem. You see, the guild regulates certain—activities in this city. The populace remains more tolerant of said activities because some control is being enforced in their favor. I'm afraid in order for you to continue whatever it is you're trying to do, you must first get a license to rant from the guild."

The woman spat at my feet.

I looked down, losing the forced smile entirely. When I spoke again, my voice was calm, but dangerous. "Listen here, grandma, I've been patient until now because you're old, and likely half crazy, but unless you shuffle your wrinkled ass either to the guild, or to the city gate, I'm going to get upset."

She spat again, leaning closer to me and pointing a gnarled finger at my chest. "You cannot escape the fires, thief. My mistress will burn you from your hole like a rat. You *murderer*."

172

My eyes flashed. "That isn't very nice, hag. I think you'd better move along now."

The woman extended her hand and her fingertip touched the center of my chest. Her face twisted with a malicious grin and she barked a garbled word.

Ruena screamed my name from the doorway of the Throat just as my chest spasmed. I tried to gasp, but no air could get in. I dropped to my hands and knees in the wet street and looked up as the woman cackled and backed into the crowd. It felt like a vice was gripping my chest, squeezing too tight for me to draw breath. My fingers clutched at the fabric of my shirt and I had to fight the urge to rip it away. It was almost as if something was trying to pull my heart out through my back.

When the pressure finally eased I sucked in a ragged breath, then another. Someone grabbed my shoulder from behind and I looked up to see Sans bending over me.

Chapter 22

"Are you alright, boy?"

Nodding, I took the barkeep's offered hand and pulled myself to my feet. The old woman had disappeared into the rain and the thinning crowd, and I followed Sans back into the bar. I rubbed my chest where I could still feel the hag's touch, even though the pain was fading away.

Ruena stepped in front of me, her face pale and upset. "Are you okay?" Her hand went up to my chest, resting over my heart on the rain-dampened fabric. "That was magic."

I brushed her hand away. "I'm fine. Just a little out of breath."

The barkeep glared at the door. "What was that all about?"

I shook my head, my chest still quivering. "I don't know, but I hope she wanders into someone else's territory next time."

He grunted. "So do I. Things like that scare people. It's not good for business." He set a mug on the bar for me.

I stepped past Ruena and picked it up, then drank deeply. When I felt a little more steady, I made my way back to the table where I'd been playing cards, reclaiming my seat and waiting for the current hand to finish. Ruena followed me like a puppy, her eyes watchful and her brow creased in worry. The room was less boisterous than it had been half an hour ago, and there were muted conversations here and there, patrons with heads bent together so they didn't have to speak too loudly. Others kept tossing glances at the door, as if they expected the old mystic to come crashing through with warnings of doom. Or at me, with worried expressions on their faces. It created a tense atmosphere, and the feeling that a shitstorm was looming on the horizon.

I played three more hands, but I was feeling out of sorts. Luck seemed to have abandoned me, and I lost almost twenty silver before I picked up my coin pouch and my cloak and wandered away from the table. Too bad Detano wasn't out yet this evening, he'd have loved to gloat over my misfortune.

Ruena dogged my heels, joining me at the bar. As Sans stepped up I dug in my pouch and produced a handful of silver, stacking it on the bartop.

"For your tab?"

"For the brat. Make sure Kash gets her some decent boots, would you? She clomps around like a horse."

"I'll see what I can do."

I nodded my thanks and slung my cloak over my shoulders, raising the hood as I strode through the room.

Ruena came after me. "Where are we going?"

"I have work to do. You stay here and help Sans."

"Awwwww! I'm supposed to be learning thief things."

I sighed and stopped at the door. "Okay. Take this—" I pulled three silver coins from my pouch "—and double it. Without stealing, or leaving the Throat." I set the coins in her palm.

"How?"

"Gamble. Trick. Persuade. Just no stealing. Sans doesn't like people stealing from his customers."

Her brow was creased and she adjusted the goggles as she stared down at the coins. "Okay."

"Good. Off you go." When I was sure she was going to listen, I stepped out into the rain. I looked around for the old woman, half expecting to see her watching me from an alley, then chided myself for acting like a little kid.

I couldn't shake the feeling of being watched. It was truly getting dark now and I made a few rounds through the district, not wanting to be followed to the shop I intended to rob. I was almost willing to mark it down to nerves, when a silent figure darted from the shadows at the edge of my vision, nearly invisible in the rain.

If I hadn't been so keyed up, I probably wouldn't have seen him at all. Even with that split second of warning, he drove me into a recessed doorway and pinned me against the paneled wood with his hand clenched in the front of my cloak, his hairy forearm pressed against my throat. My hand was on my knife at the small of my back, but the side of the alcove kept my elbow trapped behind me. When I tried to shift in order to pull it out, I felt a sharp prick at my side and froze.

I couldn't see his face in the shadows, even though his breath was hot on my cheek and smelled like rancid fish. He was so close that the edges of his coarse beard brushed my jawline.

My face was flushed in a combination of embarrassment at getting caught off guard, and anger that someone would dare jump me in my own district. I relaxed my arm, leaving it pinned behind me.

"Good man," the figure said. His voice was rough, like there was gravel in his throat. It sounded like the Red Hand from the alley where I'd found Saree. "You know who I am?" he asked.

I sneered at the shadowed face. "An overly dramatic fisherman?"

The man chuckled, pushing his blade forward a fraction of an inch under my ribs so I had to breathe shallow just to keep it from breaking the skin.

"Word is, you've been mouthing off about the Red Hands not doing their job. You've been talking about doing a little *investigating* on your own."

"Maybe if you did your job, I wouldn't have to."

"What a groundbreaking notion. Let the murderer investigate his own crimes. Why didn't we think of that generations ago?"

I growled in his face. "I didn't kill those Blues."

"And yet, all the evidence points to you."

"There is no evidence."

"Of course there is. They both mentioned going to see you. You found the bodies. They were killed with knives just like the ones you're unable to draw right now."

"None of that means I killed them!"

"Did you do it to silence them? Out of jealousy? Or did you just get a taste for it?"

I roared and tried to push him away from me. For an instant the hairy arm wasn't pinning my neck, then I felt a sharp sting across my side before I was slammed back against the door again, the knife at my throat this time.

"Don't meddle in the business of the Red Hands, enforcer. Keep your quick little fingers in purses where they belong, or we'll cut them off and turn your knuckles into dice."

I bit my lip, deciding I'd pushed my luck far enough.

The man lifted his forearm from my chest, although he kept the knife edge tight against my throat. He patted my cheek with a calloused hand and I gritted my teeth, but didn't move.

"Don't worry. We'll find enough *evidence* for the guildmaster eventually."

He stepped out of reach quicker than I could shift my weight away from the doorframe, then disappeared into the rain in seconds. I walked into the street and peered at the shadows, but couldn't see anyone.

"*Fuck!*"

I slipped a hand under my cloak where the knife had cut me. It was shallow, but stung like a bitch. Tucking my knife away, despite not remembering having taken it out after the assassin left, I wadded up the edge of my cloak and pressed it hard against the cut to stop the bleeding.

I needed to bandage this up. If I went on a hit with an open wound like this, I could bleed all over the fucking house, and I'd never hear the end of it. Normally I'd go home and do it myself, but Deidre was there and I still wasn't ready to talk to her. It was a long walk to May's and I didn't relish another confrontation there either.

I headed back toward the Throat, hunched against the pouring rain. There was a back door that led into a store room, and I slipped inside and started looking for some kind of cloth to use as a bandage, careful not to get blood on anything. When the door to the kitchen opened I expected to see Sans glowering at me, but it was Kash. She held a wooden baton with a darkened head, like it'd seen enough use to stain it deep.

I raised the hand not being used to press my cloak against my side. "Easy. It's only me."

She kept glowering. "Is there a reason you're rummaging through our stores?"

I shut the lid on the box I'd been looking in. "Trying to find something to bandage a cut. I'm in a bit of a hurry and I didn't want to bother anyone."

She set the baton down near the door and picked up a lamp instead, bringing it close. "Let me see."

"It's just a scratch really. If you can grab me some linen or something I'll—"

She slapped my hand away and unceremoniously raised the bottom of my shirt over my ribs. It pulled away from the wound where the blood had stuck my flesh to the fabric and I winced. "Hey!"

"Don't be a baby."

She peered at it closely, prodding the edges with her fingers. "You're right. It's shallow."

"Of course I'm right." I pulled away and tried to look at it myself while she went to a nearby shelf.

"How'd you get it?"

"Red Hand jumped me in a fucking alley to have a talk."

"They talk with knives?"

"Usually."

She returned with a cloth and some salve, motioning for me to hold my shirt up as she slathered it over the cut. "Did you find out anything interesting?"

"Just that they really want to pin this on me." I winced as she rubbed the salve in. "Do me a favor, and don't tell Sans I was here?"

She grunted, then motioned for me to hold a wad of cloth over the cut as she wound a strip of linen around my middle to secure it. Then she yanked it tight and knotted the ends.

I hissed and tried not to pull away. "Shit. Can you be a little more gentle?"

"I'm not a nurse, I'm a barkeep."

"Good thing."

I pulled my shirt back down and smoothed out my cloak, grimacing at the stained edge in the light of the lamp. I'd need to wash it again once I got back underground. The shirt could probably be dumped. It was sliced through and bloody, and I'd rather not have to explain it to Deidre.

I grabbed a few extra rags from the stack and got up to leave, but Kash grabbed my arm.

"Watch yourself tonight. Something seems off about the crowd."

"I won't be anywhere near the Throat."

"Doesn't matter. The Throat is the beating heart of Old Town, and when something's happening, you can tell. It's something about who's here, and who isn't. How much the people are drinking. How low the conversation is. How many eyes look to the door."

I pulled out of her grip. "I'll keep that in mind, but I have a job to do."

Before she could say anything else I had slipped out the back door and disappeared into the rain.

Chapter 23

I arrived at my objective an hour after midnight and cut into an alley to be sure I was alone before proceeding to the back door of the building. The rain had slowed to a steady drizzle. The door was locked, which didn't surprise me. Bending over to keep the rain away from my work, I pulled a lockpick from a slit in my belt. I glowered at the lock, cursing the water dripping around me that made it difficult to do the delicate task. In a few moments it clicked and I pushed the door slowly open, staring into the dark room beyond.

I slipped inside and closed the door as quietly as I could. The only person in the building should be the servant asleep in the kitchen. As I made my way to the stairs I used the rags I'd grabbed from the Throat to wipe up any water marks left by my boots. I passed by the kitchen slowly, pausing to listen to the snoring from within. The stairs were my greatest obstacle, but I stepped close to the wall to avoid making any creaking noises.

Based off reports from watchers I'd set on the house over the last weeks, the third room on the left was the one I was aiming for. It was locked as well and I went to work on it. After I entered, I shut the door quietly behind me and listened for a few minutes. The faint sound of the servant snoring in the kitchen reached my ears, but the rest of the house remained quiet. I smiled.

Moving to the dressing table of the lady of the house, I opened drawers until I found a small metal box. I snapped the decorative lock off with the tip of a knife and opened it; the faint light from the only window in the room reflected off faceted gems. Bad, bad merchant. It wasn't nice to cheat your customers.

I dumped the box into my pouch and replaced it empty in the drawer. Rummaging through the rest of the drawers, I found a fortune in jewelry,

180

but what caught my eye was a silver ring engraved with a runic script around its surface. One of the elfish rings that so fascinated the nobility these days.

How did a boot-sucking merchant in Old Town get hold of one? They weren't even being sold in the city. Deidre had asked me to look a few months ago, citing it as an opportunity to loiter around the jewel merchants, but nobody was carrying them. She'd spent a good hour talking about it, and how a lot of the escorts were trying to get one, and how she'd love to have one.

I picked it up, expecting it to give me the shivers, and was pleasantly surprised when it didn't. A fake then. Inside the band, words were scratched into the silver. It said: *lirlion nena.*

Some sort of elfish? I had no idea what it meant, and I highly doubted the merchant or his wife did either. I'd put money down that only a dozen people in Sangarie could have translated it. Since it was a fake, it was probably gibberish.

I tucked the ring into my pouch and grabbed a few more at random as well, adding other pieces of jewelry that caught my eye. I took care not to choose anything that looked too recognizable, since one of a kind pieces were hard to resell in the city. Even though I didn't have to fence them myself, the Green Hands didn't look kindly on thieves who made their job harder than it was. Making sure the pouch was shut securely, I tied it at my waist and turned toward the door.

A noise caught my attention and I froze, listening intently. Footsteps sounded from the ground floor, followed by a muted conversation, a startled cry, and then running steps.

Damn it! I crossed the room to the window, throwing the shutters open and looking out. It was nearly twenty feet to the alley below.

Heavy boots pounded up the stairs and a man yelled for help. Cursing softly, I climbed onto the windowsill and swung myself through, turning so I was able to grab the outer frame above the window. The cut under my ribs pulled tight and I winced, but kept going as the rain needled down on my face. My only options were jump or climb.

I climbed, using the timbers of the building to pull myself up. I was crawling over the edge of the roof when a voice called through the window I had just vacated.

"Stop! Thief!"

I growled and pulled my feet up, scrambling on the slick timber at the edge of the roof. The rain drummed all around me. There would be Copperguard chasing me soon, and I couldn't have that. What the Six had given me away? The servant couldn't have heard me all the way downstairs. Nothing had been out of place below except that the door had been left unlocked. And I was certain the servant had been the only one in the house, so who had he been talking to? There was no way—

"Guards! Call the guards! My master has been robbed!"

I glanced around to get my bearings, picturing the Thieves Way in my mind to fill in the shadowed areas hidden from me by the night and the rain. Taking a few steps to the right, I tested the footing and backed up as I gauged the gap across the alley.

With quick, powerful strides, I closed the distance and leaped across the gap, steadying myself with one hand as I landed, and pressing the cut in my side with the other. I didn't wait to listen to the yelling below me, taking off at a run across the rooftop. Trying to keep to the level roofs, I plotted a roundabout way toward a place where I knew it would be easy to get down and into the underground.

After just a few seconds, I could hear the Coppers running along the streets below me. They had responded much too fast. It was like they'd been waiting for something to happen. Maybe Kash had been right about something being off. I tried to keep as quiet as I could, but occasionally I had to jump over a gap and my landings weren't perfect in the rain. Eventually I was spotted and the chase was on. The Coppers were especially competent tonight of all nights, and there seemed to be a lot of them.

I changed direction, racing across the rooftops at what I knew was a reckless speed. I had to lose them or I wouldn't be able to get underground. Not even Rigel could protect me if I led the Copperguard into the guild itself. I neared the blocky shadow of a chimney and heard a zing. Chips of clay and mortar peppered my face as a crossbow bolt bounced off the bricks right in front of me.

"Fuck!" I crouched and kept going.

I would soon have a decision to make. I could jump to the left and stay with the level roofs, hoping they lost track of me before I wore myself out—or I could turn right and climb over a tiled peak, putting a solid block of buildings between myself and the men chasing me. It really wasn't much of a choice.

I cut right, grinding my teeth as I used both hands to scramble up the slippery tiles. I vaulted over the peak, set my feet, then shuffled down the other side in a barely controlled descent. I did fine until one of the rain-drenched tiles came loose under my foot and sent me sprawling onto my back, my cloak fluttering around me. I hit the roof with a thud and slid the remaining ten feet, the clay tiles cutting through my shirt, then pitched off the edge with a short cry. Tucking my arms in, I managed to twist and tumble when I hit the ground, smacking into the wall on the other side of the alley.

My breath had been knocked away and I lay face down on the ground, gasping for air. The rain pounded down on me, splashing into the puddle I was lying in. My chest heaved, causing pain to lace up my scraped back, and my shoulder was throbbing from rolling across it when I hit the street.

I couldn't stop here. They'd find me. I gritted my teeth as I pushed myself to my knees. Using the wall for support, I dragged myself up—sucking in air—and then staggered forward with one hand clenched over my opposite shoulder. I was close to an entrance to the underground. All I had to do was get there before—

A Copper jogged into the end of the alley in front of me and I threw myself against the nearby wall. I might have gone unseen if I hadn't cursed when my back touched the wall. The Copper caught sight of me, and I took off in the opposite direction with him hard on my heels.

It was much more difficult to stay ahead of them on the ground, and even worse with every step sending fire through my back. I turned onto the street and sprinted full out for a block before sliding around another corner. The next closest entrance was four blocks away, and if I couldn't get there without a guard tailing me, I'd have to find another one. I needed to run smarter, not faster.

I skidded around another corner and saw a guard standing not ten feet away. I braced my feet and slid to a stop on the wet road, catching sight of the silver insignia on his chest.

Silverguard? I scrambled back the way I'd come. My feet slipped once, and I hit my knee on the cobbles with a muffled curse, but then I was running again. A crossbow bolt whizzed past me in the rain, and I resisted the urge to cover my head.

Why in the *fuck* were they shooting at me? Guards didn't shoot thieves. It was a waste of bolts. And why were the Silverguard on the streets tonight? It felt like they were herding me, and I wondered if someone had tipped them off that the merchant was getting hit.

Every gasping breath sent pain racing across my back. I glanced over my shoulder and saw the man gaining. The next alley would be a dead-end, so I ran past it—and saw a pair of Coppers enter the street a block ahead of me. *Shit shit shit.* I careened into another alley and bounced off the wall in the narrow space, gritting my teeth as I stumbled and nearly fell, then shot out the far end.

Lionel's district was across the wide street in front of me. The streets there were more open, but the buildings had a habit of creating their own little courtyards and coves. I wasn't as familiar with it as I was with Old Town, especially not in the dark and the rain. I made for the closest tunnel entrance I could think of, but a Silverguard was standing within sight of it when I got there.

What the fuck?

I veered away and looked for another. Two turns later I stumbled over a loose cobblestone and crashed to the ground, screaming briefly and curling up as the pain seemed to rip through my back. A noise, half pant and half squeak, came out of me as I pushed myself up with shaking arms. If I couldn't get underground, I needed to find someplace to hide until they stopped looking for me.

I raised my gaze and there it was. May's.

I glanced behind me, but there was nobody in sight yet. With a last burst of effort, I sprinted to the brothel door and paused to check for pursuit before shoving it open, slipping inside, and slamming it shut again.

I pressed my hands flat against the door and bowed my head. I couldn't catch my breath. My knees were shaking.

Behind me people were whispering and shifting out of their seats. Someone ran off down a hallway. I wanted to laugh at the sight I must be providing them, but I didn't have the breath for it. My knees buckled and hit the wooden floor with a thud, and I winced as I dropped my hands to the floor as well.

I needed to get away from the door. If they came inside I'd be right here, and I couldn't run anymore.

A hand rested on my shoulder.

"Gray? Is that you?"

Oh May, you sweet, sweet soul. I gestured weakly at the door, trying to slow my breathing enough to speak. "Guards… coming…"

The old woman straightened and waved at the gathered Blue Hands. "Rede, Varin, help him to my room."

Two well-muscled men stepped forward and took my arms, lifting me to my feet. I hissed and clenched my teeth, squeezing my eyes shut over the pain in my back.

"Are you injured?"

I only nodded, doing my best not to stagger into the men. My breath was finally starting to slow, along with my heartrate. I'd be safe with May.

Chapter 24

May waved them deeper into the building and they half guided, half dragged me through the hallway into a cozy bedroom. They stopped at the bed and I leaned my knees against it, putting one hand on the mattress and waving them away. I didn't think it'd be a good idea to lie on my back.

May herself came forward and drew my cloak aside, peering at my soaked clothing and frowning. "How did you manage this?"

I grimaced, glad I was breathing at a normal rate again, even though each breath was excruciating. "I fell off a roof."

She waved someone forward and muttered instructions to them, and thin arms unfastened my cloak and peeled it away. Without the bed I think I would have fallen. I was helped onto my stomach and the madam quietly issued orders to her people. My shirt was cut away, and towels were brought and tucked along my sides. Someone mixed a white powder into a small amount of liquor and I swallowed it in one go.

A thin young woman perched beside me and started using a pair of tweezers on my back, picking out pieces of roofing tile and dropping them into a bowl, squeezing water over my bare skin to wash the rest away. I could barely feel it at this point.

"*Gray!*"

I opened my eyes as Marisso dropped to his knees beside my head. His expression was tragic and pale, and he kept glancing between my back and my face. There wasn't much emotion getting through whatever painkiller they'd used on me, but I was certain I didn't want to see him right now.

His voice wavered. "What happened?"

"I'll be fine," I mumbled. "Don't worry about it." The tweezers dug into my back and I flinched and breathed through it.

186

Marisso took my hand in both of his. I realized I couldn't feel the touch of his hands, and tried not to think about how much it *should* be hurting as the woman continued to pick shards of clay out of my back. I really hoped I'd pass out, but as time went on I doubted I'd be so lucky. At least I'd managed to shake the guards.

By the time the thin woman finished and was smearing ointment to fully numb my back, I was barely conscious. Whatever they'd given me for pain was working to drag me under. Marisso was stroking my hair back. My eyelids were too heavy to bother opening, and May's voice faded in and out. I sighed as I let go.

***

When I woke up, my mouth tasted like cotton and my neck was stiff from sleeping so long on my front. I brought an arm up and shifted onto my side, hissing and breathing through my teeth at the burning sting that stretched all along my bare back. I could feel the pull of the scraped skin, but the ointment had kept it from drying out and ripping open as I moved. It also tingled like magic against my skin, and I wondered exactly what was in it.

"Nice to see you finally coming around."

I glanced at May, who sat on a comfy chair nearby with a ball of yarn in her lap and a glass of wine at her side. She set the knitting needles down and stared at me with a soft smile. "Marisso has been beside himself. I sent him upstairs about an hour ago."

"What time is it?" I groaned as I swung my legs over the edge of the bed and sat up, gripping the mattress and squeezing my eyes shut until the pain subsided.

"We've kept you out for almost two days. It's not long past sunset now."

It didn't surprise me. I remembered them giving me something to knock me out, and when a Blue Hand wanted you to sleep, you slept. The room was dimly lit by a lamp resting near enough to May's chair to give her light to see her knitting. It was a small room, with a large bed. Even over the aftertaste of whatever drugs they'd used on me, I could smell roses.

"I'm sorry I took your bedroom away from you."

May chuckled. "When I said I wished I was young enough to have you in my bed, this isn't what I'd meant."

187

I grinned, but kept myself from laughing, because even breathing hurt right now. I looked down at my bare chest, noting the dried traces of blood they hadn't been able to sponge off me while I was on my stomach. The cut from the Red Hand's knife was starting to heal. "I would have preferred better circumstances as well."

"How are you feeling?"

"Like someone peeled all the skin off my back."

"Well you're only half wrong. That ointment should help. One of my girls gets it shipped in, and it's good for bruises and scrapes."

I imagined so. The tingle of magic wasn't strong, but it was probably enough to make things heal pretty damn fast. It had to be elfish, since even the best human healers had to rely on the natural properties of herbs. Healing magic was something only elves had managed to harness. I'd have complained more, but just thinking about how my back must look made me keep the comments to myself. "Thanks."

May picked up her knitting and started working again, the needles clacking rhythmically. "A young woman named Beth came here this afternoon. When you weren't able to see her, she went upstairs to talk to Marisso. They were up there for quite some time."

"That can't be good."

"She was looking for you—said Deidre is worried."

I sighed and nodded.

"She mentioned Deidre was hurt."

My gut tightened. "One of her clients hurt her. She wouldn't say much about it."

There was a long silence, then May spoke and her voice sounded more tired than I'd ever heard it. "I haven't seen this kind of thing since before Rigel took over as guildmaster. Back then being a prostitute was dangerous. Clients weren't always looking for simple pleasure—and we paid the price." Her needles clacked, creating a soothing noise in the quiet room. "I thought that was all in the past."

"Did you talk to Tanji about Danial?"

She sighed. "Tanji wasn't sure why he was out that night, because he wasn't on the list to work."

"A Red Hand told me Danial had mentioned coming to see me."

"Really? Tanji didn't say anything about that."

I traced a finger over the shallow cut on my side. "He was presenting evidence of my apparent guilt."

"He did that?"

I nodded, listening to the steady clacking of the needles as I stared at the floor. "The Red Hands are acting strange lately."

"Stranger than normal?"

"They're usually dedicated to finding their targets, and I've never known one to refuse to follow a lead. They pride themselves on always tracking down the right people. So why are they so willing to blame me? Plus, I find it oddly convenient that dozens of Copperguard *and* Silverguard were patrolling Old Town that night, just waiting to respond to the cries of a servant who should never have noticed I was there. Hovering near every entrance to the underground."

"You think the Red Hands tipped them off?"

"Maybe. It's not usually the way they do things, though."

She grimaced. "True. They're more likely to knife you in an alley. Maybe you shouldn't push them. Let them handle it."

"They aren't handling it!" I winced at the pull of the wounds on my back and tried to release the tension in my shoulders. "I can't just look the other way when people are dying in my district, even if they weren't blaming me for it."

She didn't answer, but the rhythmic sound of the needles wasn't as steady now. I took a few more calming breaths. It was possible the Red Hands were covering something up. Maybe they knew who the killer was, but weren't going after him? I couldn't imagine Saree or Danial having angered anyone.

May's voice broke into my thoughts. "You think it was the same person that hurt Deidre?"

"I don't know. She won't tell me who it was. She's afraid I'll do something stupid."

"I don't blame her."

I grunted.

"Be careful, Gray. Your passion makes you reckless."

I shifted the muscles in my back, wincing as it pulled tight but glad it didn't hurt as much as it had when I first woke up. "I should get home."

"You could stay here for a few more nights if you like. I'm sure Marisso would take good care of you, and I could send someone to reassure Deidre."

It was tempting, if only because I knew how painful it'd be to walk home, but I didn't feel comfortable being here. I looked around and caught sight of my belt resting on my neatly folded cloak. The bulging canvas pouch was still attached to it with the loot from the merchant's house. "I need to get back."

May folded her knitting and set it on the table beside her. "I'll go and get Marisso to help you, dear."

**

Two hours later I stood at the door of the brothel. Marisso had been subdued as he helped me into one of his own shirts, since mine had been thrown out. Now he fidgeted, twisting his hands together. "If you need anything, I'm here."

I forced a smile, giving off as much nonchalance as I could muster. Now he was here for me? What had happened to ruining his chances at escort? "I'm fine. All in a night's work, right?"

"Won't you stay?"

"I need to get home. I'm sure Deid is pacing the floor thinking of all the things she's planning to scream at me, and she should be resting."

At the mention of Deidre, his expression tightened and his gaze shifted away from mine. I sighed and set a hand on his shoulder. "Thank you. For worrying—and for the shirt. I'll make sure to return it as soon as possible."

He moved into me.

I flinched, but he wrapped his arms around my neck instead of my wounded back, one hand on the back of my head. "I'm sorry. About before." He kissed my cheek and whispered in my ear. "Please, stay... I love you, Gray."

Shit.

I looked over his shoulder and caught May's eye. She looked tired—and sad—and she broke my gaze to shuffle back into the hallway that led to her bedroom.

I lifted Marisso's arms from my neck and took a step back. My face flushed and my gut was knotted up. What could I say? I took another couple steps back, putting some distance between us. I ran my fingers through my hair and exhaled a long, slow breath. I felt like an asshole.

His eyes were wet. He pressed his lips together, his chin trembling.

I shook my head. "I'm sorry." I didn't know what else to say, so I turned and walked away before he could respond. His eyes stayed on me until I rounded the corner. Once I was out of his sight, I could breathe a little easier, but still felt horrible.

I cursed under my breath. That had been handled badly, and I didn't know if I could fix it, or even if I should. Marisso was a good man, and he didn't deserve to be left standing there in the doorway like that. I stopped in the street, going so far as to look back the way I'd come, but I still didn't know what to say to him.

I told you it wasn't serious? I'm not looking for that? It was fun for a while? Nothing I said would make this any easier.

Diedre's face popped into my head, along with a familiar squeezing ache in my chest. I shook my head and kept going.

My cloak was rolled up under my arm, and I felt more than a little self-conscious in the sheer blue fabric of the shirt Marisso had lent me. I walked stiffly, taking my time, and ducked underground as soon as the opportunity allowed. My first stop was the treasury and I emptied my bulging pouch on the table and snatched up the ring wrapped in elfish script. The Green Hand glared at me, but I ignored her as I slipped it into my pocket and went on my way.

When I finally reached my door, I paused just outside to lean on the wall and let the pain recede a little across my back. I could hear voices inside, and recognized both Deidre and Beth, but I couldn't make out what they were saying. Steeling myself for whatever lecture I was about to receive from the two of them, I pushed open the door.

They both looked up from the table at my entrance. Cards were spread between them, and Deidre sat a little more stiffly than usual, but otherwise seemed well.

I closed the door behind me and shook out my cloak, then stared at the hook just above head level, deciding it wasn't worth the pain of reaching up that high. I tossed it to the floor instead. Neither of them said a word as I crossed to the table, but Beth kept looking back and forth between Deidre and I. If I had to guess, I'd say she was actually excited. Probably waiting for the lecture Deidre was itching to give me.

I eased myself into a chair, grimacing and letting my breath even out. I didn't know how to break the silence, so I stated the obvious. "I'm home."

It didn't look like Deidre could decide how to react either. One second I thought she looked mad as hornets, the next I was certain she was going to cry. When she finally responded, her voice only wavered a little. "What happened?"

"Fell off a roof. Couldn't shake the Coppers."

She nodded, not meeting my eyes. She fidgeted with the cards in her hands and carefully plucked one out and laid it in the row in front of her. "How bad?"

I smiled, though I didn't really feel like it. "Nothing a few days won't fix."

"Nice shirt."

I snorted. My hand came to rest on my thigh, feeling the circle of the elfish ring in my pocket. Beth was staring at me with a frustrated light in her eyes—which made me strangely uncomfortable—and Deidre was doing her best not to look at me at all. My fingers clenched over the fabric, squeezing the ring.

If I handed this to her, would I see the same expression on her face that must have been on mine when I rejected Marisso? Was I reading her wrong?

I regretted keeping it. I should have left it with the Green Hand. Once I wasn't hurting so much, I'd go back to the treasury and toss it on the desk and just walk away. I wasn't sure why I'd thought to keep it in the first place. Giving something like this to Deidre would open a massive box of problems I wasn't ready to deal with.

A knock came at the door and we all turned to look, but it was Deidre who called out for the person to enter. Senyr walked inside, his mouth drawn into a grim line and his gaze hard as flint. He glared at Beth first, and she gathered her cloak from the back of her chair without a word before giving the Hand of the Master a wide berth on her way out the door.

He turned his gaze on Deidre next, but she ignored him and deliberately played another card on the table.

He scowled at her. "I need to speak with Gray."

"Then do it. This is my home and you aren't kicking me out, old man."

He growled under his breath, but didn't argue. It would have been better if he had. I would have liked to have had a few more moments while they bickered at each other, before his full irritation was turned on me.

"I thought I told you to keep a low profile." Each of the words had barbs to them. "Is this your idea of a low profile?"

"None of this is my fault."

"Oh, it's not?" He widened his eyes and placed both palms on the table to lean closer to me. "Explain how this isn't your fault. Explain how bantering with a crazy mystic outside the Throat isn't your fault. How smarting off to the Red Hands isn't your fault. How leading an entire district worth of *Coppers* on a merry chase in the rain isn't your *fault.*"

I scowled back at him. "What was I supposed to do? Get caught?"

"You were supposed to stay out of trouble!" He pinched the bridge of his nose and breathed to calm himself. "And now Rigel is making me take you off the street."

Deidre's head came up and she glanced at me.

I forgot whatever argument I was going to make and took a moment to process what my mentor had just said. He was taking me off the street? Did that mean—"Are you casting me out?"

Senyr sat heavily in a chair across the table. "No. Not exactly."

My brow furrowed. "Then what do you mean—exactly."

"No hits. No rounds."

I choked back a laugh. "Demoting me?"

"No. You're still the enforcer for Old Town."

"What am I supposed to do then?"

"You'll sit here for a few days and heal, for starters. Then you'll go sit in the Throat and play cards. You can be out, but don't get involved in anything. Anything that gets brought to you, you pass it along to me and I deal with it."

"You mean do nothing."

"I *mean* be lazy. You strive for it daily anyway. Just let me handle everything for a while, until we can figure this out."

193

I propped my elbows on the table and dropped my head into my hands.

"It's for the best," he said.

"Get out."

He sighed. "Something more than incompetence is going on here. Give us time to fix it."

"Out."

Senyr nodded and stood, hovered over me for a few moments, then strode soundlessly to the door and left without another word.

Chapter 25

I stayed in my room, partly because Deidre was insistent about me recuperating, but mostly because I didn't want to deal with my people. Even if it wasn't official, Senyr had effectively demoted me. I had no rounds to go on. I had no hits to make. I was supposed to let Senyr handle anything that came up. What was I supposed to tell people?

By the end of supper on the third night I was snapping at Deidre, and she told me to leave. My back was mostly healed, thanks to the ointment she had borrowed from May's, so I grumbled my way to the Throat and plopped myself into a chair to play cards. For the most part my sour expression kept the curious away. A couple of the other players at the table were more than happy to catch me up on the new rumors spreading about me.

Apparently a number of people had heard about me walking into the Estates, slick as you please, and showing up at a nobleman's garden party with Deidre in tow. The tales were all exaggerated, and I didn't bother to correct any of it. If they wanted to believe I stole a noblelady's undergarments right out from under her dress, or pissed in the fountain in front of the baroness's son—who was I to disillusion them?

They also talked about my last hit, where I showed up half dead at the brothel after having all the guards in the city on my tail, and hid out under the madam's skirt until they went away.

At least these rumors were better than the ones about me being a murderer.

Other than the stories, it was a quiet night, and when I finally got up from the table I was a few gold richer and a good deal less irritable. I deposited my winnings on the bar and waited for Sans to come over. He was handing off a crate of his good wine to a gangly young man that wrinkled his nose and shot disgusted glances around the bar.

After the man hurried out, Sans joined me. He spread my coins out on the bar to count with a practiced eye, then scooped them into a pocket. "Heading home?"

"Yeah." I glanced at the door. "Who was that?"

"Boy from the Running Hart. Some of their clients have acquired a taste for my wine."

"Do they know where it comes from?"

"I doubt it. Suits me fine. I don't want nobility in here stinking up the place with their perfumes and sensibilities."

I smiled. "Fair."

"That case is for Firmin himself. He's having some kind of gathering for the bootlickers at the Hart. I'd just as soon see it poured into the dirt than into their cups, but I have runt thieves to feed."

I blushed and glanced at Ruena, carrying drinks to a table in the back. "Put the coins toward *her* tab."

Sans chuckled. "I'm just giving you shit, Gray. She's a good kid." He walked away to answer the call of a customer.

I sighed and left the bar, headed home.

I was walking along Market Street when I noticed a man running up the street from the direction of the river. He wasn't running very fast at this point, and looked as if he didn't want to be running at all. To be honest, he looked like he'd rather be laid out in the street panting like a bellows. As I got closer I recognized Marko, one of my older, single bar thieves.

He staggered to a stop and set his hands on his knees to pant. I closed the distance and waited patiently for him to catch his breath. Whatever he had to say, it was going to be something I'd have to turn over to Senyr anyway.

He wheezed a couple of words out between breaths. "It's Lily."

I frowned. Lily was his daughter. She worked at Nolan's brothel, and while I'd avoided her services since becoming her father's enforcer a couple of years ago, we'd remained friends. My stomach knotted up.

The hitch in Marko's voice when he spoke again was unmistakable. "Jacky found her—she's been…" He shuddered and finally looked up at me. Tears had left tracks down his dusty face.

I knew what he was trying to say, and I knew what I was supposed to do in this situation. I took a step back and ran a hand through my hair, looking around the street. "Fuck."

"I've been trying to find you. I thought you'd be on rounds, and I was about to go to the Throat."

I shook my head. "Has someone sent for a Red Hand yet?"

Marko sniffed and dug into his pocket. "No. We thought you should come first."

"I don't think—"

He pulled out a folded and wrinkled piece of parchment with my name written on it.

The hair on the back of my neck stood on end. "What's that?"

"We found it clutched in her hand." He held it out to me.

My hand shook as I reached for it, but I doubt he noticed. He sniffled quietly and stared at the ground as I unfolded the letter. I scanned it quickly, my jaw tightening to almost breaking by the time I reached the end.

Gray, I can't do this anymore. I can't keep your secrets. It's too dangerous and I don't want to see more of my friends die for your pride and jealousy. I'm going to tell Rigel what you've done. I'm sorry. Lily

I didn't trust myself to speak. I crushed the parchment in my fist, breathing through my nose and trying to remain outwardly calm.

Marko shook his head, wiping snot from his nose with a dirty square of cloth. "My Lily didn't write that. I taught her how to write myself, and those aren't her letters."

It was odd to feel the grief and anger over Lily's death mixed with the relief of her father's confidence in me. I wanted to go to her, to see for myself what had happened and whether there was some clue about who had done it… but that was the problem, wasn't it? I was holding the clue. A clue that had been planted for the Red Hands to find.

But my people had found her first. *My* people. And my people deserved better than me walking away from this. If the Red Hands weren't going to find the killer, I'd have to. "Where?"

"Warehouses near Grundle's shipping office. On the Thieves Way."

My brow furrowed. "You found her on the rooftops?"

He nodded.

That was strange. Nobody but Black and Red Hands bothered with the rooftops. Especially in the warehouse block. Those roofs weren't connected well, and were used more for surveillance and private—

Private meetings. Like a meeting with a friend that was tired of keeping a secret. The guild would have no problem believing I'd meet someone on the Thieves Way. I met lots of people on the roofs when I didn't want to be overheard or watched.

I started pacing in the street, a tight loop just to give my feet something to do. I should get Senyr. I should stay as far away from that warehouse as possible. This is exactly what he wanted me to keep away from.

If I passed this off to Senyr, he'd shut me out of it. He and Rigel hadn't been able to do anything so far about the whole mess, and I wasn't about to sit at home and let myself get blamed again.

"Who would kill my Lily, boss?"

"I don't know."

"We need to find the bastard. We need to find him and string him out for the rats to gnaw on."

I took a deep breath, already knowing I wasn't going to Senyr. This note had been left with her body to implicate me, and she'd been left on the roof for the same reason. I needed to see it for myself, and see if any other evidence was there to help me figure this out. "Let's go."

The easiest way to get on top of the warehouses, which were taller than most buildings and relatively flat, was to go to the block you wanted and climb up. It was possible to cross between buildings, but you had to jump a good distance and catch hold of a ladder on the side of the warehouse, and most people couldn't manage the jump. Right now, with my back not quite closed up, I couldn't manage that jump either.

We reached the block that contained Grundle's and I saw a figure wave from the top of the building. I waved back, walking around to the side and starting up the ladder in the middle of the alley. I called down to Marko, "Don't let anyone go for the Reds yet. Got it?"

He nodded and replied, "There's a couple ranked people up there. You won't be out of their sight."

For once, I was glad to be watched. If someone did report me being there, I had witnesses that had brought me and stayed with me. No chance for any funny business. I winced as the climbing movement pulled at the worst of the wounds on my back. I had to stop about two-thirds of the way up and let the pain subside before I could make the rest of the climb.

Jacky met me at the top and led me wordlessly across the roof to where two men stood near the body with a lamp, then she stepped away enough to give me the illusion of privacy.

Lily was sprawled on her back. A plain knife was buried under her ribs. Her face was turned away.

I glanced at one of the men. "Did you look around?"

He nodded, his eyes avoiding the body. "Didn't find anything but that note."

I crouched at her side, reaching for her chin and gently turning it so I could look at her face. I recognized the streaky blond hair and the blue eyes, now staring vacantly up at the stars. She'd been so cheerful, and cursed better than a fisherman's wife. She might have made escort, if she'd been willing to watch her tongue around clients. Nolan's would be darker without her.

I closed her staring eyes and bowed my head, breathing through the rage in my chest. I needed to figure out who was doing this and stop them. Why would someone plant a note like that? It would have been more than enough evidence for the Red Hands to justify taking me down. Would Rigel have believed it?

My back was aching and I set a hand down to brace myself, my fingers brushing the fabric of her dress. A familiar tingle crawled across my skin and I frowned. After a quick glance at the others to make sure they wouldn't see, I reached into a pocket sewn into the folds of her skirt and pulled out a heavy coin. I didn't dare lift it to look closely, but I could feel the symbols on the sides and the taint of magic. It was one of those damn elfish coins.

"Son of a splay-legged goat." I closed my hand over it and spun away from the body, then strode across the rooftop to the ladder peeking up over the side of the building.

One of the men called out behind me. "What should we do?"

"Give me time to leave, then get a fucking Red Hand." I stuffed the coin into the pocket with the parchment and swung onto the ladder, making my way down as quickly as my sore back would allow.

199

Marko was leaning against the side of the building and he stepped out when I reached the bottom. "Boss?"

I gripped his shoulder, meeting his broken gaze. "I'll find them. I promise you."

He let out a heavy breath and nodded, stepping back into the shadows with fresh tears shining in his eyes. I left him there and headed across Old Town.

I had every intention of telling Deidre what had happened. I even practiced it in my head as I walked. I'd tell her about Lily. About how the killer had left her on the rooftops and put a damned note on her with my *fucking* name on it. How I'd found another one of those *fucking* elfish coins in her pocket.

I reached the middle of an alley and kicked at a pile of crates, scattering them across the cobbles. "*Fuck!*" I paced back and forth in the alley, running both hands through my hair and trying to get my brain to slow down and think rationally.

I had taken the note, so unless my people mentioned it the Red Hands wouldn't know about it. I wasn't sure if that was a good thing or not. At this point, the Red Hands didn't seem to be doing anything, and I wasn't sure if that was by intent or incompetence.

I'd found one of these coins near Saree. Danial's body had given no clues that I could see. A note and a coin had been planted on Lily. Three Blue Hands attacked and killed, and—

I stopped pacing.

Four of them attacked.

Had Deidre's attack been part of this? Had Deidre fought her way free of the killer? Why wouldn't she tell me who it had been? It didn't fit. There's no way she would keep silent if she could end all this. She didn't even service the same clients as the brothel workers. The likelihood of it being the same person was—

But I had helped her out before with clients. Nothing more than standing around to ensure things didn't get messy when she refused, or retrieving her when someone got a little too eager to buy more than just a night. She leaned on me as much as I leaned on her. So why wouldn't she let me know what had happened this time? Was it because she knew it was somehow part of things?

I strode through the alley, covering the last few blocks to the underground entrance as quickly as I could without running. I'd just ask again. I'd tell her about Lily, and the note, and ask her to tell me who had hurt her. She had to realize this was out of control. If it was related, I had to know.

I got to our apartment and threw open the door, the words bubbling up, and choked them off as I caught sight of Beth braiding Deidre's hair at the table. They both stared at me in shock, Beth's fingers frozen with strands of black hair held up.

I shut my mouth and took a steadying breath. I wasn't sure I wanted anyone else to know about the note, and I knew that without it I couldn't convince Deidre to talk. I needed a reason to get her away from Beth.

"Gray?" Deidre frowned.

Beth started delicately weaving her hair again, watching me from under her lashes more than she was watching what she was doing. For once she was silent.

I cleared my throat and glanced around the room, my gaze coming to rest on a bottle of wine on the counter. One of the good bottles from the Throat. That was it. Sans had mentioned the Running Hart tavern in Copperton district was hosting the baroness's son and some of his toadies later tonight. I could find out once and for all if those nobles were involved in this.

"I wanted—to tell you I was sorry for how I've been acting." I turned on the smile, quickly closing the door behind me and moving closer to the table. "I realize I've been a pain in the ass the last few days."

Deidre snorted. "The last few days? Try the last few years."

"Do you want an apology or not?"

She sighed and tried to look long-suffering, which didn't work so well while Beth was fixing her hair. "Fine. Go on."

"Anyway, I wanted to make it up to you, so I thought I'd take you out for a fancy supper. My treat."

"You don't want me to sneak you into the Estates again, do you?"

"No." My eyes tightened with the memory. "That was not fun for me."

She narrowed her eyes, probably trying to figure out what my angle was. I kept up the roguish smile and pressed a hand against my pocket where the coin was. I could just barely feel the magic through the fabric.

T. Olsen

The only connection I had to the murders was this note and coin, and the fact that the baroness's son had melted down a bucket of them, and that he was going to be living it up at the Hart tonight with some of his asshole friends.

The coin was already connected to Firmin. It was also elfish, and the only new elf in the city had been at that estate, and my gut told me they were somehow connected. I was *certain* the killer was someone at that party. Which meant they might be at the Hart tonight. And if I could get Deidre talking over a glass of wine, all the better.

Deidre sighed. "Very well. But you're taking me someplace nice, and not the Throat."

I answered out of reflex. "The Throat is nice."

She narrowed her eyes.

"But I'm not taking you there. Tonight I thought I'd take you to the Running Hart."

202

Chapter 26

The way I figured it, walking into the Hart with Deidre on my arm would get the attention of the lordling's entire group. Then all I had to do was watch them and see how they reacted to my presence. Seeing evidence of their failed attempt at killing Deidre—if that is indeed what happened—along with me apparently carefree and enjoying myself, would *have* to spark some kind of reaction. They were noblemen. Reactions were what they did best.

When we neared the Hart, Deidre clenched my arm a little tighter, leaning into me. She was smiling and her eyes were bright.

I grinned in return. "I take it my apology is accepted?"

She laughed. "I'll tell you once I've tasted the venison."

"Venison?" My eyebrow shot up. "This is definitely costing me." I reached for the door and held it for her, following close behind and scanning the room quickly to find Firmin's party and catch their reactions.

It wasn't hard to pick them out. The Hart was dignified, with small tables scattered far enough apart to give the patrons some privacy. Near the hearth, a number of those tables had been pushed together, and easily a score of richly dressed men and women were consuming large amounts of food and wine.

While the noise level was nowhere near that of the Throat—even on a slow day—the gentlepersons of Sangarie were trying. Every other customer looked subdued and vaguely irritated in contrast, and threw glances toward the party whenever laughter erupted. The chronically rich didn't seem to notice, just like they hadn't noticed our entrance.

Deidre drew in a sharp breath and stopped suddenly, so that I walked into her from behind. I steadied us both. Her face had gone pale and she was staring at the floor like it had disappeared in front of her.

I set a hand on her back. "You don't look so good."

I watched her pull the smile back on, though it trembled a little. When she met my gaze, her eyes were bright and shining again. Fake happy. "That's a terrible thing to say to a girl when you take her out for supper."

My brow creased and I was about to question her further when a waitress came to meet us. She eyed me with her lips drawn into a firm line. To be fair, while Deidre looked as stunning as always, I hadn't bothered to change out of my usual bland commoner clothes. This had been intentional on my part, because I wanted the killer to recognize me immediately. You tended to remember a scruffy nobody showing up at your garden party.

The waitress led us to a table as far away from the nobility as she could, probably more for their sake than ours. When she asked what we wanted, I told her the lady would be ordering for us both. I tried to keep my eyes on the nobles and pay attention to Deidre as she talked with the woman about what was available from the kitchen. She ended up ordering two plates of the venison, a glass of wine for herself, and ale for me. As she was finishing up the order, I saw Firmin notice us.

His first reaction was surprise, then his face flushed red. He leaned into the man next to him and spoke, and that noble looked at us as well. The stranger's expression was contemplative, and he held my gaze as he sipped his wine.

"This is nice."

I tore my gaze away and smiled at Deidre. "Yes. It is."

"Maybe we should do this more often. Go out and eat together, I mean. Not yell at each other."

"Maybe not for venison too often. I might be an amazing thief, but I'm still just an enforcer. And a neutered one at that." I took the mug of ale the waitress set beside me and drank deeply. If I was paying this much for it, I'd at least enjoy it. I looked at Firmin. He was talking to someone else, laughing awkwardly and shooting glances at our table.

After a few minutes Deidre spoke up again. "So…" She leaned an elbow on the table and set her chin on the back of her hand. "Maybe we can bring a bottle of wine home with us. Relax from everything that's been going on."

I chuckled and scanned the noble party again, making sure nobody else was showing any interest. I'd be shocked if Firmin was the killer. He was an incompetent boob. "You do realize this is the same wine I get at the Throat. We have two or three bottles at the apartment already."

She didn't answer and I shifted my gaze to her. She was staring at the table, delicate creases lining her forehead and her mouth shut tight. Her gaze flicked toward the nobles, and her cheeks reddened just enough for me to notice, then she bit her lip.

Shit. Had I said something wrong? I ran the conversation back in my head. Before I could try to salvage anything, the waitress came out with our food. The plates were heaped with roast venison, potatoes, greens, and fruit. As Deidre exclaimed over the feast I ordered another drink for each of us.

We ate with increasingly uncomfortable silence. I continued to sneak glances at the noble shitshow just like every other patron in the tavern was doing, but even Firmin had stopped paying attention to us. Maybe I'd been wrong. Maybe the nobles were just regular assholes and not killing people in Old Town.

When I thought about it that way, it sounded ridiculous. Maybe I was trusting my gut too much, stringing too many coincidences together. My intuition was good, but the more I thought about things, the more muddled they got.

And now that I *was* thinking about it, Deidre might be uncomfortable at the thought of what I would do in here with them watching. I hadn't exactly puckered my boot-sucking lips at that garden party, and I would normally have jumped at a chance to embarrass the lordling if I thought I could get away with it without being hanged. Most likely, she was either upset I was paying too much attention to them, or worried I might embarrass her and get into trouble.

I reached for another fist-sized bread roll and the bottom corner of my vest swung into the edge of the table with a muffled clink. The elfish ring was still in there. I had taken it with me so Deidre wouldn't find it, and completely forgotten about it.

She'd be so happy if I presented it to her in a place like this, over a nice dinner, drinking good wine. I was upsetting her right now, and I wanted to fix that. I wanted to see her smile—a real smile—instead of frowning at the table.

As I started to reach for the ring, I realized what I was thinking and my face flushed. Instead of going for my vest pocket, I picked up my ale and took a long drink. The image of Marisso standing in the doorway at May's crossed my mind again. I had a good thing with Deidre. I wasn't going to ruin it by trying to make it something more. We were friends.

I put it out of my mind and split my attention between the venison on my plate and the irritating laughter of the nobility. It didn't taste all that good anymore. The longer I sat there, the more sure I was that those assholes had nothing to do with the attacks. Why would the nobility care about a few Blue Hands in Old Town? And why would they bother to frame me for it?

The more I thought about it, the more certain I was that Deidre's attack wasn't related either. It didn't match up. They didn't have the same clients. Saree and Lily had both been better in a scuffle than Deidre was, so it wasn't likely she'd have fought free when they hadn't. Plus, Deidre hadn't been attacked in Old Town.

I'd still love to know who'd done it, and bash his fucking face in, but I doubted it would lead me to this killer. Showing Deid the note and the coin—telling her the killer had left it for me specifically—would only make her worry. She might go to Rigel. If a Red Hand thought it was a good idea to stick a knife against my ribs just for snooping around, what would he do to Deidre for going to the guildmaster?

No. It was better to keep this to myself for now. I needed to find out more, get a solid lead. I needed to figure out what was going on with the Red Hands and why they seemed to be involved. And why Rigel wasn't able to do anything about it.

I did my best after that to ignore the nobility and focus on Deidre. By the time we'd finished eating and drained another glass each, she was laughing again and her cheeks were rosy from the wine. I paid the serving woman and helped Deidre to her feet, bracing her with a hand under her elbow when she swayed.

"I should have stopped at two," she said.

I chuckled and let her link her arm in mine, leading her to the door. I noticed Firmin watching us, but chalked it up to him being a creepy asshole. The night air was chilly, so I put an arm around her shoulder and she leaned into me.

When we reached an entrance to the underground I stepped away, holding the door for her.

She frowned. "Aren't you coming?"

What I needed was to let the events of the evening settle themselves in my head. If I went underground with her now, she'd want to finish out the night properly, and I was in no state to do that. She'd ask questions, and I wasn't sure how I wanted to answer them yet. "It's still early. I'll be down later."

"Oh." She gazed at me for a few moments with a crease in her brow, then smiled with all the charm and beauty of an escort. "I suppose I'll see you when you get back then."

"I look forward to it."

I watched her turn and disappear into the tunnel, quickly swallowed by the darkness.

Chapter 27

The Throat seemed like a hovel after the Running Hart, but I was happy to be back in the hovel. Flirting and casual insults would go a long way to improving my mood. If I just let myself relax and stopped trying so hard, maybe I'd come up with something. Ruena wasn't there, and neither was Sans, so the place was in the capable hands of Kash. She had a mug of ale waiting for me before I even reached the bar.

Less than an hour had passed, and I was comfortably slouched in a chair playing cards with Detano and a few others, when a woman burst through the door. She paused to look around before stomping across the room toward our table.

I gazed at her from the corner of my eye as I placed my bet. I was sure I'd seen her before, but I couldn't place where. She came to a stop beside my chair, crossing her arms over her chest.

I looked up and smiled brightly. "Good evening, beautiful. Can I help you with something?"

She glared down at me and started tapping her foot. "Yes, you can. You're Culley's boss, aren't you?"

I nodded, calling the bet and tossing my hand down. The two players who had been betting against me cursed and leaned back in their chairs as I pulled the pot out of the middle of the table. I was still a little irritated with Culley. I was sure he'd mixed something into my drink at the Under Ball, and he'd been avoiding me since then. "Is there some problem?"

"Yes, there is." She flung a hand in the general direction of the door. "He's always got some barmaid's hands all over him lately. Even came home the other night with love bites. Thinks he's become this big shit criminal. He's over at the Black Bottle right now with some dirty wench in his lap, talking about what a wonderful thief he is!"

I stopped arranging the coins in my hands and stared up at the woman. My expression hardened and she took a step back, suddenly nervous.

"Is that so?" That son of a bitch. I'd warned him about keeping his damn mouth shut. "Tell me, who is he talking to about his escapades?"

She seemed a little relieved when she realized the expression wasn't directed at her, and happily answered me. "There's just a bunch of drunks around, and the leeches that hover in those types of places."

I smiled coldly, scooping coins from the table. "I'll have to step out, boys." I stood up, nodding my head at the woman. "Thank you for the information, missus."

I headed for the door.

The woman stood for a few moments, then cursed and hurried after me, grabbing my arm. "Wait! What are you going to do?"

I looked down at where she held me. "Well, Lionel says I'm not hard enough on my people. Maybe he's right." I pulled away and walked out into the night.

The woman rushed after me. "Please don't hurt him! He's just drunk and stupid."

I stopped to look back at her. As irritated as I was with Culley, I wasn't a Red Hand, and all he was doing was running his mouth after all. "He'll be fine." I turned then and took off at a brisk walk for the Black Bottle.

I hadn't made it very far before I remembered I was supposed to be leaving these things to Senyr. But then again, it wasn't like this had anything to do with the murders. It wasn't even thief work. I just needed to tell Culley to keep his mouth shut… and not to drug his boss at parties. I was still the Old Town enforcer, and if I couldn't keep my people in line, they wouldn't follow me. Besides, it was just Culley.

Old Town had its share of dives, and the Black Bottle was one of them. It certainly delivered on the promise of cheap booze, questionable clientele, and unsanitary conditions. I tried to avoid it when I could, but growing up on the streets meant I knew more about such places than anyone should. Desperation and hunger made almost anything palatable as a kid.

When I walked in, I could see the woman had been right. Of the half dozen people in the room, only the barkeep was sober enough to notice my entrance. Culley was in a chair at one of the tables with a scantily clad woman sitting in his lap, and she was kissing him while he groped her backside.

I raised an eyebrow and walked toward them, nodding at the barkeep as I passed him. The two other men at Culley's table finally noticed me and stumbled to their feet, one of them falling over a chair as he hurried away. I pulled out a chair and spun it around to sit on, propping my arms on the backrest with only a small wince as the mostly-healed scrapes on my back stretched tight.

Culley opened his eyes and looked at me for a moment before recognition dawned, then he paled and shoved the woman away.

She landed on her backside on the dirty floor, staring up at us with an indignant expression. I smiled tightly and waved my hand in a dismissing gesture. She glared at me, but got up and sauntered away, a scent of ale and food grease reaching me as she blew past. It made my stomach turn.

Culley looked across the room nervously before resting his unsteady gaze on me. "Uhm... hey, boss. I was... there was nothing... you want an ale?" He flung an arm in the general direction of the bar.

I shook my head. "I hear you've been talking about your work. Again."

He let out a shaky breath and actually looked relieved. "Oh, yeah. I'm sorry." Then he giggled under his breath.

That wasn't the reaction I'd expected. He didn't seem concerned about my accusation at all. I leaned forward, the chair back creaking under my weight. "Sorry, are you? Do you know how many people would be arrested or put out of work if the Copperguard overheard your stories?"

"Naw." He chuckled and shook his head vacantly, then noticed I was glaring at him. "I mean, yes! But there aren't any Coppers around, I swear."

"I see. Do you think it's funny to ignore me? Do you think there aren't consequences for the dumbass choices you make?"

His expression—exaggerated due to his drunken state—had gone from relieved, to confused, to terrified. His voice dropped into a stage whisper as he leaned toward me. "It's not my fault."

I pulled back from the stench of his breath. "I have no need for people who can't follow directions. If you can't even follow simple orders, how can I trust you?"

He frowned. "Are we still talking about telling stories?"

"What else would we be talking about?"

His mouth gaped like a fish for a few moments, then he nodded repeatedly. "I'm sorry. I won't do it again." He shot a glance across the room, quickly dropping his eyes to the table in front of him.

I followed his gaze but only saw a man passed out with his head on his arms at a corner table. I frowned and narrowed my eyes. The hairs on the back of my neck were up, like I was missing something. I suddenly wanted away from this place.

I stood abruptly and pushed my chair up to the table. "Come with me, Culley."

The man stood, swaying so badly he could barely remain upright. He followed me out the door and into the deserted street. I pulled a knife from the sheath at my back and held it between my hands, looking down at it contemplatively as I turned to face him.

"There are many reasons for the things I do, Culley."

The man gaped at me and dropped to his knees, clenching his hands repeatedly. "Please! Give me another chance!"

He was *really* jumpy. Maybe it was guilt for the stunt at the ball. Maybe it was the rumors that I killed people. I probably shouldn't take advantage of those rumors… but… I rotated the knife so it glinted in the moonlight. "I already gave you another chance, after the last time you acted like an idiot."

Culley sobbed on his hands and knees, his eyes bloodshot and unfocused from the alcohol.

Squatting down in front of the blubbering man, wincing as the movement pulled at my back, I tapped the tip of the knife against my chest. "I have a job to do here, Culley. My job is to make sure you do your job—" I laid the point of the knife on Culley's chest "—and that you don't fuck up."

He shuddered, and I could suddenly smell urine in the night air. I wasn't *that* frightening. At least not to my own people. He had to know I wouldn't stab him for bragging too much, or for fucking around with my drink… so what did he think I was going to stab him over? Maybe if I pressed him hard enough, he'd blurt something out and clue me in.

I moved the tip of the blade under the man's chin, forcing his head up. A drop of blood trickled down his neck. "I can eliminate all these problems tonight. I can take care of it without involving the Red Hands, or the guildmaster, or the Copperguard. It'll be one less headache for me, and the Six know I've had a lot of headaches these days."

Culley's eyes drifted from my face to something behind me, then snapped back even wider. "I'm sorry, boss. I won't fuck up again."

I shot a look over my shoulder, but there was nothing other than the dark empty street.

I reached forward, grabbing the back of Culley's head with my free hand and pressing the knife harder against his neck. I leaned close and put all the venom I had into my lowered voice. "What's going on here, Culley?"

He stuttered for a few moments, his whole body shaking. "I—uh, you're upset."

"Go on."

"Because—I—" He closed his eyes and took a shaky breath. "I powdered your drink at the ball."

I clenched my fist in his hair. "Fuck that. That's a bullshit answer. You wouldn't be pissing yourself in the street over a prank."

His fingers groped at my fist and I could hear him cursing and whining under his breath. I slid my gaze to the shadows, but there was still nothing.

"Let go. Fuck! *Let go!*"

"What's out there, Culley?"

He squirmed a little more, then bit his lip over a drunk giggle. "You'd know better than me, boss. You were there too."

My brow creased. "I was where?"

He attempted to lower his voice, but it just turned into a loud, raspy whisper. "In the labyrinth." He giggled. "I saw you."

I lifted the knife and shoved the man away. My throat tightened and my gut turned at the mention of the labyrinth. My knife was shaking in the faint light of the streetlamps and I sheathed it so Culley wouldn't notice. "You mean the ball?"

"Not the ball." He twisted so he was sitting in the street, ignoring the filth on the cobbles around him. A thin line of red was drying on the side of his throat, but he ignored that too. "You remember, don't you? You were there."

I scanned the street with my eyes lowered, half expecting to see the shadows start creeping toward me. How could he know anything about that? He was drunk. He had to be talking about the Under Ball. I wiped my sweating hands on my pants. That had to be it.

Culley put a grubby finger to his lips and made a loud shushing noise. "Don't tell em I told you. It's a—*hic*—It's a secret."

I backed away from him, putting a good amount of distance between us before I dared turn my back. Then I slipped into the shadows and left him sitting in the street.

He was drunk. And I was paranoid. Culley couldn't know anything about my trip into the labyrinth as a kid. He had only arrived in Sangarie about six years ago. He was talking nonsense. Drunk nonsense.

I hurried through the streets, darting between shadows and stopping occasionally to hide and check if I was being followed. When I found a place to climb to the Thieves Way without being seen, I did so. Up on the rooftops I felt safer... less vulnerable at least. I moved through the district like a ghost and wound up on the roof of the Throat, settling down against the warmth of the brick chimney.

I could hear the patrons within. Occasionally a raised voice could be heard, and then laugher. At one point someone started a bawdy song and was quickly jeered into silence. It was a familiar kind of noise and it quieted the thoughts splashing around in my head. I studied the shadows on the rooftop, and they were all familiar.

I stayed there, tucked next to a chimney like a scared kid, until those shadows started to fade with the false light of dawn, then picked my way down to the street and slipped underground.

Chapter 28

The next afternoon I woke from a restless sleep to the sound of Deidre rummaging through the dresser. I wiped my hand over my face and sat up in bed, frowning at her as she dug in the drawer where she kept her savings.

"What are you doing?"

She looked back at me in surprise and smiled. "I'm going shopping."

I scowled at her and eyed a heavy leather pouch she pulled out. "For what?"

She slammed the drawer shut, stood, and straightened her dress. "I ran into Marisso this morning in the market."

I raised my eyebrow, remembering the hurt on Marisso's face when I left May's. "Oh? How did that go?"

"It was nice. We talked about how you're healing up, and how I'm doing, and what his plans are once he ranks up. We had some lunch together and just—talked. He said that whenever he's feeling out of sorts, he buys himself something nice and it makes him feel a little better. He *also* said the silk merchant is trying to move old inventory, and might be willing to drop his prices."

"So you're taking a few months' worth of coin to buy… silk?"

She picked up a couple of empty canvas bags from the table. "There are a few other things I've been wanting as well." She shrugged and clutched the straps of the bags resting on her shoulder. "It sounded like a good idea, and he made a lot of sense."

"How helpful of him."

She rolled her eyes at me. "Despite what you might think, not everyone is fighting over you."

I scowled back. "I don't think that."

"Then why does it bother you if I spend time with him?"

214

"It doesn't. It just makes me suspicious that he's suddenly so helpful."

She snorted and walked toward the door.

Marisso wouldn't hurt anyone, but he wasn't above doing something petty or spiteful if he felt slighted. I had a feeling my refusal at May's had something to do with this. If I let Deidre go out there and something happened to embarrass her, or upset her, it'd be my fault.

I flung the blankets off. "Hold on."

"I'm going shopping, Gray."

"I'll come with you."

She stopped at the door and looked back at me with a shocked expression. "Seriously? You?"

I padded to the dresser and pulled out fresh clothes. She came up behind me, and I turned to face her. "What?"

"Are you sure you want to march up and down the market with me today?"

"Sure." I pulled a shirt over my head and combed my fingers through my hair. "I'm not allowed to do anything interesting, so I'll be your baggage boy."

She laughed and waited for me to finish dressing. I grabbed my vest, noting the slight dimple of the ring still in the pocket, and put the thought out of my mind. Right now I was more concerned with why Marisso would so kindly offer Deidre advice. He usually couldn't say her name without rolling his eyes.

When I finished, she handed me the heavy leather pouch and the empty canvas bags. "Take these, baggage boy."

"That was a joke you know."

I followed behind Deidre and we went topside. It didn't take more than a couple of minutes of being on the streets of Old Town before Ruena found us and planted herself in front of me with a determined expression on her grubby face and her goggles hanging around her neck.

"You're supposed to be training me."

I sighed and glanced at Deidre, cringing inwardly at the amused expression on her face. "I'm not working right now, kid."

"Well I'm still going with you."

Deidre laughed. "Oh let her. She looks like she could use a shopping trip as well."

"Fine, but no hanging on me."

Ruena's smile stretched into an excited grin.

I scowled and reached out to snap her goggles up over her eyes.

Deidre held out her hand and Ruena took it and skipped along beside her, leaving me to follow in their wake. At least Deidre looked happy. If I had to put up with the kid tagging along, something good would come of it.

We strode through the city to the New Market in Binara's district, and I kept my hand over the heavy pouch Deidre had entrusted to me. My eyes scanned the crowd as I began to second-guess my decision to go along. It was more my reputation I was worried about protecting than the gold at my side. Walking around the marketplace like this made me look horribly domesticated. I was probably over-reacting anyway. Marisso could be petty, but he wouldn't hurt anyone. Maybe he just wanted to have an ally for when he made escort. He was focusing on his career.

Deidre started at the general store, buying things like soap, thread, and salt. She bought a new lamp, a hand broom, a couple of wooden plates, and a few other things that I looked at with patiently raised eyebrows. She even used her own money to buy a few things for the kid. The merchants kindly packed everything into the bags I carried, and they got heavier and heavier.

A few hours later, as the sun was nearing the horizon, she stopped at the eighth fabric stand of the day and started rummaging, discussing her needs with the vendor and holding fabric up to Ruena's small frame.

Nothing had happened. I was entirely convinced I had followed her around like a servant for no reason, and Marisso had just been trying to be nice.

I let the bags rest on the ground, carefully rolling my shoulders to ease the ache in my back. I leaned against the post at the corner of the stand, my gaze drifting across the crowd. Several minutes passed and a glint of orange sunlight off metal caught my eye. I looked again and saw a bearded man with a crossbow leveled at the fabric stand.

Deidre! I leaped forward, slamming into her as the bolt whizzed past and sliced open my sleeve. We landed hard on the packed dirt of the square and she grunted as my weight came down on her. She stared up at me in confusion and I made certain she was alright, then looked back at the attacker. The man had turned and was pushing in the opposite direction through the crowd.

I swore as I climbed to my feet and shouted down at Deidre. "Go home!"

Ruena was already at my side, looking ready to follow me into whatever trouble I chose. I grabbed her arm and pushed her toward Deidre. "You go with her."

I took off after the man without waiting for an argument, dodging past the people in the square. He slipped into an alley and I followed, settling into an all-out run in an effort to close the distance between us. We sprinted through the streets and alleys, me slowly catching up, until the man made a wrong turn into a dead end.

I didn't slow down as we neared the end of the alley, and rammed into him, tackling him to the ground. I pinned him, sitting on his lower back and wrenching his arm around for leverage as I panted to catch my breath. "Who the fuck are you?"

He cried out as I put pressure on his arm, but didn't say anything. I caught a whiff of fish and my brow wrinkled. Why was that poking a memory?

I pulled a knife from my belt and pressed it below his ear. "Why were you trying to kill her?"

The man laughed, his voice like gravel. "Because it's my job."

My skin prickled as I recognized the voice of the Red Hand that had ambushed me in the rain and had taken care of the bodies of those Blues. It was like this bastard had nothing else to do but fuck with me. "Who ordered it?"

"Someone who didn't want to involve the guild, you moron."

My intuition screamed at me. I used the knife to slit open the back of his shirt, exposing the tattoo of a Red Hand between his shoulders with a scar in the shape of an X branded over it. An *old* scar. I stared for a second, grinding my teeth. "You were cast out."

"Now he gets it."

I growled and slammed my fist over his kidney, making him gasp and squirm beneath me. "Tell me who fucking hired you!"

The man chuckled again. "There's nothing *you* can do to him. He's untouchable."

I grabbed him by the hair and pulled his head back, leaning forward to hiss into his ear. "*Who?*"

"Firmin," the assassin spat, "Lady Karyn's son."

I froze, still holding his head back. I was breathing hard from the run and my mind was trying to grasp the fact that the son of the baroness of Sangarie could actually be behind all this. I had assumed it couldn't be him. He was too blunt and incompetent for something like this.

The man chuckled awkwardly, his breath limited by the way I held him. "Our sadistic young lordling made a mistake when she got away from him the first time."

The blood rushed to my head. Deidre's words came back to me: *You know you'll only get into trouble...* I closed my eyes, feeling helpless and hating it. What could I do against the heir of Sangarie?

"Ha!" the man spat. "It was his own fault for playing with an escort. He should have stuck to the common whores, they aren't missed as quickly!"

I hissed and punched the man in the back again, driving the breath from him. Firmin was untouchable. The politics of it were enough to make my head spin. The guild ran the criminal activity in Sangarie, but it was still Lady Karyn's city. If anyone so much as accused her precious fucking son of a crime, there'd be war in the streets.

What could I do? I needed to think. I needed to talk to Rigel... or to Senyr. They'd know what to do. They'd be able to handle the politics.

Wouldn't they? This guy was an outcast, and he'd been in the city for weeks. How could the Blades of the Master miss this? Had they already figured it out, and decided not to act? Had they been covering it up? Was that the political solution to all this? Blaming me? Was I being set up to hang for Firmin's crimes?

The man squirmed between my thighs and I tightened my grip in his hair. He was chuckling. His voice grated out, still a little breathless.

"You just keep losing friends, don't you, thief? It's dangerous for the people closest to you these days."

"Fucking bastard."

"He's got one in his bed right now. I wonder where I should put this one when he's finished with her."

My gut clenched.

"Should I have you guess who it is?"

I pulled his head back and slammed it onto the cobbles. He went limp beneath me and I staggered to my feet, looking around to get my bearings before heading in the direction of the Estates.

If I did nothing, another person close to me was going to die. If I went to Rigel or Senyr, they'd tell me to go home, and by then maybe it'd be too late. I had to do something. If I was being blamed for all this anyway, at least I could try to save whoever was about to die because they were friends with me.

I would make sure Firmin didn't hire anyone else to kill Deidre. I'd get justice for Lily and Danial and Saree. I repeated these thoughts over and over in my mind, keeping my rage burning so I wouldn't change my mind.

I kept my head down and blended into the crowds. When there were no crowds, I blended into the shadows. The sun was disappearing as I neared the inner wall separating the Estates from the rest of Sangarie. I walked toward the gate, trying to think of what to say when I attempted to go through. What excuse could I give for walking into the Estates looking like a commoner? Could I pass myself off as a messenger or a servant? Did I look as crazy as I felt?

I watched the Silverguard as I passed the last street where I could have turned aside, but he was just leaning against the inside of the gate, picking his nails with a file. His spear was propped against the gate, and his ankles were crossed. Another spear lay on its side just inside the wall, as if it had been dropped and forgotten. He glanced up at me as I came close... and dismissed my presence without so much as a grunt to acknowledge I was there.

I held my breath as I walked past him, but he made no move to stop me. Either I was convincingly invisible, or he was the laziest Silverguard I'd ever seen. Thank the gods for people who didn't give a shit about their job.

I slipped through the quickly darkening Estates, doing my best to keep to the shadows. I knew I wouldn't be so lucky with the Ironguard if I tried to use the gates of the baroness's manorhouse. But I'd been planning and replanning this break-in my entire life. It was my favorite line of thought on boring rounds.

Slipping along the stone wall that surrounded the manorhouse, I found a place where I could climb over unseen and wasted no time in doing so. I darted through the garden on the other side, making my way to the walls of the building itself.

I knew which room the lordling slept in from records back at the guild. I'd been an ambitious teen, and I had those plans memorized. When I reached the wall and stared up at the second story window where his rooms were, there was light in one of them.

Adrenaline gave me strength for the climb. The building was made of rough stone and there was plenty of purchase for an experienced thief. I made for the dark window to the right of the occupied room, and reached the window casement in what seemed to me like an instant.

I prayed to the Six I wasn't too late.

Chapter 29

Peering inside the window, I could make out a lavish sitting room in the dim light filtering in from the doorway on the far side. Deep couches and ornately carved tables were in the center, and paintings adorned the walls. It was empty. Through the open door was a lit bedchamber. Muffled voices came from within.

Silently, I slipped over the sill and to the floor, creeping across thick rugs to the open doorway, where I pressed myself against the wall and chanced a quick peek.

A naked young woman huddled on the bed, clutching a sheet to her chest. Her hair was wildly messed, and what I could see of her skin was marked with red welts and fresh bruises. I couldn't see her face.

I fought to control the rage that was bubbling to the surface.

Near a table to one side stood the young lordling of Sangarie. He was naked as well, standing with his dick flapping above his thighs as casually as if he were at a garden party. He had the beginnings of a paunch, and no musculature to speak of. He was drinking from a crystal glass as he stared at the woman.

With a toothy grin, he set the glass down with a sharp clink and turned back to the bed. I ducked behind the doorway so he wouldn't see me, unable to think of anything other than stopping what was going on in that room. Making sure this fucking asshole didn't kill again.

I heard the bed creak, then his voice rose in a slithery tone that set my teeth on edge.

"I'm not done yet. There's another handful of gold in it if you climb back over here."

The woman's voice was wavering and raspy. "Please, my lord—I'm tired."

My whole body shook with fury. Blood rushed to my head and I growled low in my throat and darted into the room, leaping for the sadistic man. I slammed into him and pushed him off the bed, rolling with him across the expensive rugs. When we stopped in a heap, the confused lordling glared at me and pushed himself to his feet.

"What the hell are *you* doing here!" he screamed.

I gathered myself and drew a knife. My voice was low and broken, and I had to force the words from between teeth clenched with rage. "You fucking *bastard*." I rushed him, slashing low with the knife and missing when he dodged back, following it with a swift uppercut punch that sent the man sprawling and nearly broke his jaw, and my hand.

I could hear the woman crying from the bed, but the only thing I could see was Firmin, and the faces of the Blues—of my friends—dead and cold. And Deidre's face as she stared up at me in pain with blood matting her hair. I rushed in again, slashing him across his bare chest and opening a shallow cut that bled down over his belly. The lordling staggered back, his hand raised to the wound. He fell against the wall beside a small table, which rattled with the impact. A glass of liquor fell and shattered on the floor.

I had to stop this now. I had to keep him from killing Deidre… from killing anyone else I cared about. I rushed in, and the lordling fumbled against the table as he tried to dodge so that I only cut open his arm, revealing bone and sinew.

He screamed as I moved forward again. With a furious growl, he grabbed the little table and swung it like a club. I raised an arm to protect my head and the table broke as it slammed into my shoulder, staggering me.

Firmin swung a follow-up punch that connected with the side of my face and sent me sprawling to the floor. The ring that had been in my vest pocket tumbled out, bouncing in front of me on the expensive rug and coming to a stop a foot from my face. My chest tightened as I thought of Deidre, injured and frightened. The rage and frustration from the past few weeks flared even brighter. I grabbed the ring with my free hand and scrambled to my feet to face the nobleman.

Firmin advanced on me with a small weapon in his hand. I let out a short, barking laugh at what looked more like a decorative letter-opener than a dagger, and darted forward. The lordling swung at me, and I blocked it by stabbing my knife into his arm. He screamed as I levered my blade up and his little dagger fell from nerveless fingers, dropping to the rug. My eyes blazing, I pushed the lordling up against the wall.

The man stared at me in terror. "Wait! I'll give you gold! There's gold over there. The purse is on the dresser. How much do you want?"

I sneered back. "I don't want your gold." I shifted my balance and drove my knife up into the man's gut.

Firmin jerked, eyes widening.

I leaned forward and whispered, "You won't kill anyone ever again."

His face screwed up in pain and confusion. "What are you—talking about?"

I yanked my knife out of his gut and he squealed. He started to fall and I braced my fist—knife clutched tightly in it—against his shoulder to hold him up. The ring bit into my other palm where I held his opposite shoulder. "You have the balls to ask that, with your next victim sobbing in your bed?"

He tried to slow the blood trickling from his abdomen with his hands. "I wasn't going to kill her. I just like to see them cry." He gasped and leaned his head against the wall. "I paid her well for it."

The rage in me sputtered, and I glanced across the room at the woman. I didn't recognize her. She was pressed against the headboard, staring at me in horror.

Staring at *me* in horror.

I pushed harder against his shoulders as my arms started to shake. "But the other Blue Hands are dead. You killed them and had their bodies dumped in Old Town."

"What?" He coughed and blood splattered my shirt. "I didn't kill anyone!"

I shook my head, all my assumptions falling apart, a growing fear in my chest. "No." That outcast—he said he had dumped the bodies. "You hired a man to kill Deidre, because she got away."

The lordling's breathing was rattling now, and he would have fallen without my fists pressing him against the wall. He looked shocked at my words. "I would never... I didn't know she would get hurt." He drew in a wet breath. "Loring... I didn't realize what he would do. I wouldn't have sent her to him." He coughed up more blood and his chin sank to his chest, his voice breathy. "I never offered her this deal."

I shook him. "What deal?"

"I paid them… so I could hit them. They wanted the money."

I looked back at the woman. She had stopped crying now and was staring at me with wide eyes.

Firmin went limp and I let him slide to the floor. He looked up at me, his voice sputtering. "I'd never hurt Deidre." His gaze wandered. "She is so beautiful… Too beautiful for the slums."

There was blood all over the floor between us. All over my hands. All over me.

Tears flowed down Firmin's face, streaking the faint rouge he'd been wearing. "I didn't… kill—"

I stepped back as the lordling's breath faltered and his eyes grew distant. He took a couple shuddering breaths—nothing more than reflexive gasps—then was still. His empty eyes stared at the ceiling, and his jaw slackened.

The full realization of what I'd done hit me, and my legs shook. I'd taken the word of an outcast Red Hand, and killed the baroness's son. Firmin was a sick and worthless bastard, but he really hadn't done it. The outcast had lied to me, and I'd swallowed it without question.

I staggered back. The blood squished in the rug under my boots, and I dropped heavily to sit on the bed. My entire body was shaking as the last of the rage failed me and fear set in. I stared down at the body of the lord without actually seeing it for several moments.

The woman touched my shoulder and brought me out of it. "What have you done?"

What had I done? I'd signed my own death warrant. I'd killed the heir of Sangarie. I could still hear his last choking breaths, and feel the warmth of his blood spilling over my hand as I held the knife.

I'd crossed a line. Leaped across it.

The events of the past few weeks kept popping up in my mind as flashes of memory, trying to sort themselves out and make some sort of sense. I tried to justify it to myself, to explain why I had to do it.

But Firmin hadn't killed those Blues.

I opened my palm and stared at the ring in my hand, bloody and dull in the lamplight. I slipped it back into my vest pocket and let my shaking hand drop to my lap.

The outcast was a Red Hand. He was already a killer. It was no great leap to assume he'd done it himself and dumped the bodies, but why Old Town? Why be so careless? The Red Hands could make a body disappear and never be found, so he must have wanted them to be found, and to be found by me... to be blamed on me. I mean—one of them had my damn *name* on it.

To get to Firmin? To trick me into killing him? But *why*? I didn't know this outcast, and I certainly couldn't remember having pissed off a Red Hand this much. Was someone else using him?

The woman beside me swayed and I caught her arm to steady her. She was back to sniffling quietly. "I want to leave," she whimpered. She glanced worriedly at the door.

"Right. What brothel are you from? I'll get you back there."

The woman's brow creased. "I'm not from a brothel. I'm a maid. I just want to go back to my room, sir."

I stared at her a moment, my gut sinking even further down, if that was possible. "You aren't a Blue Hand?"

"Of course not." She looked at the body of the lord with a mix of fear and disdain. "Even *he* wouldn't treat a licensed whore like this. The baroness would have been furious if he damaged her politics with the guild."

The woman's eyes widened even more. "Are you going to turn me in for getting paid for it?" She edged away from me, twisting her arm to get it out of my grip. "I earned it! You have no idea how—how hard—"

"No, I'm not going to turn you in. Fucks sake." I glanced around the room, saw a massive wardrobe, and shoved the roiling thoughts to the back of my mind so I could function enough to get away with the woman. "I *am* going to bring you someplace they can patch you up though."

"You're bringing me to a brothel?" She staggered off the bed and tried to back away, but her legs were wobbly and she had to lean against the wall.

"They'll take care of you, and then you can leave. They have experience in handling injuries like this. I won't tell them anything about the money."

She nodded and started gathering up her clothes, struggling to dress.

I rummaged through the wardrobe until I found a couple of long, rich cloaks with deep hoods. They had fancy trim around the edges, but not so much that a nobleman's servant couldn't have worn them. One for her, to hide her injuries. One for me to make me look more like a rich servant. I had no idea how much the guards were in on this disgusting activity, but I couldn't just send her out into the manor like this. I couldn't carry her out over the wall, so we'd have to walk out.

I slung the cloak around my shoulders, wrinkling my nose at the smell of musky cologne and sweat, and my eyes happened to drift toward the table where a leather pouch rested. A glint of gold shone in the lamplight from a large coin next to it.

I recognized it before I was halfway there. As I picked up the elfish coin and the tingle of magic crawled its way up my fingers, I was positive there was more to this than an outcast getting his revenge. I believed Firmin had been telling the truth about his part in things, but our idiot lordling had been just as much of a pawn as I was.

I pocketed the coin and grabbed the pouch, then turned and held it out to the woman. "Ready?"

"That's too much."

"I don't think he'll complain."

She nodded, clutching the pouch beneath her cloak like it was a precious child.

I took hold of her upper arm and headed for the door. My hood was pulled so low I couldn't see much more than the floor, but if I raised it enough to see faces, they'd be able to see mine as well.

Chapter 30

I tugged the woman into the hall and saw two pairs of boots from the shelter of my hood, and two more further down. I didn't hesitate, pulling the frightened woman forward quickly enough she was thrown off balance, and she let out a muffled cry when I squeezed a little too tight to keep her from falling. The feet of the Ironguard shifted, and I could hear the creak of their leather armor, but they didn't move from their posts.

I walked as quickly as I thought an impatient servant would have done, passing the second pair of Ironguard before I'd drawn half a dozen breaths. My ears were straining to pick up any sound of pursuit, but other than a grunt of disgust from one of them, there was no other reaction.

I relied on my memory of the layout of the manor to get us out. It wasn't perfect, since the drawings I'd referenced depicted a manor from ten or more years ago, but it was enough to get me to a side door.

I hurried through the lamplit grounds of the manor, through the darkened streets of the Estates, and reached the same gate I'd entered from. The same Silverguard was there, and he tossed me a sloppy salute and went back to picking his nails. I slowed automatically, my intuition finally telling me something was very wrong now that I wasn't running on rage.

From this side I could see a man in an undershirt sitting slumped against the wall a little further down, right at the edge of the lamplight brightening the gate, a mug spilled on the cobbles next to him. The owner of the fallen spear I'd noticed earlier? It would explain why the Silverguard wasn't fussed with stopping people coming and going. He wasn't a real Silver. Or at least he wasn't concerned with guarding anything right now if he was.

I thought about confronting him, because he was obviously involved in some way, but that would give me away and attract attention. Instead I walked through the gateway like I hadn't noticed, and kept the woman moving as fast as she could. As we walked, I whispered to her to keep quiet about everything. About me, about Firmin—especially about him being dead. I had no doubt the Ironguard would figure it out soon enough, but I didn't need them to track it back to me so easily. Or to her.

I brought her to the nearest brothel I could find and pounded on the door until an irritated man answered. His eyes widened and I pushed the woman forward and spun on my heel, leaving her trembling in his arms.

As I continued on, the Warden's bells rang out over the city, calling up the guards for an emergency. They'd found the body.

I looked down at myself. I was covered in blood and sweat under the rich cloak, and was trembling like a crazy man. I couldn't walk the streets like this, so I found the nearest entrance to the underground and went beneath the city. As soon as I was below, I shucked off the cloak and left it on the dirt floor. The tunnels were mostly empty, and I made my way through them as quickly as I could, trusting to the dim light and speed to keep people from looking too closely.

I'd reached the door to my apartment and had my hand on the knob when I heard Deidre pacing inside. I paused, listening to her footsteps and her muffled crying. She would occasionally mutter something I couldn't make out in a high-pitched and wavering tone, like she was saying it through tears. Ruena's voice answered, consoling her in the only way she knew how—by telling her how amazing I was and that nobody could beat me. That I'd be back soon. I let my hand slip from the doorknob and kept my head bowed just outside the door.

I could feel the last of the tension finally draining out of me... and a strange calm.

If I stayed here, they were going to hang me. They might torture me first, but it would most certainly end in hanging. The guild wouldn't be able to protect me from this. If it had been some minor nobleman I might have been able to hide until it blew over, but it had been Firmin. All I could do was wait for the Warden to come for me.

Or leave. The thought of leaving Sangarie—everything I'd ever known—was uncomfortable, but the thought of leaving Deidre was painful. An ache rose up in my chest, and I blinked past the stinging in my eyes. I set a hand lightly on the wooden door, still able to hear her pacing inside—waiting for me to come home.

If I went in there, she'd try to help me. A part of me wanted it. Maybe we could find some other city… start a new life… But what if she didn't want that? What if I tried to take her with me and she ended up hating me for it? What if I ruined what we had, trying to make it something else?

I dug in my vest pocket and pulled out the elfish ring. My palm was still stained with blood, and the ring was blotchy with it. I could just flick it under the door before I left.

I rolled it between my fingers, wondering whether it would be a comfort to her or a burden. Muffled crying came from inside the apartment, and I slipped the ring back into my pocket. I turned away from the door and forced myself to walk away. One foot in front of the other. Just leave.

I didn't make it far before I caught sight of a figure lounging against the tunnel wall. *Senyr*. I drew in a steadying breath and walked up to him.

He stared at me, his eyes unreadable. "Going somewhere?"

"Thought I'd take a walk."

He gazed at me for a moment more, before easing away from the wall to stand in front of me. "Lord Rigel can't ignore this. He ordered me to send the Red Hands after you."

My gut tightened and I clenched my hands to keep them from shaking. "Already?"

"I think you've got about twenty minutes before I can find one in this damn rat warren."

I let out the breath I'd been holding, light-headed with relief. I was ashamed to admit I'd had my doubts about him, but if he'd been involved I wouldn't be walking away right now. "Thanks."

"Once you're outside the city we can't hurt you. Lady Karyn can send her own guards, but the guild has no jurisdiction outside these walls, so Rigel won't order the Red Hands past the city gate. You'll have a chance."

I nodded, turning my gaze to the floor. "I thought he'd killed those Blues."

"Why?"

"There's an exiled Red Hand sneaking around the city. He tried to kill Deid in the marketplace." I closed my eyes, realizing how weak my excuses sounded now that the rage had died down. "He told me it was Firmin."

"I see."

"I thought—" I swallowed back the words. *I thought you and Rigel had played me*. But without Firmin's guilt, that line of thinking made no sense. They'd have no motivation. I was back to not knowing what was going on, and now it didn't matter.

Senyr's voice was tired. "What were you thinking?"

"I couldn't let him do it again. The Red told me... he'd said the next victim was already there."

There was another long silence, and I kept my eyes on Senyr's boots. When my mentor finally spoke, I could barely hear it.

"I might have done the same."

I chuckled and looked at my hands, still covered in dried blood. "But you'd have done it better, right?"

"I don't know why you've been acting so stupid, boy. It isn't like you." He shook his head and sighed. "But I can't let them hang you for it. The bastard deserved it, even if he wasn't the killer."

"That Red Hand. I knocked him out in an alley and left him. Scruffy beard, gravely voice, breath like fish."

"I'll have them start searching for him, too. I'm guessing Rigel will have words with the Blades of the Master about the integrity of their investigations."

I nodded.

He set a hand on my shoulder. "I'll make sure Deidre is okay."

I smiled and my gaze drifted back toward my apartment. "She doesn't need anyone to take care of her. She's the one that took care of *me* most of the time."

"Good thing someone did."

I swallowed against the ache in my chest. "Check in with Sans for me? And tell him I'm sorry about the tab. And May. Tell her not to worry a—"

Senyr grabbed me in a rough embrace, thumping me on the back.

I stiffened reflexively, shocked at the uncharacteristic display of emotion. After a moment I hugged him back, and he pulled away.

"Right. Get out of here so I can keep looking for those pesky Red Hands. They're never around when you need them."

I looked down to hide the flush on my cheeks. "Yes, sir."

He walked past me and I listened to the sound of his footsteps for a few moments before I realized I could *actually* hear his footsteps for once. I smiled and started walking.

Chapter 31

I took the least used tunnels, coming up as close to the northern city wall as I could, then snuck the remaining distance, hiding whenever I heard the clanging armor of guardsmen or caught sight of torches being carried through the streets. Along the way I stole a clean change of clothes, a cloak, and a loaf of honey bread. I had a little time before the Red Hands would be after me, but the Silverguard at the gates would already have been alerted, so I couldn't chance meeting one of them. A number of buildings hid secret doors through the wall, and I chose one that didn't have a Yellow Hand hanging around.

The door rattled on rusty hinges and scraped against stone, and moonlight streamed into the building across the floor. Looking out onto the riverside plain, a lump rose in my throat. When I was younger I'd always talked about leaving, adventuring in the world, but I'd found a niche in the guild and that was really all I needed. Now it was all gone.

I slipped my bundle of clothes out the opening and squeezed through after it. I tried to close the door, but one of the hinges was halfway pulled out of the stonework and it would have been too noisy to force it, so I left it hanging in the breeze. Keeping to the shadows made by the wall, I edged my way closer to the road that led north along the river. When the guard atop the wall turned in his rotation, I slipped away and used the bushes alongside the road as cover until I was comfortable he couldn't see me in the dark.

Once I was away from the city I settled into a walk. It was a few hours until the sun came up, and I needed to pace myself. With the urgency having bled away, I didn't think about anything but where I was putting my feet. My mind was numb. I'd never been farther outside the city than just down the river, and I passed that point in less than an hour.

The sun came up slowly on the plains, starting with a muddy purple, then building up a pink glow until I realized it had been daylight for a while. Dragging my feet in weariness, I scanned the road ahead for someplace safe enough to lie down. By the time I came upon a thicket near the river I could see people in the distance. I found a cluster of bushes to squirm into and pushed my bundle ahead of me until I came to a more open area in the center. It wasn't big, but I'd be able to stretch out and sleep without branches scratching my face.

Pulling the hood of my new cloak as low over my head as I could, I used the rest of the bundle for a pillow and was asleep almost instantly.

I woke in the early evening, lying where I was until the sky darkened and I could no longer hear people on the nearby road. When I figured it was safe, I crawled backwards out of the bushes.

The blood had dried stiff on my clothes, and I peeled them off and washed it from my skin the best I could in the river. It was freezing cold, and I was shivering by the time I felt clean enough to put on the stolen clothes. I stashed the bloody ones under the bushes, mourning the loss of one of my best vests.

I sat on the bank for a while, eating the honey bread and wishing I had grabbed some jerky or cheese at least. The moonlight frosted the ripples on the water, and the sounds of the night were much different than inside the city. Oddly, it was louder out here, where there was nothing but grass and trees and river. This was going to take some getting used to.

I dug in the pocket of my new vest—a little looser and lighter colored than what I'd have chosen normally—and pulled out the elfish ring. Deidre must know I was gone by now. Senyr wouldn't keep her in the dark, and I was sure he'd have gone to my—her—apartment shortly after finding the *elusive* Red Hands. As part of his duty in trying to find me, if nothing else. He'd have explained everything.

I hoped she understood. I hoped she wasn't too angry with me. Most of all I hoped she'd be okay. I turned the ring in my fingers, watching the moonlight slide along the etchings. My chest ached. What would she have said if I'd asked her to leave with me? If I'd told her I loved—

Damn it.

I sighed and flicked the ring into the river. It hit with a *ploop* and was gone.

After pulling my boots back on, I slung the cloak over my shoulders and started off again, no particular destination in mind, just knowing I had to keep walking. I could find another city maybe, work my way up in another guild. Thankfully the moon was barely past full, or the countryside would've been much darker than I was used to, with no street lamps or glow from windows. Sure, the alleys of Sangarie could be black as the abyss, but nothing was ever this empty. The darkness went on for miles.

A few hours later I was scuffing my feet along in the dirt, not thinking about much of anything, when a voice startled me. I jumped and had a knife in my hand within seconds, peering into the dark grass at the side of the road.

"Who's there?" I demanded, keeping my voice low.

A hunched figure walked toward me and I tightened my grip on the knife. As the figure came close enough for me to make out the features, I recognized the old woman I'd confronted over a week ago in Sangarie. I lowered my blade, but kept it ready.

"What are you doing all alone in the dark, grandma?"

The woman leered at me and I backed up, unsure if it was out of instinct or disgust.

"This isn't guild territory, is it, enforcer?" The old woman looked me up and down, and chuckled. "Are you lost, or did you finally catch up to your destiny?"

I grunted and shoved the knife back into its sheath at my back. "Your mystic babbling doesn't impress me." I turned away from her and started to walk down the road. "You should hope we don't meet again, old woman. You bother me, and I just might fix that more permanently next time."

She didn't answer, and I didn't bother to look back as I trudged away, ignoring the prickling sensation of her gaze on my back. I quickened my pace until I no longer felt her stare, then settled back into what I hoped was a mile-eating trudge.

My thoughts shifted into automatic as I moved. Occasionally something coherent would muddle its way to the surface, but I really didn't care to deal with any of it at the moment. It wasn't my problem anymore. Senyr would handle it.

I kept walking, feeling an ache in my calves at the pace I'd set myself. Walking like this was nothing like doing rounds in the city. I shook the thought from my head. It wouldn't do me any good to think about the past. Or about how many people I'd failed.

Eventually I heard a faint melody of thumping noises, and it took a moment to realize it was the sound of horses cantering down the dirt road behind me. Had they found me already? I looked around frantically for someplace to hide.

In the city I could have disappeared in a few heartbeats, sliding into an alley, slipping through a door, merging with a crowd. Here on the open river plain, the only thing I saw higher than my knees was a clump of bushy trees a couple dozen paces ahead and a few yards off the road. I made for that, having no clue how long it would take the riders to reach me. I could only hope they wouldn't notice me in the dark. I glanced back as I skidded around the concealing branches.

I'd just made it. I panted softly as I backed further behind the tree, and nearly jumped out of my skin when a wheezing cackle rose behind me.

Spinning around, I found myself only a few inches away from the wrinkled old woman I'd left behind on the road over an hour ago. My eyes widened and I opened my mouth with the beginning of a curse as I staggered back, but it was cut short. The woman thrust her gnarled hand forward and placed her fingertips on my chest as she snarled a harsh, unintelligible word.

Despite my quick jerk backward, I didn't have enough time to escape her touch before the spell took effect. It felt like she'd punched a taloned hand *through* my chest and taken hold of my heart in a vise. I would have screamed, but there was no air in my lungs. Instead, I clutched at the place she had touched me and fell to my back in the grass. The hag scurried away, her touch broken, but my chest was convulsing and keeping me from drawing any breath. I clawed at my chest as I tried to draw in air.

I dimly heard the horsemen leave the road and trot around the clump of trees.

When the pain finally faded and the pressure released, I opened my eyes, gasping for air as I looked at the men on horseback surrounding me. They didn't have the uniforms of the city guard, but that was the

235

only thing reassuring about them. There were eight of them, and each one had a sword strapped to his hip and held a light club in his hand while they watched me with less than friendly expressions. My eyes shifted beyond them in a habitual search for an escape route, but found only grass stretching for miles... and one pompous looking nobleman.

The nobleman nudged his horse closer and peered down at me. I narrowed my eyes, searching my memory for his face. Firmin's guest. Had he come after me himself to avenge the lordling's death?

"Would I be correct in assuming you're Gray, a former enforcer of Sangarie?"

I was breathing heavily from the aftereffects of the mystic's spell, but I rolled and pushed myself to my knees, wondering how I was going to outrun mounted men. I ignored the nobleman for the moment, since the guards were more threatening. They shifted in their saddles as I staggered to my feet with one hand still pressed over my heart. They'd spaced themselves out around me and were swinging their clubs menacingly. I didn't need the visual to know how much it would hurt if they attacked.

The nobleman spoke again. "I asked you a question."

"I'm aware of that, asshole."

The nobleman frowned. "I'll take that as a yes. I'll need you to come with us, Mr. Gray."

I couldn't go back to Sangarie.

I had no idea what was on the road ahead, and I couldn't outrun horses. My best option was trying to avoid the clubs and get to the river, then hope they didn't throw themselves in after me. If I could put the river between us, I might have a chance.

If I didn't drown trying to cross it. My experience swimming had been clawing my way out a few times as a kid when someone bigger threw me in.

But it was either running or giving myself up to be hanged.

"Mr. Gray—"

I spun on my heel and took off, aiming for the gap between two riders where the river glinted beyond a sea of waving grass. With a dodge to one side and an off-balanced twist, I managed to avoid the first two attacks as the riders swarmed me, but the swing of the third landed on my back and sent me face-first into the grass. Pain shot across my right shoulder blade and my arm tingled and went partially numb.

I had to get up. The riders were surrounding me again, and I grunted as I propelled myself to my feet and wheeled away from the nearest attacker. The rider I'd turned into on my other side took a swing and the club whizzed past my face as I bent backward, then I darted forward and past the horse. The nobleman was screaming orders, and I dodged one more attack to find myself with a clear shot to the river.

I sprinted forward and was halfway to the bank when one of the horses rammed into me from behind. I stumbled and rolled, flinging my arms up to protect my head as the horse charged on over the top of me. The hooves struck me in the ribs as the animal stumbled, and pain flared across my side, adding to the renewed pain in my shoulder. The horsemen surrounded me, trotting back and forth, raising a cloud of dust that I sucked in as I coughed to regain my breath.

The nobleman dismounted and walked to where I was trying to get farther from the ground than my hands and knees. He held his hand out and one of the riders passed him a club. With a disgusted expression, he took aim and bashed me across the head.

I didn't even feel myself hit the ground.

Chapter 32

The first thing that came back to me was a fuzzy feeling in my head, followed by a queasiness in the pit of my stomach. All my other senses faded in and out, refusing to let my mind catch up to what they were telling me. A quick succession of light slaps on my cheek straightened it out though, and I jerked to full consciousness with a moan, wincing at the ache in my head. I realized immediately that my hands were tied behind the chair I was sitting in, pulling my injured shoulder back. The second thing I realized was whoever had tied me up had taken my vest and belt beforehand. All my hidden picks and blades were gone.

With my vision focusing in on the scene in front of me, I twisted my wrists, disappointed to find that whoever had tied the ropes had known exactly what they were doing. It'd take me hours of undisturbed time to loosen them, and I didn't seem to have any undisturbed time. In front of me stood the nobleman who'd led the riders on the road. He was staring at me with just the hint of a smile on his face, his dark eyes seeming to glow in the torchlight.

"Welcome to my home, Mr. Gray."

Clearing my throat, which felt as if I'd swallowed sand, I glared up at him. "A little dark and dank, isn't it?"

The man smiled wider, playing with a club he held in his hands. "Very well. Welcome to the dungeon beneath my home, if that suits you better."

I focused on my surroundings again. My ankles were tied to the legs of the chair, and the chair had been placed in the center of the room, away from anything that might have helped me escape. The room itself was bigger than any jail cell I'd ever seen... maybe eighteen feet square. There were two brackets with lamps, one on either side of a large wooden door centered in the wall facing me. The walls were brick,

238

painted a dingy white. The chair seemed to be the only furniture in the room, though I couldn't see the area directly behind me without craning my neck and causing myself even more pain.

And there was magic somewhere. I could feel it crawling over my skin, raising the hair on the back of my neck. I didn't know what it was, or where it was, but I didn't like it.

"I'm surprised you aren't asking where you are, or why I've brought you here."

I shifted my eyes back to the man's face, keeping my own expression as blank as I could despite the stabbing pain in my shoulder and ribs. "It really doesn't matter, does it?"

The man's face flashed his disappointment, and my mouth twitched with a smile I quickly hid. I wasn't going to give him the satisfaction of seeing me grovel. If he wanted to torture me for what I'd done, so be it, but I wasn't kissing his boots.

The man had regained his shifty grin quickly though, tapping the club he held gently against his leg. "Oh, I think it matters. You see, we're in the Estates of Sangarie."

I knew my indifferent expression had slipped. I glanced at the door without meaning to and the man chuckled.

"Oh yes! I've smuggled you back into the heart of the city, Mr. Gray. You see, there's a job we want you to do for us here."

A job? This wasn't about Firmin?

I eased back against the chair, doing my best to stare at the man with the same calm expression I used with my people back in Old Town. I looked him up and down. "I'm sorry, mister whoever-you-are, but it's against guild law to take a contract without the guildmaster's permission."

The man actually laughed. "Guild law? I'm afraid it's no longer a question of guild law, Mr. Gray. You see… you no longer belong to the guild."

I had honestly forgotten. In my own defense, it had been only a day or so since I'd fled the city, and I'd been in a daze most of that time, hardly admitting to myself what had happened. I may not have been branded an outcast, but if I showed my face on the city streets again, a Red Hand would put a crossbow bolt in my neck. I had no doubt they'd have been given standing orders to kill me on sight.

"And since you no longer belong to the guild, you are free to take employment with us." The man smirked at me, searching my face for a reaction. "We've gone to a lot of trouble to get you to this point, and I'm afraid saying no isn't an option."

I let the silence lengthen.

It was their doing. My head hurt too much to fit all the pieces together right now, but this nobleman had access to Firmin. He could have brought in the outcast Red. The knight... They must have been getting help from someone, but if all this was to ruin me just so I'd steal something for him...

I raised my aching head and stared into the man's eyes. "I have no intention of working in this city ever again."

"Would you rather I turned you over to Lady Karyn? I'm sure she could find a suitable punishment for the man who killed her son and heir. It may end with your head on a pike, but I'm almost positive there would be worse things before that."

I stopped myself before I shrugged my shoulders, remembering just in time that I was already injured. Instead I settled for raising an eyebrow and turning my gaze toward the door. If he was bluffing, I'd call it. If he wasn't... well, I was pretty sure what the Red Hands could do to me was worse than what the Ironguard could come up with. "Go right ahead. I'm not doing anything for you."

The man moved forward, placing the end of his club beneath my chin and levering my head back. "Aren't you even a little curious as to what I want you to do?"

"No."

The man growled under his breath and swung his fist. My head snapped to one side with the blow, pain flaring across my cheek and blood trickling inside my mouth. I spat it out on the floor and looked up at the man. "You hit like a little girl."

Snarling, he raised the club over his head.

From behind my chair, a harsh voice told him to stop.

My heart jumped into my throat at the sound. I hadn't even realized someone had been standing behind me the entire time. Not just any someone either... the creeping tingle of magic grew stronger as the wrinkled old woman walked around the chair at last and stood facing

240

me. Her eyes were rheumy and sunk into her head, but they peered at me with malicious delight.

The nobleman sounded pleased with himself. "Ah yes. Sela. I believe you've already met?"

I tried once again to twist my wrists and loosen the ropes binding me. I didn't want to be helpless while facing this mystic. I could feel the strands cutting into my skin, but they didn't give at all. I grunted at the pain in my ribs and shoulder, trying to get a better angle so I could reach a knot with my fingers.

The old woman shuffled forward, leaning on a staff that was almost as gnarled as she was. A grimace had distorted her features even more than normal, and her lips parted in a raspy sigh. One of her wrinkled, blue-tinged hands reached toward my chest.

I slid right past my calm façade and into panic. My arms and legs shivered and the blood drained from my face. With a desperate jerk, I tried to pull my hands free, crying out at the sharp pain in my shoulder. The chair didn't even rock. It must have been bolted to the floor.

The old woman placed her knobby fingers on my heaving chest and barked out the word that activated the spell. The magic ripped through my chest and twisted itself around my heart as it had before, squeezing and cutting off my breath at the same time. It felt as if my heart was about to burst with the pressure and I arched my back against the chair trying to relieve it. *Stop! Gods, stop!* I writhed against the ropes holding me down and the spell crushing my chest. I couldn't even draw enough breath to scream.

Then the pressure lifted and I went limp. I sucked in a shuddering breath, not able to choke back the whimper that followed it. My head tipped forward and I breathed heavily, trying to stop the tremors that shook my body. The fresh pain in my ribs and shoulder was a welcome sensation, and I swallowed back the feeling of nausea that followed. I was aware of something trickling down the inside of my wrists and into my palms, but I wasn't sure if it was sweat or blood. I knew it was sweat that ran down my neck and pasted my shirt to my back.

A hand gripped my hair and pulled my head up, bringing me eye to eye with the nobleman.

"What do you think of my offer now, Mr. Gray?"

I was still gasping for air, but I wouldn't have answered anyway. If I took a job in Sangarie I was as good as dead. Too many people here knew me, and I'd never be able to sneak around unnoticed. I'd rather die in this ridiculous excuse for a dungeon.

"I asked you a question, thief."

My mouth curled into a snarl. "And I already answered it, didn't I?"

The nobleman growled and swung the back of his hand across my face.

I glared up at him, my stomach turning at the taste of blood from the inside of my cheek. An ache spread across my jaw and I opened and closed my mouth, trying to ease the pain, then I gave the man a dark look and turned my face away.

Sela whispered harshly at him before he could move again, but I couldn't pick out the words. My ears were ringing and blood pounded under my skull, making it hard to concentrate on my hearing. The pain in my head muted everything else.

There were no brilliant plans coming to mind for escaping from this mess. I did the only thing I could think of, and kept twisting my wrists against the ropes binding me. From the sharp pain the motion caused, I guessed it was blood that trickled into my palms. It was providing a more slippery surface though, and if I could just loosen the ropes some more, I might be able to slip one of my hands out.

I saw the man coming toward me again and looked up, watching with narrowed eyes as he ambled around behind the chair and out of my line of sight. His voice was strained, but calm.

"I don't think you understand the position you're in, Mr. Gray."

I snarled. "Will you quit calling me that?"

The man walked back into view on my other side and I turned to watch him. He held the club loosely in one hand, the other sliding along the length of it lightly. "Let me explain something to you." He reached out and placed the blunt tip of the club against my chest. "You're a thief."

He gestured between himself and the old mystic. "We need something that someone else has."

I rolled my eyes and looked toward the opposite side of the room.

The man growled and took hold of my hair again, then bent back my head. "You will listen!"

242

I spat in his face.

He turned red in fury and raised his club to strike, his whole body shaking, but the blow didn't fall.

I stared up at him, waiting, tensed in anticipation of the pain.

The man shook his head, lowering the club and stepping back. A malicious smile spread over his face. "No... there are better ways." He motioned at the old hag that watched nearby and she grinned.

The color drained from my face and I glanced back and forth between the two of them. Being beaten I could handle. I didn't *like* it, but it was familiar. I'd been beaten enough in my youth to know what I was in for. Magic was something else. Magic was unnatural. My heart started racing and I pulled against the ropes as the woman stepped closer. "Get away from me!"

She walked past me, moving to stand behind the chair, and I tried to lean forward. The ropes around my wrists tightened to the point that I could no longer feel my hands at all, and still I could only move a few inches.

When her wrinkled hands came to rest on either side of my head, I froze. I was hyperventilating, and had broken out in a cold sweat. Her bony fingers shifted on my temples. I closed my eyes and clenched my teeth.

I heard the word she croaked just before my senses exploded. Everything disappeared except the searing pain in my head. I could see nothing and hear nothing past the pain. My body strained against the ropes holding me and I screamed over and over.

When the hag's fingers finally lifted, I sagged in the chair, my head lolling back as I blinked through red spots up at the ceiling. I gasped for air and fought the shudders that pulsed through my body, trying to keep myself from shaking apart.

The man spoke from nearby, but I didn't catch any of the words. The room blurred and twisted in my vision and I gagged once before fighting down the need to throw up. Someone slapped my face hard, and I winced as it echoed through my head.

A hand in my hair brought my head forward again and I desperately tried to focus on the face before me.

"This can get worse, Mr. Gray. Sela can do things you wouldn't have imagined in your wildest nightmares. She has a gift for delivering pain, you see. A very useful gift."

I breathed hard through my nose, teeth clamped down against the nausea. From behind me the mystic's hand slid across the back of my neck and a chill went up my spine. The bony fingers crawled their way around to the front of my throat and I shuddered, squeezing my eyes shut.

In the darkness of my own mind I was that little boy again. The pain of being flung across the cobbles... the choking terror of a monster pressing down on me... the first ever surge of magic burning through my body until I squealed.

The old mystic's touch sent echoing tingles through my neck, and when I spoke, my voice cracked. "Stop!"

The fingers froze, gently wrapped around my throat where my pulse raced just beneath the skin. I sucked in air and whispered again. "Stop."

The man leaned closer. "Are you going to steal for us?"

I swallowed and nodded slightly.

Sela pulled her hand away and the nobleman let go of my hair. I glared up at him, panting and trembling.

He drew himself up, staring down at me with a sneer. "I want to hear you say it, thief."

I took a couple of steadying breaths and held his gaze. My stomach rolled in disgust—at his smirk, at this situation—at *myself*. He was waiting with that pompous confidence all nobility had when they believed the world belonged to them.

Maybe it did.

I did my best not to let my voice shake. "I will steal for you."

"I'm glad you've come to your senses. I'll have my associates see you to a room where you can rest."

The sound of boots scuffing on stones came from outside the room. I flicked my eyes to watch as the door opened and two large guards walked inside.

"Oh, and Mr. Gray? Don't even think about trying to leave."

Chapter 33

One of the burly guards walked around and began to saw at the ropes binding my wrists, the other bent to free my legs. When the restraints fell away, my arms dropped and I raised my wrists to look at where the skin had been torn open by the rope. My hands were covered in blood. Again.

The two men each grabbed one of my arms and hauled me to my feet.

The room spun and my vision narrowed as my legs refused to hold my weight. I dropped, my shoulders wrenched upward as the men tightened their grip until I hung between them. Pain flared across my chest.

The nobleman's voice came from behind me. "Give him a moment, boys."

I struggled to stand, cursing my weakness. The pressure on my chest loosened as I supported my own weight, and the nobleman held the door open for us, smiling as if we'd just shared a lovely evening of drinks.

I half walked, half stumbled down the corridor and up the stairs into less dark surroundings. If it hadn't been for the two men helping me, I wouldn't have made it at all. They brought me to a room with a bed and a chair. It was smaller than the one I'd just left, but paneled in wood and warmer.

They stopped at the door and I walked into the room on my own wobbling legs. I didn't look back as they closed the door, but I could hear the latch click, locking me in, and only one set of footsteps walking away. I staggered to the bed and fell into a sitting position on the edge.

With a moan, I laid down. I tried to work out everything that had happened, but my thoughts scattered whenever I concentrated. All I knew for sure, was three of my friends had died to force me into this situation, and those deaths weighed heavily in my thoughts.

245

As exhausted as I was, sleep wouldn't come. I alternated between lying flat on my back and curled on my side, but I was in pain no matter how I tried to settle. I attempted to get up and pace the floor once, but standing made me reel and I quickly laid back down.

It had to have been a few hours later when I heard soft words outside the room and listened as the latch clicked and the door creaked open. I turned my head, raising myself partially off the bed, but stopped when I saw who entered.

It was the elf.

Her heavy, night green cloak was still missing, as was the hardened leather she'd been wearing in the garden. Now she was dressed only in pants and a simple tunic, embroidered with silver thread at the hems and at the cut-off sleeves near her shoulders. She was a little smaller than a human, but the muscles in her arms rippled beneath the skin as she tossed a bag onto the bed beside me.

I could see the green tint of her skin better now that she was indoors instead of locked in a cage in the garden. Tattoos of vines and elfish script flowed down her arms. Her face was smooth and unmarked, other than what appeared to be light brown freckles on her greenish cheekbones.

The warm glow of the lamp flickered as the door was closed behind her, and just for a moment her face was in shadow. Her eyes stared out from it, a brilliant green, hard and angry. It dredged up the memory of that place of nightmares. The shadowy figure that haunted my dreams and threw green lightning, with glowing eyes just like that. And pointed ears just like hers.

I shook the thought away.

Her voice was richer and much more biting than I expected, almost slithering through the room between us. "I remember you from the garden."

I pushed myself into a sitting position, using the wall beside the bed as a backrest. It took an embarrassingly long time to get settled, and I was sweating by the time I'd finished, holding an arm tightly to my ribs to help me breathe. "What do you want?"

"Loring ordered me to tend your wounds. So I brought bandages and salve." She pointed at the bag next to me. "It is there. Do it yourself."

I ignored it, keeping my gaze on her. "What are you doing here? In Sangarie."

She narrowed her eyes. "I was brought here. Just as you were."

"Loring?" I pulled the bag closer, wincing as the fresh scabs around my wrists pulled tight. The name caused a current of anger in me, but I couldn't remember where I'd heard it. Everything swirled in my brain right now.

"The nobleman." She crossed her arms in front of her chest and looked away from me.

I dug in the bag and found a few different tins, rolls of clean cloth, and some other healing supplies. I opened the tins one at a time, trying to read the faded labels and smell them to figure out what to use. Each one made my fingers tingle just a tiny bit as I held it, but I remembered how helpful the ointment from May's had been and decided I'd suffer through it if the pain would go away faster.

The elf finally sighed and pointed at one I had set aside. "That will help your wrists." She pointed at the one in my hand. "Use that on broken bones."

"Broken bones? What's ointment going to do for broken bones?"

"Then do not use it." She recrossed her arms over her chest and leaned back against the wall. "I do not care."

I mumbled my thanks and gooped the first one onto my wrists, wrapping strips of cloth around the raw skin. I couldn't tie a knot with only one hand, so I tucked the ends of the bandages in to secure them.

I glanced at the elf a few times as I worked, but she was determinedly ignoring me. I expected to feel her standing there, like when you can feel lightning just before it strikes, but other than a general sense of apprehension—and a whole lot of nausea—there was nothing. Either elves didn't spark off my talent, or she was too far away.

I picked up the tin she'd indicated for broken bones and looked at it more carefully. It looked like normal ointment. I scooped it out with my fingers and immediately felt the tingle of magic on them. I hesitated a good long while, just staring at my fingers and the greasy ointment, imagining the magic seeping through my skin, through my body, into my bones. I shuddered—and it hurt—which was enough to convince me I didn't have the luxury of being squeamish right now.

247

I pulled up the bottom of my shirt with one hand and started slathering it on. The skin was red and purple in places, and it hurt to work the ointment over it, but I clamped my teeth together and powered through.

When I had finished, I packed everything back into the bag. "Thanks for the help."

She was staring at me, her emerald eyes narrowed. "You are the thief they have been seeking."

"Is that so?"

"*Humans* talk in front of me. Like they do in front of an animal."

She said the word *humans* with contempt, like humans were lesser beings. Something disgusting she had to put up with. Her nose wrinkled as she looked me over. "You do not seem... special."

"I assure you, I'm not." I thought about the tingle of magic still wrapping my wrists and ribs and grimaced. I supposed in that way, I was special, but I didn't know how they could have found out about that. Or why it would make them want me this badly. It was a useful, but minor talent.

"They said they had to remove you from the guild, or you would not agree to anything. There was an elaborate plan, but I did not bother with the details." She tilted her head and I couldn't help but feel like I was being measured. "I am not convinced their effort was worth it."

I bristled at the insult, but didn't argue. My brain had jumped at the phrase "remove you from the guild" and I thought again about the reasons I'd left the city. Saree... Danial... Lily... they died to manipulate me. Their deaths were meant to get me cast out. That Red had probably killed and dumped them himself, then conveniently been the one called to the scene.

I narrowed my eyes. "Have you seen an ugly bearded man with fish breath helping them? An assassin?"

"There are many humans here. I can not remember them all, nor do I want to."

I let my head fall back against the wall and closed my eyes, swallowing the lump in my throat. The fucking bastards.

The elf spoke as if musing to herself. "Why do they want you so badly?"

I chuckled bitterly. "I wish I knew."

She stepped forward and grabbed up the bag. "Well. I do not care. As long as you do not get in my way."

I opened my eyes and watched her moving toward the door. She looked grimly determined, and not at all happy. "In your way for what? What's this all about?"

She turned at the door, her eyes flashing in anger. She spit the next word with enough venom to silence anything I might have said in response. "Destiny."

Chapter 34

I still wasn't able to sleep. I had no idea what time it was, since there were no windows in my room, and I didn't know how long I'd been out before waking up in the nobleman's makeshift dungeon. I wished I had thought to ask the elf about food.

I did my best not to think about anything—to quiet my thoughts and rest. It wasn't working. My mind was going in circles trying to figure out what was going on and why I was involved. What could they want me to steal that couldn't be stolen by any other decent thief from any other city? Surely it'd be easier to bring in a stranger than to execute this convoluted plan.

Being able to sense the presence of magic set me apart, but only Rigel and Senyr knew of that particular talent. Even as a kid I'd known not to let *that* slip. And as much as I bragged about being the best thief in the city—there were a couple I considered better than me. Senyr was one, even if he was getting older.

It had to be something else. Some connection I had? Some experience with the target? Until I knew what I was supposed to steal, I had no idea.

By the time footsteps approached my door again, and the lock clicked open, it had been hours. I looked at the door without sitting up and saw a bowl pushed inside on the floor and a waterskin dropped beside it. Then the door was shut and locked again.

At least I wouldn't starve.

I expected the stabbing pain in my ribs when I sat up, but it was nearly gone. I took an experimental deep breath and was pleased and a little disturbed to find it felt more like a mass of bruises, rather than anything broken. Hooray for magic ointment.

My mouth was still cut inside, and my headache wouldn't go away, but I ate anyway. I left the bowl and empty waterskin as far away from the door as I could, just out of spite. Maybe I could finally sleep.

***

The sound of the door opening woke me. I opened my eyes without moving, expecting to see the burly guards, but it was only the elf. She tossed the bag to me once again, and I sat up and started unwinding the bandages from my wrists.

She leaned against the wall, her bare green arms crossed over her chest, watching me. Her jaw was tight and her eyes hard.

It was my best chance at information. "Heard anything else about this job?"

"No."

Helpful. I peeled the last of the bandages from the sticky ointment on my wrists, biting my lip as it pulled at the wounds. "Maybe if you tell me what you know, I can figure out a way for us to get out of here."

She snorted. "I do not want to get out of here."

"Why not? Aren't you a prisoner?"

"I am where I need to be. I would prefer not to be a prisoner, but if it brings me to my destiny, it is what I must be for now."

I didn't bother concealing the sarcasm. "Inspiring." I rummaged for the tin I'd used last time, slathering it on and wishing I had some water to wash my hands. They were still covered in dried blood. Maybe I should have used the water they sent with my meal, but I hadn't thought about it at the time. "You might be happy to hitch a ride in the Warden's wagon, but I'm not. Can you tell me anything that might help me figure out what's going on?"

The elf raised an eyebrow. "Humans are so concerned with their immediate comfort. I doubt you would be able to escape this place before the quest begins."

"You see, you do know something. When is this hit taking place?"

The emerald green eyes flashed in irritation. "I know a great many things. I am not required to share any of them with you."

I sighed and wrapped fresh bandages around the wounds. "I'm going to take a wild guess and assume we end up working together. If this is your destiny, don't you think it'd be easier to be on good terms with each other? I mean, I don't like the idea of working with an elf any more

251

than you probably like working with a dirty human, but you play the cards you're dealt." *Or the ones you slip into your sleeve.*

She stared at me for a few moments, chewing it over. I took the opportunity to smear more of the magic ointment on my ribs. I didn't know if it would fix the bruises too, but if I was going to try anything foolish I wanted to be as close to the top of my game as I could get. My headache had dulled to a mere throbbing.

"Three nights from now."

A response was on the tip of my tongue—politely mocking and probably enough to piss her off—but then my brain finished guessing what day that would be and my face paled. I had been caught at night on the road. If only one more night had gone by since then—that meant three nights from now was the Night of Shadows.

My throat was suddenly dry and I licked my lips and made my voice as casual as I could. "What is today?"

"By the human calendar? The fourteenth day of Everbitt."

My hand clenched reflexively and the tin shot out of my greasy fingers. I fumbled for it and missed, watching it bounce across the wooden floor.

The Night of Shadows. This bastard nobleman wanted me to do a hit on the Night of Shadows.

It made sense, in a twisted kind of way. I was marked by the guild, and it would be nearly impossible to move around the city except on the one night when the streets would be empty. Nobody worked on the Night of Shadows. Even the Red Hands put away their crossbows and knives and stayed under their rocks.

I set my elbows on my knees and rested my head in my hands. Shit. Shit. Shit.

"Are you feeling unwell?"

I snorted. "You could say that." I had wanted to escape before, but now I had to. There was no way I could pull a hit on that night. I'd rather bare my ass to the Red Hands.

The elf stepped closer to pick up her bag. "We all must face our futures, human."

I ignored her. She sounded like a fucking mystic.

She moved away without a sound and knocked on the door, and it opened to let her through. I could only hear the footsteps of her escort as she was taken away to wherever they held her.

Chapter 35

There was only one guard outside my door. If I could get him to open it and somehow overpower him, I'd have a chance to run. I'd have to run blindly through the house and find an exit, then escape the Estates, then cross the entire city without alerting the beggar spies or the roving Red Hands. Going away from the river would be my best option, even if it meant crossing the least familiar districts. It was shorter and I was less likely to be recognized. If it was day, I might blend into the crowds. If it was night, I could use stealth.

I stood up and paced the room for a while, examining the furniture for anything I could use as a weapon. My life on the streets had taught me to make do with whatever I could get my hands on.

The chair beside the bed wouldn't be of any use unless I wanted to bust it up, which might draw a little too much attention. I stopped next to the bed and grabbed hold of the mattress, lifting it up to see what supported it. Rope crisscrossed between the sides of the frame like boot laces. No wonder it was so damn uncomfortable.

I stepped out the length of the room, thinking if I got into a scuffle I'd need room to maneuver. The door, when I examined the handle from the inside, had just a simple knob. There was no lock to pick even if I had the tools. There must be a separate latch on the other side.

I walked the perimeter of the room, rapping lightly on the wall every few feet. It was good construction. The paneling was thick and there was no hollow sound behind it. It was likely filled with brick between the layers of paneling. The door was set into a sturdy wooden frame as well. The hinges were on this side, but the guard would quickly figure out what I was doing if I tried to take them out.

I stopped tapping on the wall and set my palms flat against it, letting my head fall forward until my forehead touched the smooth wood. I'd go crazy locked in here for three more days. I turned my head, gazing at the door. Maybe I could shake things up a bit, get them to open the door and see if I could get past them.

"Guards!" I shouted. I stepped away from the wall and toward the door. "Guards!"

Walking up to the door, I pounded against it with the heel of my hand. "Guards! Open up!"

From just outside, an annoyed voice came back to me. "Quiet you!"

I pounded harder. "You can't keep me locked in here forever!"

No answer.

I cursed and walked over to the chair, grabbing hold of the back. Taking a few quick steps sideways, I dragged it across the floor and used the twist of my body to spin it up and fling it at the door. My ribs twinged, and I pressed a hand to them as I staggered to keep my balance.

The chair bounced off the door with a splintering crash. The frame twisted and one of the legs broke off as it clattered to the floor.

The guard's voice rose from outside. "*Hey!* I said *quiet!*"

I swore and kicked the chair leg across the room. Apparently I needn't have worried about making noise. I moved to the bed and laid down, staring up at the ceiling. It was hours since the elf had left. When did she plan on coming back?

I closed my eyes and tried to think about something else. I could sit for hours on a hit, watching people or listening to the sounds of the city. The problem was I could hear nothing in this room, and there was nothing to look at other than bare walls. I flung an arm over my eyes. To occupy my mind, I started thinking of scenarios I could use to escape. Each one involved someone opening the door.

When the door actually opened, I thought I might have been imagining it. But a dented metal plate was pushed inside with some soggy meat and mash, accompanied by another waterskin. The door closed without me seeing more than an arm, and footsteps receded again.

I crossed to the meal and wrinkled my nose at the smell of the food. I would have preferred the stew from the day before. With a sigh, I picked up the plate and took two steps toward the bed before I stopped and looked down at it.

It was metal. Not sharp, obviously, and not heavy enough to use as a weapon, but it would make more noise than the chair. I dumped the soggy meal on the floor just inside the door, careful not to step in it. When I swung the plate at the door it clanged nice and loud. I swung it again, adjusting the angle so it clanged louder. It vibrated in my hand and I swung it again, grinning at the shouts of the guard just outside.

A couple dozen hits later I finally heard the click of the lock on the door. I ducked to the side, making sure to slip behind it so it blocked the guard's view of me.

When he stepped inside, I swung the plate at his head. He raised his hand to block it and lunged for me. His foot hit the food on the floor and his arms pinwheeled.

I tried to slip past him, but he caught the fabric at my shoulder and jerked me back inside. I staggered into the far wall, pushing away from it as I darted for the door a second time, but he'd regained his balance quicker and held his arms wide.

I balled up my fist and aimed a punch at his jaw.

It was over in a matter of seconds. He caught my arm and twisted it up behind my back, shoving me chest first against the wall opposite the bed. I grunted, tipping my head back to keep my face from being smashed into the wood paneling, wincing as he wrenched my arm back even further.

He hissed in my ear. "Think it's funny to cause trouble, do you?"

I smiled, but was careful to keep from sounding too pleased. "Well… there's not much else to do in here."

"Would you prefer I send you down to rot in the dungeon?"

"I'm a valuable guest. Wouldn't your master be cross with you?"

The guard reached up and gripped me by the hair at the back of my head. "Don't push your luck, thief."

I did. "Looks like I finally found a way to entertain myself. How long is your shift?"

He pulled my head back and slammed it forward into the wall.

Pain exploded in my forehead, and I saw stars as I squeezed my eyes shut. When he pulled me away from the wall I staggered and tried to keep my feet as I was shoved toward the bed.

Putting my arms out to break my fall, I managed to catch the bed with one hand, but the other slipped off and my shoulder was wrenched

256

as my chest hit the edge of the mattress. Pain sliced through my mostly healed ribs. I grimaced, rolling my shoulder and struggling more than was necessary to right myself so I could slip a hand under the bed for the broken chair leg that rested just a few inches away.

I came up and moved immediately for the guard, who was ambling toward me. Stabbing forward with the chair leg, I aimed for his chest where a steel breastplate protected him. I didn't want to kill him, just get past him. He flinched, and the wood struck the steel and scraped along until it caught a leather strap.

He made a grab for me again but I dodged, jumping out of reach. My foot narrowly missed another piece of the broken chair, and when I caught my balance I hooked the toe of my boot under it and kicked it up at his face.

He raised an arm to block the chunk of wood and put a hand on the hilt of his sword, growling curses under his breath. But I had already bolted for the open door.

He shouted after me as I shot through the doorway and bounced off the far wall to run down the corridor. There had to be a window somewhere. I couldn't remember what floor I was on, but if there was any kind of handhold at all, I'd risk it.

The corridor turned ahead of me and I careened off the opposite wall at full speed, wincing at the throbbing in my ribs. I just needed one window. Maybe I'd get lucky and I could jump.

Doors lined the corridor and I slowed down enough to try one. It only rattled. Locked. The guard was running down the corridor behind me now. He was slower, but didn't have to search for a way out. I ran flat out and looked for a staircase instead, hoping I didn't encounter anyone else in the house. I made one more turn and the hall dumped me into a wide room with a grand staircase, lit by the orange sunlight of late afternoon.

The stairs went both up and down, and the narrow windows on the wall closest to me reached from floor to ceiling. I was on the second floor, and a wide expanse of garden was just outside. The windows were the good kind of glass, thick and solid. I remembered going past this staircase when I visited the Estates with Deidre.

I had two choices, and they flitted through my mind in an instant. I could take the stairs and hope to outrun the guard and get to the garden on the main level, or I could try to jump through the glass here at a bad angle. I'd have to curve around to come at it straight on, or else I might just bounce off. Then there was the fall to the ground outside.

I sighed and went for the stairs. If I incapacitated myself by jumping out a window, they'd just carry me back in at their leisure. It was better to get outside in one piece.

I took half the stairs as fast as I could, then jumped the remainder, landing hard on the floor and rolling to come back up to my feet. Pain spread across my ribs. As I started to sprint away, my boots slipped on the polished stone and I set a hand on the floor to steady myself, then took off at speed down the wider corridor. I heard shouting from behind and risked a glance back to see two more guards passing the bottom of the stairs after me. Probably the ones from the front door.

The garden had been down this hall and through a large sitting room. I skidded to a stop at the first door I saw and tried the handle. It opened into a room full of couches and high-backed stuffed chairs. On the opposite wall was a row of smaller windows overlooking the garden, but no door.

Close enough.

I darted inside and swung the door shut, running for the windows as the guards slammed into the other side of the door. Raising my arms to protect my head, I prepared to launch myself at the glass.

And saw Deidre outside.

My stomach dropped. I skidded to a stop, staring at her and lowering my arms.

She was standing in the garden, dressed in blue satin with her hair curled in dark ringlets and pulled up to cascade over her shoulder. She was laughing, and her hand came to rest on the arm of a well-dressed man. His face turned enough for me to recognize him as Firmin's guest, Loring.

Loring.

I remembered where I'd heard that name before. Firmin had said it right before he died.

I was panting from the run, and my heart pounded in my chest. It was Loring that had hurt Diedre. Firmin's ramblings made sense now. The strange look Firmin had given us at the Running Hart... not guilt at his own misdeeds, but at having introduced her to Loring.

Why was she here?

Loring raised a hand and brushed a loose curl away from her face, and she blushed and edged closer to him, tilting her head up to speak. Her face was radiant.

I vaguely heard the guards behind me burst through the door.

Loring slid a hand behind her head, clenched a fist in her tumbling curls, jerked her head back, and kissed her.

My chest tightened—and a club came down across my back.

Chapter 36

With a grunt of pain I staggered forward and dropped to my hands and knees. A booted foot slammed into my gut and lifted me a few inches off the floor, and my breath whooshed out. The next kick sent me sprawling onto my side and pain shooting across my chest. A club came down on my shoulder and another on my hip, and I think it was a boot that grazed my forehead. I wrapped my arms around my head as the beating continued, unable to draw more than a wheezing breath between blows, squinting my eyes shut.

Eventually, one of the guards put a boot between my shoulders and forced me face down on the thick carpet. They wrenched my arms back and one of them tied a length of rope around my wrists, over the bandages already there. He stood and spit on me, then aimed one more kick at my ribs.

Dizzy and aching, each breath stabbing painfully through my chest, I stayed still and listened to them argue about what to do with me. I forced myself to breathe, when all I wanted to do was curl up and die. There was blood in my mouth again, and the side of my head was wet.

Two men came to stand over me and grabbed my upper arms from behind. I tried to tense up before they lifted, but none of my muscles would actually do it, and when they hauled me up I groaned in pain. They didn't wait for me to try to get my feet this time, just dragged me across the room. I tried anyway, pulling my feet up one at a time like they had weights tied to them.

They dragged me through corridors, but not stairs, so when they dropped me onto my face on a stone floor I knew I was still on the ground level of the manorhouse. I slipped in and out of consciousness, and couldn't make sense of the voices around me anymore.

Then I was outside. There was a breeze, and I smelled horses. They heaved me into a wagon and I curled up the best I was able with my hands still tied behind my back. A blanket was thrown over me, cutting off the light.

I had never had the opportunity to ride in a wagon. I'd stolen from them many times, and used them for cover, but never been on one while it was moving. It was more jarring than I would have thought. Each cobblestone we rolled over was painful. I'd have preferred being pushed down the stairs—or off a roof.

I wasn't sure if I stayed conscious the entire time, because the trip was mostly a painful blur, but I was awake when they flung the blanket away inside a large room. There weren't many buildings you could drive a wagon into, so I figured I was in a warehouse or shop of some kind. The room was barely lit.

Hands grabbed my legs and dragged me to the back of the wagon, then lifted me out and carried me across the room. I passed into what looked like a jail cell, and they dropped me to the stone floor and walked off.

It took a few minutes to breathe through the pain, and I tried to move as little as possible. Then I heard the rattle of the cage door, departing laughter, and finally silence.

I twisted my wrists, testing the rope binding me. It felt about the same as having my arms twisted off. How the fuck was I going to get out of this? At least I couldn't work in this condition, so I'd avoided that disaster. I was trying to decide if I could pass out when I heard a voice directly behind me.

"Thief."

I jerked in surprise and choked at the pain that spiked through my shoulders and chest.

The elf stepped around where I could see her, squatting on the stone near enough to touch. Her mouth was pressed tight, her eyeteeth dimpling her lower lip, and her eyes narrowed in irritation. "That was stupid."

"Yeah." I wheezed and rested my head on the floor, closing my eyes. "Can you untie me?"

She sighed and moved around to the knots at my wrists.

261

When the ropes came off, I dragged my arms forward and wrapped them around the front of my chest. Maybe that way I could hold my ribs together while I breathed. "Thanks."

She looked like she wanted to say something, but backed up and shook her head, moving to the other side of the cage to sit against the bars and stare out at the mostly dark room.

The cage was bigger than I expected, now that I bothered to look. It was centered in one wall of the building, covering maybe twenty-five feet of the thirty-five foot wall, and extended at least eighteen feet from the wall. There were small dark piles in one corner, and judging from the smell it was animal shit, but dried and dusty. It must have been a holding pen at one time.

The rest of the room beyond the cage was vast and empty. I guessed it was twice as deep as it was wide. I saw no sign of the wagon they'd used to bring me here. In one of the far corners was a desk and some empty shelves covered in a thick layer of dust, with a couple of simple chairs scattered nearby. A massive set of doors was in that far wall, but they were now closed. The ceiling was at least two and a half stories, although the cage stopped at about twelve feet. A number of windows near the ceiling provided the dim light, which filtered down through the dust hanging in the air.

Eventually I must have passed out, because I woke curled up on my side to the sound of someone dramatically hissing my name. I lifted my gaze to look and my chest tightened when I saw Ruena kneeling outside the cage, her hands wrapped around the bars and her face pressed tight between them. Her pearly white eyes were wide and her face was flushed.

She glanced from me, to the elf, and back again. "Gray?"

The Six be damned. I swallowed a couple of times and carefully cleared my throat before I could croak out a question. "What are you doing here?"

"I saw them bring *her* in, and wanted to see who she was. Then I snuck inside and saw you." Her white eyes filled with tears and her chin trembled. "Where did you go? You've been gone for days!"

I tried to roll onto an elbow and groaned, sinking back to the floor. Everything had stiffened up. I was pretty sure more of my ribs were broken than weren't. She couldn't stay here. If the building was guarded she'd be caught, and who knows what Loring would do to her. "Rue—get out of here."

"I'll get you out."

"No."

She scrambled up and moved to the cage door, trying to force the latch.

I closed my eyes and sucked in a breath, then rocked to my knees. "Rue!" I dropped to one elbow and paused to steady myself and wrap an arm around my ribs. "Get the fuck out of here."

"Not without you. I'll see if there's a key somewhere."

The elf snorted and I glared at her. Ruena's footsteps echoed through the warehouse as she ran to the desk to search for a key. Damn kid. She got into more trouble than I ever had at that age. She was going to get herself killed.

Sure enough, a door set into the far wall creaked open and light spilled across the floor. Four guards filed in, catching sight of the girl even though she dived behind the desk. They surrounded that corner and one of them moved in.

Ruena didn't wait for him to get there. She rolled under the desk, coming up in front of it in a cloud of dust and cobwebs. I was impressed with how quickly she regained her feet, but she wasn't fast enough to slip past the guards. One snagged her around the waist and pulled her—kicking and screaming—to his chest.

They didn't bother to quiet her. One of them snorted at the noise and another chuckled. They carried her toward the cage, one of them digging at his belt for a set of keys. They hadn't acted at all surprised at her arrival. Either they'd seen her sneak in, or they'd been expecting her. As convoluted as my capture had been, I didn't doubt they knew exactly who she was and what she was doing.

The guard carried her into the cage, rather than throw her in like I expected. His fellows remained outside and closed the door, then leaned against the bars to watch.

That made me nervous.

I knew I couldn't stand. It was hard enough just kneeling and sitting back on my heels with my arms wrapped around my middle. I looked over my shoulder at the elf, but she had her knees drawn up and her arms draped over them, staring out into nothing as she ignored everyone. No help there.

The guard dropped Ruena. She staggered to keep her feet and shot him a dirty look before ducking behind me. She clutched the back of my shirt, trembling hard enough I could feel it in her grip.

The guard spoke. "I have a message from Loring."

I glared up at him. "What does that asshole want?"

The man sneered, closing in until he was within arm's reach. I recognized him now. It was the guard I had attacked in my room earlier. The scratches on his breastplate from the broken chair leg were clearly evident. "He wanted me to tell you the lady hopes you enjoy your stay."

My thoughts shot back to Loring and Deidre in the garden outside the sitting room. An avalanche of emotions hit me all at once, and I lowered my gaze trying to sort them out. Anger, jealousy, disbelief, betrayal…

The old mystic had ranted about her mistress bringing down the guild. Loring had used the words "for us" when he asked me to steal. There's no way the nobleman could have gotten so much inside information on the guild without someone working within it.

Deidre?

She'd been acting so odd lately. She'd been constantly worried about where I was going and what I was doing. All the strange, distant looks I'd noticed—and the fake smiles. Had she been playing me this whole time?

The guard chuckled, then spit on the floor in front of me. "He also said the whore tastes pretty good."

My eyes flicked up and I drew in a shuddering breath. I wanted to launch myself at him—rip that sneer off his face. I clenched my fists at my sides. "*Fuck* your master. And fuck you too."

The guards outside the cage laughed, and the one in front of me grinned. "He's probably all fucked out by now."

I had to force the words through clenched teeth. "Won't you be disappointed not to get bent over when you get home?"

Ruena was right behind me, so I didn't try to dodge the fist that came at me. Not that I could have anyway. Pain flared across the left side of my face and I fell to the side.

The laughter sounded far off and echoing.

Everything hurt.

Chapter 37

"Gray?"

I didn't want to wake up.

"Gray."

Someone was shaking my arm. It brought back all the physical sensations I had been avoiding by sleeping. Not that I really had much choice.

I blinked, bringing Ruena into focus, and the elf beside her. Every time my heart beat, the image blurred a little at the edges. I hurt in so many places I couldn't even tell them apart anymore. My entire body was one massive ache. I'd hoped to just die in my sleep. No such luck.

"Drink this."

The elf forced my mouth open and a splash of liquid hit the back of my throat. I gagged and my chest tightened painfully, but the worst feeling was the tingle of magic going down my throat as I swallowed.

My eyes widened and I grabbed her wrist, staring at the tiny bottle in the palm of her hand. "What was that?" It tasted sweet, and left a numbing film behind that made me want to shove a scouring pad down my throat.

She pulled away and stood, brushing herself off. She was dressed in her armor again, and her hair was freshly braided. "That was a healing draft. It was the last one I had. I hope you appreciate it."

I waited for something to happen—to have my body contort into some other form, or melt into the floor, or have my mind turn inside out—so it was a relief when the aches and pains just faded away. Within a matter of minutes I felt perfectly normal again, other than feeling like I hadn't eaten in days.

I relaxed against the stone floor and closed my eyes, enjoying the sensation of breathing without pain. However, I quickly realized I was now capable of pulling a hit again, and my brain was no longer distracted from my situation by the injuries.

Ruena took my arm. "Are you okay now?"

"Yeah. I think so."

I sat up as she dragged over a small basket. Inside was bread, jerky, and hard cheese, along with a couple pieces of fruit. My stomach growled and I pulled out a chunk of the jerky, then gazed pointedly at the goggles around her neck.

She blushed and glanced across the room. "They already know."

A trio of guards were at the desk in the corner, seated on chairs and playing cards. Two more leaned against the wall near the big double doors, chatting quietly. The elf, as I'd noticed before, was kitted out in her armor and even had a rucksack near to hand. Ruena pulled over a small bundle and set it solemnly before me.

I unwrapped the cloth, finding my belt and stolen vest, along with all my lockpicks and knives intact. Why would they give me back my weapons? Unless—

"Rue, how long has it been since you got here?"

She hugged her knees, staring up at me. "A couple of days maybe?"

The elf spoke from where she leaned against the cage bars. "It is close to sundown on the night you call Shadows."

Shit. I climbed to my feet and slung my belt around my waist. It felt good to have my possessions back, and I checked the two knives in the sheath at the small of my back. The smaller blades that had been taken from the lining of my boots were also there, and I secured them too. The stolen vest was last. I wished I had the heavier version I used when I expected trouble, but this was better than nothing.

Ruena sniffled from the floor and I glanced at her in time to see her wipe a hand across her eyes. I sighed and squatted beside her. "You shouldn't have come."

"I'm sorry."

"If you get a chance, I want you to run away. Got it?"

She nodded. "Gray?"

"What."

"Are you scared?"

I gazed back at her, forcing a smile. "I'm the best thief in the city. I'm not afraid of anything."

266

"Nothing?"

"Well, maybe Kash. She's fucking scary."

Ruena smiled and wiped away a tear that ran down her cheek. "She's not *that* scary."

I nudged her hard enough to rock her sideways. "Are you kidding? She could kick my ass."

She giggled, then moved toward me and wrapped her arms around my neck, snuggling her face into my shoulder.

I caught the elf's quiet stare before she looked away with a frown on her face. I cleared my throat and pulled Ruena's arms away. "Enough of that. Thieves don't hug."

The door into the warehouse opened and I stood quickly, shoving the girl behind me. A troop of guards walked in and spread out, followed by the old mystic woman. The hair on the back of my neck stood up and I itched to pull one of my knives. The only thing keeping me from flying into a suicidal flurry was Ruena's hands tugging at the back of my vest and the thought of what would happen to her if I did.

Sela passed through the group of guards and stopped in front of the cage. Her rheumy gaze shifted to each of us in turn, then locked on me. "It's almost time. Are you ready to do your part in fulfilling my lady's desires?"

I pulled my mind away from an image of Deidre in Loring's arms, and stared back at her. "If I'm not?"

She cackled. "Then you'll probably die trying."

I crossed my arms. "Not sounding like such a bad option right now."

She squinted at me, her eyes calculating. "But are you willing to let more friends die due to your failure?"

I glared in return, conscious of the little girl hiding behind me, and bluffed. "I'm a criminal, remember? Scum of the city? Appealing to the goodness of my heart won't help you."

Ruena peeked around me, her face screwed up with a fierce little snarl. "Yeah. We're criminals. And you're a fucking asshole."

I grimaced and shifted her back out of sight.

Sela chuckled and waved the guards forward. "Bring them."

Chapter 38

Guards moved up to unlock the cage as Sela slipped back outside the building. I thought about making a break for it then, but I couldn't leave Ruena behind. They prodded me out first—separating us—and I glanced back to see her slip her hand into the elf's. The stern expression on the elf's greenish face slipped, and she didn't pull away.

The guards shoved me forward. I stared at the door leading outside and did my best to squash down the panic already creeping up. When the door was opened, the red-orange sky was already darkening into purple and the city streets were in shadow. It was sunset, and time for the Night of Shadows to begin.

Panic wouldn't help me. Panic would make me freeze up, make mistakes. I'd just steal whatever it was, give it to Loring, and hopefully be done with the whole mess. I just had to be careful… avoid the blue glow of the labyrinth…

My eyes darted into every shadow, down every street. The city felt empty with everyone locked inside for the evening. We weren't in the Estates, obviously, and this wasn't Old Town. I would have recognized the streets of Old Town immediately. If I had to guess, It was the Lower Yard to the south of Old Town.

It didn't take long to reach our destination. A narrow, twisted alley emptied into a wide courtyard where a building had once stood. I could see the signature of ash on the surrounding walls, and figured they hadn't bothered to rebuild after the fire that had taken it, but had cleared the debris instead and used the space for storage. The entire block seemed like it was hardly used, so it was probably not far off from being torn down and replaced by something that made more money.

Guards stood around the edges of the courtyard, watching the entry points. I was led through and stopped in the middle by a guard extending

268

a hand in front of my chest. Loring stood to one side, flanked by a pair of men. Two more people walked into the circle of guards, chatting casually with each other, and my face flushed in anger when I recognized them.

One of them was the outcast Red Hand that had tried to shoot Deidre in the market. The other was Culley.

All the anger I'd felt at Deidre's betrayal bubbled to the surface. Not only had she played me for a fool, but one of my own people—someone I had vouched for and worked with—had been in on this. I slipped past the guards in front of me and launched myself at the thief, a knife already in my hand. "*Culley*! You son of a *bitch*! I'm going to cut your fucking balls off!"

The Red Hand was faster, and he grabbed my wrist and threw his weight into my ribs to flip me over his shoulder. I landed hard on my back on the cracked cobbles and we struggled for possession of the knife, rolling in the gravel.

He pulled a second knife from his belt and raised it above me, a deranged gleam in his eyes.

Loring's voice cut through the buzz of the garden. "*Waren*! Enough!"

The butt end of a spear jabbed into my side. I folded up and the Red Hand chuckled. He climbed off me and sauntered a few steps away.

The knight in tarnished armor stepped closer and held the spear out for one of the guards to take back. "Revenge can wait until after the quest is finished, thief."

I didn't answer. I coughed and glared at Culley, who at least had the decency to look sheepish standing behind the knight.

The Red Hand, Waren, tossed my knife onto the cobbles beside me. "Get up," he snapped.

I rolled to my knees and picked up the knife as I got to my feet. Ruena darted to my side and grabbed my arm.

I looked up as Loring stepped forward.

"I won't waste time with speeches. Find us the stone in the center of the labyrinth and bring it back before the night is over. You all know what's at stake if you disappoint us, or if you're late."

I stared at the nobleman, a shudder going up my back. "Wait—in the center of the labyrinth?"

The outline of a gateway began to appear, the blue glow hanging in the air around the courtyard, and the tingle of magic washed over me, making my hair stand on end. My gut clenched and my heart raced. I shuffled a few steps away from the gateway solidifying nearby, dragging Ruena along, but a guard's spear blocked me from retreating further. "Not a chance," I snapped. "Just kill me now, Loring. Find somebody else to jump into the abyss for you."

The man shook his head. "We went to great lengths to get you all here. Now you will get us that stone. You've been there before, so this should be easy for you."

My eyes narrowed as I took a few steps toward the nobleman. "No way am I—"

The pain came without warning. One moment I was bearing down on the haughty face of the noble, the next I was blinded by agony and on my knees, holding my head in my hands. I screamed, trying to keep my head from ripping itself to pieces.

Then it was gone, fading into a dull ache that was just a reminder of what it had been. I took a couple of deep breaths, fighting back nausea, staring at the cobbles between my hands. Gnarled fingers trailed across my hunched shoulders and ruffled the hair on the back of my head as Sela walked past me to stand at Loring's side.

Loring's voice drifted down to me. "You realize if you don't go willingly, I will have you thrown in like a sack of grain, screaming in pain the entire while."

I raised my head to glare up at the man.

Loring continued. "I'm not sure what you'll find on the other side, but I don't think you'll want to announce your presence by screaming like a wounded animal."

Ruena knelt on my left side, taking hold of my arm. "Gray?"

A hand touched my right shoulder as well, and I turned to look at the cloaked figure of the elf as her pale green features reflected the eerie glow of the gateway opening nearby. Her eyes had hardened, more like the eyes of a fighter than a mystic. She was now holding a scythe-like polearm with a red wooden shaft and an etched blade.

It poked something deep in my memory.

"We have little choice," she whispered in her lilting accent.

I shrugged them both off and stood, my legs shaking, turning to glare at the nobleman once more. She was right. The only way was to move forward and hope I saw some way out. "A stone?"

Loring smiled and nodded. "The Enhali Voga Surai."

The elf beside me growled low in the back of her throat and her narrowed gaze focused on the nobleman briefly before she turned it to the gateway. A new sense of determination—maybe resignation—set into her face. The name of the fabled stone had meant something to her.

I ground my teeth, wanting nothing more than to slide away into the night and disappear. My hands were shaking, but I clenched my fists and took a deep breath. "Do you know anything about how it's protected? What we'll face?"

"Culley will guide you once you reach it. He's been there once before."

I shot a glance at the thief. He'd been in the labyrinth too?

Ruena leaned against my arm, and I glanced down to see her shielding her sensitive eyes from the magic of the gateway. I looked back up at Loring. "Let the kid go. You don't need her."

"She has a gift. It could prove useful in there."

The words were on my lips to tell him my curse would be enough, but old secrets were like rusted gates. Two decades of hiding it and the thought of saying it out loud in front of dozens of people had my tongue in knots. I glanced down at Rue as she clutched my arm.

Too many people had died for me already. "You don't need her gift. I can do the same thing. Let her go."

Loring's eyebrow went up. "Is that so? How convenient. What else can you suddenly do? Breathe fire? Fly?"

I wanted to laugh. He didn't believe me. "I'm serious, asshole. How do you think I'm so good at what I do? I don't need her. She's just a kid." I shrugged Rue's hand off and stepped away from her.

His eyes narrowed and he gazed back at me. "Nice try. She was right about how much you care about your people." He fluttered his fingers at Ruena. "This one will be useful for keeping you on task. It'll keep you motivated to succeed, since you're so eager to die instead of face the shadows. If you die in there, she can die with you."

I shook my head.

"Or I could send her in alone. How would you like that? What's one more body added to the list of people you've killed?"

"I didn't kill—" The reply was automatic, but cut off as I realized that—in a way—I *had* killed them. They'd died because they were close to me.

The lump rose in my throat and I merely clenched my jaw and turned without another word, facing the gateway that now stood in the center of the courtyard. The outer rim glowed blue as if it were on fire. The gateway itself was a rolling cloud of black smoke. Here and there I could glimpse images of the labyrinth beyond... ruined stone walls, cobbled paths, jagged pieces of timber on the ground.

I was shaking and breathing fast. Fear threatened to overwhelm me.

The nobleman's voice called out behind me, arrogantly cheerful. "Good hunting."

"Fuck you." I watched as both Waren and Culley stepped through the gateway, followed closely by the knight.

The elf took a step forward and glanced back at me, nodding her head once in tight-lipped encouragement. Then she walked forward with her polearm gripped tightly in both hands and stepped through the smoke, fading into the labyrinth.

Ruena slipped her hand into mine and I looked down. Her pearly white eyes were squinted nearly shut as she flinched away from the gateway and tears flowed from them. "Thieves aren't afraid, right?"

"Right." It was such utter bullshit, but it's all I had to say.

"Gray?"

I forced a smile. "Yeah?"

"I can't see... The magic is too bright."

I squeezed her hand and stepped forward, leading her. I just had to do it—without thinking about it—or I'd balk. I knew if I was going to end up in there, I wanted it to be on my feet, rather than squealing like a pig being slaughtered. Silence was a thief's friend, after all.

Loring called out as I got closer. "Just a reminder, *thief*, this is the only gateway that guarantees you'll return home. Remember where it is."

I shivered, forcing myself to keep moving.

Chapter 39

The magic rolling across my skin as we stepped up to the gateway was like ants crawling all over my body. I resisted the urge to rub my arms to get it to stop, knowing it wouldn't help.

Just step forward.

I hesitated, my muscles locking up as I tried not to hyperventilate. The old unreasonable fear washed over me, making my legs feel weak.

Just. Move.

I trembled, and then Ruena stepped forward into the gate and pulled on my arm, dragging me after her. As I crossed the threshold, I sucked in a breath.

My entire body twisted up like a towel being wrung out, forcing all the air from my lungs. As I took the next step, it went back to normal and I found myself stumbling into the ruins of the labyrinth. I gasped, nearly choking on the ash and dust. My legs were shaking, but my thoughts were shockingly clear.

Every noise sent my eyes darting in a different direction. A patchy wind scattered small stones and made jumbles of debris creak and moan. Farther afield a faint scream raised the hair on the back of my neck, but was suddenly cut off. Gravel crunched as the three men and the elf walked around the ruined courtyard.

Ruena was coughing beside me and I glanced back at the gateway, catching fleeting glimpses of the people standing on the other side. Then Sela passed through and stood on the broken cobbles in front of the rolling black surface of the gateway. She met my gaze and grinned, showing her stained teeth.

"You didn't think I was letting you run off alone, did you, thief?"

"I could only hope."

She spoke a garbled word and a red crystal brightened at the tip of the staff she carried, spreading a bloody glow around her. She shuffled forward, the gnarled wood clicking on the stone. "We only have until sunrise." Her voice rose and cracked as she called out to the knight. "Lead the way, Kincaid."

I turned to look out over the labyrinth and frowned. My nightmares were full of this ruined darkness, the smells and the eerie screams, but looking at it now made my brain itch. As a child, it had been huge and terrifying, and those memories had been overwhelming, but now I saw it with the eyes of a master thief. "This place looks familiar."

Sela grunted as she walked past me.

I gazed across the skyline, watching the last rays of the dying sun shining onto the high places of what looked like ruined buildings. I could see the highest point of the labyrinth, rising up on a hill in what I assumed was the center. "That's the palace?"

Sela didn't bother to look. "Get moving, thief."

Ruena tugged me into motion and I started walking. The sensation of magic was a constant tingle over my skin, maddening and setting me on edge. It was like the very air was filled with magic.

The elf walked up beside us. "This place is dead."

"What do you mean?"

She squinted at the hill. "I am not certain. It just feels dead." She turned to look at me, her thin lips tilting into a half smile. "You are Gray?"

I nodded. "That's what they call me. Are we suddenly friends?"

"I told you before that I needed to be here. Now that I am here, I am free to find my destiny." She bowed her head in a regal motion. "They call me Nissa."

The mystic screeched back at us. "Move! We only have a short time until we're trapped in here."

I gestured rudely at the back of her hunched form as she hobbled quickly after the men.

The elf—Nissa—lifted the corner of her mouth in an amused smirk. "I will take the rear guard. My scythe will protect our backs."

I didn't want an elf at my back, but I wanted the labyrinth at my back even less. "Suit yourself."

Looking around at the broken walls, I didn't think this shadow realm looked much like a labyrinth. It looked more like the shell of a city. It had a blackened look, like something had burned everything away but the bones of the buildings. Crumbled stone was strewn around, and bits of wall stood up from the rubble like jagged teeth. A few thick wooden timbers remained in place, but looked charred and brittle.

I heard another scream on the wind, full of terror, and it keened on for a few heartbeats then ended abruptly. The men in front of me didn't react, and Sela continued her hobbling steps without pause. I glanced back at Nissa. Her face was grim.

We quickly reached a large wall that ran across the direction we needed to go, but an opening was cut through it, leading out into a maze of passageways through the debris. I looked up toward the presumed palace as I crossed through the opening, thinking again that the skyline looked eerily familiar.

Ruena dropped back to walk beside me, leaning close to whisper. "Everything here was broken."

"I can see that."

"No." She pointed at her eyes. "I can *see* it. Everything here was broken with magic. It coats the rocks like dust."

"Well," I said, looking out over the debris, "nothing natural would have done this. So that makes sense."

She tugged at my sleeve and I looked at her again.

"There are trails through the dust."

I shuddered and peered through the faint light cast by the mystic's staff. "Stay close, Rue."

We walked for about half an hour, having to wind our way around fallen stones and climb over rubble. Sela's staff, combined with a hazy glow from the partially obscured full moon above, gave us enough light to see. There looked to have once been wide pathways, but most of them were clogged with fallen stone. At one point, after doubling back for the third time, I called out to stop the men in the lead.

"Hold up. This is useless."

Sela glared back at me. "We need to keep moving," she hissed.

I pushed Ruena behind me and walked forward, glaring at the old woman. "You brought me along because I'm a master thief. Maybe you should listen to me."

She looked like she wanted to rip my heart out and eat it, but instead she nodded and stepped back. "Fine. Lead the way, thief."

"First," I said, looking around at the walls, "we need to get our bearings." Picking my route, I walked over to a tumble of stone against a wall that was as tall as a building. I reached out and set a hand to the debris, shivering at how cold it was even though the air around us was warm.

I climbed up, testing each hold before putting my weight on it. The broken stones kept shifting, sometimes threatening to roll out from under me entirely, but I managed to get to the vertical part of the climb. That was the easier part, as the stones were still locked together and didn't move as much. I finally got a hand on top of the wall and pulled myself up, swinging a leg over and straddling it.

I looked out over the labyrinth from about twenty feet up, and what little moonlight breached the haze bounced off stone and left the paths in shadow. I could see blue-rimmed gateways dotted throughout the landscape like blazing mouths, reflecting off that same haze and casting their glow everywhere. There were so many more than I'd ever seen. Hundreds of them. The magic they put off was prickling continually on my skin, but I was getting used to it, letting it fade into the background of my senses.

I'd spent many years on the rooftops of Sangarie, and I could read the city like a map. It didn't take more than a few moments to recognize the landmarks. I could trace the lines of the districts, pinpoint the docks and the market squares, and follow the widest streets, which looked like rivers of darkness from my position. With the collapsed rooftops spread out around me, my heart tightened.

This wasn't a labyrinth from the ancient past. This was Sangarie, ruined and dead.

Chapter 40

A voice came from the group below, and I looked to see them all peering up at me.

The knight spoke again. "Well?"

I looked out over the city, and back the way we'd come. The gateway must have sent us to the ruined version of the warehouse courtyard. If I looked where I remembered the baroness's manorhouse rising over the walled Estates, I could see the dark outline of it now. That was the center of Sangarie.

Here and there movement caught my gaze, but when I tried to focus on it, there was nothing. The shadow was so complete between the ruined buildings that anything could be moving in there. In places, the shadow seemed too deep. Impossibly large to be cast by the ruins around it.

Like it was a thing of its own.

I shuddered and swung my leg back over the wall to make my way down, sliding the last few feet and dusting myself off. "This is Sangarie."

Everyone stared at me blankly, and the knight finally responded. "We *were* in Sangarie, yes. I thought you were supposed to be the smart one."

"No, *this* is Sangarie." I glared at the mystic. "I don't know how, but this is the city. It's been destroyed."

Sela stared at me with narrowed eyes. "What trick are you playing?"

"I've walked these streets my whole life," I snapped. "I think I'd recognize the layout."

The knight looked back and forth between us. "So it's not an ancient labyrinth. That makes it easier. We know where we're going."

I looked at him incredulously. "Easier?"

"Yes. We know our path."

T. Olsen

"The path isn't the problem. Have you ever been in Sangarie during the Night of Shadows?"

"I don't place much faith in superstition."

I walked up to him, waving my arm to indicate the ruined city. "What about this? Does this look like superstition?"

"It looks like magic."

I glared.

The armored man pointed at the manorhouse towering in the distance, addressing the rest of the group. "If this is Sangarie, then the center of it is the manor of the baroness. We go there." He turned and started down the ruined street with Waren and Culley following after him.

The mystic turned to follow as well, and Ruena started to walk past me but I pulled her back and called after the men. "Hey—knight! I'm not done here!"

He shouted back. "Time is short, thief."

"Lives are short!" I jogged forward, pushing past the men. I reached the knight and grabbed his shoulder, spinning him back around. "We need to think about this."

The man shrugged me off. "We need to complete this quest. I know where we need to go."

"I'm not going to blindly follow some mercenary in a tin suit."

"*Mercenary*? I'm a knight, and you need to learn some respect!"

"Look," I gestured back at the group, "we aren't the only ones here. There are things in this place we don't want to meet."

He shoved me back and I staggered on the uneven stones, but kept my feet.

Culley spoke up, his voice hesitant and wavering. "He's right. You don't want to meet what hides in this place."

The knight sneered, resting an armored glove over the hilt of his sword. "I don't need to sneak up on my enemies. The people here will know that Kincaid of Araneth is coming, and they should run or prepare to face me."

I let out a short laugh. "People? You think people are what's in here?" I turned and looked straight at Sela. "Did you tell him anything about this place, hag?"

She smiled, showing her teeth, but it was Kincaid that answered.

"She told me stories. Commoners are good at telling stories to scare themselves. They make up monsters in the dark and ancient curses to explain everything."

I snarled back. "I grew up on the rooftops of Sangarie with a good view of what happens on the streets below. Not all those rumors are made up."

He walked toward me, jabbing a gloved finger on my chest. "Real men don't skulk in the shadows or believe in bedtime stories. I told them you weren't needed." He jabbed me in the chest again, shoving me back half a step. "All I really need is someone to warn me of magic and someone to pick locks. You're a waste of time and effort."

"Then why am I even here?"

The knight sneered and pointed at Culley. "Because your stupid thief saw you here last time he tried to get the stone. So they think you're the key to reaching it this time."

I looked over at Culley, who was scowling into the shadows and pacing with nerves. He'd seen me here? His drunken muttering at the Black Bottle made a little more sense now, but I didn't know how he could have seen me in here, or even recognized me. Last time I was here I'd been smaller than Ruena.

The knight droned on. "But you're just a lazy, good-for-nothing criminal. I told them not to bother with you, that I could do it myself with just the little brat and that worthless lockpicker." He poked his finger into my chest one more time. "You can't even do things right on the other side of the gateway."

A knife was in my hand before the last word was out of his mouth, but I never got the chance to respond. From somewhere nearby came the clatter of stones crumbling from the walls, and the sound of something heavy scraping across the cobbles.

The entire group went silent, glancing warily around the ruined street. Ruena had grabbed hold of Nissa, who was quietly removing the girl's arms from around her waist and motioning for her to stay back. I stepped away from Kincaid and spun in place, staring out into the darkness.

A distant scream made the hair rise on the back of my neck. It sounded like a person, and I thought about the thousands of blue portals I'd seen from high up on the wall. How many people had wandered into this place, and were even now trying to survive against the monsters I knew were out there?

A rock the size of my fist bounced out of an alleyway, skittering to a stop in our midst. We all looked in that direction, and Waren drew a wickedly curved knife. He motioned Kincaid forward with him, and the two faced the alley, waiting for something to come out. My traitorous thief fumbled a short sword from his belt, but didn't move.

I glanced at Nissa as she came up beside me, holding her polearm. She whispered in the flowing language of the elves, and a glow started on the blade. As she brought it forward and held it with both hands across the front of her body, the blade curved and lengthened, the metal glowing a brilliant green as it slithered and stretched.

She stopped chanting and the glow dimmed somewhat, but didn't go out. The blade was now a deadly-looking scythe, at least three feet long and extending in a graceful curve away from the wooden shaft. I could feel the increased magic from a few feet away, adding to the prickling sensation from just being in this place.

She looked over at me, her face glowing eerily in the light of the blade. "Shadows can only be defeated with light."

"At this point," I said, "there's nothing that could make this place worse." I turned my head, searching out Ruena.

She had her back to us a few paces away, and was staring out into the dark city, shifting her gaze between two directions. I narrowed my eyes. "Rue?"

She didn't respond. Nissa turned to keep both the girl and the alley in her sights, nodding faintly at me. I walked quietly up behind the girl and repeated softly, "Rue?"

She wrapped her arms around her chest, hugging herself and shaking her head. "They're watching."

I looked out in the direction she was staring, feeling a shiver run down my spine. Reaching a hand out, I rested it lightly on her shoulder. "Rue, what do you see?"

She shook her head. "Trails in the dust. Lights in the shadows."

The hair on the back of my neck stood up. I was about to lead her back to Nissa's side when she jumped against my chest. "It's coming!" she squeaked, pushing me back.

I staggered backward as she pushed against me, staring out into the darkness with my heart pounding. My mouth had gone dry and my hand tightened around the handle of my knife. "Where? I don't see anything!"

She pointed at a dark hole in the side of a ruined building, grabbing my shirt and swinging around behind me. I looked, but there wasn't anything there. My fingers flexed on the knife handle and I shook the stiffness out of my arm, not sure the weapon would be any use against the monsters here.

Nissa came up beside me, her scythe held ready.

The creature wasn't completely invisible. When it finally moved I saw it like a mirage against the surrounding darkness. The form resembled that of a bull-man that lumbered forward on its hind legs, arms twice as long as they should be so they dragged on the broken cobbles. It seemed to have no color of its own, and I knew if it stayed still, it'd disappear from sight again.

I pushed the girl behind me, scrambling out of its reach, but it didn't advance. It hovered at the edge of the circle of red light cast by the mystic's staff, its claws scraping along the ground as it paced. It made no other sound, not even a growl or a grunt. The silence was filled only by the scraping of claw against stone—and the uneasy movements of our party.

Sela let out a wheezing laugh. "It works. The staff works!"

It repels them. I edged closer to the hag, more afraid of the creature in the shadows than an old woman's magic. The shadowbeast sniffed the air and abruptly backed out of the edges of the light. I strained my eyes but I couldn't even catch a glimmer of movement. It was gone.

Sela turned and started walking toward the baroness's manorhouse. "We should go. Others will come."

Culley whispered in the silence. "She's right. Let's keep moving."

I sheathed my knife and joined Ruena in trailing behind the mystic and the three men. Nissa drew up beside me, her polearm once again a normal soldier's weapon. I gazed carefully at it, noticing the tiny runes engraved into the blade. From farther away they would have seemed nothing more than decorative edging. The wooden shaft was a varnished red, showing whorls of darker knots, but it was simple and unadorned. The magic must be in the blade itself.

She noticed my attention and brought the weapon forward, twisting it to reflect the moonlight. "It was given to me by my grandfather. He fought darkness, too, in a different place."

I resisted the urge to flinch away from the magic I could feel leaking out of it. "Creatures like that one?"

"No, but all shadows fear the light, no matter their source."

Chapter 41

I kept my gaze on the street around me, watching for the blue glow of gateways, but I glanced often at Ruena. I was guessing she'd see the danger with her magic eyes long before I would. As for *my* senses, the uncomfortable tingle of the magic surrounding us was so constant it had become a dull prickle, like an ache you just grew used to.

As we walked, we passed very close to two gateways, and I swore I could see the real streets of Sangarie on the other side of each of them.

Ahead of me, Ruena tripped and fell to her knees. I reached forward to help her up, but she scrambled back into my legs, staring at the ground where she'd fallen.

The red glow of Sela's staff revealed the upper half of a man. Everything below the waist was missing, and one arm was gone. The light shone off a puddle of blood and viscera, and with my next breath I could smell it and gagged.

I scooped Ruena up, setting her on her feet and urging her past it. "Don't look."

The man had looked normal enough, other than the mangled state of his body. Middle-aged. Common clothes in an outdated style. Had he wandered through a gateway and found a tragic end? So many screams drifted on the wind in this place... If they all were unfortunate visitors, why so many? People knew better.

Most people.

Nobody spoke, but everyone walked a little closer to the mystic. We avoided the gateways as much as possible, but they seemed to be everywhere. So many more than I'd ever seen on the streets. Some of them looked out onto a Sangarie that bothered me. The buildings didn't fit quite right, and the styles were wrong. One showed a farmer's garden plot where I knew I should be seeing a line of darkened shops.

When Ruena grabbed my arm again, I nearly jumped out of my skin. I took a deep breath to calm myself and looked down at her. She pointed into an alley, her face pinched in the light of the mystic's glowing red staff.

I followed her gesture and squinted, trying to see if there was more depth to the shadows there. Nissa looked as well, frowning.

A scraping noise set my teeth on edge, and stones crumbled from the walls on either side of the narrow corridor. The noise came again after a short pause, as if something massive was inching its way forward. I backed up, still peering into the alley in an effort to see what I faced.

Nissa's voice whispered beside me and her blade began to glow.

A fast clacking noise came from the alley, as if the glowing weapon had angered something hidden there. I recognized that noise. My gut clenched in fear and my heart thudded hard against my ribs.

I dragged Ruena closer to the red light of the mystic's staff. Then the clacking noise grew louder, and the stone walls at the mouth of the alley groaned as shadowy tentacles wrapped around the corners and spilled out onto the street directly into the pool of red light, without hesitation.

"*Run!*" I grabbed Ruena's hand and took off in the opposite direction, nearly pulling her completely off her feet.

Nissa and the men sprinted after me, and Sela shimmered before her form shot like a falling star past us, appearing again a few blocks down in front of me and Ruena. She gazed back at the thing crawling out of the alley, her wrinkled face pale and frightened.

I ran past her.

Ruena strained to keep up with me, and when she tripped and reached out her free hand to break her fall, I dragged her back to her feet. Nissa drew up beside me, glancing back over her shoulder. "It will catch us."

I nodded and began looking for a place to escape, to hide. The knight was right about one thing, thieves liked to skulk in the shadows. If it kept me alive I'd crawl into whatever hole I fit in.

A pair of dark tentacles shot between me and the elf, then swept to either side. I leaped more from instinct than anything, vaulting over it. Ruena didn't jump, and the writhing shadow caught her and pulled her back, ripping her hand out of mine.

"*No!*" I twisted to grab for her and landed hard on the street in the dust and ash. The tentacle lifted up and I scrambled to my feet and launched myself toward her. My fingers brushed the bottom of her boot and I dropped back down and fell to the cobbles.

I gasped for air, vaguely aware of Nissa sprawled on the ground nearby. My gaze wasn't drawn to her, though. It was drawn to the sight we'd been running from.

Towering over the walls of the street behind me was a creature of nightmare. It looked like one of the giant monsters from stories told by sea merchants, a shapeless body the size of a three storey building that shifted in and out of sight as it moved through the shadows, dozens of tentacles long enough to wrap entirely around a market square and waving in the air like they had minds of their own. The clacking noise came from somewhere below the body, where the giant maw waited.

The old fear took hold. I wanted to cower... to run... to scream... but I forced myself to stand firm.

Well... to stand.

I was shaking like a little kid and my hands were clenched into white-knuckled fists. I *wanted* to run to where Nissa was getting to her feet, using her polearm like a staff, but my legs just shook.

Waren and Culley ran past me, their faces white with fear. I had the urge to follow them, get as far away from this monster as I could. Instead I cursed, taking a deep breath and grinding my teeth as I all but threw myself into a stumbling jog to Nissa's side, shaking enough to make my teeth rattle.

Ruena screamed and the sound told me she was a good ways above the ground, but I refused to look. Instead I drew both knives and went to stand back to back with the elf, trying not to hyperventilate. I couldn't leave Rue.

One of the tentacles darted toward me and I raised my hand, the knife held backwards in my fist, and stabbed it as I shoved it aside. The knife met no resistance, but my fist deflected the tentacle up and over my head. Out of the corner of my eye I saw the flash of the elf's blade, but I couldn't spare a better look. I was sure she was doing better than I was at any rate.

I sliced at another tentacle as it whipped out at me, but my blade passed through it like smoke, throwing me off balance so I stumbled backward into Nissa. She staggered, but didn't fall, and I caught myself.

285

A battle cry came from closer to the monster's body mass and I risked a glance to see Kincaid charging the creature.

I couldn't help but feel a small desire to see the monster eat him.

Another tentacle came sweeping straight at me, and while I thought I could dodge it, I knew it'd carry through and hit Nissa in the back if I moved. I spun and grabbed her around the waist, diving for the cracked cobblestones. The tentacle passed over close enough to brush the fabric of my vest.

Nissa scrambled out from under my arm, bringing her scythe around. "This is not working! We need to get out of here!"

I pushed myself to my feet and stared into the dark sky above the monster where most of the tentacles waved, fighting back panic at the sight. "Not without Rue." I wouldn't lose her, too. I wouldn't.

She sighed, but nodded.

I clamped my teeth shut, taking a deep breath through my nose and slipping my knives into the sheaths at my back. Steeling myself, I glanced at the elf. "Can you cut her down? I'll catch her."

"Yes, if we can get close enough."

I started walking toward the monster, my muscles vibrating with stress. "Rue!" A tentacle swiped at me and I rolled across the pavement, coming back up and darting closer. Every instinct I had was telling me to turn and run. "*Rue!*"

A hoarse scream came from above and to the right, near the wall of crumbling buildings. I broke into a run, staring up at the darkness above where flashes of light shone off rubbery skin.

A tentacle shot toward me and I dove over it, rolling over my shoulder and coming back to my feet. "Rue! Where are you?"

"*Gray! Help me!*"

I peered up into the dark and caught sight of a flailing leg. "Elf!"

She stepped up beside me. "My name is Nissa, human."

I ignored her and pointed. "There, do you see her?"

She ran forward, following the tentacle with her eyes, and leaped into the air swinging her scythe. The blade glowed more brightly as it struck the rubbery skin and cut clean through it.

I watched the entire tentacle falling, and its grip on the girl loosened enough for her to squirm free. I reached up as both fell on me, knocking me to the ground.

The feeling of the tentacle on top of me, even dead and unmoving, nearly drove the sense right out of me. I rolled the girl off my chest and kicked the rubbery flesh away, scrambling back and breathing fast and shallow. One of Nissa's slender hands came into my vision and I grabbed it and let her pull me to my feet.

"Go!" she shouted.

I grabbed Ruena's hand and ran. We ducked into an alley, out of sight of the monster, and continued to run through the streets until I no longer heard the clacking of the jaws or the sound of stones being crushed by the tentacles.

After we'd stumbled to a stop, I let go of Ruena and leaned forward with both hands on my knees, breathing hard. I looked back to see Kincaid clatter to a stop behind us. Sela was nowhere in sight.

Kincaid staggered forward. "What *was* that thing?"

I glared at him. "A bedtime story."

Nissa spoke up from my other side. "It was a shadowkraken."

"And it's *exactly* why we have to get out of here." I turned to get my bearings. "If we can make it back to the gateway we came through, maybe we can surprise the guards on the other side."

The darkness in front of me flashed and Sela staggered to a stop, propelled by her magic. She stepped close, raising her glowing red staff and glaring at me. "Did you think you could just run away? That you could escape that easily?" Her gnarled hand shot up to grab for me and her fingers brushed my temple as I jerked back, but it was enough.

I clamped my teeth shut just as the pain hit and dropped to my knees, screaming with my hands on either side of my head. Some part of me realized the noise was a bad thing, but I couldn't stop. It was like the screams were being ripped from me by the magic, or maybe it was just my own body trying to keep my head from bursting from the pressure.

When the pain finally stopped, I still heard screaming. As I knelt on the broken cobbles, I was pretty sure I wasn't making the noise. I looked up, letting my eyes regain their focus, and saw the old hag standing over Nissa now. That's where the screams were coming from.

I growled low in my throat and reached for one of the knives at the small of my back. With a twist of my upper body, I threw it directly at the mystic, watching in disbelief as it lodged in her back with a solid thunk.

Deep down, I'd assumed her magic would protect her from such simple attacks.

The screaming died out as her control fell apart. She turned and raised her eyes slowly to mine, fury burning inside them. "I... curse..." she gasped.

I made the sign against evil, scrambling up and backing away from her as she toppled. The staff hit the ground and the red crystal shattered into a thousand pieces across the broken cobbles.

Chapter 42

In the silence that followed, it was easy to hear Ruena's sniffles, and the click of Nissa's scythe as she set it to the stone and climbed to her feet. The shadows on the street behind them shimmered.

My gut tightened and I took half a step toward them. "Behind you!"

Nissa spun and met the slashing claws of the shadow creature with the blade of her scythe. It snarled in her face, its muzzle curled back over pale teeth. The claws wrapped around the blade, keeping her from using it and pushing down at her.

Her arms were shaking from holding the beast back and I darted forward, taking advantage of the beast's distraction to stab one of my knives up into its unprotected belly.

My knife disappeared into the flesh like it wasn't even there, and the beast didn't react at all. I sliced sideways with the knife, watching it cut through the hide like smoke, and leaving no trace of damage.

It finally flung the elf's scythe away, and her with it. She landed a few paces back, scrambling to her feet.

I backed up a step as the creature turned to growl at me. My heart thumped hard against my chest and I gripped my useless knife tighter, holding it in front of me. When the beast lumbered toward me I slashed at its muzzle and staggered as it slid right through with no resistance.

The claws swiped down and I threw myself back, barely avoiding them. With another roar, the creature gathered itself and leaped. I tried to get out of the way, but a heavy claw smacked me to the ground and drove the breath from my lungs. My knife skittered across the cobbles and I squirmed, acutely aware of the claws flexing on my chest and the breath like hot smoke in my face.

Ruena's scream came from where Sela's body had crumpled. My eyes darted that way and I saw Kincaid carrying the struggling girl in his

289

arms, her feet kicking in the air. He was following Culley and Waren as they headed down the street.

She reached out with one hand. "*Gray!*"

I gritted my teeth and heaved at the arm above me, but it had me pinned. Its other claw came up and spread wide in preparation to crush my head.

A cry from Nissa made it bring its head up and the scythe slammed down to lodge in its back. With a squeal of pain it dissolved into smoke. The scythe dropped as the beast disappeared and I flinched, but the elf stopped it a few inches from my heaving chest.

I shuddered, then pushed the blade aside and stumbled to my feet. There was no sign of the knight, the men, or the girl. I took a few heavy steps in the direction I thought they'd gone, but Nissa grabbed my arm and pulled me up short.

"Do not run into the dark with no weapon."

I shrugged her off. "I have to go after her!"

"You will die."

Dropping my gaze, I raised both hands to rub at my face. "Shit."

The elf crossed to where the mystic's body lay, kneeling to rummage in her ragged clothing. "Why do you care so much? She is not yours."

I ran my fingers through my hair, and the dusty remains of the beast drifted to my shoulders. "I promised I'd take care of her. Besides, she's just a kid." I searched the ground for my knife.

"They said you were a criminal."

The light of the elf's scythe flashed on steel at the base of a fallen archway. I walked over and picked it up, shoving it back into the sheath at the small of my back. "I am."

She stood up, gazing at me over the mystic's body and brushing the dust from her knees. Two knives and a pouch were in her hands. She slipped the pouch into a bag slung across her chest as she crossed the broken cobbles to me. She handed me back my knife, red with the blood of the mystic on the blade, and held the other up. "This has magic. It might work better than the ones you carry."

I gritted my teeth as I took it. The hilt was bone, and the blade silver, etched with runes and sharpened on both sides. The balance was wrong, and it felt warm and tingling in my hand, even over the constant thrum of magic here. My first instinct was to throw it away, but I sighed and tucked it behind my belt.

"Gray—"

"I know all the reasons not to follow them. If you want to go back, I'm sure you can retrace our steps. I'm sorry I can't help you with the guards on the other side of the gateway, but I can't leave her in here."

Nissa walked forward coolly, passing me by. The light from her weapon moved against the walls around us. "They likely went toward the manor. The knight will want to finish his quest."

I jogged a few steps to catch up to her, pacing her. "You don't have to."

She arched her eyebrow. "I will find my destiny there."

I walked in silence, keeping eyes and ears alert for any sign of the monsters roaming the ruined city. The magical scythe gave me a bubble of brighter light to see by, but it made me feel like a target in the darkness.

Nissa spoke, the words mumbled as if she were speaking to herself. "So much destruction of life."

"What do you suppose this place is?" I waved a hand toward the manor rising over the ruined buildings ahead of us and to the right. "I mean it's obviously Sangarie, but not the real Sangarie."

"It is real."

"It can't be real, the real Sangarie is back there, through the gateways. Besides, this place only appears one night a year."

The elf bent to pick up a chunk of broken stone, holding it out to me as we walked. "Is this not real?"

My eyes narrowed at having my words thrown back at me. "It could be a trick. Maybe it's some kind of illusion."

"That would take too much power." She tossed the stone aside.

"Then what is it?"

"I do not know, and that makes me uneasy."

I grunted. "Welcome to the party."

We passed a wide, dark street and dust blew past, carrying with it the scent of smoke and ash. A high-pitched scream came from far off in the darkness. I looked over my shoulder, the hair on my neck and arms standing up.

I heard the creak of leather just before the elf barreled into me, knocking me to the ground as a black tentacle whooshed over my head. My heart jumped into my throat and I scrambled out from under her arm, pulling the little silver dagger and searching for the body of the shadowkraken. It filled the large street we had just passed by, heaving itself forward now with writhing tentacles, some of which were nothing more than oozing stumps. The same one we'd fought before?

Nissa rushed past me, swinging the glowing scythe over her head and screaming in elfish.

I clenched my hand on the mystic's knife. I had survived as a thief because I trusted my instincts and knew when to run away. Every thread of sense I had was telling me to run away now, and not stop running until I was back in my own Sangarie. I watched the elf leap onto a tumbled chunk of wall and launch herself into the air, doubling up with the strength of the next swing and slicing open a nearby shadowy tentacle.

I was a damned fool. I darted forward, sliding under a flailing tentacle and cutting deep into the rubbery flesh as I went by. I twisted on the other side and ran for the main body, hoping the tentacles wouldn't be as maneuverable close to the base. I could hear the monster's maw clacking, and did my best to shut out the part of my mind that was sobbing in terror at the sound.

The light of Nissa's blade brightened and dimmed as she fought, making it hard for me to see the flailing monster properly. I dodged an appendage that smashed into the street beside me, and another that swooped over me. I was just a few paces away from the main body now, and I wondered what I was going to do when I got there.

A thickly muscled shadow darted in and wrapped itself around my waist, lifting me off my feet. I cried out in surprise and the knife nearly slipped out of my hand when I was dragged backwards off the ground. As the monster's grip tightened, I gritted my teeth and stabbed the tentacle with the knife. It spasmed and tightened even more, forcing my breath out in a wheezing rush and making my ribs creak. My stomach flipped as it turned me upside down and raised me higher. I stabbed again.

Then it let go and I was falling. I twisted in the air, seeing movement beneath me. Flinging my arms out, the knife gripped tightly in one hand, my chest hit a tentacle. I immediately started slipping off and scrambled to get a grip on the leathery skin. The enchanted knife bit deep and I angled it like a hook to stop myself falling.

The tentacle quivered, then bucked beneath me. I hooked a leg over it and gripped the handle of the knife in both hands as the blade was jerked through the flesh. The thick tentacle moved in a wave and I rode it as I dug the knife in. The metal sliced it open like gutting a fish and it jerked, flinging me off in a shower of whatever black, oozing fluid passed for blood in the creature.

My back hit a solid chunk of stone wall and the breath was forced out of my lungs again, then I fell to the pile of rubble at the base of the wall. I shook my head to clear it. I still clutched the knife in one hand, and the broken stone cut my other palm as I pushed myself up, but the dust and darkness prevented me from noticing much else. I choked as I tried to breathe, the rubble making it hard to keep my footing.

The shadowkraken clacked loudly and keened, then I heard the enormous creature retreating. I shoved the knife under my belt and used both hands to crawl to the edge of the debris.

Nissa walked toward me, her scythe glowing green. "Your fighting style is reckless."

I slipped on a loose stone and sprawled in the rubble, cursing and holding an arm across my ribs. "Yeah, well I'm used to fighting *people*, not monsters."

She reached out a hand and I took it as I looked up at her, then froze. This was the face from my nightmares, dripping black ooze from pointed ears and chin. She was drenched in it, and her large elfish eyes shone out from her face, glowing emerald in the green light of the magical weapon.

Chapter 43

My voice broke. "You—"

"Are covered in ichor. Yes, I am aware."

My heart raced and my thoughts went in circles trying to explain what I was seeing. All these years... I had told myself it wasn't real, that it was a fever dream or a nightmare. But the figure I'd seen in the labyrinth as a child stood before me right now. This elf—how could she have been there?

A thin scream echoed through the street and I flinched. A child's scream. Much too young to be Ruena.

Nissa looked in the direction it had come from, then at me, stepping back and pulling her scythe around. "Get up. We have to keep moving."

I shook my head and scrambled off the rubble, staggering to my feet and wincing at the pain that shot through my back. "You can't be—"

The scream came again and everything snapped into place in my mind. "No." I looked at her again and then in the direction of the screaming, in the opposite direction of where we were meant to be going. "No no no."

I took off at a run down the street. *Years ago, before I'd joined the guild and when I still lived on the streets, I'd been very brave and very stupid.*

I jumped a crumbled pile of stone and darted into what had once been an alley, hearing the elf close behind me. The alley was choked with splintered beams and debris, and one beam rested like a ramp along the side wall. I leaped onto it and ran up, scrambling onto the top of a broken wall. In the dark I could barely see the narrow stretch of stone under my feet.

A gateway had opened in an alley on the Night of Shadows, and I'd taken a dare from the older kids to step inside. I remembered the sound

294

of clacking in the darkness. Turning around and seeing the monster made of waving arms of shadow, coming closer.

There was the courtyard and the shadowkraken that had so recently fled from us, just as they were in my nightmares. I stumbled on a loose block, putting a hand down to catch my balance, then sprinted for where the wall ended in darkness.

I remembered a man leaping from above to attack the monster. A man with dark hair and a scruffy chin—wearing a vest—wielding only a knife.

Planting my foot on the last six inches of wall, I leaped for the monster with the mystic's knife in my hand.

I hit the main body and the wind was knocked from me as pain spiked across my back, but I focused on the knife as it stuck in the leathery hide. My weight was ripping at the wound and I shifted the blade enough to let the sharp edge slice into the flesh. It opened and gushed fluid as I slid down the side of the monster. Once it realized what was happening it shook itself and my knife popped out of the widening hole, dropping me to the street below.

I landed hard on my feet and fell backward, feeling the shock all the way to my knees. The stones were slick with ichor and a tentacle was coming down on me faster than I could get out of the way. I flung my arm up as a flash of light followed the tentacle, and when it landed, it wasn't with the crushing force I expected, but a dead weight.

I heaved it aside and scurried to my feet, looking toward the blue glow of the gateway tucked back in an alley. A child stood at the edge of the courtyard, frozen in fear, dressed in rags with a shaggy mop of dark hair.

I was a scrawny little brat back then.

I remembered seeing the dark figure with glowing green eyes— though I hadn't known what she was then. *I remembered her throwing lightning—* although the part of my brain that was putting everything together realized it was the glowing scythe I'd seen, flashing through the darkness. *Then I remembered seeing the tentacle coming at me, and a man shoving me out of the way.*

I ran for my younger self, catching sight of the tentacle waving at the edge of my vision. I snatched up the boy and dove out of the way, my free hand cradling his head as we rolled beneath the flailing appendage.

It was like I'd wrapped myself around a bolt of lightning. Heat and magic flared between us. I tensed, expecting to be burned to ash like one of the shadow monsters, but the sensation merely left me curled around the unconscious boy in my arms with magic pulsing through me in waves.

I tasted blood in my mouth. Nissa screamed, a high wailing that set my teeth on edge. I eased the boy onto the blackened cobbles and got to my knees, gasping at a sudden sharp pain in my ribs and bracing myself as I took a couple of breaths. The magic was dizzying.

I tapped the boy's cheeks, smeared with ash and tears. "Hey kid."

His eyes fluttered open and he stared up at me in confusion and terror.

The gateway. I had to get him through the gateway and back to Sangarie where he—where I belonged.

I forced myself to my feet and grunted in pain, but grabbed the boy's arm—my arm—and dragged him toward the glowing blue gateway. Memories made vivid by the rush of adrenaline gave me the confused sense of being myself and being him at the same time. My hand was soon numb to the elbow from the magic sparking between us. I wanted to say something, to warn myself about the mystic or about being an idiot and killing a baroness's son, but I caught sight of the shadowkraken lunging toward us and shoved the boy toward the light. "Go!"

The tentacle swept through and I had time to tuck my head behind my raised arms before it hit me. I slid and rolled across the cobbles, coming to rest on my back and thinking about just letting the monster squish me. My chest hurt when I breathed and every part of my body ached.

At least the painful pulse of magic was fading now that I wasn't so close to the kid.

"Gray!"

Shit. I rolled to my knees and searched the darkness of the market square for Nissa. The shadowkraken was forcing its bulbous body into an alleyway, multiple tentacles waving ichor-spraying stumps. With a clacking and hissing, it sank away into the dark. Nissa ran toward me.

I sat back down and pressed on my lower right ribs, breathing carefully. She stopped in front of me and looked at the gateway glowing from the alley.

"Did the small human go in there?"

I nodded. He'd be heading toward May's by now, sobbing and sure the monsters were chasing him.

And from that night on, he'd be able to feel magic. I flexed my fingers, shaking off the last of the numbness. Fuck. I'd done it to myself.

She stared at me, streaks of ichor on her face where she'd tried to wipe it off. "You are acting strange, even for a human."

I chuckled and immediately regretted it as pain shot through my chest. "You have no idea." I put a hand on the broken cobbles and lurched to my feet, taking her offered shoulder.

"Are you badly injured?"

"A few broken ribs, thumped head, enough bruises I'll turn purple by morning."

She wiped the ichor from her cheeks with the bottom of her cloak. "If you can not walk, you can not fight."

I let go of her shoulder and turned toward the center of the city, holding my forearm across my ribs. "I'll be fine. Let's go."

She followed me, her polearm tapping against the street but her footfalls silent. If it wasn't for the sound of the weapon against stone I wouldn't have known she was there.

How was it possible this was the same place that had traumatized me as a child? Loring had said to return to the gateway in the courtyard if I wanted to come back home. Had they sent us back in time to fetch the stone? If I went through the wrong gateway would I find myself in the Sangarie of my youth?

I stumbled on a loose cobblestone and swore under my breath, riding out the shooting pain in my ribs. When Nissa gripped my arm I jumped in surprise and glared at her.

"We should stop and tend your ribs at least." She dragged me to the side where a chunk of wall had fallen into the street and I had no choice but to follow. Pressing me to sit, she pulled her satchel forward and rummaged inside. She brought out the little tin of bone mending ointment. "Lift your shirt."

"I don't think—"

"Do not argue. There is no time. We have to be out of this place by morning."

Sighing, I loosened my vest and pulled the bottom of my shirt up as far as I could. The touch of her hand was gentle, but the ointment was cold and I flinched when it hit bare skin.

She paused and raised an eyebrow at me.

I breathed through my teeth and sat with my back straight, refusing to meet her eyes. She worked quickly, massaging the salve into the skin over my ribs. At first I had to grit my teeth with the pain, but it quickly numbed into a dull ache, then was gone entirely. Even with the constant tingle of the magic in the air, I could feel the specific pulse of the healing salve at work.

"Did I get it all?"

I nodded, my brow creasing. "It doesn't even hurt anymore."

"It is elf magic. The ointment binds together what is broken. With a little help," she wiggled her greased fingers at me, "it works more quickly."

"I see." I touched my bare skin, feeling the oily slickness and rubbing it between my fingers. Taking a deep breath, I found no pain at all. I dropped the bottom of my shirt. "Elf magic, huh?"

"Do you have any other injuries?"

"Bruises. They'll be fine."

Nissa put the little box away. "You do not like my magic."

"I don't like any magic."

"Why?"

I stood and straightened my clothes, grimacing at the ichor that streaked my pants and had soaked into the fabric of my vest. I glanced in the direction we'd come from, where I could still catch a faint blue glow from the darkness. "Magic has brought me nothing but trouble."

She stood and followed me as I started off again. "Magic is a part of life," she said.

I snorted, making sure not to outpace her because her polearm was the only thing lighting my way unless I stayed close to the gateways, and I didn't want to do that. "Magic is unnatural. It's a perversion of life."

"Not elf magic."

I pointed to the left, where a gateway glowed blue in an alley. "That isn't natural."

Nissa sighed. "This place is an abuse of magic. It is a human creation."

298

"How do you know that?"
"Because an elf would have closed the gateways."

Chapter 44

I left her comment alone and led her onto what had once been Market Street, weaving my way through the disturbingly familiar city. Once in a while the street was blocked with debris and we had to circle around on the side streets, but it was easier going than anyplace else had been. With each passing minute I grew more and more uneasy, my shoulders tense and my eyes darting everywhere.

It was the emptiness. Sangarie was a bustling place, and even at night there were beggars stationed to keep an eye on things, and lights shining out from under doors. Here, there was nothing but far-off screams and the feeling of being watched. Occasionally we'd find a fresh body, but never any that were more than a few hours old. At times I heard a terrified sobbing drifting from the surrounding ruins.

Eventually the wall separating the estates of the nobility from the surrounding city loomed above us. I stood before the west gate, staring at the mangled slabs of metal that had been the gates themselves now flat on the street. A pile of rubble in the opening blocked the way, and a dark splatter of blood was at the base of it.

Nissa stepped up beside me. "There are other gates?"

"Yes, and secret doors, but it will take time to reach them and there's no guarantee they won't be ruined too." I peered up the wall, taking note of the crumbling stone. "I don't suppose you have a rope in that bag?"

"Should that not be a tool of *your* trade, thief?"

"It's not something I keep in my pocket, and they didn't let me go shopping before we left." I motioned her to follow as I picked my way to the left of the gate. "Can you climb?"

"Of course."

I nodded and scrambled up the debris at the base of the wall, digging my fingers into the cracks between blocks that were even more prominent due to the damaged stone. The green of the scythe winked out as Nissa put it away to follow, leaving us to rely on the faint moonlight and the reflected glow of blue gateways.

It was an easy climb for me, even in near darkness. The mortar was loose and the damaged stones provided plenty of holds. I reached the top and eased over the edge of the parapet. The wall was over six feet thick and a narrow walkway stretched between the inner and outer parapets. It was intact, at least in this section.

There wasn't a lot of light, but the glow of the many portals was enough to give me a view over what had once been the estates of the most rich and powerful people in Sangarie. It looked like a terrible wind had come through and leveled everything.

The manors were little more than patches of rubble, smeared across their lawns in a radiating pattern, as if the wind had come from the baroness's house itself. The garden walls were mostly gone, and the streets seemed relatively clear, until I looked down at the base of the high wall I stood upon.

Blackened rubble had piled against the inside of the wall nearly to the top. A set of stairs that had once led down to the street level was buried. It stretched in a slope that extended at least a hundred feet out, peppered with broken stone and jagged pieces of timber. All the debris from the estates themselves, washed against the protective wall like so much trash on a riverbank.

I peered back over the side of the wall, searching for Nissa's cloaked form in the shadows. I could hear the fall of gravel as stones shifted under her weight and the occasional scrape of her boots. Her hand soon gripped the parapet beside me and she swung herself over.

I was impressed. "Are you sure you aren't a thief?"

"I have been climbing trees since your grandfather was suckling."

I chuckled and gestured at the debris that descended to the street. "How about climbing mountains?"

She unwound the polearm from the bag over her shoulder and activated the magic to send light across the slope. It cast dangerous pockets of shadow and made the timbers that stuck up look like snapped grave markers. I wasn't sure if it would help our decent or hinder it, but it was better than being in darkness.

We went carefully, not wanting to break an ankle in the rubble. Once at the bottom, it was just a matter of pushing through the scattered debris to the relatively cleared streets, then it was an easy walk toward the center. The wall surrounding the baroness's manorhouse remained standing in the distance, but large chunks of it were missing.

We walked in silence for a few minutes before Nissa looked at me again. "We may face our deaths in this place."

"Did that just occur to you?"

She grabbed my arm and pulled me to a stop, peering out from the streaks of ichor dried on her face like warpaint. "If we are to die here, I would like you to know my name."

"Your name isn't Nissa?"

Her nose crinkled and she pulled away her hood, revealing her snow white hair, braided tightly against her scalp and disappearing into the back of her cloak. Her ears swept up close to her head. "That is what humans call me."

I realized I was staring and flicked my gaze to our surroundings as a blush crept up my cheeks. "Well, I'm human."

"My people believe we are given strength in the next world by our names being spoken in this one after we die. I would like you to know my name, so if you survive this place you can speak it when you tell others what happened here."

I raised an eyebrow. "Oh."

"My given name is Nissephriana Silvertree."

"That's a mouthful."

She stiffened.

I held up my hands. "Sorry. I think this place is getting to me. I didn't mean to be rude."

"Say it, so I know you will remember it."

I repeated the name perfectly. My training as a thief had prepared me for remembering things when I needed to, no matter how little sense they made.

Nissa raised her eyebrow and nodded. "That is correct." She stared at me for a few moments, her head tilted to one side. "Do you want me to speak your name if you die?"

"Sure. Every great thief wants to be infamous."

"What is your full name then?"

I chuckled and continued walking. "It's just Gray."

She followed beside me. "The human girl said that was a nickname, like Nissa is for me."

"It is, but it's all I use."

"You claim no other name as true?"

"Nope."

"It is a strange name. How did you come by it?"

I shrugged. "I didn't have a name when I was a boy, or at least I don't remember it. One day I decided if I was going to make a name for myself as the greatest thief ever, I would need one."

"And you chose Gray?"

"Gods no. I chose The Black Viper. But the thieves at the Throat laughed and started calling me Gray. Said I wasn't good enough to be black anything yet. It stuck."

"Would you like me to remember you as The Black Viper?"

"No, it's a stupid name. Sounds like something a kid came up with."

Nissa smirked and shifted her grip on the polearm, sending shadows bouncing over the blasted lawns of the elite. We walked unchallenged to the manor's outer wall and I stopped a few paces from the gaping hole where the gate used to be. Through it, across a garden of blackened stumps of trees and ash-covered marble crushed to rubble, the manorhouse itself could be seen rising into the dark sky, surprisingly intact.

My gaze was pulled to a window on the second floor. It was as dark as the others. I half expected to see Firmin's light on, mocking me.

I wondered how much the lordling had known of Loring's plan. Was he as much of a pawn as I was, or had he gotten himself in too deep with someone with bigger ambitions? I was finding myself uncomfortably remorseful for killing the depraved bastard.

"Is something wrong?"

Nissa's lilting accent brought my attention back to the ruins. I stepped through the crumbled frame of the gate, my boots making popping noises on crushed stone despite my best efforts. "No. Nothing."

Nissa walked beside me up the cobbled path to the manor itself. Her blade was in her hands, lending a green glow to the stones. "You seem to be thinking about something that troubles you. It is not my concern, except we are on a dangerous quest and your inattention could prove fatal."

"It won't distract me."

"This place is already distracting you. You keep secrets."

I snapped back. "Want to stop and build a campfire so we can tell life stories?"

She narrowed her eyes and stopped. "It is blood."

My momentum carried me a few paces further before I stopped as well and glared back at her. "I said it's nothing. Just leave it alone."

She pointed at the ground between us.

I glanced down and saw a smear of blood on the cobbles, dark in the greenish light of the scythe.

Oh.

I knelt and ran a finger over it, smearing it across the stone. "That's fresh."

"I know not what stories haunt you, human. For now, set them aside."

"We need to get Rue and leave. Let me worry about what's rattling around in my head."

Chapter 45

We walked in silence to the front door of the baroness's manorhouse. In any other town it would have been called a castle, but the nobility of Sangarie styled themselves as modern, and had to set themselves apart.

The windows were mostly broken, and some of the roofs had holes showing black against the shadowed tiles that remained intact. A few parapets were caved in. The delicate architectural details had been crushed and sheared off, and there were huge scrapes down the sides of the building. It looked like something massive had been climbing all over it.

I swallowed the fear rising in my throat and dropped my gaze to the front door. One problem at a time.

Nissa whispered as she scanned the grounds. "This place fared better than the rest of the city."

"Somehow that makes me even more uneasy."

The double front doors, each five feet across, were open wide. One of them was askew on a single hinge. Past the doors was darkness, and Nissa muttered a few words under her breath to brighten the glow on her scythe. As I crossed the threshold, I peered to either side and winced at the echo of Nissa's scythe tapping on the marble floor, then chided myself for being ridiculous.

There were no Ironguard to rush out of the halls and arrest me. There was no baroness, and certainly no sadistic lordling. Just shadows and death.

I took the lead, pulling up my memory of the layout of the building. Footprints crisscrossed the dust coating the cracked marble floor—more than three men and a little girl could make. At the end of the front hall a grand double staircase rose to the second level, while an archway led to the audience hall beyond.

The building had mostly escaped whatever had destroyed the city, like the calm eye of a magical storm of destruction. Here and there I even saw signs of the panicked exodus that must have been underway. Furniture toppled, personal items dropped and trodden on, a discarded weapon coated in dust, doors ajar. Prints led off in multiple directions through the dust.

I peered down and slid a finger along one of the steps, pushing a path into an undisturbed layer of dust and ash. "The stairs haven't been used. Let's keep to this level for now." I dusted my finger off on my pants and followed the elf between the staircases, spinning to keep an eye out behind me.

As we passed through the arch, the terrified scream of a man came from the right side of the audience hall where another archway led into a corridor. I hurried in that direction with Nissa on my heels. The corridor contained a handful of closed doors before it widened into a library. A pedestal was in the center with a marble statue of a naked man barely covered by his flowing marble cloak, but a thick layer of dust hid most of the features. Four doors were spaced around the room, one of which was open.

At the sound of another scream, I went directly to the open door and saw a richly appointed sitting room where Waren was being driven to the ground by a shadow creature inside. Culley was groping along the wall, pulling on torch brackets and fixtures. Kincaid held Ruena with one hand and his sword with the other, urging the thief to hurry.

"Rue!"

The little girl twisted to look at me, trying to pry the knight's armored fingers from her forearm. "Gray!"

I darted inside, going for the knight rather than the creature busy ripping into the assassin's chest. Culley crowed and slammed a lamp bracket to the side, causing the paneling to slide open in front of him to reveal a descending stairway. He ducked inside immediately.

Kincaid looked at the shadow creature, then at me, and smirked. "Take care of that, would you?"

I roared as he ducked into the opening and ran to follow, but the shadow creature had finished its kill and leaped for me. I looked just in time to drop to the floor so the creature sailed over my head and crashed

306

into the wall beside me. I scrambled to my feet and away from the flailing claws.

"Down!"

I ducked as the glowing green scythe cut the air above me. It missed the creature, but forced it back to the wall again. I pulled out the magic dagger and launched myself toward the shimmering black belly of the monster, slicing open its gut. The scythe came down above me, lodging in the creature's chest, which stopped its forward motion. I scrambled out from under it as it turned to dust.

I ran for the secret passageway. "*Rue!*"

Nissa hissed behind me. "You will bring more monsters down on us, human."

I ignored her and darted into the opening, taking the uneven stone steps two at a time. This wasn't on the plans I'd memorized, but there was no time to pause and think about it. I turned with the walls, winding down into the belly of the manor, deep, deep into the ground.

At the last step it dropped into nothing. I caught myself at the edge of the stone and windmilled my arms to keep from pitching forward. Nissa caught the back of my vest and tugged me away from the edge, and I panted and looked across the twenty foot gap in the floor.

Nissa's voice was angry now. "You can not run blindly through this place."

I set a hand on the wall and nodded as I caught my breath. She was right. I was well beyond the point of catching them with speed and needed to pay attention to my surroundings. I didn't remember anything like this existing in the baroness's manor in *my* Sangarie, so it was either something the guild didn't know about, or something that didn't exist in my time.

I knelt and peered into the darkness of the pit. "Can you shine that scythe over here?"

In the green light of Nissa's weapon I could see the bottom, at least thirty feet down and littered with the remains of the broken floor and two bodies. Neither of them were Kincaid, Culley, or Ruena. The trap must have been sprung before they arrived.

A closer look at the walls revealed that the floor hadn't entirely crumbled away. There were solid chunks that stuck out like teeth from

307

the wall and could be navigated even by an armored knight dragging along a little girl. I stepped onto the first tooth.

Nissa followed me with ease, and in a few seconds we stood on the other side. It continued for about twenty feet, then branched in either direction. I peered around the corner, seeing small piles of rubble, along with more blood and corpses.

Nissa bent down and examined the floor. "They went this way. There are prints in the dust." She frowned. "This destruction looks recent, and caused by weapons."

I went a few paces in, checking the first body. It couldn't have been more than a few hours old. Upon closer inspection, the piles of rubble were hacked up statues. "I'm not sure I want to know what happened here."

Voices came from further ahead and I could make out Culley's whine. I motioned Nissa to follow and crept down the corridor, sliding along the wall as it curved. As I went, a prickling sensation started at my fingers where they touched the wall. I recognized it as the presence of magic, even over the general discomfort of the labyrinth. It was odd, feeling it coming from a wall. The corridor ended at an open door and I tightened my hand on my knife as I peeked around the corner.

Chapter 46

I noticed the treasure first. I was a thief after all. The light of half a dozen lamps reflected off silver, gold, and steel, and danced on the facets of gemstones of every color. It was piled on the floor, against the walls, spilling from boxes and bags. Enough wealth to take my breath away. The little boy in me wanted to squeal in delight.

Then I noticed the pulse of magic across my body had increased dramatically. It made sense that a treasury like this would have a significant amount of magic in it as well. It was strong enough to make my teeth ache.

My eyes slid past the treasure to the far wall. Kincaid stood with his arms crossed over his chest, watching Culley work on a lock in the middle of a massive door. The entire back wall, and the door itself, were gilded with lines of gold that met in the center at the lock. It traced intricate patterns on the stone wall. A man's body, stiff and purplish in color, was off to the side.

I saw no sign of Ruena.

I pulled back from the doorway and glanced at the elf. "She's not there."

"There is no place else. She must be there."

My brow furrowed and I flexed my fingers over the handle of my knife. "Let's go ask."

I took a deep breath and straightened up, then stepped out boldly into the middle of the doorway. "Hey, tin man, where's the kid?"

Kincaid turned to look at me, that entitled sneer spreading across his face again. He kicked a large trunk next to him and I could hear muffled cries from within.

I growled and took one step into the room before Nissa grabbed my arm and pulled me back. I shrugged her off, but didn't go any further. "Let her go. You have your treasure so you don't need her anymore."

"We're not here for treasure, we're here for the stone." He swung an arm toward Culley and the door. "And it's behind that."

I grunted. "Looks like you have a thief already. So you don't—"

A buzzing noise interrupted me and I glanced at the door. White sparks zipped along the gold lines that decorated the wall, and Culley suddenly stiffened and cursed. He jerked his hands away from the door and held them in front of him, staring at them in horror.

He began to breathe with heavy gasps, and dropped to the floor on a pile of scattered gold coins. When he turned to look at the knight I could see his face changing from red to purple, his tongue already so thick it was protruding from his lips. He reached toward the knight, but toppled over and wheezed a couple more times before he grew still.

I swallowed and clenched my jaw. Poison was never a good way to go. No thief in the guild ever wished that death on one of their own.

Kincaid let out an amused grunt. "Well. Maybe they were right about needing you after all." He sneered over his shoulder at me. "Your turn."

"I don't care about your stupid stone. Just give me the girl."

He lifted the lid of the trunk and Ruena straightened up, her eyes squeezed shut and her face streaked with tears. He grabbed her arm and set the point of his sword where her neck met her shoulder above the hanging goggles. "Get me the stone, and you can have her. Otherwise I'll just run her through now."

I narrowed my eyes. I didn't think I could throw a knife well enough to hit a weak point in his armor and kill him, and I wasn't fast enough to attack him hand to hand before he could kill Ruena. There was no waiting him out, because if the sun rose before we got back to the gateway we'd be trapped here. It was already getting late as it was.

Nissa stepped up beside me. "Can you open the door?"

"I don't know."

"Perhaps you should try."

I stuck the knife under my belt and walked to the door. Culley's body was still sprawled in front of it and I squatted beside him and looked at his hands without touching him. A large bead of blood in his palm was probably where the poison had entered.

I peered at the lock. There were no holes around it for needles to come from, so it must come out of the lock itself. The trap had been triggered twice, judging by the other body in the room, so it would reset itself.

Culley was not a very good criminal. He was lazy and cowardly, he had no social finesse, and a drunk bard could sneak up on him, but he could work a lock in his sleep. That didn't bode well for my chances.

Maybe something else was a factor in this trap. I ran my fingers over the edge of the locking mechanism, feeling the residual static from the lightning sparks that had run through parts of the wall when Culley triggered the poison, as well as a thread of magic. I was surprised I could pick it out with all the other sources making my hair stand on end.

Had the trap gone off before or after the sparks? I looked across the wall for the origin of the static, expecting to see some kind of magic writing or runes, but the gold lines were the only things that looked out of place. They were embedded into the stone like rope, and disappeared into the side walls.

I ran my finger along one of the lines, stopping when I reached a break. There was a deep, narrow groove in the wall there, as if someone had stabbed the wall to cut the line. As my finger bridged the space I felt a zap and jerked my hand away.

A knot of dread twisted my gut as I examined my hand, but there was no mark, no blood, and nothing seemed to be happening to me. I blew out in relief and thanked the Six. I ran my gaze across the lines and found three more places that had been broken. Maybe the trick wasn't to pick the lock. Maybe the door wasn't locked at all.

I stepped back to look for something to bridge the gaps in the lines, and realized the answer was all around me. I snatched a handful of coins out of a box and went to the first gap.

The coin wobbled, not quite filling the space. Cursing under my breath, I tried to wedge a second in beside the first, but that was too much. I backed up and looked for something else, and my eyes lit on a mound of the strange elfish coins that had been popping up the last few weeks. I scowled and picked up a tingling handful.

They were thicker than human coins.

I grumbled and jammed one of them into the gap. It fit like it had been slotted specifically for that reason. I fixed two more of the breaks, but when I slapped the fourth one in it zapped me again so that I cursed and shook my hand out.

But it worked. The lock turned on its own and the door split in two and separated, revealing a stone corridor about five feet wide and eight feet tall. I could see the corridor split further ahead, leading off in both directions.

Nissa stepped up beside me. "Impressive."

"Not really," I whispered, "I just didn't want to try that lock." I tossed the remaining elfish coins to the side.

Kincaid's voice came from behind us. "Bring me the stone, and you can have the girl."

I looked over my shoulder at the huddled form in the open trunk. One red-rimmed eye peeked out at me. Tears glistened there, and she was whimpering. I nodded encouragingly at her.

"Ok," I muttered. "Let's do this."

Chapter 47

I took a step into the corridor and light brightened around me. Not the wavering yellow glow of lamps, or the greenish glow of Nissa's scythe, but a cold white light that created sharp shadows. I didn't see a source for the light, it was just suddenly brighter. The prickling sensation of magic that had become so constant was joined by normal goosebumps.

The corridor was made of tightly fitted stone blocks, set together without mortar so that the only gap was at the gently rounded corners of the blocks. Even the floor was stone. I set my foot down on one and felt it give, heard a tiny click, and threw myself back just as three metal rods as big around as my little finger shot out from each side of the corridor. They quivered in the air in front of me, barely a handbreadth from my chest. They didn't quite meet in the middle, but it was close enough it wouldn't have mattered.

My heart thumped wildly against my ribs and I let out a breath as I set a shaking hand against the wall.

Nissa stepped around me and reached out to touch one of the rods. "I have seen this before."

I wanted nothing more than to turn around and leave, but a glance behind me showed Kincaid watching with a lazy smile from the treasure room, one boot propped on top of the now closed trunk. As I stared at him, he raised a gauntleted hand and shooed me onward.

"Where have you seen it?" I asked through clenched teeth.

Nissa bent to inspect the stone I had stepped on, now recessed a fingerwidth into the floor. "In an ancient elfish stronghold."

My brow furrowed and I moved to the wall where the rods stuck out of the little bit of space at the corners of the blocks. That same space was on every corner of every foot-long block, so there was no telling which ones held death behind them. "Why would elfish architecture be underneath the baroness's manorhouse?"

"I know not. But I would like to find out."

"You wouldn't perhaps like to go first, would you?"

She raised her white eyebrow at me, her emerald eyes steady. "You are the thief."

I sighed and scanned the wall ahead. "It was worth a shot." I crouched to move under the rods in front of me, then crept forward until I found the stone that triggered the next set. They sprang out with the sound of steel on stone and a muffled thunk behind the wall, then quivered in front of me like the others had. "This might take a while."

"I suggest you hurry. We have only a few hours until sunrise."

I made my way carefully through the corridor, examining the walls and the floor every inch of the way. When it branched off, I continued left, figuring it would keep things simple for finding my way back out.

In addition to the occasional wall trap, I discovered some that shot darts from the ceiling, and some that thrust long rods up from the floor. The floor rods had come up on either side of my foot, and I counted my thief's luck as the only thing that kept me from having my thigh impaled. Even so, I borrowed Nissa's polearm after that to explore the floor ahead of me. It buzzed in my hands, but it was better than being skewered.

We hit the end of the left turns and doubled back, checking the multiple right-side tunnels. None of the traps seemed to reset themselves, but I didn't want to take any chances, so it was slow going. After more than an hour we had crisscrossed a roughly square maze and found no doors other than the one leading back to the knight in the treasure room. There were no outlets.

There was, however, a life-sized relief of an elf on the side opposite the entrance, occupying its own shallow alcove. It was carved of the same stone as the blocks, and the expression on its face was full of sorrow.

Nissa stood before it, her jaw clenched, as I slid to the floor to lean against a wall. My back ached and my eyes watered from peering so closely at every crack and block. The corridors around us were full of steel and discarded darts. "This is a maze without an exit. Maybe it's only here to keep people busy until the sun comes up."

"It must be a puzzle. The stone is here somewhere."

"A puzzle."

She nodded, glaring at the walls. "Elves enjoy puzzles. If we built this, we would have tried to be clever."

"What about that statue?"

She reached out a greenish hued hand, setting it reverently on the figure's chest. "The Eternal Son. He was thought to be the first elf to master magic, and unlocked the secret to long life. His memory is honored among my people."

I sighed, dragging myself to my feet. "Well, it's the only thing in here that isn't flat stone or spiky metal. Let's have a look."

She moved away, standing nearby with her arms wrapped around herself as I inspected the relief. It wasn't a full statue, being sunk into the wall about halfway. It was a single piece of stone, though. No large cracks. No moving pieces.

I braced my hands on the figure's chest and put all my weight into it, but it didn't slide back or to either side. I even lifted, and nothing. I touched every inch of it, tried prying my fingernails into the edges, and finally just stood and said every version of "open the fuck up" I could think of.

Finally I stepped back. "Did I mention I hate elves?"

"Even me?"

"I haven't decided yet."

She snorted and shook herself out of whatever reverie she'd fallen into at the sight of the figure. "There is a way through it. We just have to find it."

I walked back to the passage leading into the alcove and ran my finger over the edge of a recessed stone that had set off one of the dart traps. I couldn't imagine how much skill had gone into making this one little maze. Everything was put together so perfectly. I'd love to see behind the walls, and pick through all the gears and springs that made this deathtrap tick.

Behind the walls.

I hurried to the nearest cluster of steel rods on the wall. Gripping the middle one in both hands, I started wiggling it and shoving it back and forth, trying to pry it out of the wall. Nissa came to watch, but didn't move to help. I pushed on the bar, tugged it back with all my body weight, pushed it again. It grated against the stone. I tried to twist it with no luck. "Damn it. Come out of there you—fucking—"

It let loose all at once and I fell back into Nissa's hastily outstretched arms. I grinned and flung the bar to the floor, wincing at the echoing metallic rattle, then peered into the hole it had come from. "Can you shine your light in here?"

Nissa lit up her scythe and held it over me. I could see empty space beyond the eight inches of stone block that made up the wall. Shadows revealed parts of a mechanism. How to get back there, though? The blocks were sealed tight.

"What do you see?"

"There's space back there." I moved through the corridors, no longer worrying about setting off traps, mapping the walls out in my head and trying to figure out how much space was between them. If they were all about eight inches thick, that meant most of the space was inside the walls themselves.

There had to be a way to get into it. Wouldn't they need to reset the traps somehow? I glanced in the direction I knew the treasure room to be, frowning. It was possible they entered through another room, but if I was being clever I'd want the answer to be closer to the puzzle. If this was indeed a puzzle, then solving it should be possible in here.

"Look for blocks we can move. There has to be a way to get behind the walls." I ran my hands over the blocks as I went, looking for anything that hinted at a secret door.

"We have been moving blocks this entire time."

I stopped, looking over my shoulder at her in shock. Of course we had. The pressure plates. And there was one spot where I'd nearly died because they put three of them in a row and I wasn't expecting it.

I ran to the far left corner of the maze, dropping to my knees beside the three recessed stones lined up in a row on the floor. Plenty big enough for a person to squeeze through.

I tried to pry up one of the stones using my knife, but only bent the tip. "We need to smash it. Was there anything heavy back in that treasure room?"

Nissa reached down to the center block and dusted it off. There was the faintest hint of a rune painted on the dull stone. Her thin fingers traced the lines, a crease deepening on her green forehead. She spread her fingers over it and pressed her palm to the stone, closed her eyes, and began to chant.

My skin crawled as I listened to the strange words, immediately thinking back to the mystic and her magic. This seemed different though. Her voice wasn't gravely or scratchy for one thing. But even the words weren't as harsh, and they rang in my ears like chimes. A light was growing between her fingers and the stone. After a few moments the light flared briefly and there was an ear-splitting crack as the stone shattered. She sat back and blew the dust off her palm.

I swallowed back the unease I was feeling at seeing her use magic, and smiled instead. "Well—aren't you useful."

The other two blocks were easy to remove now, and soon I was looking down into a space about six feet deep, filled with metal and wooden bracing and machinery. There was light coming from somewhere below and ahead, casting shadows and making it look even more tangled. I took a deep breath and looked at her.

"I'm going inside. Wait here so I can find my way back."

She nodded and lit her scythe so the gentle green glow showed through the hole.

I took off my vest, not wanting it to catch on all the metal and wood below, but left my knives on. Sliding into the hole was easy enough, but it immediately got a lot harder to move as I squeezed through the bracing and wedged myself past metal contraptions. The light was poor. I could see the green from Nissa's scythe, and yellow coming from somewhere ahead, but there was so much shadow in between that I was constantly knocking against things and working myself into places I couldn't get through.

It took a long time to go about twenty feet, at which point I hovered over a hole in the bottom of the floor that opened into some kind of cavern. It dropped hundreds of feet to smooth water and sand bars.

Chapter 48

"Nissa!" My voice echoed in the confined space of the floor.

"What is it?"

"A cavern. It's a big drop, can you see if there's any rope up there?"

I heard her move away and the green light disappeared. I took the time to wrap my legs around a brace and pop my head through the opening, peering around to get a better idea of the size of the chamber.

It was a huge natural cavern, and a good chunk of the ceiling had been covered by the close-fitting blocks of the maze, supported by a lattice of beams. The light was coming from a number of yellow globes strung throughout the space. There were massive rock formations thrusting up from the floor, flat on their tops and connected by ropes and flimsy bridges, like a web hovering a hundred feet off the floor.

An underground river flowed from one large tunnel below, splitting into dozens of smaller flow sections that weaved between the pillars before converging and exiting through another tunnel at the far side. It flowed lazily, winding through the cavern, clear enough I could see the submerged depths lit from below the surface of the water with the same yellow globes. The banks looked like a silty beach with scattered boulders.

Near one side of the cavern was a formation with a pedestal on it and a bluish white glow in its center. I would have laid bets *that* was the stone we were after. Even from here I could feel the buzz of magic stronger in that direction.

"Gray, I have rope."

I pulled myself back into the hole and maneuvered my way to the green glow of the scythe. Nissa thrust a coil of rope into the opening above me and I grabbed it and slung it around my shoulder. It smelled like blood and I wrinkled my nose. "Where did you get this?"

"One of the corpses had it."

"Of course it did." I wormed my way back to the hole in the floor and tied one end of the rope around a sturdy brace, then dropped the rest through the opening. It bounced and wiggled to a stop about fifty feet down. Nowhere near enough to reach the floor, and there were no platforms directly below the hole.

"Fuck." I hooked my legs around the bracing again and lowered myself to look around the roof of the cavern. There were the massive timbers that supported the maze, and each of them had a long metal bracket holding a globe of light. I twisted around, checking the location of the platforms. If I could hook one of those brackets with the rope, I could swing to a platform.

The problem was getting back up if I didn't have the rope anchored in this hole. It wouldn't do me any good to get the stone if all I could do was sit there and hold it while the sun rose. "Nissa!"

"What?"

"The rope doesn't reach, is that all there was?"

"It was all I could find."

"Any ideas on how I get back up once I go down there?"

"Fly?"

I grimaced. "I've made up my mind. I do hate you."

I pulled the rope back up. I didn't have any other options available, and at least if I left the rope attached to the hole I had fifty feet worth of chance to escape. I moved deeper into the innards of the floor until I found a metal bar I could pry out, then made my way back to the opening. I tied the bar to the end of the rope and dropped it back through the hole.

I shimmied down it until my feet hit the crossbar at the bottom, trying to ignore the creak of the strands. I was about thirty feet away from the edge of the closest platform, and eight feet higher than it, but if the rope snapped I'd be falling well over a hundred feet to the boulder-strewn shore below. I started swinging.

When I had some momentum going, I slipped the rest of the way down the rope and dropped to hang by my hands from the bar. It got me a little bit closer. It was still going to hurt.

When I figured I was swinging the best I could, I let go just before the apex and led with my feet. I had about three inches to spare as my feet touched down and I rolled forward and skidded to keep from falling off the far edge. The rough rock of the platform was worse than cobblestones, and when I slid to a stop I stared up at the cavern ceiling for a moment and just groaned.

The rest was relatively easy. The platforms were all connected, even if some of them were only held together by a single rope. After growing up on the rooftops, I was used to heights and precarious handholds, and at least down here I wasn't surrounded by monsters and tin-suited assholes. The hardest part was the continuous buzz of magic, growing stronger the closer I got to the pedestal. I shook myself every chance I got, rubbing my hands over my arms and the back of my neck, restless even when I was resting.

I finally reached the platform with the stone and took a few minutes to sit and calm myself. My hands felt raw from the ropes and my arms ached. I couldn't rest long, or my muscles would stiffen up. I listened to the sound of dripping, the gentle lapping of the lazy river far below me, and a light wind that twisted out of a hole somewhere and made the ropes sway and creak.

I heaved a sigh and pushed myself to my feet, walking to the edge of the carved dais in the middle of the platform—and stopped. There were runes on the floor, and the presence of magic crawled over my skin and made my teeth buzz. A white glow softened the dais, not bright enough to shine on its own, but enough that it blurred the edges of the runes. I took the time to walk around the platform, peering at every piece of the dais and the stone on the pedestal without actually touching anything.

I didn't understand magic, and I couldn't tell what was dangerous. If only Nissa had been down here with me, I might have been able to rely on her elfish instincts. Time had to be getting close. If I didn't do something now, I might as well sit down and wait to starve.

I stood at the very edge of the dais and shook my hands out beside me, bouncing a little on my toes. I breathed deep, blowing it out slowly. Before I could give in to my common sense, I gritted my teeth and stepped onto the dais.

Nothing happened.

I laughed and rubbed my hands over my face, trying to get rid of the tingly feeling. "Ohhhh shit. If I get out of here I am never leaving my apartment again."

320

If I ever *saw* it again. I was still a wanted man in Sangarie.

I shoved the thoughts aside and walked forward, staring at the stone. It pulsed a bluish white from its bed on the pedestal. The pedestal itself was unadorned. A simple cylinder of rock with a shallow indent in the top where the stone rested. I touched the side of the basin, but it was just cold rock.

"Fuck it." I reached out and picked up the stone, squeezing my eyes shut.

Chapter 49

I got the disturbing sense that it recognized me. I couldn't explain it, and the feeling was gone almost as soon as I noticed it. For the space of a few heartbeats I waited with my eyes shut for something more to happen. The stone felt alive in my hand, which made me want to drop it like it was a spider and flail around, but it wasn't actually *doing* anything.

Then the world crashed into my brain.

I saw myself, as if I was looking up from my own hand. I seemed older, more ragged. There was no sound, but it looked like I was shouting and gesturing with the other hand, red-faced and panicked. I could even see the edges of my fingers, as if I held my eyes in my hand. The only noise was a steady, quiet pulsing… like hearing your own heartbeat underwater.

My perspective swung wildly as the me in the image moved its hand, focusing in for brief moments in the chaos. Images of the manorhouse as I remembered it from back home, full of men and women running in all directions. Guards and servants. Walls sliding past in a jolting rush, as if I was being carried at speed. A sudden view of the sky, starting to turn orange with the sunset to one side, and flickering with flame from the other.

Nissa in full armor, standing with her face an emotionless mask—except for her eyes, which already screamed loss. Her hair was chopped short, so the wind whipped the white strands about her head. It was like I was looking at her from waist height, still clutched in my own hand.

Beside her, a young woman stood at the parapet on the roof of the manorhouse, her hands gripping the stone edge. She twisted to look over her shoulder at me and I recognized Ruena—years older—her pearly white eyes steady and her face as calmly tragic as Nissa's. She nodded once.

I joined them at the parapet, my body in the vision standing between them as guards surrounded us. But the guards weren't paying any attention to us. They were peering out over the city, screaming at each other and readying weapons.

Then I was raised up, and everything exploded.

***

I groaned and rolled onto my back. My eyes fluttered open, and I expected to see the evening sky on fire, but the ceiling of the yellow-lit cavern greeted me. My hand and forearm were numb, my fingers convulsed around the faintly throbbing stone. A dull ache filled my head.

I pried my fingers off the stone—terrified at how I couldn't feel anything below my elbow—and it dropped to the dais with a thunk, flickered a couple times, and went dark.

The soft glow was no longer making the dais hazy. The runes were carved crisp and clear on the surface, but held none of the power they'd seemed to before. They'd been turned off along with the stone, and the buzz of magic that had been assaulting me since I entered the cavern was gone. I had no idea what that meant, but it probably wasn't good.

For a few minutes I sat there, massaging feeling back into my wrist and hand. There was still the tingling magic just from being in the labyrinth, but occasionally it would stop for a moment, like it was faltering. I stared at the fist-sized stone lying dark next to me.

Had I broken it? Would the knight know, and kill us all here in this ruined version of Sangarie?

No. That was stupid. There was no way the tin man would know a magic stone from a rock I picked up off the riverbank. The real worry was whether he'd believe that dark lump of stone was what he was after. It didn't look magical anymore.

I shook the last of the numbness from my hand and stood, staring down at the stone. Logically, it had done whatever it was going to do to me already.

I held my breath and stooped to pick it up.

It flickered, just barely, and I could sense the sluggish weight of magic. It wasn't overwhelming... and I got the sense it was deeply asleep somehow. I fumbled at my belt and shoved the stone into a pouch, then trotted off the dais and started making my way back across the platforms.

My muscles were definitely sore, and it took longer to get back beneath the hole in the ceiling the than it had to reach the stone. By the time I stood on the platform closest to the hanging rope I was sweating and shaking with fatigue.

How was I supposed to reach it? I'd need another rope to bridge the last thirty-five feet or so.

I looked over my shoulder at the two ropes connecting this platform to the next and smiled.

Getting over to the previous platform was easy. I used a knife to cut one of the ropes from the edge and let it drop to hang from the far side. I had to wrap my arms and legs over the single rope remaining and inch my way across, stopping once in the middle to hang for a few minutes and catch my breath.

When I crawled onto the final platform once again and hauled the rope up, I was starting to worry I wouldn't have the strength to make it all the way up to the ceiling. My shoulder muscles burned and my hands were bleeding. I left the rope tied to the platform on one end, and twisted the other end into a multi-knotted lump to give it weight.

It took over a dozen tries to throw the knot well enough to get it to tangle over the bar hanging from the maze. Then I played with it to swing it back to me and pulled it taut before tying it off, connecting the hole above to the platform I stood on.

I didn't waste any more time. My hands stung as I climbed, but I kinked the rope at my feet and put most of my weight on that, using my arms to pull myself up in short bursts. It seemed to take hours. When I reached the bar I swung both legs over to sit on it, hugging the rope to my chest so I could rest my hands.

Almost there. I climbed the rest of the way, relieved to see the tangled braces and machinery in the floor of the maze. I sprawled in the bracing and waited for my hands to quit throbbing, looking toward the green glow.

"Nissa, you awake?"

"Did you succeed?"

"I have it. Give me a minute."

"Are you hurt?"

"I'm fucking exhausted."

There was no answer, and I rested a few more minutes before groaning and making my way through the braces. After I crawled out of the hole in the stones, Nissa helped me to my feet. She steadied me and raised her eyebrow as she looked me up and down.

I untied the pouch from my belt and tossed it to her.

She opened it to look and her face turned grim. "This is a powerful magical artifact."

"Well I fucking hope so. It wasn't fun to get."

"I had thought it a myth."

I frowned. "You've heard of this rock?"

"The Enhali Voga Surai. Roughly translated it means First Among Stones." She lifted her gaze to mine. "We can not let them have it."

"We can figure it out later. We need to get Rue and get out of here."

She put a slim hand on my chest. "Wait." She handed me back my pouch and dug in her own.

I tied the pouch on my belt and looked up to see her holding a tiny bottle. My eyes narrowed. "You said there wasn't any more. What's that?"

"This will not heal any wounds, but it will give you back some strength."

I was so tired of magic, but I held out my hand. "Fine. Give it here."

It tasted like bile. I gagged, but kept it down and handed her back the bottle. "That was disgusting."

"Making it taste good would dilute the effects."

I gagged again, holding my hand up to wave her off and bending over with my other hand on my knee just in case. My mouth was watering like crazy and I swallowed a few times until I was sure I wouldn't vomit her magic potion all over the floor. "Ok." I wiped my hand across my mouth and ran my tongue over my teeth, making a face at the aftertaste. "Let's go."

As vile as the potion was, it worked. I felt more like I had when we'd entered the manorhouse, as opposed to being ready to turn into jelly on the floor. It hadn't fixed my raw and blistered palms, or any of the bruises, but I had energy again. I shuddered at the thought of how much abuse my muscles were taking from this.

It was just a few quick turns to the door leading to the treasure room. I couldn't see either Kincaid or Ruena inside, and I jogged forward with a curse on my lips.

I caught a glimpse of movement to one side as I passed the threshold and managed to duck under the swing of the knight's sword, letting the blade clang against the gold-inlaid door. Kincaid growled and swung his gauntleted fist down like a hammer. I raised my arm over my head to block him, and his fist crunched into it and drove me to the floor.

I screeched and rolled away from him, cradling my forearm. A bright spike of pain shot through it every time I moved, and nausea clenched my gut. It was definitely broken, but there wasn't much I could do about it right now. Being skewered by the sword would kinda make it a moot point.

Kincaid laughed and advanced, spinning his sword in slow circles. "Here we are, thief. Just you and me."

I scrambled to my feet, sending golden cups, silver plates, and stacks of coins flying across the floor.

Kincaid shifted to swing, his armored boots grinding coins into the stone floor.

I dodged, then ducked beneath the return swing. I grabbed a goblet with my uninjured hand and flung it at his head.

"Knave! Hold still so I can end your pathetic life."

Nissa ducked back into the maze, but I could see her crouched near the opening and watching. I scooped a handful of coins and tossed them in the knight's face, taking advantage of the distraction to place myself opposite the door where she waited. "I'm rather fond of my life."

Kincaid growled and took a few wild swings, forcing me back until my feet hit a pile of coins that slid out from under me. I had the sense *not* to catch myself with my broken arm, and landed sprawled on my back instead.

He grinned and extended the point toward my chest. "If you die quietly, perhaps I'll petition the goddess for your salvation."

I raised an eyebrow. "You're a *church* knight?"

He frowned.

I chuckled. "I thought you were just a crazy man in a tin suit."

"Don't mock me, thief."

"But it's so *easy.*" I slid one of my knives from the sheath behind my back and flung it at his face.

He jerked his head to the side so it flew by and clanged against the wall before dropping with a muffled jingle on a pile of coins. Then he sneered and attacked.

I avoided the first swing and grabbed hold of a jeweled rod, raising it in both hands as the sword came down on me again. My broken forearm gave out and pain spiked to my shoulder as I screamed. The blade slid off the rod, barely missing my fingers, and smashed into a pile of goblets next to me.

Kincaid reached out a gloved hand and wrapped his fingers around my throat, holding me down on the treasure and raising his sword.

I pulled my second knife and plunged it into a gap in the armor at his waist. The fingers on my throat tightened and I couldn't breathe, but I refused to let go of my knife, instead twisting it deeper. My eyes met his and I knew I hadn't hit anything vital. He might die in a few days, but that would be a little too late for me.

His body suddenly jerked and his eyes widened in surprise. The hand around my throat loosened as the armored body toppled to the side in a racket of falling treasure to reveal Nissa standing behind him. She lifted her scythe and leaned on it like a spear, gazing down at me.

I relaxed against the pile of cups and coins, gasping for air.

"Are you badly injured?"

"You waited long enough," I croaked.

She didn't answer, but pulled me to my feet.

I staggered and turned to look for Ruena. "Let's get out of here." Maybe she was still in the trunk. "Rue?"

I grabbed the first massive trunk I saw and opened it. It was half full of coins. I dug in and pulled some of them out, my hand tingling as I stared at the strange markings. This trunk was dragonoak. I looked around the room and counted four of them in total. Nissa was helping Ruena out of one of them.

Four dragonoak trunks full of elfish coin. If this was the same Sangarie, but not the same time... was this the same four dragonoak trunks? Why were they in the baroness's manorhouse and not in the guild treasury?

"Gray?" Ruena stood, staring up at me with her eyes squinted almost shut. "It's so bright. There's so much magic here."

"I know." I wrapped my good arm across her shoulders and she hugged me around the waist, burying her face against my ribs.

Nissa trudged through scattered coins and treasure to join us. "Sunrise will be upon us soon."

I ignored her comment and nodded my head in the direction of the trunk full of coins. "Have you seen these before?"

She glanced down and stared for a moment. I caught the tightening of skin around her eyes and the twitch at the corner of her mouth, but her expression didn't change. "No." She took Ruena's hand and pulled her toward the corridor.

Well, that wasn't at all suspicious. I scanned the room again, a tightness in my chest at the thought of the riches I was leaving scattered on the floor. "Shouldn't we take some of it?" I called to her.

Nissa shouted at me to get moving and started down the corridor.

I took two steps toward the door, then cursed and bent to open one of the little wooden coffers. Gold and precious gems winked back at me in the torchlight. I quickly picked out the gems and opened a few other boxes to find more, stuffing them all in my pockets.

Weapons poked out of the piles here and there, and I scowled at an etched knife with a blackwood handle as I rummaged through another coffer. Yeah it was gaudier than I typically used, but it was a far sight better than the mystic's bejeweled dagger. I wrapped my fingers around the handle and the tingle of magic crawled over my skin.

"Gray!"

"I'm coming!" I tossed the mystic's bloody dagger aside and stuck the new one behind my belt, then grabbed a coffer box on the way out.

Chapter 50

We ran to the pit and stepped carefully along the wall to the stairway. I counted the steps as we went up, wondering if my own Sangarie had a secret stairway in the manorhouse. If it did, I might need to have a talk with Rigel about updating our maps.

We came up to the library and Nissa paused to search through her bag.

I blocked Ruena from seeing the bloody remains of Waren in the corner and scanned the handful of doors leading out of the room. "What are you looking for?"

"The ointment that can fix your arm."

The room shook and the sound of glass shattering and stone cracking could be heard deeper in the manor. Ruena put her hands over her face and hunkered down against a bookshelf, sobbing into her palms. I bent down, pressed the little wooden box to her chest, and wrapped her arms around it. "Hold onto this for me, kid."

She stared at me with her pearly eyes, sniffling and clutching at the box. "Did you steal it?"

I grinned. "Of course. We're thieves."

She smiled through the tears. "Yeah we are."

Nissa cursed and dug more violently through the bag as the rumbles continued. I stared at the swaying chandelier above us. "Let's take care of that later. We need to get out of here. Now."

She huffed in irritation, but grabbed her polearm from where it'd been resting against the wall. I pulled Ruena up and led her into the entry hall with the massive staircases. Shadows moved across the upper windows. As we neared the double doors leading outside the manor, a black tentacle slid past the opening outside.

Nissa stopped and held her arm out, blocking the way. "Shadowkraken."

The windows above had lost their glass, but the frames creaked and stone crumbled from the sills. I pushed Ruena behind me, peering up to where shadows flickered beyond the empty openings. "We have to get out of here."

"If we run, it will see us."

"If we don't, we won't get back before sunrise."

A black tentacle thrust into one of the upper windows and chunks of the frame and stone around it fell to the shattered marble floor. I took Ruena's arm and ran for the double doors. Nissa ran beside me, chanting to make her scythe glow.

I burst into the front garden and kept going. When I risked a look back, three of the massive shadowkraken were crawling over the manorhouse, hovering at the front parapet wall. One of them turned and undulated down the front façade, stretching its tentacles forward. The sky, hazy before now, was roiling with smoke and allowing the stars to peek through, as if the haze was being blown away. That sky held the deep purple color of pre-dawn.

It was nearly sunrise.

I returned my focus to the street, pulling Ruena as fast as I dared over the broken cobblestones. I held my forearm tight against my gut and clenched my teeth with the pain. The green light of Nissa's scythe danced over the stone around us.

"*Jump!*" Nissa's voice rang through the street.

I pivoted and slammed into Ruena, rolling into the base that was all that was left of a garden wall nearby. A slimy black tentacle crushed the cobbles where we'd been running. I pushed myself up and cried out as my broken arm took my weight, dropping me back to the street. Grinding my teeth, I used my other arm to stand and grabbed Ruena again to continue running.

"We need cover," Nissa shouted. She paused to swipe at a tentacle, leaving the tip of it flopping in the street behind her.

"If we can make it into the next district we'll find some."

We ran. A glance back showed nothing but blackness beyond the light of the elf's scythe, but I could hear massive things moving in the dark, and the clacking of the shadowkraken's jaws. It was being more cautious now.

In my head I tried to plot out the best route back to the gateway in the courtyard. It kept me from panicking about what was chasing us. Staying on the main streets would be faster, and the best route back to the Lower Yard was out the south gate and down Tinner's Row.

I led them south through the estates. As the gate finally loomed out of the darkness I staggered to a stop at the base of the debris slope. I'd forgotten about that.

I looked down the length of wall in both directions and grimaced. "Climb. It's the only way."

Nissa took the lead, climbing over crushed and broken stone, using upthrust timbers to pull herself forward. Ruena was right behind her and I took up the rear, glancing often to check on the shadowkraken's pursuit. I stumbled a few times, remembering to catch myself with only one arm and sacrificing the skin of my knees to do it. When I reached the top I saw Nissa looking down the opposite side, her scythe held out over the edge to shed more light.

She shook her head and said, "We will have to climb down."

"My arm is broken. I can manage it, but you need to help Rue."

"We should have fixed that."

"Do you have a cream in there to fix being trapped in a deadly shadow labyrinth? If not, we might have to wait with the broken arm."

Nissa crouched and urged the girl to climb onto her back. I turned to scan the estates and thought I saw shadows moving between the ruins, but it was too far away to tell if they were murderous shadows or normal ones caused by the turbulent clouds.

Nissa swung herself over the wall. Ruena clutched the scythe and the coffer box under one arm, and her other arm was wrapped around the elf's neck. I walked a few paces to the side and swung myself over, doing my best not to use my broken arm. The climb had been simple going up, but I couldn't even grip the stone with one of my hands now, so I had to be very careful where I dug the toes of my boots into the mortar.

Nissa reached the bottom and Ruena climbed off her back. They both stared up at me, casting anxious glances into the streets leading deeper into the city. I moved as fast as I dared, grimacing as I used my broken

331

arm to brace myself while I moved my good hand to another stone. I was only about six feet from the bottom when a thud shook the entire wall and my boots slipped.

I instinctively gripped the stone with both hands and my weight came down on my arms. The injured one gave out and I lost my grip and fell to the cobbles below. My feet hit first, and I fell onto my backside and then to my elbows, screaming in pain.

Nissa lifted my shoulders, pushing me to a sitting position. "Get up! Hurry!"

I took a deep breath and let her help me to my feet. My arm throbbed and I cradled it with my other hand. "This way."

We fled down Tinner's Row, ducking around obstacles and darting between shadows. This district had been full of large official buildings, and some of them had fallen into the street, littering it with loose stone. My breath was coming in heaving gasps and I shrugged off the supporting hand of the elf.

The shadowkraken were once again in pursuit, but hindered by the buildings. I could hear stone crashing on the street behind us and the clacking echoed through the ruined city.

Ruena tripped and fell, crying out as the box she held clattered to the street. I pulled her up by the arm and swiveled my head to search for enemies as she gathered up the box, then we were running again, moving toward the warehouse with the gateway.

I did my best to avoid the other gateways. I'd considered using one of them to escape instead, but there was no telling where we'd end up. There was at least one gateway that led to my childhood in here, and I had no desire to go back there. Besides, with magic it was better to do things the way you're told.

My legs were shaking as I rounded a corner and slammed into one of the shadow creatures. It knocked me and Ruena to the street and I flung my good arm over the girl as the creature took an instinctive swipe at us and missed.

Nissa leaped over us in a green blur. She whirled her scythe, forcing the creature back and opening its chest. The next swipe took out one of its eyes and it roared in fury. She dispatched it quickly and it disappeared into dust.

Behind the drifting dust, a man was scrambling to his feet. For a moment I didn't recognize him because his beard was trimmed and his hair was shorter, but it was definitely Culley. A very shaken and blood-covered Culley.

He looked at me, recognition in his eyes, then shock. "Boss? What are you doing here?"

But Culley was dead. Purple and bloated back in that treasure room.

Nissa grabbed my shoulder and pulled me around. "Let's go!"

I turned back to Culley, but he picked up a bucket of coins—heavy as shit judging by the way he staggered with it—and disappeared into a nearby gateway, and whatever version of Sangarie it led to. I took one step toward him, wondering how he had come back to life, and looked down to see a single gold coin on the blackened cobbles. I picked it up and rubbed my thumb over the strange markings—like the ones from the treasure room—and from the bucket of coins the goldsmith had been melting down. A bucket exactly like the one he'd been carrying.

I stared after him.

"Gray, *come!*"

I looked at the elf and caught a shimmer behind her. "Duck!"

She wasn't fast enough. The claws came down and sliced open the back of her shoulder. She screamed as she dropped to her knees and I pulled the etched knife from my belt and ran forward. I took two long steps and jumped to a chunk of fallen wall next to the kneeling elf, pushing myself off to gain height before coming down with my knife in both hands at the creature's face.

The blade went into its eye and stuck there, just before I slammed chest-first into the beast, screaming as pain flared through my arm. The creature howled, one claw swiping at the knife buried in its eye socket. I pushed off with both knees and the knife came loose with a popping sound. My arms flailed and I dropped onto my back with a grunt as it turned to dust around me. I was spread-eagled on the street with my muscles twitching in protest, the dagger still clutched in my good hand.

I stared up at the sky, mostly clear now, the stars shining brighter than they ever had over Sangarie. If I ignored everything around me, I could almost pretend I was home. I watched the last of the swirling clouds, shivering at how quickly they were just disappearing into nothing, revealing the faint red light of sunrise in the east.

333

As I lay there, the magic that had filled the air since I entered the labyrinth faded out for a moment, then returned. Then faded out again long enough for me to count to three before coming back. Just like the clouds that were breaking apart in the sky. "The magic is dying."

Nissa scrambled to her feet, using her scythe to support herself as she hunched forward. "What did you say?"

I turned my head to look at her. "The magic that's here, it's fading away."

The elf scowled at me. "I thought you were bluffing about being able to see magic like the child."

I chuckled and it turned into a cough.

Ruena knelt beside me, the box clutched under her arm. She set her hand on my chest, her little face screwed up in worry. "Don't die."

I snorted and rolled onto my side, then put the knife away before letting her help me to my feet. "I can't see magic, but I can feel it." I put my good hand on Ruena's head and made her look up at me with her pearly white eyes. "Don't tell, okay?"

She nodded, staring back at me with a grin.

Nissa raised her eyebrow as I walked past her and took the lead again through the maze of streets. Twice Ruena tugged me in the opposite direction I'd chosen, and I found another route that satisfied her. When I caught sight of the ruined courtyard with its gateway, I let out a sigh of relief.

I stumbled through the debris of the surrounding buildings, pulling Ruena along with me. Nissa was right behind me. I risked a glance at the nearest wall and saw a looming darkness begin to slither over it, tentacles dislodging stones. It was framed in the orange of the rising sun, and I wasn't sure which of the two terrified me the most right now, the sunrise or the monster.

I clenched my hand over Ruena's and ran faster, stumbling as stones turned beneath my feet. The gateway loomed before me.

I thought there was no way I could be more terrified right then. The glowing portal of my nightmares in front of me, the shadowkraken and the ticking sun behind me... but then the portal flickered out for the space of a few frantic breaths and I was certain we were too late.

It popped back, a little less stable, a little more transparent. It was fading.

I put everything I had left into dragging Ruena forward. At the last instant I closed my eyes, held my breath, and leaped.

Chapter 51

The magic twisted me up, forcing out my held breath and wrenching at my other senses. The last time I'd been through had hurt, but this time felt like someone had grabbed my injured arm and tried to twist it off. I stumbled out the other side and fell to the cobbles, then found enough breath to scream as I doubled up over my broken arm. I was afraid to look at it, in case it had been mangled like it felt.

I was dimly aware of the jangling of armor as guards closed in on me, then everyone else started screaming as well. I lifted my gaze to see black tentacles poking out of the gateway, blotting out the dimmer, more familiar stars of Sangarie, flopping through the ranks of guards and smashing into walls.

Nissa grabbed my good arm and pulled at me, trying to drag me to my feet. I bit my lip and let her help me stand, looking around for Ruena. The girl ducked between us, and Nissa pushed us both toward the alley. Some of the guards were attacking the tentacles, but most were scattering in panic. Loring was screaming orders from off to the right. The flickering glow of the gateway was nearly smothered by the mass of writhing tentacles sticking out of it.

I ducked into the narrow, twisting alley and raced around the corners, hoping there weren't guards stationed ahead of us. If we could escape in the chaos, we could disappear into the city. When it dumped me out into the street, I staggered to a stop and scanned both directions, then the rooftops. Nissa and Ruena came out right behind me. I could still hear the screaming of the guards in the courtyard we'd left behind.

I pushed up to the closest building, taking advantage of the dawn shadows. "We shouldn't be out here. It's still the Night of Shadows, and those smaller beasts can come through until the sun is up."

She nodded. "I am unfamiliar with this city. Where can we go?"

336

An image of the underground flashed in my head and I'd already thought of two entrances close to the southern wall, then I remembered I had a price on my head. I shrank into the deeper shadows of a covered doorway, thankful the Red Hands weren't dedicated enough to be out right now.

Nissa gestured at the city again, her voice edged with panic. "They will be after us soon, where do we go?"

I took a deep breath and nodded. "We can find an empty warehouse close by for now. It will get us off the streets and let us figure out what to do."

"Go."

I shivered and forced myself to walk into the street. Between the dangers of possible shadowbeasts and the threat of hidden Red Hands with crossbows, I felt like I was crawling out of my skin. The only thing keeping me moving was the clean line of rooftops in the dark, the smell of the city, and the sight of candles in the windows. This was Sangarie. *My* Sangarie.

I reached a likely warehouse and checked the front door to find it locked, then went around to the back. The back door was locked as well, but it was more sheltered, and simple enough to pick even in the dim light with a broken arm. I opened the door a crack and listened, peering inside for any muffled light sources that would indicate the place had a night guard. When I finally waved Nissa and Ruena forward, they slipped inside and I closed the door behind them. Nissa whispered a few words of magic and I grimaced when a light brightened in her palm.

Fucking magic. The tingling had finally disappeared and she had to make more.

The warehouse had been converted from an old merchant's shop, and goods were stacked along the walls to either side. There wasn't much, and I picked through the piles briefly to find clothing, rough canvas, various used and worn household goods, and discarded boxes. But I did find a couple of lamps, and a quick look near the door netted me a striker to light one with.

I carried the lamp to the back of the building where there weren't any windows and sat against the wall. Ruena curled up beside me, her arms wrapped around the coffer like it was a stuffed toy. I lifted my good arm and she leaned into my ribs.

Now that we were back in the right Sangarie, I noticed how awful I looked. My vest had been left in the stone maze beneath the manorhouse. My shirt and pants were covered in black ichor that had dried to a tacky, tar-like consistency. Ruena's hair was already sticking to it where her head rested against my chest. My hands were bloody and raw and covered in the stuff as well, which burned in the wounds.

Nissa walked up with a tin in her hand. "I found it."

"The broken bones ointment?"

She sat cross-legged on the floor in front of me and pushed up my sleeve, revealing my swollen forearm covered in a darkening purple bruise. I winced and clamped my teeth shut, trying not to show how much it hurt just having her touch it.

She went to work quickly and silently, smearing the ointment over the swollen area with that extra tingle of magic that meant she was pouring a little of herself into the healing. Ruena watched without a sound, her eyes tracing the elf's movements with wonder. I wondered what the magic looked like to her. Did it flow from Nissa's fingertips and sink into my skin? Did it spread across the surface like the ointment and slowly fade? I looked away from them both, fighting the urge to pull my arm out of her grip.

When she'd finished, she let go and scooted back. I flexed my hand and bent my elbow, but all I felt was a lingering soreness and the ache of the bruise. "Thanks," I mumbled.

"You are welcome."

I cleared my throat and settled more comfortably against the wall. There was a long stretch of silence while Nissa tended the claw marks across her shoulder, otherwise ignoring us. Ruena fell asleep against my side. I would have told her to go nap somewhere else, but the kid had been through a lot tonight. I'd been half her age and all I'd done was *walk* into the labyrinth, and I hadn't taken it nearly as well as she was.

I leaned my head back against the wall and stared at the dusty cobwebs in the rafters above. Now what? The sun was already shining across the floor, even if it had to filter through years of built-up grime, so the Night of Shadows was over. The gateways would be shut for another year, and the guards left in that courtyard would be wondering where we'd gone. They were probably already looking for us.

338

Every inch of my body ached. I was covered in bruises, scrapes, and rope burns, not to mention black ichor. All I wanted was to find a hole to crawl into and sleep the day away.

And to forget everything that had happened during the night.

Bits and pieces kept popping to mind, trying to fit themselves into some semblance of order. Seeing Culley—a younger version of Culley—had me teetering on the edge of the truth. I could feel it. I had walked through that gateway twice now, and both times I'd ended up in the exact same place and time. Maybe Culley had been through it twice as well. He'd brought back the coins. He'd told someone about seeing me there.

Now that the magic of the labyrinth wasn't bombarding me, I could feel the orb humming at my side, and the pressure of the etched knife tucked under my belt. I pulled the knife out and tensed to throw it across the room, but the lamp reflected off the etchings of the blade and I paused. Elfish script?

Nissa spoke up from where she was slinging her bag across her chest once more. "I have seen that knife."

It still tingled in my hand, but the grip was perfect and the weight was comforting. "Yeah. I took it from the treasure room."

"No. I mean that I have seen that knife in my homeland."

I turned it in the light, angling the blade's edge to her. "What does it say?"

She bent closer and her brow creased for a moment. Then she raised her eyebrow and lifted her gaze to mine. "Walk through darkness to find light."

How appropriate. I huffed and rolled the handle in my fingers. It'd be a shame to just throw it away. As I was weighing the desire to keep it and the discomfort of having a magic knife on my person, a loud crash echoed through the building from the area of the back door, and dust rained down from the ceiling.

For one terrifying moment, I feared the shadowkraken had followed us here, but that was ridiculous. I dragged a startled Ruena to her feet and pushed her toward Nissa, clutching the etched dagger tight. "Out the front! Go!"

The back door crashed open and three of Loring's guards tumbled inside. They peered through the dim interior, shouting at us to stop.

Nissa grabbed her scythe and took Ruena's hand. We'd barely covered half a dozen paces when the front door was flung open as well and two more guards stepped inside, followed by a woman in a simple dress.

I stepped past Nissa to get a better look and scowled. "Beth?"

She looked at me, smiling winsomely. "I knew you could do it, Gray."

My jaw tightened. Was everyone I knew working for this asshole nobleman? "Care to explain what in the name of fuck is going on?"

She chuckled and motioned at the guards. Four of them stationed themselves around us, but one remained at her side. "Give me the stone and you can leave."

I caught Nissa's low growl beside me and drew myself up taller. "I don't have it."

Beth tsked and played with the amulet at her throat. "You're such a liar, Gray."

"That's rich, coming from you."

Her smile twisted into something more like a sneer. "Do you really think you have the time to play with me? How long before the Red Hands catch your scent now that the Night of Shadows is done?"

I squashed down the little knot of panic. She was right. They were probably already on the streets, and even if she let me go Loring had probably tipped them off. I had to keep her talking, give me time to think of something. "Why this convoluted game? Why me?"

"I knew it would be you. Three years ago I tried, and failed. But when that worthless thief of yours came back alone, he told me he'd seen you in the labyrinth. I knew what I had to do then. You'd been there before, you could navigate it again."

Beth had been responsible for this? For all of this? My brow creased. "What have you done?"

She smoothed the front of her dress and adjusted the way her breasts rode in the corseted top. "I had to get a little dirtier than I thought I would, but it was all worth it." She turned a shoulder to me and brushed her hair aside to show the Blue Hand tattoo with a single bar, partly exposed beneath the strap of her dress. "A small price to pay to get close to you. I knew I had to look the part."

I tried to keep the guards in sight as I squeezed the handle of the etched dagger. "Did you make a deal with Loring? Was it for gold?"

340

She laughed, a sound much more confident than I'd ever heard from her. "My dear thief, Loring made a deal with *me*. That stone will make me the most powerful mystic humanity has ever seen, and my brother Loring will rule the kingdom. Now give it to me." She reached out her hand.

"Your *brother*?" I shook my head, frowning as I tried to rearrange everything I knew in my head. "Did *you* kill those Blues?"

"Oh—you're finally putting things together, aren't you?" She grinned and took a few steps in my direction. "Let me help. To be fair, Waren did the actual killing. The first one was to protect my secret. Saree caught me having a private conversation, and refused to let it go. But a stray comment about her sneaking out to meet you gave me the idea of blaming you for her death. If I could get you out of the guild, I could use you."

I shook my head, sickened at how excited she sounded as she laid it all out before me.

"The second death should have made you even more suspect, but those whores at Tanji's didn't believe you could have done it. I had to get you to make a scene at the ball, show them you were losing your mind a little." She spun her finger alongside her temple and clicked her tongue. "Culley didn't want to, but it's amazing what a little gold can do to soften a person's morals."

It had been aimed at me all along, like I'd thought, only I'd been *so* very wrong about where it had come from.

"The third... well, no matter how I tried, the right people just weren't willing to condemn you. I had to make it more obvious. I had to get Rigel to kick you out, so I could convince you to work for me."

Nissa touched my arm, but I shrugged her off. My chest tightened and I thought of the scene in Loring's garden. *Deidre*. Beth had been alone with Deidre so often for weeks. Had they been working together, or had Deidre been played as well? Was that attack staged? Had Deidre been protecting her? Either she had betrayed me, or I had wrongly believed she could.

My mouth was dry, but I had to know. "Deidre?" I asked. "Was she involved in this too?"

She looked shocked for an instant, then laughed outright at me. "Oh that's precious. You think that bitch was in on it? So much for trust between criminals. It's sad how quickly you turn on each other."

My eyes dropped to the floor and I lowered the knife to my side. "I saw her at the manor with Loring."

"Ah yes. She was looking for answers. Poor thing. Even willing to return to his painful embrace. My brother isn't known for his gentle disposition. Firmin appreciated his tastes, though. And that made it easier to set up here." Beth's eyes lit even brighter. "Imagine her reaction when I told her everything. It was so satisfying after playing dumb all these years. She really was as blind as you."

I took a ragged breath over the ache in my chest. "Fuck you."

She heaved a sigh. "Honestly, you almost ruined everything when you killed that idiot Firmin. I didn't expect that from you. Well done." She took a few more lazy steps forward. "Storytime is over. Now, give me my stone."

Ruena put her arms around my waist and pulled me back, and I stumbled numbly a few paces. Deidre had been hurt because of me, too. Loring had hurt her, and she'd gone back to him for me. She'd put herself in danger to find me... If Deidre knew everything... did that mean Beth had killed her too? My chest tightened even more.

Nissa raised her polearm and stepped up so her shoulder rubbed mine. "Pull yourself together. We can not let her take it."

Beth grinned. "You don't have a choice."

The four guards moved all at once. Nissa stepped away to meet the two on her side, and I looked up as the one to my right took a swing with a shortsword. I watched it come, not really seeing it, but at the last moment Ruena yanked me backwards and I stumbled to keep my balance.

"Gray!" Her voice was panicked and she tried to step in front of me as the guard advanced again, his sword raised. She stood as tall as she could, defending me.

There was no way I was letting her get hurt because of me. I clutched her to me and raised my knife to catch the downward stroke of the sword, then twisted to knee the guard in the balls. He went down like a sack of grain.

I shoved Ruena behind me and told her to stay back, then stepped up to meet the next guard as he howled and rushed me. I blocked the sword, but he stepped in close and bore down, moving me backward.

I pushed up under his guard and drove my knife between his ribs. The heavy jerkin wasn't enough to stop the magical knife, and the guard spit blood over my shoulder and slid to the floor.

Nissa had dispatched her guards and was advancing on Beth, whose face was twisted in rage as she backed toward the door, clutching her pendant. She ordered the last guard forward, but he turned and ran out the front of the warehouse.

She screamed at him to come back, and even after he'd gone she yelled threats at the empty doorway. Then she glared at the elf and backed up, shifting her gaze to me. "Do you know what I had to do to get you here, Gray? You're mine! I stole you from the guild and you work for me now."

I strode past Nissa, warning her off. My hands were shaking and I couldn't unclench my jaw, but I was not letting Beth get away now. I strode right up to her and pressed her against the brick wall, then set the tip of my dagger under her throat.

"Where's Deidre?"

She looked surprised for a second, then laughed at me. "Still thinking with your cock?"

The tingle of magic crept over me. Everything started getting fuzzy on the edges, and the sound of Nissa and Ruena shouting was muffled.

Desire flared up within me, burning through my veins and pulsing through my core. It made me gasp, and my knife fell from nerveless fingers as I leaned into her. I gripped her arms and marveled at the way the freckles on her skin seemed to be pulsing. My breath was fast and my heart was racing.

Beth's voice buzzed warm against my ear. "Now that you brought me the stone, I don't need you anymore."

My brow furrowed. I needed her. I wanted her. My grip shifted to her waist so I could pull her even closer...

The crawling feeling of magic across my skin made me hesitate.

A flash of steel at the corner of my vision gave me just enough warning to shove myself away. The knife sliced through my shirt and grazed my chest, and the pain broke her spell so everything snapped into

343

focus. I touched the wound as I staggered back a step and my fingers came away bloody.

She pulled back to strike again. "You insufferable—"

I side-stepped a thrust of the knife.

"—lecherous—"

She swung at my chest and I staggered back another step.

"—bastard!"

She howled and grabbed the pendant with her free hand, ripping it from her neck. Her face was flushed and twisted in rage, and she was panting. She held the pendant out in front of her, gripping it so hard her fingers were white and blood dripped from her closed fist, then she began to chant.

I had a really bad feeling about—

An invisible weight hit me from above, knocking me flat on my back. Air whooshed out of my chest. My arms and legs were pinned to the floor, but nothing was there. I tensed my muscles, but couldn't even expand my chest. It was like something was slowly crushing me.

I strained and wheezed for breath, tried unsuccessfully to slide my arms or roll a little. My chest was starting to burn. Beth walked into my line of sight, a sneer on her face and a dagger raised. "Hold. Still."

Shit.

I tried to heave myself up, but it did nothing.

She stepped closer and crouched over me, the dagger glinting in the lamplight.

The sharp curve of Nissa's scythe buried itself in her back up to the shaft, protruding from her sternum a good six inches. For a long moment Beth stood curled around it, slowly lowering her gaze to the etched surface, then she dropped the dagger and the pendant. The metallic clinks echoed through the warehouse.

Nissa jerked the scythe free and Beth was tugged a quarter turn and collapsed to the floor in a pool of blood.

I sucked in a sharp breath, then another, gulping like a fish and coughing. The weight was gone, and all I could think was if Beth died right now I wouldn't know if Deidre was alright. I rolled to my knees and crawled to her limp form, panic in my chest. "Where's Deidre?"

Beth focused on me briefly and her mouth curled into a little sneer, then her eyes went glassy.

Chapter 52

I shook her. "Beth!"

Nothing. Blood still poured out of her chest, soaking my knees, but she was gone. I sat back on my heels and looked up at Nissa, trying to sort through the emotions coursing through me. I wanted to scream. I wanted to curse. I had no idea if Deidre was alive or dead. I wanted to find her—but at the same time I recoiled from the thought of facing her.

The elf extended a hand. "We have to leave."

"I need to find Deidre. I need to know—"

"Later. When we are safe."

I took her hand and she pulled me up. Ruena joined us, clutching the wooden box to her chest and pulling her goggles up without being asked. She stared at my chest.

"You're bleeding."

I pressed an already bloody hand to the wound. "It's not that bad." I looked back at the four dead guards. Nissa must have finished off my first one when I wasn't looking. She was right, we needed a safer place than this.

I wasn't willing to leave Sangarie until I knew Deidre was okay. So safe would have to be negotiable. "Let's go."

I led them out the back door again, mapping out a route in my head that would keep us mostly out of sight. We started down the alley. It wouldn't be long before people would be walking the streets, going about their business. I couldn't be seen. Maybe we could find another warehouse—

I had no warning when a lump of rags burst into motion and drove me face-first into the wall of the alley. I swore, then felt the prick of a knife at the base of my skull and froze.

345

The voice directly behind me made my blood run cold. Neffery calmly ordered the elf and the girl to stay back, or he'd drive his dagger into my brain.

If it had been a low level beggar it's possible I could have bluffed my way out of it, but Neffery knew everything. The point of the dagger broke the skin and I pressed my forehead against the brick, holding very still. Neffery was as fast as I was on a good day, and after the exertions of the night I was far from the top of my game. "Neff, I can explain this."

"You're marked, Gray."

"I know that."

"But you still show your face here. You got balls." He pressed me harder against the wall.

"Not by choice," I growled.

Neffery's voice was as slow and collected as ever. "You keep strange company these days. And that girl has a box full of gold or I'm an elfish princess."

Shit. I swallowed and thought fast. "I was kidnapped and brought here. You know I'm not stupid enough to come back on my own."

"You telling me these ladies kidnapped you? An elf and a little girl?"

"No, a nobleman. These two are with me."

"A nobleman kidnapped a thief. There's a switch."

"Neff, I swear to the Six if you don't let me go I'll—"

"You'll what?" The knife pushed a fraction of an inch deeper and I hardly dared to breath. "Why would anyone kidnap you and bring you back here, unless it was to sell you to Lady Karyn?"

"Reach into my pocket."

Neffery shifted and I felt a bandaged hand slide into my pocket. There was a fortune of gems in there, but also the strange gold coin I'd picked up on the way out of the other Sangarie. The knife didn't move as the beggar searched.

"Impressive. Are you trying to bribe me, Gray?"

"Fuck no, those gems are mine. There's a coin."

"I don't come that cheap."

"Just take it out and look at it."

Neffery pulled out the large coin and held it up in the light, turning it over and peering at it closely. "This is one of those funny coins from Rigel's vault."

"The nobleman sent us through a gateway into the labyrinth on a hit."

This time the knife pulled away enough that I risked turning my head to look at the beggar out of the corner of my eye.

"Are you insane?" Neffery asked.

"There was very little in the way of choice for any of us. But we found a ruined version of Sangarie, and where the ruined manorhouse stood we found four trunks full of those coins."

Neffery gripped my shirt at the shoulder and spun me around, slamming me back up against the wall and setting the tip of the knife against my throat. "If you *did* go there, then you've gone mad. Are you saying these coins have been leaking out of some treasure in the labyrinth?"

"The nobleman who kidnapped me has been spending them. He sent someone in before us, and they brought those back with them."

"If that's true, why did he need you?"

"I don't know."

"Convenient how much you don't know."

I smirked. "I'm no beggar spy, all I do is steal things."

Neffery held up the coin. "Which is why I don't trust you."

"You don't have to trust me. You just have to tell Rigel what you've seen, and let us go."

"I already told you," Neffery said, "you're marked."

"By the Red Hands."

"Yes, by the—" Neffery narrowed his eyes. "You *are* trying to bribe me."

"Pretend you didn't see us."

Neffery grunted. "Pretend not to know something?"

"Fine. Just take your time informing the rest of the guild."

Neffery pulled the knife away from my neck and stepped back. "What are you offering me?" He gestured at my pocket. "I have enough jewels."

"Information. I'll tell you anything you want to know about the labyrinth, as well as the nobleman that kidnapped me, and those coins."

Neffery rubbed a bandaged hand on his chin. "What else?"

347

I frowned. "What do you mean, what else?"

"While it'd make a good story, that information is useless to me."

"What else do you want?"

He narrowed his eyes. "The truth, for one. You're lying to me."

"I'm not."

"You are. You're very good at it, but I'm better."

I straightened my blood and tar-covered shirt and brushed my hand over the pouch containing the orb. I could feel the magic even through the leather. "It was Beth. She infiltrated the guild to trap me into stealing something from the labyrinth. She got Culley to go along with it the first time. And—" I dropped my gaze.

I didn't want to admit having doubted Deidre. I never wanted her to know I had given in to that voice in my head.

"I already know about Beth."

I glared at him. "You do?"

He spit on the ground, his beady eyes flashing. "I'm the Eyes of the Master. It's my fucking job, Gray." The silence stretched for a few moments, then he looked away. "Although I didn't know why she was playing at being a Blue Hand. She'd been spending a lot of time around you just before that spat of killings. I wanted to talk to you about it but you went and killed the fucking baroness's son. We thought you had disappeared. Then I trail after that bitch and find you here."

If he'd been trailing Beth… I swallowed past the lump in my throat, knowing I had to ask. "What about Deidre? Have you seen her?"

"She went into a manor in the Estates and we haven't seen her come out."

"She's in Loring's manor?"

Neffery gestured at me with his knife. "So what else?"

I shook my head and started to move to the side. He shoved me against the wall again. "Not so fast."

"I have to go back and find Deidre."

"We're haggling here, in case you haven't noticed."

"Neff—" I took a breath, trying to calm my thoughts. "She's either trapped in there, or dead."

"Are you sure?"

I nodded.

The old beggar narrowed his eyes in thought. "Maybe we should find out."

Nissa stepped forward and held out her hand. "If you plan to go back there, give it to me."

I tugged the pouch from my belt and tossed it in her direction. "Keep the fucking thing."

She caught it and stowed it in her bag, then held out the blackwood handled knife. "You dropped this."

I stared at it for a few moments, then took it and shoved it under my belt.

Neffery didn't even hide the shrewd look as he watched our every move.

Chapter 53

As I pressed a wad of cloth over my bleeding chest, watchful for the glint of sun off crossbow bolts, Neffery questioned the elf. He was much more polite with her, and didn't resort to poking her in the neck with a dagger. I thought it was a little unfair, but I kept my mouth shut. Eventually Neffery joined me, tossing over a bundle of rags in the form of a cloak.

"It's just you and me, Gray. You try anything and I'll kill you myself."

"That's a little extreme, don't you think?"

"I'm still not entirely sure you aren't feeding me a line of bullshit."

"All I want is to find Deidre." I slung the makeshift cloak around my shoulders and pulled the hood forward, concealing myself like a Yellow Hand. The wound over my chest stung and started bleeding a little again.

I followed him toward the Estates, growing nervous in the light of early morning. Here and there I caught sight of a familiar face, and I pulled my rags tighter around me. I knew I wouldn't recognize a Red Hand before there was a bolt in my chest, and I wasn't sure Neffery's presence would guarantee my protection. At least my exhaustion made me walk like a beggar.

Neffery led the way, slipping through one of the secret doors into the Estates to avoid using the gates. He made us leave our rags behind at the wall, stowing them in a trunk and pulling rich robes from another trunk that would cover our common clothing. We left the small outbuilding on the inside of the wall and made our way to the first concentric street.

It felt strange crossing into the inner city in the daylight after fleeing for my life in the ruined version. Blackened images of the blast that had torn through it superimposed themselves in my mind, and I shook the thoughts away.

We walked in plain sight to Loring's manor, and I felt like I was being watched the entire time. When Neffery walked up to the front door, I wanted to protest, but didn't want to draw attention. He merely turned the knob and walked inside.

It wasn't locked. I glanced out at the empty street, then ducked inside and closed the door. The place was eerily quiet, like it had been abandoned. They clearly didn't care about watching over anything here, and my anxiety spiked. I didn't want to think about why they saw no need to guard a prisoner.

I led the way to the makeshift dungeon. We weren't trying to be quiet, but a thief and a spy don't make a lot of noise, so we got into the basement itself and were checking rooms before Deidre heard us.

A door rattled on its hinges a couple rooms down and I saw her fingers wrapped around the bars in the little window at eye level. We were out of her line of sight, though.

"You fucking little *bitch*! Get your fucking ass over here and let me out!"

My eyes widened and Neffery put a finger to his lips. He walked with more weight in his steps toward the room and I followed silently.

She banged the door again. "Tell me where he is, you traitorous bitch! If you've hurt him, I'm going to skin you alive and throw you in the street for the dogs. How *dare* you do this to your own—" She sobbed and slammed her hand on the bars. "To your friends... You were a Blue..."

I started to move past Neffery, but he held me back.

She was crying now as she yelled. "How dare you. We trusted you. *I trusted you!* How could you do this to them! How could you sit there and pretend to cry about it? You lying *fucking* bitch!"

That was enough. I shoved Neffery aside and strode up to the door. "Deid?"

She gave a shuddering gasp and stuck her hand through the bars, reaching for my shirt before noticing I was covered in blood and black ichor and stopping short. Her face was streaked with tears and her eyes wide. "Gray? Oh gods are you okay?"

I squeezed her hand once and bent my head to look at the lock on the door. "I'm fine."

351

"What happened? She said you were on a hit. She said she was sending you—she was sending—"

"I'll tell you about it later. Let me get this open." I bent to work the lock, but she kept talking.

"She had those Blues killed. She said she had to get you out of the guild, so you would agree to steal for her. She said you worked for her now."

"Under protest."

"Where is she? I'm going to beat her senseless. I'm going to carve the ink right off her back."

"Dead."

For a couple breaths all I could hear was her sniffling, then the lock clicked and I pulled the door open.

Deidre rushed into my arms. She wrapped her arms around my neck and sobbed into my shoulder, and I finally felt my tension release. I held her tight, burying my face in the dark waves of hair near her neck, taking a deep breath of her familiar scent. My heart was racing, but at the same time I felt an intense relief at having her in my arms.

Neffery came up beside us and cleared his throat. "Time to pay the beggar, Gray."

I turned my head, but didn't loosen my hold on her. "Go ahead and shoot me, Neff."

Deidre pulled away, her clothes stained with blood and ichor from my chest, and put herself between me and the beggar, holding me in place behind her as she glared at him. "Don't you dare."

He glowered back. "I wasn't going to. I'm taking him to Rigel."

Chapter 54

Several hours later, I stood before the guildmaster's dais, in an audience hall packed full of thieves and beggars, prostitutes and assassins. I wasn't bound, and I was still covered in gore, my clothes stiff and beginning to smell like rancid blood. Deidre stood next to me with her hand firmly in mine, but I could feel the keen eyes of the Red Hands on my back, and likely their crossbow sights as well. The room hummed with whispered conversation, but I kept my eyes on the guildmaster.

Rigel was lounging in his chair, staring at me with narrowed eyes, tapping his finger on the armrest. He'd been that way since Neffery walked me in and announced me. The old beggar had given me one last long look, then disappeared into the crowd.

Rigel finally straightened in his chair and motioned me forward.

I slipped my hand from Deidre's and strode up the steps, stopping a few paces short of his chair. The activities of the night were finally catching up to me and I was visibly shaking, just hoping my legs held. The hours that Deidre, Nissa, Ruena and I had waited in a small room nearby—watched closely by a pair of Red Hands with loaded crossbows—had done nothing to allow me to rest.

When he spoke, Rigel's voice was pitched so only I would be able to hear it. "You've put me in a tight spot, Gray."

"I know."

"Lady Karyn was a little upset about the death of her son."

"That's a pity." I held the guildmaster's gaze, realizing it wasn't giving an inch. Reluctantly I added, "Sir."

Rigel sighed. "You also helped expose not one, but two traitors to the guild; you found an exiled Red Hand working inside the city that makes me question the loyalty of a great many people who should have realized

353

it themselves; and you pulled off what's probably the most impressive hit I look forward to hearing more about."

I didn't respond. I wasn't sure where he was going with this, and I didn't want to make things worse. The room had gone so quiet trying to hear the exchange, that I could almost believe we were alone.

"You realize I can't put you back out on the streets."

There it was. I straightened my back a little more, determined not to react. He'd already exiled me. I'd been cast out, and I'd returned. I knew what that meant.

"Jashon is planning on retiring to his grandson's farm on the other side of the country. He's looking forward to shucking peas, or slabbing butter, or some such nonsense."

I blinked and opened my mouth, but wasn't sure where the conversation had gone. Jashon was one of the Hands of the Master, the three highest ranked thieves in the guild. What did—

"Senyr can explain the details of your new duties."

I stared at him, and he stared patiently back. Maybe I was more tired than I thought. "Sir... are you telling me—"

"I'm giving you a promotion. Say thank you."

"Thank you," I mumbled automatically.

"See to it I'm not disappointed. It cost me a fair amount to buy your pardon from the baroness."

He bought... My brow creased and I couldn't help my next question. "What did you give her?"

Rigel stared at me without expression. "Four dragonoak chests of elfish gold."

The blood drained from my face.

Rigel stood and looked at the assembled crowd, raising his voice to be heard throughout the room. "Gray is a Hand of the Master. As my personal envoy, he is absolved of all accusations." He waved his hand carelessly. "You can all go spread the word."

The crowd bubbled over in conversation. The guildmaster nodded at Deidre and walked out through a side door, and still I didn't move. Deidre stepped up beside me and hugged me, laughing with tears rolling down her cheeks.

He'd pardoned me.

I absently wrapped my arms around Deidre's shoulders and my eyes came to rest on the figure of Senyr in the shadows behind the dais. His weathered face was set in a wide grin and he winked at me. People started coming up, congratulating me, asking questions about where I'd been and what I'd done. I ignored them all.

He'd *promoted* me. That bastard.

Chapter 55

The next day, it was still early enough the road outside Sangarie was empty. There was dew in the grass and an owl hooted near the river. I handed Nissa a sack holding provisions I'd taken from the guild's stores. "Are you sure about this?"

She nodded beneath the deep hood that hid her features from view. Even her hands were covered with new gloves to hide the greenish tint of her skin. "I have places to visit. I need to discover why this artifact appears in a human city in the future."

"Future?"

"When the skies cleared in that place, I could finally see the stars. Those stars will not be in this sky for another five years."

"So that was five years in the future?"

She nodded.

Anxiety tightened my gut. "That's what Sangarie will look like in five years?" The vision the stone had given me when I first picked it up flashed in my head. I had looked older. Ruena had looked older. In her teens.

"Possibly. These things are best discussed by elders and scholars."

I nodded. I couldn't even begin to guess what could cause all the destruction we'd seen in the ruins of the city. All the bodies had been fresh, and I would have laid bets they'd come through the gateways and weren't part of the explosion itself. There'd been no bones, no signs of battle. And there had been an elfish puzzle under the baroness's manorhouse, with that stone at the end. Was it waiting there now?

I gazed at the pouch hung on Nissa's belt, where I could still sense the stone. Just the barest hint of magic, like it was sleeping. "What is that thing?"

"Powerful. And thought to be lost."

My vision returned to mind. Being carried through the manorhouse. Some kind of battle happening. Exploding. "Powerful enough to destroy Sangarie?"

"And to send echoes of that destruction through time, yes. The Enhali Voga Surai is a piece of magic itself, pure motherstone. It is the First Stone. The keystone of this world. It is more than dangerous."

She pursed her lips and looked over my shoulder at the city. "A few years ago, most likely when your friend saw us in there and returned to his time, our elders started having visions of me going there. They knew I needed to be there, but not why. Now it is done, and I want answers. I do not enjoy being manipulated by destiny."

I looked toward Sangarie, seeing the smoke rising from thousands of homes into the morning sky. "The stone will be safer with you. Honestly, I don't ever want to see it again."

"I will show it to the elfish scholars. They will know what to do with it."

"Better in the safekeeping of the elves, than the possession of a thief."

"The lady may be dead, but your spies saw the human noble leave the city. He will not give up so easily. He spent considerable effort to find this stone and may try to search it out again."

"Well it's not here anymore, so I'm done with it."

"It *will* return here. We have seen it."

I knew that. I'd seen the visions it had shown me in the cavern. It was the one thing I hadn't told anyone… not even Nissa. "I'll deal with that when it happens. I hope you give me a little warning when it's not in elfish possession anymore."

She inclined her head gracefully. "What will you do until then?"

I waved my hand at the city. "Keep things running, apparently. The guildmaster has a special interest in my career."

"Are you certain staying in this town is the wise thing to do?"

"Wise?" I chuckled and hooked my thumbs in my belt. "I've never been wise."

Nissa sighed. "You could come with me. The scholars may be able to tell you why you can sense magic, even without the blood. Bring the child if you like. She carries the legacy of my people within her."

"Deidre is already attached. She'd skin me alive if I took the little brat away. Besides, I think living with the elves would be a bad idea for me."

Nissa's green eyes sparkled in the light of the rising sun. "Because you do not like elves?"

"I like you." I shrugged. "I don't particularly relish the idea of being poked at by your people."

She smiled and adjusted the sack on her shoulder. "That is fair. Do not forget my name, human. It may be useful someday."

"And you can tell stories about me, too. Make sure they're flattering ones."

I watched her walk away, the dust billowing from under her boots. She never looked back, and I waited until the gates opened behind me and people started going out into the surrounding farms, then strolled back into the city with a polite nod at the Silverguard scowling back at me.

I was headed to the Devil's Throat. It was still early enough I wouldn't catch any of the regulars, but I'd agreed to tell Neffery the entire story from start to finish as long as he bought all my drinks.

Well—most of the story.

www.ingramcontent.com/pod-product-compliance
Lightning Source LLC
Chambersburg PA
CBHW061938130726
47909CB00013B/2032